MY LIPS, HER VOICE

MY LIPS, HER VOICE

L.L. MADRID

Creature Publishing
Charlottesville, VA

ISBN 9781951971342
LCCN 2025930085

Cover design by Luísa Dias
Spine illustration by Rachel Kelli
Author photo by Sommer Koweek of Solstice Photography

CREATUREHORROR.COM

@creaturepublishing

For Elora, may you always find your way.

Chapter 1

Audrey
Present Day

It's the darkest time of night, and I'm alone in the woods.

A harsh shriek shatters the quiet. Above me, a pale heart—the face of a barn owl—watches from a crook in the cottonwood tree. Her onyx eyes glisten with starlight as she shoots from her perch. I stumble backward, imagining those talons sinking into my skin. She dives at a rodent, scooping up the creature with ease.

"You frightened me, lovely," I whisper to the bird. This is my forest, and I shouldn't be afraid, but so much has changed, and I don't remember coming here. I shiver, my nightgown is tissue-thin, and my bare feet are collaged with leaves and dirt. My skin prickles as unseen eyes linger. Something—someone—is watching. Waiting.

"Hello?" I call. The air has gone cold. I peer into the darkness, dreading a flash of movement, a crunch, or the tingle of electricity. With only a scattering of stars for light, I glimpse a dense fog coiling between the pikes of trees, slithering closer to the edges. To me.

In the distance, the owl screeches. A voice whispers:

Audrey.

My soul seizes at the sound of my name.

He's there.

"Who's there? What do you want?" I don't know if I'm asking the voice or the forest. Maybe there isn't a difference. There isn't an answer anyhow.

A wave of energy emits from the woods, rippling across my skin like a million gnats. I flail against the unknown until it recedes. The thicket's dark shapes are familiar. There's the outline of the crumbling staircase to nowhere, the lone relic of some long-ago homestead. Beyond the landmark, the path is clear; ten minutes at a quick trot and I could be home safe.

A sharp crack rends the night, and nighthawks spit out from branches. I freeze mid-step, turning as a form flitters through the shadows, following a trail that leads to a cluster of condemned cottages. Nausea twists my stomach. Whatever that is, it beckons me to follow.

Home. Home, I have to run home! But my legs are stiff, and my heels root into the ground.

It's him.

My left leg jerks forward as if being yanked by a rope. The right follows. No, No! I plant my feet, toes raking mud as I fight the pull of the invisible tide. Something is controlling me from the inside. I want to rip it out. To scream.

Another jolt from within, and my body lurches toward the wrong path.

I pitch myself forward to stop whatever's happening to me. On hands and knees, I cling to the loamy earth. I won't go any-where near whatever is in those branches.

I need to see.

My legs kick as if trying to run without me.

"Stop!"

There's no answer, but my feet cease their twitching.

I fumble to standing and a thud snaps the silence. I run home.

Pink and orange frost the horizon with dawn's arrival as I break past the tree line. Doubling over, I fight to catch my breath at the twisting road that borders the forest and my front yard.

The windows are dark; my parents must still be sleeping. I wish they were awake; I imagine them with their arms outstretched, ready to embrace me with a promise to fix whatever it is.

But they can't.

The front door is locked, so I move to the side of the house and spot pale blue curtains fluttering out my open window. The dandelions directly below are all smashed.

The bent stems set off a fresh prickle of panic. I'm not the type of girl who climbs out of windows. Why don't I remember leaving? Momma once told me I used to sleepwalk when I was little, but that's not what happened.

I look back one last time before dragging a lawn chair over and hoisting myself through the window. Dirt falls from my legs onto the hardwood floor. My feet and shins are coated with muck and scratches.

The floor creaks as I tiptoe to my bathroom and gasp at my reflection. Violet shadows hang under my eyes, and mud trails across my chin. My blonde hair hangs in clumps matted with leaves and sticks. Something happened. But what? All I know is that I can't tell anyone. They won't understand. *I* don't understand.

Momma blames a blend of sorrow and fear for giving me nightmares, but I'm certain this isn't one of the stages of grief.

It's been a little over two weeks since my cousin Mara vanished and five days since they found her body in Copper City's old mine. Someone took her, held her captive, and then . . . got rid of her. My stomach turns. That alone would've given me bad dreams. But it gets worse.

There's a thirty-minute gap in my memory from the day she disappeared.

I was in the woods, and then I wasn't. Just like tonight, something unexplainable happened. I told my parents and the police everything. No one believes me. They don't think I'm lying, not exactly. They think I'm traumatized and *imaginative*. Until I find those lost minutes and understand what happened to me tonight, I'll keep quiet. Otherwise, they'll think something is wrong with me—but it *isn't* me.

Chapter 2

Shirley
55 Years Ago

The vision arrived in fragments while Shirley was sneaking a smoke. The snippets swirled together in a kaleidoscope of images. A leveled chain-link fence. A pair of towheaded toddlers—possibly twins. A school bus careening into a vast pit, flipping to the bottom. A black-and-white portrait of a pretty girl with curly hair.

Blinking, she sank to the earth; these things always gave her the worst migraines. The school bell clanged in the distance and, for the millionth time, Shirley considered quitting the squad just so she could have a cigarette in the lounge with the other seniors, as Coach Hoffman forbade her cheerleaders to smoke while in uniform.

At least there were no witnesses; the telltale aura had appeared as she'd ducked behind her favorite tree. The Lucky Strike lay snapped in her palm, and cold sweat pricked her upper lip.

She took a deep breath, closed her eyes, and conjured the vision again. It took practice, but she'd learned to call up her library of premonitions. Though it made her nauseous, the repeated viewings often answered questions, as she could slow down the pieces and make better sense of them.

On the second watch, she looked past the grounded fence and puffs of dust rising between its links and recognized her town's copper pit. The toddlers looked alike, though not identical, as they played on a yellow crocheted blanket similar to the zigzag afghans Shirley made with her grandmother. The bus was from Copper City High—Shirley's school. She couldn't see the faces, but at least a dozen people were aboard. Her eyes flew open, and her heart punched against her ribs.

Grinding her teeth, she viewed the crash again, looking for more clues. This time she spotted fuzzy red dice hanging in the windshield. If she couldn't stop it, people would die. Shirley vowed to watch for the dice. The school only had three buses, and aside from a few rural kids, no one used them except for field trips.

She lit the remains of the Lucky and took a drag. There was more to this vision than the bus. The desire to understand kept her from heeding the tardy bell's toll in the distance. She exhaled a plume of smoke and closed her eyes again.

The photograph at the end of the vision was a senior portrait; one of those wallet-sized ones friends traded when they went off to college, stuck into corners of mirrors and used as bookmarks. Shirley focused: The face was distantly familiar, like it belonged to a classmate's cousin or someone from the next town over. But no one wore their hair like that, all big and puffy. Shirley tried to imagine the girl younger but still couldn't place those eyes or that upturned nose.

Another wave of nausea rocked her as stars burst in her head, and then:

A tree root that looked to be made of metal. A rusty pickaxe. A flashlight rolling in a cavern.

Hot pain jolted through her head. The cigarette fell into a pile of leaves as Shirley pressed her palms to her eyes, bits of tobacco sticking to her lids. Burning foliage dragged her back to the present, and she stomped out the smoldering brush, dirtying her cheer shoes.

Already late, Shirley pulled a composition book from her bag and logged everything. There wasn't much else to do. A couple of her premonitions had made sense months later, but what good was after-the-fact confirmation? There was no need to add another drop in the well of crazy McBennett stories folks swapped like recipes.

Her mother had complained about ghosts for years. No one believed her, so she took to exorcising them through drink. Shirley's brother, Kurt, was twenty-eight and always a loner, but once he returned from Vietnam, he was different, strange even. Shirley heard the whispers about battle fatigue, recognized the hollowed-out look in his eyes, and she, too, came to avoid her brother, or would if he ever left his tiny apartment over the antique shop.

Still, people liked Shirley, who, try as she might to fit in, was counted among Copper City's eccentrics. So, she didn't tell anyone about the visions. After all, her mother saw terrible things, and no one believed her, even when the poor woman screamed for hours. These days, vodka and pills muffled the shrieks to whimpers.

Shirley didn't want this *gift*; the future was none of her damn business. All she wanted was to be crowned homecoming queen, go to college in California, and spend four years on the beach before returning to marry some nice boy.

When she was little and didn't yet know how strange it was for her mother to have imaginary friends and for her grandmother, the town's midwife, to keep a tidy stash of poisons in the cupboard, she'd had her first vision. It came like a flash flood, unexpected and full of fury: A burst blackberry inking over a landscape of lumpy reds, oranges, and yellows.

The sight had knocked her down, and she'd split her lip. Her mother's expression turned so fearful that five-year-old Shirley swore she'd only tripped. That night, and every night since, Shirley saw the burst blackberry right before passing into sleep. Instinctively, she knew it was important but could never figure out why.

She shut her notebook and shuddered as dark shadows wove about. Grandma Dottie warned dreary thinking in the woods allowed the devil to worm his way in, so Shirley closed her eyes and envisioned a warm glow haloing her body in protection. When she looked again, dappled sunlight bathed the forest floor in a golden shimmer. Cicadas vibrated loudly, invisible in the trees. Shirley paused to gather jimsonweed, slipping the trumpet petals into her saddlebag. She scanned the path on her way back to school, looking for the odd root.

Chapter 3

Audrey

Mara's funeral is the second I've attended. The collar of my dress rubs against my throat, irritating the skin, just as it did six months ago at Grandma's service. My fingers fumble, tugging at the fabric, conjuring the memory of Mara scowling at me and buttoning up her peacoat because our funeral frocks were too similar. She loathed the idea that anyone might think we purposefully dressed alike. Though she was taller than me, we looked nearly identical. I suppose that can happen when your mothers are twins. I loved having a doppelgänger, but she . . .

Mara hated me. I didn't want to annoy her; I was just desperate for us to be friends. Sometimes people don't like me because they think I'm weird. Really, I'm just shy and a little awkward, but there was more to Mara's dislike. To her, my anxiety was a sign of weakness, that's why she started calling me Angsty instead of Audrey.

"Sweetheart, you don't have to look if you don't want to." Dad's words are soft in my ear, bringing me back to the present. Momma huddles with Aunt Robin at the far end of the old church, blotting out the rainbow light from the stained glass, their shared moans echoing throughout the chapel.

"Is it . . . bad?" I ask.

"They brought a specialist in. It'll look like she's sleeping." Dad reaches for my hand and squeezes it.

I meant, is it bad if I didn't go up at all, but the words slip down my throat before I can speak them, so I squeeze back and keep my eyes on the worn burgundy carpet as we walk to the dais.

We stop, and my breathing goes shallow. Beside me, Dad sniffles, and tears slip down his face. I never saw him cry before Mara went missing. I take a gulp of air and—

—a scream cuts through the doleful piano music. I freeze. Dad rushes past me. Murmurs slip through the pews, and the stream of mourners still filing in sputters to a stop.

Aunt Robin is on her knees, her hands ripping through her hair, her mouth pulling as if yanked by hooks as she calls Mara's name. Momma tries to hold her sister as the contents of her purse spill across the floor. Dad wades through onlookers to help while Uncle Tim stares out the window, his face as blank and pale as paper.

No one is looking at me or at the cherry casket that somehow contains Mara, a girl who always took up more space than her fair share. I lift my head, exhale, and look.

I'd never noticed before how small Mara's hands were. They were always in motion, gesturing with every word or twirling pens between her fingers—she was never still, not like now. Her right hand is fisted with the left positioned over it to hide her missing thumb. According to the leaked coroner's report, it was cut off while she was still alive.

My eyes travel up over the long-sleeved high-collar dress that covers up to her jaw. Her face, a near copy of my own, is waxen. My lungs frost with dread. This is what I look like dead.

An electric surge rips through my body, and I grip the edges of the casket to keep from falling as my vision blurs.

Someone is bellowing, a howl so loud it chisels into my skull. I whirl around, shrinking away from whoever's raging grief fills the small church. My parents are gone; they've taken Aunt Robin outside. Other than soft sobs and whispers, no one is crying out, not like this. Why isn't anyone else reacting?

I scramble away from Mara and slam into the next mourner, Mr. Walls, my principal. He grips my elbow, steadying me with fingers that are too tight. I shake him off.

Eyes dry and serious, he mouths "Are you okay?"

Nodding, I stumble back, grateful when he doesn't follow. My head pulsates with the horrible sound. Realization roils in my gut. No one hears the shrieks because they're in my head.

I rush from the main building into a vacant hall. The bellow turns into a whimper, and then:

No, no, no.

An icy fist of fear clenches my heart. I recognize this voice and can't deny it anymore.

"Mara?" The name scrapes against my throat.

The response I'm dreading comes on the heels of my whisper. *Angsty? What's happening?*

Dread turns to horrible certainty. I feel her inside me—it was Mara last night in the forest.

"You're—you're dead."

She starts screaming again. Her cries throb in my head, and I struggle to catch my breath; she's using up all of my air. "Stop, I can't . . . "

Mara rages, howling like a wounded beast as I stumble blindly past the Sunday school rooms. My head pounding, near exploding, I open a random door and collapse next to a mop bucket.

"Mara, calm down," I beg her, but I am not calm. I want to

scream too. I should scream, but when I open my mouth, a futile rasp aches out.

Grandma warned me about ghosts and said to never let them in. I never thought to ask what to do if they were family. "Mara, please stop. It hurts!"

She isn't listening; her terror thrashes about my insides like she's trying to escape. I slam my hands against the tile floor and ride the wave of pain surging from within.

The door opens, and a girl sinks beside me and pulls my body into a seated position. Her arms wrap around me, and she sways, rocking me like a baby. "You're not alone."

Inside, Mara stills.

Zadie.

"You need to breathe."

I can't.

"I-I can't."

"Sure, you can." Zadie's tone is gentle and warm. Like breathing is easy, and there isn't a dead girl taking all my air.

Mara whimpers.

Zadie tucks the curtain of hair behind my ear before miming holding something in her hand. "Smell the flower."

Zadie! Desperation punches inside me.

I gasp as Zadie holds the invisible flower under my nose.

I breathe in, and Mara curls fetus-like inside me. Weeping.

"Good girl. Now blow out the candle." She purses her lips and lets out a stream of breath. "Again."

We stay in that janitor's closet, our backs pressed against cases of Kleenex, practicing the art of breathing until I don't need flowers or candles anymore.

"Was that your first panic attack?" Zadie asks, picking at a run in her black tights.

I *am* panicked. Either my dead cousin is inside me, or my brain is broken. "I think so."

"I get them too." Zadie shuts her eyes and leans back. "Nothing will ever be the same, will it?"

No.

"How could it be?" I wipe my face with my sleeve. My phone vibrates in my pocket, probably my parents wondering where I am. I'm about to answer when Zadie sniffles. Her display of strength moments ago evaporates as tears roll over her apple cheeks.

"The last time I was with Mara, we broke up."

A protest bubbles inside me, but they're not my words, so I swallow them down. I witnessed their argument. I wasn't trying to spy; they just didn't know I was there. "I'm sorry. Do you think the breakup would have lasted?"

Zadie snorts as a flush heats my face and my insides prickle. Like always, I've said the wrong thing.

"I'm sorry, I meant—"

"It's cool. We've been on and off since seventh grade. This time felt different, we've been fighting about what to do after graduation, and she thinks—thought—a friend of mine wanted more than friendship."

Rhea. The word sounds like a sneer, and my heart skitters against my lungs. Oh god, Mara really *is* inside me.

My phone buzzes again. "My parents—"

Zadie stands and stretches her hand out to me. "I'll walk you. Listen, my mom wants me to go back to school, senior year and all, so if you want to, sit with me, okay? Don't wait for an invite. It's gonna be weird, but we're sisters in sorrow now."

Warm gratitude builds in my throat, and I can't form words but manage a small smile, which Zadie returns.

"I gotta work tonight, but we can hang out after if you want."

Yes! Mara's eagerness wells up inside me, overwhelming my hesitancy—I nod. My evening plan had been to hide out in the kitchen, seeing how many kinds of fudge I could make before running out of sweetened condensed milk. But now, I'm grateful I won't be alone with a voice in my head. It's easy to understand why Mara was so in love with Zadie, and I want nothing more than to have her as a friend.

Longing blooms inside me, but the feeling isn't mine. And there's something else too. Cold fear douses me as I register a new emotion from the spirit I didn't mean to welcome in—Mara resents me for living.

Chapter 4

Zadie

Tourists visit Copper City because they're either into ghosts or serial killers with handlebar mustaches. Our lone industry is feeding these culture vultures, and because I need the money and don't mind taking it from actual ghouls, I show them where we hide the bodies. They get a bite-size thrill and enjoy their sample spoonful of horror.

Mara's parents had more than their share, so they shoved what they could in their Subaru and left town an hour after burying their only child. I wish I could leave.

Mom told me to call in, and my boss offered me the night off. But the truth is, I want a distraction, and it's easier to dissociate from life when there's a costume involved. Besides, Mara loved messing with tourists, so I give them my best customer-service smile. This is just until I get out of Copper City. I don't believe in ghosts, but I know what it is to be haunted.

My boots clack along the cobblestones, each footstep a death knell as I lead tonight's strangers closer to the source of Copper City's nightmares. I'm used to the tight, murky alley, and I know where the trash cans lurk. The visitors stumble and squeal. Most of the pack smells like they've had a few drinks.

We reach the entrance of the old saloon that once was the only bar in town. Now it's a tourist trap that sells watered-down and overpriced concoctions like the Wyatt Earp Slurp, Copper Miner's Mule, and the Bloody Jasper.

The sightseers gather behind me, and I wait for their whispers to fade. When all is silent, I remove the heavy iron key from my skirt pocket and raise it like a talisman.

"This is the original skeleton key that the Copper City sheriff carried. It still opens many of the historic buildings."

My skirts rustle as I turn. Though it's been dark for hours, the day's heat holds steady. Sweat beads along the edges of my expertly rolled and puffed Gibson girl hairdo. I'm rethinking my pioneer woman costume. It worked fine in the winter, but it's already too hot in the spring. I may have to ditch my pride and switch to a saloon girl outfit. I twist the key in the lock and fling open the door.

"The Rusty Spur Saloon has a rich paranormal history. When the mines first opened, there were only three businesses in town: this saloon, a brothel, and a church."

I wait for chuckles that don't come. Weeknight crowds are always tough, and this one is no exception. It's a trio of couples on spooky dates; a mother and daughter who, judging by their glares, aren't speaking; and a solo guy named Jimbo, who I pretend not to know.

"In 1897, Jasper Dodge strolled in, drenched in blood from his final killing spree, and ordered a whiskey. A panic ensued, leaving five bystanders dead, including the piano player. One of the saloon's most common paranormal occurrences is the plinking and plunking of piano keys."

I stifle a yawn. I've worked as a Graveside tour guide for six months, and it's been less than spine-tingling. My boss Jennifer would fire me if I said this aloud, but our ghosts suck.

As we weave through tables, I offer bits of lore, moving about the room as if laying place settings. I pause and call out to the ghosts by name. There're no knocks or creaks in reply tonight; the old building doesn't feel like groaning. I gulp down disappointment. Any activity means better tips, and tonight, the place is extra dead.

After a final dusty tale, the group ducklings behind me out of the saloon, and we gather on the front steps under the twisted neon letters. I appraise their faces, tinged red from the lights, and guess who wants more.

"That concludes our tour. Any questions?"

"Zoe, do we get a refund since we didn't see anything paranormal?" asks a blond guy who spent the entire tour trying to scare his girlfriend by pinching her butt.

"It's Zadie. As stated in the tour waiver you signed, we do not guarantee ghosts. However, you get ten percent off your next tour."

He shakes his head and whispers something into his girlfriend's ear. She snickers.

"Aren't we gonna go into Bloody Jasper's mine? Isn't the Devil's Domain the most haunted sight in America?" the loner, Jimbo, asks. His voice is too loud, too insistent.

I give him a hard look. "I'm sorry, sir. Our tours don't go into the mine. It's dangerous, especially at night."

"Aren't mines always dark?"

For the first time during this tour, I feel the group's interest grow from giddy ghost hunters to actual intrigue. "I'm not—"

"My buddy did this tour two months ago. He said they went into the mine and heard screams coming from the pit."

My breath catches on the mention of the pit. The miners

weren't the only dead tossed in there. I shouldn't be doing this. Mara's murder is too fresh. I lift my head to look straight at him. "That's not part of the tour."

"He told me that if everyone pitches in ten bucks, the guide will risk it." Jimbo holds up a crumpled bill.

I scan the silent group; their eyes glisten under the old-fashioned streetlamp. One guy reaches for his wallet. They want to see something. All they got on the tour were a few creaky steps and a slight temperature drop.

A cocktail of fear and excitement swirls in my belly as I think of the lockbox under my bed containing stacks of crumpled fives and ones. "Twenty each." With Mara gone, I plan to get my diploma and leave this town, but my "adios, Copper City" fund needs serious padding. "Cash."

"We're in." The blond guy fist pumps his wallet into the air. The girlfriend nods solemnly.

"If we do this, no one can blab about it around town. It's not something we're supposed to do."

The mother-daughter duo exchange whispers before slipping away into the night. The rest of the group buzzes with excitement.

"I'll grab the keys."

I rush into the back room of the saloon. Not bothering to turn on the lights, I yank off the heavy skirts, fling them into my locker, and pull on my boy jeans. Girl pants piss me off. You can't fit anything in the pockets. These jeans hold my cell, wallet, lighter, and mini-Moleskin. I leave the high-neck blouse on. Once, a wolf spider crawled down my top in the mine, and I haven't gotten over it. I snatch up the keys and an industrial flashlight. Before I rejoin the group, I send a text to Audrey.

Got a bonus-tour. Meet up at the mine trailer after?

At the mine entrance, their cell phones glowing like fireflies, the group huddles together.

"Do we give you the money now or after?" Jimbo asks.

"Now." Bags and wallets open, and the people offer fresh-plucked bills. The wad of cash in my hand gives me confidence. Money can take you anywhere, and I want to go someplace where my girlfriend's murderer isn't roaming around. I fold the bills and slip them deep into my pocket, my fingers brushing against the cool metal of the Zippo I carry for luck.

"Stick close. You don't want to get lost in these tunnels—there's no cell reception." The key cranks inside the padlock and I yank it off and push the metal gates open, interrupting the night-time chorus of crickets. "Every few years, a tourist or two disappears in Copper City. We've lost a Girl Scout, and dozens of hikers. They're never found. So, don't go panicking yourself into a pit."

Someone gulps audibly.

My speeches on the bonus-tours are more satisfying than the pun-filled monologues Graveside has me spewing. This is a meatier performance—and I relish it. I give each person a long stare. Jimbo winks.

I let my eyes narrow on him, offering a silent threat. "If anyone wants to back out, this is your last chance."

No one speaks. I nod and step into the void.

The mine smells of mildew and rot. While I love performing, I don't want to do *this*. But I'll be eighteen soon, and there isn't some magical trust fund waiting for me. "Everyone got their flashlights?"

There are clicks and bobbing beams from the Graveside Tours souvenir flashlights. They're cheesy, but they do the job. "Remember, if anything happens, stay calm. Don't run."

We follow the rails as the narrow entrance passageway slopes downward into the belly of the mine—the temperature drops with our descent. We've gone about seven hundred feet when we reach a fork in the tunnel. We're getting closer.

Stepping in front of the smaller entrance, I wait for laggers and clear my throat to get their attention before heading into the dark. "We're going this way. You'll notice there aren't rails here. It isn't meant for visitors, be careful."

A hush falls around me as beams of amber light gather on the chiseled letters above my head, and someone in the back reads the words aloud:

THE DEVIL'S DOMAIN

DO NOT ENTER

"Over one hundred years ago, sixteen miners disappeared, one by one. Their bodies were discovered through here." I shine my light behind me. "The mine was going bust, and Jasper Dodge used his pickaxe to eliminate the competition."

A roll of yellow police tape lies forgotten by my feet. Blood thrums behind my ears; this is my first time in the mine since Mara disappeared. I'd blocked out that this is where her body was found, cold and alone. I silently apologize to her. She'd understand that I need the money to get out. The bonus-tours were Mara's idea back when we were plotting our escape to any big city with a music scene we could vibe with.

"This way." My voice cracks as I turn away and walk into the black.

The tunnel widens. Thick wood supports appear, lining the walls like rotting teeth. The once-boisterous group is silent but for their falling footsteps until a shriek sounds behind me.

"Something is in my hair! Get it out!"

Spinning around, I throw a splayed hand over the shrieker's mouth. "Shush."

I scan her head with the light and find nothing. "It's gone. Probably a bat," I whisper, running my light over one of the beams. Hundreds of tiny brown bodies hang from every nook.

"Disgusting!"

"Quiet. If you freak them out, they'll swarm. Come on, we're almost there." I grit my teeth; we're steps away from where they found Mara. The air is sour with decay, pairing well with the stone of guilt in my throat. The passageway narrows again, forcing us to walk single file into the main cavern.

An expansive natural cave is in the middle of the mine with a pit scooped out like a halved avocado. I shine my light into the bowl. "They found the bodies at the bottom. Stick to the path and watch your step."

A skittering silences the murmurs of awe and fear; I hold my breath and steel my soul.

"What was that?" A woman's fingers tug at my shirt like a child's. The people behind me cluster together. Hands clench, and breaths are held as I pan my flashlight toward the sound. The beam cuts through the darkness to a catwalk opposite us. A shape is illuminated.

Terror shreds my heart. It's Mara.

She stares at us, her eyes as wide and blank as a baby's. Her hair glows white, and her mouth rests in a little pink O. She's wearing the same overall dress as the picture in the missing person flyers. Like a marionette's, her arm floats up, and her hand flaps once in a small wave before stretching out as if reaching for us.

There are gasps. A man yells.

The specter bares her teeth and gives us the finger before crouching as if about to jump—to fly—across the chasm to get us. The flashlight slips from my hand and clatters against the pounded-stone ground, rolling away. More screams as flashlights scatter light over the cavern. I grope for mine, find it, and shine it back on the catwalk and into the pit.

Mara is gone.

A clang sounds in the distance—a metal door slamming shut. There's chaos as the tourists push and shove in a mad scramble of bodies leaving the Devil's Domain.

"Don't run!" I call.

They hardly slow as flapping wings follow in pursuit. Ducking and dodging through the hailstorm of bats, I force my way to the front of the pack. I don't want anyone getting lost or falling into a bottomless hole.

Placing two fingers between my lips, I let out a sharp two-beat whistle. The bats slam against the cave walls like pinballs, but I've startled the humans into silence.

"Single file! Keep low, put a hand on the shoulder of the person in front of you, and march," I say in my fiercest tone. If working for Graveside Tours has taught me anything, it's that freaked-out folks want to be bossed around; people feel safer if someone appears to be in charge. The journey out of the mine is swift, and the group keeps quiet except for the whimpers and gasps that come as bats dive-bomb the line.

There's a collective sigh of relief when I open the gate and we exit the mine. Above us, the sickle moon hangs like a warning. The metallic residue of fear still tangs at the back of my throat. I thought she was going to jump. Her face was so full of fury that I was sure I was about to lose Mara again.

It wasn't real, though. It *wasn't*.

There's no such thing as ghosts.

But what actually happened?

Around me, the tourists laugh in relief. Jimbo snuck back before we got to the pit, but no one notices his absence. A lady asks for a replacement flashlight.

I blink, realizing I'm shaking, staring at nothing. I clear my throat. "Sorry, only one per customer. They sell them in the gift shop if you want another one." At fifteen bucks a pop, they aren't worth it. The only difference between our flashlights and those sold at the dollar store is a tombstone logo and the words *A light from beyond*.

No one else asks me anything. They're all too busy rehashing the sighting.

I lead the tittering group to the old bank, which is now a bar called Safehouse. Some look like they could use a stiff drink.

"Not a word to any of the locals," I warn the group. "Trespassing in the mine is a felony." Ignoring their gaping faces, I double back toward the copper pit.

Jimbo waits in an alley with a six-pack of the local Spirit Brew. He gives me a goofy grin, and I know he turned back long before we reached the Devil's Domain. Jimbo isn't a fan of the mine and skips out once the tour is underway.

"You didn't have to lay it on so thick." I hand him a few crumpled bills—his share of our little scam. The mine has to be the group's idea. If I bring it up, the bit loses authenticity. That used to be Mara's job. She recruited Jimbo into the con because he has access to beer.

Jimbo's two years older than me, but with his flop of hair, and all knuckles and Adam's apple physique, he's got a dorky-little-brother vibe. He works as a barback, and his dream is to get promoted when Gus, the bartender of the last fifty years, retires or dies.

"Good money tonight." He flashes his crooked smile.

"I guess." It's okay money, but I need more if I want to leave after graduation. I have to remind myself that Mara would be fine with what I did. Wouldn't she?

"Audrey's gonna meet us, right?" Jimbo holds up the six-pack. "Do y'all like this stuff?"

I shrug. I can't shake the image of Mara in the mine.

Chapter 5

Audrey

*A**ngsty?*

I'm lying corpse-still on the Copper City Tours's trailer floor. I press my palms to the gritty linoleum, trying to hold on to something, but there's nothing. I don't want to talk to Mara right now. I'm not ready to face her continued existence.

Instead, I count the hard hats lining the industrial shelves. Twenty-seven. Then, I watch as passing headlights cast a cemetery of shadows behind rows of flashlights. CCT is a sister company to Graveside Tours; both businesses are part of the Orlich Family Corporation, just like Dad's job at Bloody Saloon Shooters. Grandma used to tell me that everything in this town is connected. What she didn't say—and what you figure out if you pay attention when everyone forgets you're there—is that it's not always a good thing.

So, I don't like being in here without permission, even though Zadie assured me that the key isn't stolen because she put the original back after making a copy.

Audrey, you can't ignore me.

"Why am I wearing your dress?" I murmur. I should be freaked out. I *am* freaked out, but I don't want to make a scene.

Mara stretches inside me, moving catlike along my ribs. *I gave*

25

it to you. Remember? My mom wanted me to wear something girly in my last school pic. Joke's on her cause it just looked like overalls.

"It's what you're wearing in the missing posters. What were we doing in the mine?" My head rolls to the side as if to look at someone. "Stop! Don't make me move."

You're not the only one who's freaked out. I'm dead. I wanted to see where I ended up. Scaring the tourists was just for funsies. They really thought you were me.

I inhale sharply, realizing what she's saying. She's admitted to taking over my body and abandoning me in the dark. I bite my lip to keep from telling her to leave. To just be dead. It isn't really what I want—I want her to be okay and me to be okay. Hysteria bubbles to the surface, and it's all my own.

Smell the flower. Blow out the candle. My voice shakes only a little when I reprimand, "It's not funny. Don't ever do that again. Please."

Mara sighs. *It's hard. I wanted to find out what happened, how I . . . It's like trying to remember a dream. All I know is my killer had big hairy hands. It was so dark. I know I should've asked, but you'd say no.*

"I wish Grandma was here. She'd know what to do." I go still. Mara's here, maybe Grandma . . . I close my eyes and imagine peeling back a veil, hoping to catch the scent of her homemade creosote soap.

Inside, Mara prickles. *Grandma's not here.*

"How do you know?"

She was too good.

"Mara?"

When I died there was a bright light, but something—she stops. Nausea flips my stomach.

Then there was just a void. A black hole dragging me—I didn't want to disappear—nothing but fucking dark. It got me. It felt like teeth all over. It was trying to eat me.

"Please," I whisper, sensing hot spittle and sharp edges along my skin.

But then there was this tiny light, like a dying match. I ran to it. When I got closer, the dark broke apart and I saw you in the woods, and somehow, I latched on.

I struggle to keep centered as I remember every search party. A shiver dances down my spine. Grandma said to keep your guard up in the woods, your emotions even, and never to exude desperation or fear. Searching for Mara, I was frantic with the desire to find her. I'd left my soul wide open during the last search party, and a strange feeling struck me on the trail and I'd nearly fainted.

Yup. That was me. I didn't know what I was doing.

"Wait, you hear my thoughts too?" My hysteria returns. Nothing private, nothing mine. Not even my own body. I know I'm not good at taking up space. Grandma was trying to teach me before she—

You think loud. I want to tell Zadie that I'm here, that—

She's interrupted by the old Shave-and-a-Haircut knock on the door. My hand fists and gives the two-bits reply. "Mara!" I protest, and feel her shrug in response.

The door opens, and Jimbo Lorenzini and Zadie slip in.

Mara groans inwardly at the sight of Jimbo. A daydream flashes before me, Mara and Zadie having a reunion—she's been planning this all day—and Jimbo's presence destroys the fantasy. To her credit, she doesn't make me scowl.

Jimbo is the closest person I have to a friend. We met in the library when I was a freshman. We both liked to hide in the stacks to eat lunch. Sometimes I'd bring him a sample of whatever I baked the night before. He still brings up the sticky date pudding

I made last year. We never talked much, just read side by side. Like everyone in town, he knew Mara, but he never *knew* her. It's nice having someone around who thinks of her as my cousin and not the reverse.

Zadie's eyes fall on my outfit. I watch her shoulders drop in what appears to be relief before concern splashes over her face. Her brow furrows as if deciding something before she offers me a simple, "Hey."

"You want a beer?" Jimbo asks, cracking one open and setting it next to me.

Zadie grabs a bottle and takes a swig. Though drinking is a common pastime here, I've never done it. I sit up and take a tiny sip that tastes like sour bread. "Thanks."

"Guess who showed up at my place last night?" Jimbo asks, flicking a bottle cap, spinning it across the floor.

"Chief Uckleman?" Zadie quips as she fiddles with her hair, releasing her dark waves from a bun.

Jimbo cringes. "Uckleman broke up a party we had a coupla months ago. You'd think it was a satanic ritual instead of a kegger by the way that dude showed up all Hulk-like. But no, it wasn't him. Audrey, you wanna try for the win?"

"Principal Walls?" I ask, regretting my guess as Mara groans inside.

"Nope. It was the one, the only, the *Great Big Asshole Jim Lorenzini!*" He shakes his head. "He was supposed to have the gig for a year, and he barely lasted a week. He's back and crashing on my couch."

Until he left, Jimbo's dad, Big Jim, the Great Lorenzini, was Copper City's biggest star.

"Big Jim's in a bad way. He wants me to drive him everywhere but doesn't wanna admit they took his license away. He won't even cop to getting fired, thinks he's too good to get shit-canned."

I set down my beer. It smells too much like over-fermented dough. "Maybe he can get a different job?"

Jimbo's dad is a world-class hypnotist, but I've never liked his show. It's unnerving. People volunteer to give him all their control, and his smooth-voiced suggestions and finger snaps lead them to do humiliating things.

"Orlich will give him his show back. It's not like they found a replacement," Zadie says, tapping her fingers on the neck of the bottle as her eyes shift to me.

I know she wants to ask about the mine, and Mara is practically squirming inside, demanding I make Jimbo leave. "So, will he ask Mr. Orlich for his act back?" I ask, and Mara swears.

Jimbo snorts. "Said he's got a new gig. He's starting a true-crime podcast about Copper City. He's gonna ask to interview you two. The living room's full of all sorts of junk now. Didn't ask or even offer to throw in for rent. And he ate all my peanut butter."

"That's lame," Zadie says. "I've never met my dad, but if he showed just to eat my snacks . . ." Her gaze meets mine.

Mara stirs inside, forcing my spine up straight. My fingers flex with her impatience. But Zadie won't believe Mara's here; she barely knows me. It isn't the right time.

There is no right time. There's only now.

I grip the sweating bottle.

Mara twitches, her frustration bubbling.

Not now. I'm not ready.

The bottle presses hard against my mouth. I taste Mara's anger as I squeeze my lips together. Cold liquid dribbles down my chin before I give up and take a swallow.

"You okay, A?" Zadie's brown eyes shine with concern.

My thumbnail scrapes the label, shedding it. It takes all my concentration to stop ripping the paper. My fingers cramp; Mara wants to smash the glass. I push it away and silently beg her to stop. To let me have my body.

"I'm fine. Thank you." My eyes water with the effort of containing Mara.

"Hey Jimbo, I think Audrey and I need some girl time." Zadie's meaning is unmistakable.

Jimbo stands. "Want me to wait outside to walk you home?"

I shake my head. It's all I can manage.

"Thanks, but we're good." Zadie smiles and pats his back.

Jimbo hesitates as if trying to find the right words. He's the only boy I know that's not always rushing to speak. Finally, he settles on, "Text if you need anything. Oh, and watch out for snakes."

Zadie salutes him. "Sure thing, boss." The trailer door clicks shut.

I shove my hands under my thighs, sitting on them like a child desperately trying not to fidget. I need to regain control.

"What's going on, Audrey?" She rests her hand on my shoulder. "You're dressed like Mara. In the mine, I was scared you were gonna jum—fall."

"I-I didn't . . ." Inside, Mara flinches.

I turn my face to the ceiling. How many gestures has she manipulated without my knowledge? What else can she do?

My belly sloshes as Mara slinks down, not wanting to provide answers. Zadie's skin is golden against the starch-white blouse. Mara's yearning is ravenous. *I'll tell her*, I think firmly. *But no more making me do things.* Mara gives a slight nod beside my heart. My knees knock as I push her down.

I lied. I never lie—it feels gross, and besides, I'm not good at it. But I'm not ready to tell, and Mara isn't taking no for an answer.

I don't want to scare Zadie, and I don't want her to pity me. Most of all, I don't want to ruin this budding friendship. "I don't know why I did that in the mine. I don't even remember putting on this dress. Maybe I wanted to feel closer to her."

Zadie's concern washes into relieved sympathy. "Mara always liked messing with tourists. I actually thought it was her for a minute." She drapes an arm over my shoulder. "It doesn't feel real. Maybe it never will. She'd still be here if we didn't have that fight."

"Don't say that."

She looks down, studying her hands. "She ran off, and no one ever saw her again. She would've been safe if . . ." Zadie swipes her hand across her eyes.

"It's not your fault. Mara's always had a temper."

Zadie lets out a small laugh. "True."

We lapse into silence. Even Mara's presence is quiet.

I swallow. It's nice to talk to Zadie like this. Nice to have a friend. "What did you fight about?" When Zadie's shoulders tighten, I hurry to add, "You don't have to answer."

"Naw, it's cool. Rhea Uckleman." She sighs. "God, it's stupid."

I tilt my head attentively as Mara bristles at the mention of Chief Uckleman's daughter.

"Mara thought Rhea had a thing for me. Didn't like that we hung out sometimes. You know Mara, fiery in the best and worst ways. She wanted us to leave to go on tour before graduation. My mom woulda killed me. Besides, we didn't have enough money saved. But she thought I wanted to stay longer because of Rhea. That was the fight."

"You would've made up," I say, half in response to Zadie's bitterness and half to appease Mara, who's making my fingernails dig into my palm.

Zadie pales. "Probably? Promise you won't think I'm a bad

person?" she asks, biting her lip.

Though I'm wary of Mara's reaction to whatever it is, I nod. People don't tell me secrets—the ultimate sign of friendship—and I want to know how it feels.

"I do sorta like Rhea. I wouldn't cheat on Mara, it's just we were always arguing. And Rhea, she's so calm, and we text sometimes, nothing more, but it's nice."

"But you love Mara."

"I always will." She exhales and looks away. "I doubt anything will happen between Rhea and me. I can't stay in Copper City praying to wake up from a nightmare when it's reality. I need to move on. Literally."

"You're going to leave me?" The words aren't mine, but they claw into my soul.

"Audrey . . ." Zadie's eyes glisten with tears.

Mara is motionless. A fire deep within snuffs out. I open my mouth to speak, but Mara wails now, and my body vibrates with her grief, my thoughts drowning in an ocean of hurt.

We bolt from the trailer, from Zadie, from the pain that splinters us. I couldn't stop her even if I wanted to. And I don't want to. It was such a whisp of a wish. To have just one friend. For someone like Zadie to want to spend time with me. Too much to hope for. First Grandma, then Mara, and now Zadie too.

Outside, I don't watch for snakes. The night is cool and dry, and I can't tell which shards of sorrow belong to me.

Chapter 6

Zadie

It's late when I get home. Creeping inside, I turn off the porch light, signaling my return. When Mara went missing, every bulb blazed as if all she needed to come home was an illuminated path. Now, clicking off the light triggers a dull pain.

Tonight was extra weird. I'm not the only one who sees Mara when I look at Audrey. There's a whole whack of tourists who just mistook her for a ghost based on Mara's now-famous senior picture. But there were moments I felt like she *was* Mara. And that's all sorts of messed up.

Then she ran off after I told her about Rhea. That shook me more.

Audrey texted that she was fine, just overwhelmed. I get it, grief's great at giving surprise smackdowns.

My phone pings with a text from Rhea: *Ghost emoji.* Her way of asking how work went.

Guilt and excitement war with each other every time I think of Rhea. Tonight, I don't answer. Mara and I were on the outs, but it doesn't change that she's the only one I ever loved—still love—and I'm scared I'm a bad person because I want to move on. I *need* to leave all this behind. Mara, Copper City, everything.

After grabbing a sleeve of crackers from the cupboard, I head to my room to get my guitar. Mom's bedroom door is shut, and she doesn't call to me, meaning she's out cold.

My body zings with adrenaline and I'm hours from falling asleep. Our house—an old miner's casita—is tiny, with walls that barely hold a whisper. It's not ideal for late-night jam sessions, so I sling my tobacco-burst Vega across my back and head out to the porch. It's easy to get onto the roof; you stand on the railing, throw your elbow over the lower beams, and pull yourself up like you're climbing out of a swimming pool. I've done it so often that it takes only seconds, even with a roll of Ritz dangling from my mouth and a guitar on my back.

From the top of our hillside cottage, you can see all of Copper City nestled in the valley below. Contained by cliffs and the ridge of the quarry pit, the town is basically isolation island. Thickets of cottonwoods spread like forest fingers clenching us tight. The amber glow of streetlamps dots the winding roads, but there's no visible light outside our borders. It's like no place else exists.

Settling into my spot next to the dormer window, I twist the Vega's tuners and strum a few chords before trying to start a song. My fingers are clumsy, and my mind is too full of memories to let the music come. I shut my eyes and wait for the sensation of being lost in composition. Tonight, I need the escape. I squeeze my eyes tighter, breathe in, and position my fingers on the frets. Exhale. Ready now, I open my eyes and freeze.

A faint green light emits from the last place I saw Mara alive.

Deep in the trees, past the remains of a staircase and down a twisted trail, there's our spot. A hollow encircled by a wall of thick pines and red boulders. Mara and I claimed the clearing as ours and promised to keep the spot a secret. Even the historical society seems to have forgotten the clearing, along with the old brothel at its edge. Now it's spewing toxic-waste green.

I reach for my phone and snap a picture; the auto-flash washes out the strange light. I swear, shut off the flash and refocus, but the glow is gone.

I don't know what I saw. I *could* follow the splintering short-cut through the woods to find out. But I haven't been back to our spot since Mara went missing. I can't even walk past the giant ironwood that marks the trail to the clearing. A volunteer found pages ripped from our shared notebook hanging on that trunk, the paper spiked on the tree's thorns. The lost cover has *The Zaras— Keep Out!* scrawled in Sharpie. The Zaras is our band name. We filled nearly every inch of that pad with song lyrics, notes, and our collection of secrets. We had rules about our songbook, and we took turns carrying it.

The rest of the red spiral notebook is still missing. I hate that her murderer has it, and I hate that the FBI kept the other pages as evidence. Those scraps were private bits of Mara and me. The day everything changed, I was supposed to have the notebook.

I choke down the reason Mara had it.

Memory is a bitch that haunts like no ghost can.

Chapter 7

Shirley
51 Years Ago

Death had a way of derailing dreams; thus, Shirley never made it to the beach. The morning after graduation, Shirley's mother took a bath and a bottle of pills. Out of kindness, the coroner listed the passing as accidental. Condolence casseroles filled the fridge, but for over a week, Shirley ate only the *Congrats, Grad!* sheet cake her mother had bought.

Dottie, Shirley's grandmother, who'd always been strong when her daughter couldn't be, deteriorated rapidly—both in body and mind. Shirley stayed in Copper City, working as a saloon girl bringing folks whiskey and sarsaparillas while smiling suggestively for tourists' cameras. In her off-hours, she walked the forest paths, following the old woman's instructions on which herbs to gather to brew medicinal teas. Soon, Dottie's requested ingredients were for numbing rather than healing.

On her last night, Dottie pleaded for oleander, desert thornapple, and hemlock. Shirley's brother, Kurt, brought over a jar of raw honey to sweeten the brew. They sat on either side of the bed while Dottie called out to long-departed friends and family, but Dottie's last words were reserved for the siblings.

"Keep the light."

*

Time moved swiftly around Shirley's indecision of what to do now that she had no family besides her brother. The decade age gap had kept the siblings apart when they were young, and now, when Kurt wasn't at work maintaining the old mine, he holed up in his tiny apartment.

Dottie's house hadn't been worth much, but the bit of land brought in a small sum of money that the siblings split. Kurt paid for his apartment over the antique shop in full while Shirley saved her share and moved into her best friend Franny's spare room, just until she got her head straight. There wasn't much time, as Franny was pregnant, and soon the room would be a nursery. Besides, Franny's husband, Michael Hennessey, grunted and scowled whenever he found the women laughing. Franny claimed that men's foul moods were a part of marriage. So Shirley vowed to stay single and kept clear of the bickering.

She filled the hours wandering the forest, collecting herbs and foraging for mushrooms. Claiming the dark woods as her own, Shirley explored every path, visualizing light wherever she went, just as Dottie had taught her. When she found herself on an overgrown trail with an odd tingle of electricity in the atmosphere, she ignored the goose bumps rising across her flesh and followed the unkempt route until she came to a clearing. The sun shone on the space as if welcoming her. She walked the perimeter with everything feeling both lovely and wrong.

A row of trees nearly concealed an old building at the far edge of the clearing. The unease fluttering about her stomach intensified as Shirley moved toward the structure. She peered through the cracks of boarded-up windows and saw toys scattered about: a shiny Slinky, Matchbox cars, a toy gun with a roll of orange caps.

She moved to the door and checked to see if any boards were loose. She got a nasty splinter trying to budge a plank, and couldn't figure out how a little kid could've gotten in. Dust coated everything except the toys. A strange notion pulled at her: She was seeing something she wasn't supposed to.

Her temples throbbed as green and black auras swirled, blurring her vision as she stumbled from the building. The urge to get away grew with a droning, terrible hiss like an intrusion of cockroaches emanating from the old boards.

She couldn't hold on to her light. She had to leave. Now.

Shards of premonition assaulted her as she blindly fought through the clearing, fumbling to find the path home. The visions came like a photo carousel rapidly flipping through images.

Bus. Fuzzy dice. The girl. Toddlers. Blanket. Root. Blackberry.

Shirley crashed through the trees and into the forest. Her splayed hands came into focus first; the earth beneath them was dark and loamy.

A glint of metal sparked as the blade of a pickaxe crunched into the ground by her fingertips before dragging along to rest by a pair of black boots.

Don't be afraid, darlin'. The voice was a contradiction of velvet and grit, an intruder comfortable in Shirley's mind.

Fear rooted her to the forest floor, her body quaking as the specter bent, leaning closer.

Let me in.

The words sizzled in Shirley's head. "No." A whisper was all she could manage as an eruption of pain shot through her skull. Pressure built behind Shirley's eyes, and she feared they'd explode as flashes of her mother's dangling arm, her grandmother's waxen skin, and her brother's blank face popped into her mind.

All her pain—emotional and physical—melted to nothing, leaving her numb. A hot presence wormed into her ear as Shirley succumbed. The scolding call of a cactus wren jilted her back.

Her eyes flew open, and she gasped, her breath icing the air despite the summer's heat. The man kneeling before her wore old Levi's and a shirt drenched in blood. With soot-blackened fingers, he tipped his hat as his cracked lips parted, revealing sharp ocher teeth.

Shirley screamed, the pain returning with a vengeance as she managed to stand—to run. She looked back only once as the figure broke apart like bats flapping through smoke. Shirley tripped and fell hard, skinning her chin against a rock, but she scrambled up and ran, not daring to turn again until she was out of the woods.

Chapter 8

Audrey

Dread keeps me from sleep. Mara might take over and bring us to the woods. I can't let her do that, she doesn't understand the balance, doesn't sense the subtle shifts in the air. Grandma tried to explain Copper City's supernatural undercurrent, but Mara never listened. I didn't always understand her instructions about golden light and soul shielding, but Mara outright scoffed at them. Maybe it'll be safer if I sleep on my parents' floor like I did when I was little.

Angsty, chill. I said I'd leave our body alone.

"You also said you wouldn't listen to my thoughts." I fling off my sheet and go to the window, pushing the glass up and letting in a blast of spring air.

I said I'd try.

Taking a grounding breath, I move to the closet and pull down the heavy cardboard box where I keep Grandma's things. It's too late to bake, and I need comfort. At the top of the box is a faded pink fanny pack. I hold it to my face and breathe in the lingering scents of lavender and rosemary. As long as I can remember, Grandma wore this on all her strolls, using it as a catch-all for her roots, herbs, and other forage.

Are you gonna wear that on your first day back at school? The dead granny look isn't a vibe.

Ignoring Mara, I set the fanny pack on my nightstand and start pulling out Grandma's books: a collection of books on spiritualism, the occult, and other spooky stuff I don't have the stomach for. I prefer to curl up with a fantasy or one of my vintage cookbooks, but these aren't for reading; I kept Grandma's books because she wrote in the margins of everything. The idea that she'll never form another word makes all her scribblings precious.

You miss her *more than you miss me.*

"That's not fair. You're still here and—"

Grandma was your only friend.

"Stop, Mara." Tears well behind my eyes.

I didn't mean . . .

I plop back on the bed, pick a book at random, turn the pages until I find Grandma's heavy marks, and run my fingers over each letter, losing myself in the ritual of seeking bits of her.

Angsty?

"Please, I know it's weird, but this helps me cope."

Relax. I wasn't gonna call it weird—I mean, it is—but these are Grandma's, right?

I sigh, pick up another book, and page through it.

Mara sits up straight, knocking my shoulders back at attention. *Why was Grandma taking so many notes on possessions?*

The page rips under my tightening grip. I scan her marks and run my eyes over the passages she'd underlined. Mara's right. "Wow. It's like she knew you'd possess me."

What? No. I'm not *possessing* you. *I got stuck with you on accident.*

The feeling of hope, of being little and waking from a bad dream and finding Momma's light on, fills me as I flip through the books. Maybe there's something here on how I can get rid of her, something—

That's cold. Mara sounds small, and I barely feel her now.

"I didn't mean it like that."

I'm not some parasite. Maybe I'm supposed to do something, and I need your help.

"With what? Chasing demons in the forest? Playing ghost in the mine?" I feel her shrink. I was always so in awe of Mara. She was effortlessly cool, funny, and never cared what anyone, especially me, thought. Since we were small, I'd always wanted her to like me. She was the closest thing I had to a sister. I loved that we looked so much alike and wanted us to pretend to be twins, to share secrets, but companionship, with me at least, never appealed to Mara.

Now, her hurt radiates in my bones. "I'm sorry, but I don't understand. Why are you here? Grandma isn't."

Mara is quiet, so I pull the remaining books—a stack of composition books—from the box.

There was no place else to go.

A chill slips down my spine.

Maybe I'm supposed to get justice? But I can't remember my death. Just that, oh Audrey, it was . . .

My vision blackens, and terror ices my lungs before I sense Mara shaking like a dog tossing off rain, and the light returns.

Maybe, I'm here to say goodbye. If you let me talk to Zadie, that'll wrap up my unfinished business, and I . . .

"Zadie doesn't believe in ghosts."

She'll believe in me.

"I don't really believe in you. You're probably a mental breakdown. No offense."

The energy shifts in the room, and I stand and walk jerkily

toward my bathroom. My knuckles turn white against the sink. I'm not in control. In the mirror, my head cocks with a bored confidence I don't possess. "Zadie will believe me. I can tell her things. Things only I know."

I gasp. It isn't my voice. The husky alto belongs to Mara.

A sly smile cuts across our lips. "See? I—*we* could convince her. Wouldn't it be nice to have one less person to keep secrets from?"

I shake my head and watch my expression change to a big-eyed pleading look.

"My parents left town without me. There was so much I wanted to say. Can't you just let me tell Zadie the truth?"

"Mara . . ."

"Come on, Angsty."

"I'll think about it but not if you do anything while I'm asleep. And you need to stop moving me around."

Deal. And listen, I can help you too. There's loads of stuff you're dying to do but too shy or scared or whatever. I feel it in you. Give me a chance and I can help whenever you need a confidence boost.

I'm too tired to imagine how Mara could help me, but I agree and head back to bed.

I've spent years trailing after Mara, and suddenly our souls are intertwined. It feels like my fault. I've made an embarrassing amount of wishes in my life, always yearning to have someone to share my secrets with, and now I have no choice.

*

"Mornin' darlin'," my dad drawls. The cowboy accent is fake, but he's a method actor and has been putting on the twang for the tourists for so many years I can hardly remember what he truly sounds like. I peer up from my tea and toast and manage a sleepy greeting in response.

He sits next to me. "Your mother's still asleep. She had a rough night."

I try not to stare at the Copper City sheriff's badge that my father wears for work. It's an antique, one of the few remaining originals. The star is slightly uneven, and the letters are all hand-etched. Dad is proud of his badge—all the other reenactors wear reproductions. I've never told him or anyone, but sometimes when I look at the badge, it's coated with blood.

Like now.

I nibble my toast and mentally list the ingredients in my sun-flower seed bread: flour, yeast, honey, butter, salt, warm milk, and seeds. When I look at the badge again, the blood is gone. I don't share what I see with others; I only trusted Grandma. She taught me the distraction trick. Counting and recipes keep me sane.

Dad drums his fingers on the table. "Your mother wants you to wear your tiger's-eye pendant."

I nod and sip from my mug.

"Good girl." He squeezes my hand before standing. Neither of us buys into Momma's rocks, but I know it's her way of telling me to take care today. "Do you want me to walk you to school?"

I smile. That's Dad's way. "No, thanks."

"It's the spurs, isn't it?" he asks, stroking his handlebar mus-tache.

"Maybe a little."

He takes off his white cowboy hat and playfully bonks me on the head. "Learn somethin'."

"Have fun shooting Bloody Jasper."

Dad tips his hat and is about to leave when he pauses. "Today . . . well, it'll be harder than most days. If you need anything, call me."

"Thanks, Dad."

We say nothing else, but we don't have to. The door clatters shut.

I finish my tea and squint at the dregs—I don't see anything in the dark clumps despite years of Momma insisting I should.

She wants me to carry on the family tradition of fortune-telling; she says I have the sight. Sometimes I see snippets, but they're gone in a blink. Since Mara's return, it's gotten worse, like my cousin left the door to the spirit world open behind her. Those snippets linger now. I do *see* things, things I don't want to, but nothing foretelling the future. At least, I don't *think so*. As far as I can tell, the flickers are of the past.

Mara hasn't said a word since last night, but I feel her inside, stewing about how the entire world is moving on without her.

In case she's listening, I whisper, "If you want to talk about anything, I'm here."

Duh. Where else would you be? There is no spice in her words. Mara sounds sad. *Thanks, or whatever, but I'm going to lie low.*

It feels like she's hovering outside of me, clinging like a loose hair or a shadow. She doesn't go too far. I'd be afraid of floating away like a lost balloon, but Mara would never admit to fear.

Outside, the sky is clear, the wind calm. Since Mara is somewhere in the ether, I walk by her mother's bakery, Robin's Nest. The hanging sign—a speckled egg—creaks in the breeze as if nothing's wrong. A closed sign is taped to the door, and butcher paper covers the windows to deter reporters from using the bakery as a backdrop for their quaint-town murder-mystery stories.

I can't help but picture the oven's warm glow and puffs of powdered sugar and flour drifting like clouds. Mara never took an interest in creating confections, but I did. I helped out for extra money around holidays. First, prepping and mixing, but before long I'd mastered frosting florets and sculpting fondant designs. Last summer Aunt Robin promised that she'd take me on as her business partner one day. Though it's disappointing to Momma, I have no desire to spend my hours meeting strangers, and worse, having to talk to them. I like the quiet, and baking doesn't give me anxiety. Sure, there's the occasional collapsed soufflé, but you can always start over with a new recipe.

This is my favorite place—it's always warm and golden sweet inside. I press my palm against the door. A year ago, my future was solid. I'd stay in Copper City and help run Robin's Nest. Eventually, I'd take over, expand, and add a tiny tea shop. My dreams were so safe and certain. Now . . . I don't think Aunt Robin and Uncle Tim are coming back.

"Excuse me, do you know where we go to buy tickets for the mine tour?"

Blinking, I turn to find a woman gripping two small, wriggling boys by the wrists.

"We don't wanna see the mine! We wanna see cowboys killing bad guys!" the slightly bigger boy screeches.

"I told you, Landon. The shoot-out isn't until later."

I give the woman directions to the Copper City Tours ticket center as the smaller boy sets his fingers into a gun shape, points at me, and mouths *pew-pew.*

The streets are filling with tourists. I check my phone; I have time before first bell. I cross the street and slip through an alley where the bricks are painted in psychedelic swirls. In less than a minute, I'm at the tree line. Though I fear the forest after dusk, the woods still call to me.

The forest changed after Grandma died. When I was small,

I spent my afternoons walking the trails with her. She taught me the names of the trees and birds. We'd collect herbs and plants like yarrow, bits of sagebrush, and petals of evening primrose that Grandma tucked into her pink Las Vegas fanny pack.

We were always looking for something on our walks. What exactly, she never told me. She'd only say that the place was troubled, and she was searching for the root of it. Grandma led the way, often off path, following scents I couldn't catch and speaking to people I couldn't see. Softly suggesting "It's time to move on. Seek out the light." Or scolding "Leave this place. You aren't welcome." She promised to explain everything when I was older, but I thought it was part of our game.

Grandma was the town's fortune teller before Momma took over. She didn't like what Momma did to the shop, adding thousands of crystals and telling people what they wanted to hear instead of what they *needed* to. Momma made more money than Grandma ever did. That didn't bother Grandma, though. She never claimed to see the future. Her predictions were cleverly worded pieces of advice she gave after listening to what people said and noting what was left out.

In the same way, as if the trees had stories strung between them, we spent our walks looking for spots with fewer insects and pausing in areas where birds didn't chirp. Grandma would grip my arm with her calloused hand and whisper, "Hear that?"

"No."

"Exactly."

After she died, I never stopped wondering what we were searching for. I still look, hoping I'll find it instead of inheriting madness.

I let my backpack slide from my shoulders and drop to the ground. I kneel next to it to remove a worn leather pouch containing a set of twenty-five uniquely carved runes crafted from deer knucklebones. Grandma wanted to teach me how to use them, but the idea of reaching into a pouch of bones made me queasy—I never told her no but made excuses and remembered plans when she brought it up. The runes were too precious to her for me to dare call creepy.

The first time I let my fingers wade among the knuckles, I was terrified I'd feel sticky blood or hear the clap of bullets. But I only smelled sweet grass and tasted morning dew. The deer of these runes were not murdered; they'd simply passed.

Now I use them to try to talk to Grandma.

I do a mental scan of my body, searching for signs of Mara. I don't feel her; this moment is mine alone. Satisfied she isn't waiting to spring up and scare me, I whisper, "Grandma, what should I do about Mara?" and shake out a single bone from the bag.

Sunlight winks on the polished surface of the lone blank rune—Wyrd.

Unknowable fate.

Sighing, I put the runes away. Grandma always said I needed to learn to decide things for myself. Though my knees are wet from the grass and pebbles poke at my shin, I don't get up. My spine straightens, and I hold my breath—I feel someone in the woods.

"Grandma?"

A warm breeze rustles leaves in response.

My body tingles, and my breathing goes shallow.

A bird stops mid-chirp, and the air around me stills. Through the pines, a pair of black eyes glower at me. I can't move. A grim smile curls the man's thin lips as he twirls a pickaxe; the blade catches the sunlight as it—and the man—winks out of existence.

Electricity shoots up my spine, and I kick over my backpack, spilling its contents as I fumble to my feet. The man is gone, leaving behind the coppery scent of blood. Grabbing my bag and the books, I ignore the scattered pens and other debris and run.

When I get to school, I gasp for breath, squeeze my eyes shut. I've never seen him before, but in my bones, I know he's the spirit Grandma warned me about.

Chapter 9

Zadie

Z adie!" Mom's way too shrill when I enter the kitchen. "You're just now getting up?"

My response is a cross between a groan and a yawn.

"The bell rings in twenty minutes."

Violet crescents underscore her eyes. She should learn that sleeping in never killed anyone. "Relax. I can get to school in ten minutes."

"Zadie-doll, we gotta talk."

"Is there any coffee? I—" I stop, taking in two dirty wine glasses—the nice ones—on the counter.

Mom steps in front of them, forcing me to meet her stare. "I called ASU about payment plans. They said you canceled your registration."

My gut drops. I knew that would come out sooner or later, but I was banking on later.

Mom's arms flop to her sides, and she sighs, looking close to tears. Her lectures are easy to tune out, but a Mom breakdown is never good.

Mom likes to throw around phrases like *income* and *job security* and wants me to pursue a practical degree, but I'm gonna be a singer-songwriter. So what if hardly anyone makes it? Some do. Besides, you never know how long you have.

"Oh, Zadie, what were you thinking?"

"It'll be okay, Mom. I promise."

She runs her fingers through her bleached-blonde mom-bob. She's younger and more single than most of my classmates' parents. That's why she got stamped with the label *tourist tramp*. Mom may be hooking up with historians and ghost hunters, but at least she never lets anything get serious. Still, she must be lonely with only me and our sometimes here, sometimes not cat, Hobo.

Mom had me when she was in her early twenties—nine months after a girls' trip to Rocky Point, Mexico. She met my dad on the beach, had a "magical" night, and promptly lost her phone and forgot his last name. Basically, I'm a souvenir.

The Copper City gossips love using Mom as a cautionary tale. She's perpetually single, obsessed with CrossFit, and is always showing cleavage. I'm sure my less-than-studious approach to school doesn't help the Slade family image. I swear I'll send Mom on a cruise or buy her a ridiculous car when I make it. But now, I'm having trouble making eye contact with her.

Mom reaches out like she's going to tuck my hair behind my ear but stops short. "If you need time or more sessions with Dr. Pham . . ."

I blink and force my eyes to meet hers. "Okay."

"A reporter asked to interview you. The Quinns fled town, so they want the girlfriend. I told him to interview our lawyer. If anyone approaches you, tell them to shove off."

"Who was it?"

"It doesn't matter. Mara deserves to rest in peace."

Outside the window is a golden morning, and it feels like a betrayal. Mara always said she'd be famous one day, and I guess she was right. But she'd hate that her murder is fodder for amateur psychics and true-crime TikTok. Her life reduced to only her death. Our town booms with the notoriety that comes with slayings. Mara's corpse wasn't the first to wind up in the Devil's Domain—just the most recent. "I bet they'll add her to the ghost tour someday."

"Oh, Zadie." Mom looks at her watch. "I gotta get moving. I think the yogurt in the fridge is still good."

I plop on a stool and check to see if Rhea's texted me. Nothing. I feel guilty for being disappointed, but we're just friends, and honestly, I don't have many of those. I'd made Mara my entire life.

My new thing is imagining a parallel universe where Mara never went missing. Mara is alive, and we sneak out at midnight and climb the clock tower to wish on stars.

In my game, that last day never happened. If I could delete just a few hours from existence, Mara would be here. We'd still be together—like we always promised.

We were the weird girls, but that didn't matter. We had what we wanted—each other. The last day before the nightmare, we sat cross-legged on a yellow blanket as we practiced our latest song. Mara's husky alto sounded sultry and grown-up compared to my girlish soprano. Still, our voices melded together.

Anything was possible.

We ate chocolate-almond fudge that Mara had swiped from her family's bakery. She broke a chunk in half, handed me the bigger piece, and said, "My mom says you look like Linda Ronstadt."

"Who?" I asked around a mouthful of crumbling chocolate.

"Some singer from the seventies. I Googled her, and it's true. She was pretty."

"How dare you Google another woman?" I fluttered my hand

against my chest in mock horror.

"You're a dork." Mara grinned. Sunlight shone on her blonde hair, and her skin glowed. It was the right time, a moment I'd been planning.

I grasped her hands and studied her blue eyes with specks of green around the irises. "Mara, I love you. After graduation, I think we should get a place together."

My heart crept up my throat in the seconds she took to respond.

"I love you too—let's do it!"

I kissed her and slid my fingers into her hair. At that moment, every sense was heightened, important. The scratch of the blanket against my bare skin, the wind cool and thick with pollen. She tasted like salted chocolate.

When I pulled away, her eyes were wide with excitement. "I have news." She held me by the elbows and gave me a wicked grin. "Remember that band from Phoenix we met on Insta?"

"You mean the witchy one—was it The Craft?"

"The Coven. Anyhow, they got a bus, and they're going on a cross-country tour, and drumroll please, they've asked us to go as their openers."

"Seriously?"

Mara sucked in her lips and blew out a big breath. "Do you think Katherine will let you?"

"My mom can't stop us! We'll be grads, true adults. We won't need permission."

Mara broke off another piece of fudge and pressed it to my lips. "Chew on this."

Mouth full of chocolate, I gestured for her to go on.

"Here's the thing, the band that was going to open for The Coven bailed. That's why they asked us. We'd need to be on that bus next weekend."

The fudge was thick in my mouth and hard to swallow. There were almost two months left of the school year.

She held her finger to my lips. "Graduation, I know. Our parents will freak, but I propose we just do it."

"What?"

"Seriously. We go, they'll panic for a few days, but then we'll call and explain that we're on tour, and we'll come back and do summer school or something."

"Mar—"

"Oh, come on, Zadie. It's why we started The Zaras, to be musicians and get out of this damn town. Chances like this are rare, like once-in-a-lifetime-comet rare." Mara spread her arms wide above her and grinned like she knew I'd say yes.

"No."

Her face fell. "We gotta do this. We're in love and about to have our big break. It's destiny. I know it. Don't you trust me?"

"Come on—" My phone cut me off with a series of alerts, the screen glowing from the blanket.

"Rhea sure texts a lot." Mara stood. "Maybe she's why you suddenly don't want to do what we've spent our entire lives planning." Her lower lip trembled until she bit it hard enough for a tiny bubble of blood to bloom.

"Mara."

She shook her head, turned, and ran. I called out to her, but she didn't look back.

That was the last time I saw Mara alive.

Outside, sirens wail, breaking the spell of memory. It sounds like all five of the squad cars are out. There are only a few scenarios that warrant this level of commotion. I swallow. Maybe they got Mara's killer.

My phone chimes with a message from Rhea:

Morning Sunshine. Hurry up and get to class! It's boring without you.

I smile, but thinking of Mara's hurt face, I don't text back.

Chapter 10

Shirley
50 Years Ago

Franny looked twelve months pregnant instead of seven in her pastel tent dress. She pressed a paper sack into Shirley's hands. "I made you some egg salad sandwiches for the trip." Then she grabbed Shirley, pulling her into a hug, the bag smashing between them as Franny wept.

"Oh, Franny," Shirley whispered into her hair.

"You're leaving because of Michael, aren't you? I'll get him to be nicer, I promise."

Shirley sighed; they'd already had this conversation. "I have to make a change."

"But why now? You turned into a nervous Nellie overnight, and suddenly, you're moving to Vegas. It's crazy."

Shirley pulled out of the hug and glanced over at Michael and Kurt arranging the last of her things in Kurt's VW Splitty van. She tugged Franny to the mailbox, just out of earshot. Smoothing the hem of her plaid minidress, she took a deep breath. "Remember my mother's"—Shirley swallowed—"problem?"

Franny wiped her eyes with a handkerchief. "Michael says she had schizophrenia."

"She was haunted." Shirley grabbed Franny by the elbows and

looked at her dead-on. "I see things, too, snippets of the future. That I can deal with, but there's this thing in the woods and—"

"You're grieving, I'm sure—"

"No. I know what I saw. That's why I'm going to Las Vegas, where it's never dark, never quiet. I can't live like my mom. I don't want to die like her either."

Franny sucked in her lips as tears trundled down her face.

Shirley let go of her friend's elbows and wiped the trails from her cheeks. "I need you to do something for me."

Franny gave another small nod.

"Watch the buses. If there's ever a pair of red fuzzy dice in one, it means something horrible is going to happen. Do whatever you can to keep people from getting on that bus."

Franny's eyes widened with bewilderment, and Shirley felt no relief from sharing the burden of the premonition. A horn honked, and the women turned to see Michael pulling away from the VW's open window. Kurt stared down and kicked at a rock.

"I'll call you every week," Shirley promised as she held her best friend before bending to kiss her belly. "He's going to be a wonderful person."

A slight smile played at Franny's lips. "He?"

"Yes, he. Just promise you won't name him after Michael."

The horn blasted again, and Kurt muttered a swear and walked over to Michael. Shirley gave Franny one last squeeze and joined her brother.

As they drove away, Shirley leaned out the window to wave goodbye. She didn't roll it back up after settling in her seat; instead, she breathed in all the mountain air she could.

"I hope it works," Kurt said, his pale blue eyes on the road ahead.

Shirley regarded her brother, his long fingers at ten and two on the wheel, and how stiff he held his lanky arms. He was tall but too thin, and his ginger hair gave him a boyish appearance, even now that he'd let it grow to his chin.

"Hope what works?" she asked.

"Leaving." His voice was soft but certain. "I've seen them too."

Shirley reached out and gently touched the worn flannel on Kurt's shoulder. "You don't have to go back."

Kurt chuckled. "No one will hire me as a showgirl."

"That's not what I'm planning!" Shirley's face went hot. It wasn't far off—her Vegas plan was to be a cocktail waitress until she could scheme up a new strategy.

"You can live with me, and we can both start over."

"Thanks, Shirl, but I can't survive in a place with all those lights and the noise. I gotta keep where it's quiet."

"Sometimes it's too quiet."

"In that case, let's find some Credence." Kurt flipped on the radio and spun the dial, producing a series of static sizzles and snaps.

Shirley shook her head. "You can't always expect to find CCR."

Kurt gave the knob another counterturn and whooped and drummed his palms on the wheel as "Lookin' Out My Back Door" sputtered from the speakers.

"How'd you do that?" Shirley laughed.

But Kurt only shrugged and sang along. Shirley joined in, and they didn't speak of their hauntings again.

*

After they unloaded the van's contents into Shirley's new apartment—smaller and dirtier than the agent promised over the phone—Shirley bought Kurt dinner from a smoky diner and asked if he was certain he didn't want to stay the night.

"Thanks, sis, but I won't feel right until I'm back home."

It was nearing dusk, and the street was lit with neon, diminishing the sunset. On the walk back to Shirley's apartment, regret hitched around her heart. She'd promised her grandmother she'd look after the woods. Dottie swore that the forest needed a gentle presence to drift through it, to keep bad energy from gathering like cobwebs. Dottie taught Shirley to steward the forest, claiming it as their dominion. Shirley's mother never ventured into the wilds, and Shirley hadn't understood why until she encountered that nightmare entity and heard him speak inside her head.

Forcing the memories away, Shirley pointed at a souvenir shop. "Do you mind if we go in? I'd like to get something for Franny."

"Sure," Kurt said, but his face was uneasy.

"It'll only take a minute, I promise."

The tiny store was bright and overstocked with colorful trinkets, mugs, steins, novelty pens with dancers whose costumes vanished when tilted, furry red-and-pink lingerie, and racks of T-shirts. Shirley glanced at her brother; his eyes were wide and his mouth narrow. She'd have to hurry. She looked at the handbags first. They cost too much, but she found an affordable pink pouch with a golden scrawl of *Viva Las Vegas*. Trying it out over her shoulder, Shirley frowned.

"It's a fanny pack," the salesgirl called from the register. "It's European. You wear it around your waist."

"Oh, thanks!" Shirley smiled; Franny would never go for that, but it would be perfect for gathering herbs. Her soul twinged with loss. She wouldn't be doing that here; there weren't even trees besides the palms. She put the fanny pack back.

She wandered past beer mugs and shot glasses to a small selection of baby goods and picked out a pastel bib embroidered with the phrase *Mommy's Good Luck Charm.*

Still, she wanted a gift just for Franny. Kurt was at the register buying something, probably hoping it would signal her to leave. She scanned the shelves again and spotted a beautiful figurine of a showgirl dressed in peacock-blue feathers. She gasped at the price, but then spied the orange 75 percent off sticker and wondered if Vegas would bring her luck after all.

The bell over the door tinkled, and Kurt went outside and leaned against the window. Shirley took her items to the girl—Becky, according to her nametag—and added jerky and sunflower seeds to give Kurt for his drive back.

"First time in Sin City?" Becky asked, snapping her gum.

"I just moved here, actually."

Becky paused in wrapping the doll in tissue paper, reached under the counter, and pulled out a business card with an illustration of a hand with an eye at its center. "Then you should go to my babushka, Inga. She's the real deal—she specializes in periods of transition."

"I'm good. Thanks, though."

Becky snapped her gum. "See her anyway. She's next door to the temp agency, and she'll tell you who's hiring and who pays the best without charging a finder's fee." She dropped the card in the bag and handed it to Shirley.

When they reached the van, Shirley gave Kurt the gifts to pass on as well as his snacks. "Thanks for everything. If you change your mind, I'll make room for you."

He smiled sadly, and they both knew he wouldn't leave Copper City. "This jerky's my favorite. I got a little something for you too." He opened the bag quickly, and Shirley caught a flash of something red and fluffy. Her cheeks flushed as she pictured the furry bras and wondered if Kurt had a secret girlfriend.

He handed her the pink fanny pack, and Shirley's eyes welled with tears as she threw her arms around Kurt's bony shoulders. She'd finally gotten to know her brother, and she was leaving him and everyone else she loved behind, all to escape an inheritance of ghosts.

Chapter 11

Audrey

I run and run and don't stop until I make it to the school's court-yard. Inside me, Mara uncoils. I feel her toes stretch and her mouth open in a feline yawn.

Why are we out of breath? I was in a nice nothing space before you flooded it with nervous energy.

"I-I didn't want to be late."

Jeez, Angsty. The world won't end if you miss morning announce-ments.

"I like to be punctual."

Gross. I'm going back to the nothing.

I don't dare think of what happened, not until after I sense the last twitches of Mara settling into the ether. But then it's too still. The gathered crowd turns as one and all eyes land on me. Voices fall silent as I enter the building and walk to home ec. People turn away. They click their lockers closed gently instead of slamming them. A low murmur follows me. Someone says something about how awful it must be for me to look in the mirror. Every whisper, every exchanged glance slices into my thin skin. I'm a sideshow.

I used to be invisible in these halls. Mara was the opposite, soaking up attention like a flower poised to the afternoon sun.

Now, I wish she'd say something, share just a tiny bit of her spunk, but Mara is quiet, just a fuzzy sensation way down at my ankle.

Outside the home ec classroom, I imagine Zadie's flower and breathe in and out. Entering is like diving off a cliff. The chatter fades to whispers and the soft taps of texts patter like raindrops. It's too late to turn back, a dozen eyes pin me in place. If our fates were reversed, Mara would make a joke or even call out the silence. In awkward situations, she'd flip her discomfort onto others.

I wish I had the guts to speak out. Instead, I duck my head and slide into a seat at the only empty table in the front, the one dead in the center. If they're going to stare, I prefer it to be at my back.

Waiting for the bell, I pull out one of Grandma's notebooks. I've looked at them before but never deeply, and after last night I wonder what Grandma was up to. The notebooks are dated like diaries and are filled with strange lists. I think they might be dream journals, but I suspect there's more to it.

When Mrs. Delaney walks by, I slide the notebook back into my bag and pick up the embroidery I started after finishing all the other projects planned for the semester. Even though I missed the last few weeks of school, I'm still ahead. For me, handicrafts are like baking. I adore the process; it's easier to plan a project and create it than it is to hold a conversation with my classmates.

The classroom door creaks open. Zadie's creeping in fifteen minutes late, and my stomach flickers with butterflies that belong to Mara.

Zadie gives me a tight smile and goes to grab her project from the monster rack in the back. She's alarmingly behind, but I don't think she cares. She drops a heap of fabric on the table, sits down, and works her deep brown curls into a messy bun.

"I'm glad you came." My words sound stiff, and I feel a flicker of annoyance from Mara.

"Well, you know. Misery loves company." Zadie yawns. "You okay?"

I nod and twirl the embroidery needle. It's cold, and the half-finished pattern feels like it was made by someone else. Someone who could control how the stitches flowed together. My fingers tremble too much to push the thread through the needle's eye. Inside, Mara prickles.

"Hey, Zadie. Hi, Audrey. It's good to have you back." Rhea Uckleman stops in front of us.

"Hey." An easy smile spreads across Zadie's face.

Rhea leans over the table and lets her long fingers trace over a stripe of stitching on Zadie's project. "Looks good."

"Um, thanks." Zadie chuckles.

It isn't good. After a beat, I realize Rhea is flirting.

She shifts and smiles again, turning Zadie's cheeks pink. I feel like an intruder.

Her body pointing toward Zadie, Rhea rolls a scrap of felt. "Geo's having a party tomorrow night. Nothing big, but his parents are out of town."

The effing audacity. I'm barely in the ground, and Rhea's making her move.

My chest tightens as I pick up a pastel skein of embroidery thread and tie a little knot, followed by another. It helps to keep my hands busy, under my command. There's an unmistakable electricity between the girls, a sizzling enchantment. Mara swells inside. Six. Seven. Eight knots now.

Zadie replies, "I hadn't heard about it."

"You can come with me." Rhea touches Zadie's arm so quickly I'm not sure her fingertips landed.

My belly tightens with unease, and invading emotions scrunch my forehead into a scowl. It's bad enough to be a lonely bystander while Zadie and Rhea exchange sly glances, but Mara's turning me into her angry avatar. Twelve knots.

"You too, Audrey." Rhea's smile isn't unkind, but I have to clench my hands together to keep Mara from taking a swing.

"No thanks." I manage to say it without spite, but my teeth grit.

"I have to work," Zadie says. "But . . . I can stop by after."

"Great. I'll see you there. Text me." Rhea saunters off with Zadie's eyes tracking her movements across the room.

Inside, Mara's desperate rage courses through my veins like lava. My fingers twisted the thread into a useless lump, but I still have control. The last thing I need is Mara's jealousy surging through me, washing over my face.

But a trace of something must be there because Zadie frowns, and her brows knit in concern. "Are you okay? Wanna sneak out when the bell rings—hang out in the woods?"

The flashing teeth of the apparition are fresh in my mind, so I shake my head before letting out a gasp as a bead of blood bubbles around the embroidery needle embedded in my finger. I hadn't meant to do that.

When I pry the needle out, red spirals into the grooves of my fingerprint. My eyes lock with Zadie's and she looks away first.

The classroom door opens, and an administrator rushes over to Mrs. Delaney and whispers something. The pinking shears drop from Mrs. Delaney's hands as the color drains from her face. She stares at them for a long moment before speaking. "Put up your supplies. We're going to the cafetorium."

Zadie squeezes my hand, and it's hard to let go.

Twenty minutes later, the entire school—all two hundred of us—

gather in the cafeteria slash assembly hall. A new marble plaque hangs on the entrance wall, it's an etching of Mara's yearbook picture along with the words *Forever in our hearts.*

More like forever in the lunchroom. Gross. Mara sinks inside.

Mr. Walls, the principal, taps the microphone. He doesn't give his usual gruff comments about respect or remind us to stack the chairs afterward. Instead, a croak emits when he opens his mouth, and he sobs.

Someone in the back hoots before the room falls quiet. The grown man's magnified cries echo throughout the school. The vice principal, Ms. McGill, jogs over to him, her heels snapping like gunshots. She wraps her arms around Mr. Walls and leads him off stage before returning to the microphone.

She grasps it with both hands. "Students . . . Isabel Walls has gone missing."

Chapter 12

Zadie

No!" My cry causes a beat of silence. On stage, Ms. McGill continues, but I can't make sense of her words. Mara was missing nine days before her body was found. The search teams and reporters left, but no one bothered to take down the missing posters and purple ribbons.

There are no suspects, only whispers. Another girl is gone, and the town can't pretend Mara's death is some one-off tragedy. People in the surrounding rows turn to stare at Audrey and me. It's happening again.

"Zadie?" Audrey's face is slick with tears. She's tugging at my arm. I'm standing. Everyone else is sitting. Audrey gives my arm one last pull, bringing me back to my seat.

I bite the inside of my cheek until it hurts enough that I know this isn't a dream. "Isabel Walls?"

Audrey nods. Buzzes of silenced texts fill the space, and no one tries to hide their phones.

At the microphone, Ms. McGill mentions that counselors will be available. "School is canceled for the remainder of the week. Your parents have been notified. If you have information about Isabel, contact the police." She points to the media screen overhead.

My eyes blur as I focus on the school picture of the smiling middle-school girl with light brown hair, hazel eyes, and tan skin. My stomach twists; it's Isabel's turn to have her face on every storefront. Her picture turned into a plea.

Ms. McGill honks her nose into a handkerchief as she exits the stage. Silence turns into wary murmurs. Maybe this is a nightmare.

We've all been here before.

Tunnel vision leads me to the nearest exit. It's an emergency door, but the alarm's been broken for years, and no one's ever bothered to fix it. Audrey skitters behind me. I march with tears drying on my face. Red tinges of anger explode at my temples.

Poor Isabel Walls. They didn't take it seriously when Mara was stolen. Sure, there were searches in case she was hurt in the woods, but I'd told the police about our fight. I'd trusted them and told them everything. I never said she ran away, but that's what they decided after my interview. It was my fault. When her body was discovered in the mine—a historical mass murder site—reporters flocked. People only took it seriously when it was too late.

Isabel Walls's parents are well respected. She's a "good girl," so maybe she'll have a chance.

Audrey is squeaking something. I move faster. My bones want to rip from my skin. I feel like I'm about to explode. Or shatter.

Is there a difference?

I run, pumping my legs like if I can get away fast enough, this won't be happening. I crash blindly through the forest path, my body taking me someplace familiar. It doesn't register how far I've gone until I see the brothel. This was our special place.

A rustle sounds, and I whirl around. Mara breaks through the trees and into the bright light of the clearing. She's running, her face full of fear. But it's too late. I didn't help her. She's dead.

The world around me is a blur of blonde and trees. I scream.

Fingers wrap around my arms and yank. My knees hit the ground.

It's Audrey. She's squeezing me. Pale hair blocks out the surroundings. She kisses my cheeks, wet with a thousand tears. Her fingers glide down my face. It's as if she doesn't hear my cries.

I'm jolted back by a crash. My face burns. Stings. Audrey is on top of me, grim-faced. I want to raise my hand to touch my cheek, but her knees are on my arms. "You slapped me," I gasp, throat burning.

"You wouldn't stop screaming." She doesn't apologize. "It's what they do in the movies." Her voice is different, husky and cool.

"Get off."

She slides onto the ground beside me. I sit up, but she pulls me back to the warm grass and cradles my head. "Breathe, babe."

I dig my nails into my palm until my hands stop shaking. Audrey is acting strange. "Do you think she's dead?"

"Not yet. But she might as well be."

I swallow a gasp. "Audrey—"

"It's Mara."

"Audrey!"

She squints skyward, her lips pursed as if annoyed by being asked to explain herself, a Mara-esque gesture.

I would have never pegged Audrey as an actress before now. She's having some sort of breakdown. Hell, I'm in the middle of my own. I thought she *was* Mara a minute ago. But that's different than her saying she is.

"There is no standard way to experience tragedy. Or to express grief." Dr. Pham said that to me after I confessed to only feeling numb to Mara's death, that I couldn't accept she was really gone.

I fight the anger building inside me and try to replace it with empathy. I let out a slow breath. "Don't joke like that."

We sit quietly. Birds tweet like there's nothing wrong with the world. A bee buzzes between us, oblivious to the tension.

Audrey breaks the silence. "Remember when we went skinny dipping in the Millers' aboveground pool because we thought they were out of town—but they hadn't left yet? And we had to hunker down naked for a full hour when the whole family decided to eat dinner on the porch? They said grace and everything. It was freezing. They never noticed our clothes on the other side of the pool."

Audrey spinning the recollection like it belongs to her is a gut punch. I didn't know Mara shared our stories. It hurts to be surprised; I thought I knew Mara better. I thought I knew Audrey too. "Why are you doing this?"

"It's me. Zadie, I swear." Her blue eyes almost have that greenish tint that Mara's did. Her voice is a perfect imitation, and it breaks my heart.

My voice cracks. "Audrey, please stop."

"That same night, you got attacked by mosquitoes, and you got that hellacious bite on your tit. I wrote an ode to your third nipple. Remember?"

Tears slip down my face. "Audrey—"

"*Mara*! It's me. I'm still here, in Audrey, but I swear it's me." She grabs my hands, clasping them in hers like a prayer. "Please believe me."

She leans forward and kisses me, a long press ending with her playfully nipping my lower lip, Mara's signature hello.

It's an impossible thing to believe. But I do.

*

At home, Mom's door is shut. When I press my ear to the wood, the unmistakable sounds of crying filter through. I grip the knob for a moment but let my hand fall before stumbling into my room. These last hours have felt like a fever dream. Another girl taken, and this time I'm sure of the outcome. What happened to Mara shattered my naïve belief in happy endings.

Mara.

I sink onto the bed. I've imagined so many alternate universes where she was somehow still alive, but living inside Audrey wasn't one of them. When I was with her, it felt so real. Now, I'm not sure. It's all so insane. Tonight, the three of us, if there indeed are three of us, can sort everything out. There's so much to say, to try to understand.

My phone chirps with a text from Rhea, and I can't bring myself to look at it. After Mara died, Rhea knew what to say. Her mom passed years ago, and Rhea was one of the few people who didn't offer me trite condolences or shy away from my grief. Without her encouragement, I wouldn't be working to move on and out.

But now, answering her text feels like a betrayal.

There are so many questions. I asked Audrey—Mara—the most important one already: if she knew who killed her. I assumed the answer before she said it; Audrey would have gone to the police if Mara did. But it's still a blow.

Lying on my bed, I put on a playlist and let the notes wash over me, and my eyes fall on the Vega. My throat tightens. My mom tutored Isabel Walls. I mostly ignore the parade of kids who come on weekends and evenings for one-on-one algebra lessons, but I remember Isabel.

She showed up one Sunday afternoon a few weeks ago when I was sitting on the porch playing some old folk songs. Lost in the music, I didn't acknowledge her straight away, as she didn't move up the steps or utter a word. She watched my fingers with such intensity, I fumbled a chord change and put down the guitar.

"Can I help you?" I asked.

Isabel ducked her head and murmured something.

"What?"

She looked up; her cheeks were rosy. Isabel wrapped her arms around herself in a dead-on impression of Audrey at her most awkward. "I like your guitar." Her voice was a soft and clear soprano. "I-I'm here for tutoring with Ms. Slade."

Mom wasn't home. I gestured for Isabel to join me and called Mom's cell. She swore and told me she'd forgotten and was fifteen minutes out. I relayed the message to Isabel, who shyly asked if she should come back later. Her gaze never shifted from my guitar.

"Do you play?" I asked.

She shook her head.

"Wanna try it?"

Her eyes brightened, and a smile twitched across her face. I motioned for her to join me, and I set the guitar on her lap and looped the strap over her head. "The first chords you wanna learn are C, G, and D. You can play thousands of songs with those."

Tears prick at my eyes as I recall the warmth of Isabel's back as I stretched one arm behind her, positioning her fingers along the frets. She let out a tiny gasp of delight when she managed to sound a pure C. Isabel had an ear for music. We worked on those three chords until Mom pulled up, breathless and apologetic.

Isabel gave me her phone number, and I promised to text her and give her another lesson. I never did.

Guilt creeps over me like a rash, and I punch my pillow. Mr. Franklin, my old guitar instructor, once told me I'd be a great music teacher, and I took it as an insult. I didn't want to be like my mother, working behind the scenes of someone else's success. I wanted to be a headliner.

Now, I'd give anything to go back in time and set up lessons with Isabel.

My ringing cell pulls me from my regrets. I know it's Jen, my manager at Graveside Tours. The only people who call instead of text are her and my mother, but Mom's still in her room trying to hide her freak-out. I don't feel like talking to anyone, but it's work, and Jen's probably calling to cancel tonight's shift.

"Hello?"

"Hi, Zadie. I wanted to touch base with you. You're scheduled tonight, but I can fill in if you need time off in light of . . ."

"People still want to go on the tour?"

"Triple the usual amount. You know Mr. Orlich won't turn away customers."

Audrey. I bet it's her appearance as Mara that triggered the extra reservations. There are whole forums where ghost hunters swap hot spots. "I can work." The idea leaves a bad taste in my mouth, but I need a distraction, and it's more money for my get-out fund.

"You sure?"

"It's fine."

After hanging up, I sweep my thick curls into a puffy bun. My stomach flips and twists as I slide in the bobby pins. It's messed up to scam people when a girl is missing. But triple the usual crowd size? Even without a bonus-tour, that'll be good money.

I text Jimbo, and after a moment's thought, Audrey.

I sigh—Mara will be the star of this show, and I have a feeling she'll be an eager participant. This has nothing to do with poor Isabel. I hate myself when I look in the mirror.

I look like a fraud.

Chapter 13

Audrey

Inside me, Mara is so joyful she's practically skipping.

I told you she'd believe me! No more secrets. Thank you for letting us be together like that. Today was the first time I've felt happy—actually happy—since I came back. I can't wait to see her tonight, and the three of us can talk about everything!

My insides knead with fury as Mara tap dances with glee. "I didn't *let* you. You forced your way out."

No, I didn't. You shut down when we were in the clearing and Zadie was freaking out. You didn't do a damn thing. So, I asked if I could take over, and you said nothing.

My tongue feels thick in my mouth. She isn't lying. The disappearance of Isabel Walls is a soul shock. "I froze. But you didn't have to take over."

Mara is quiet; I don't sense contrition, only calculation.

Fine. Next time, I'll wait.

I think about telling her there won't be a next time and feel her prickled reaction. She's listening.

I told you, you think loud. Besides, I'm excited. I felt alive.

"Did you forget about Isabel already? She's only been missing a few hours." It's cruel to ask, but there's a meanness fermenting in me—it may belong to Mara, but I let it rise.

Of course not. Mara turns liquid. It feels like shame.

"What do you remember about—" I swallow. "Your killer?"

She exhales. Ripples. *Tall, massive, really. Big hairy hands. I never got a good look. It was always dark.*

"Do you think he's the one who took Isabel?"

Mara twists hard and sharp. *Don't act stupid. You know he is.*

We both fall silent. The walk home has never felt this long.

A tinkling sounds; it's Dad's ringtone. Grateful for the distraction, I answer.

"You alright, honey?" Stripped of his faux twang, he sounds younger and uncertain.

"Yeah. What are you doing right now?"

"On break between shows. I'll take off if you need me."

I hold my breath, picturing us on the couch streaming episode after episode of *Steven Universe* like we did between searches and police interviews after Mara vanished. It's tempting, but I know better now. Binge-watching comfort television won't help anything.

"Thanks, but I'll be okay."

"Listen, keep the doors locked. Both your mom and I work late tonight, but I'm gonna keep my phone on vibrate. Call me, even if I'm shooting Bloody Jasper, I'll answer. If you need me, I'll come home. No questions asked."

I don't mention I plan on meeting up with Zadie after she gets off, and thankfully he assumes I'll be at home like always. After we hang up, I don't feel any relief at not being found out. It makes me sad that he couldn't tell I was keeping something from him.

As I often do when I'm feeling lost, I find myself in the kitchen. The pantry is in desperate need of a restock but I'm not looking for anything complex. I crave simple and sweet. Thinking of Dad, I select a sleeve of saltines.

My father is an easy man who eats the same oatmeal each morning. To me, he always smells of maple. Outside of the occasional barbeque, he doesn't spend much time cooking. Still, his recipe is my go-to for a fast fix of sugar and salt. I preheat the oven and toss sticks of butter and brown sugar into a saucepan. After the bubbling mixture caramelizes, I drizzle it over rows of crackers, and at last, my hands are calm, my heartbeat steadies.

The doorbell rings as I'm setting the baking sheet to cool on the counter. I stiffen. No one else is home, meaning it's up to me to answer. With all that's happening, I can't just ignore it, can I? The bell sounds again, and I tiptoe to the door and hold my breath as I peer through the peephole; the glass distorts Jimbo's lean figure. He's never been to my house before. I step back, considering not answering, which is silly. Even though we've never actually hung out, he's as close to a friend as I have.

"Audrey?" Jimbo calls, sounding concerned.

"Just a minute," I answer before counting to ten and opening the door.

He raises a hand in greeting. His standard grin is missing; instead, he wears a small, tight smile.

"Why are you here?" The words fall like rude toads from the sky. "I mean, it's okay that you're here." That wasn't much better.

"I heard about Isabel Walls. Are you okay?"

"I don't know. I haven't let myself realize it yet." The statement is odd, but it's true. I've been too worried about Zadie and Mara to wonder about my own feelings.

"I get that. I made this for you." He holds out a cereal bowl filled with a cake-like substance. "Microwave mug brownies. I didn't have exactly the right ingredients, but it's probably edible."

"Thank you." I join him on the porch, tears threatening my

eyes. It's been a long time since someone's done something nice for me without wanting anything in return. My lips part but no words come out. Fragments of thoughts tumble in my mind and I fight the urge to tell him everything: The thirty minutes of missing memory from the day Mara disappeared. The apparition in the woods. Mara's return. How she'll destroy my life, and how lonely I'd be without her.

"You don't have to eat it." Jimbo shakes his head at the bowl. "It sorta looks like meat loaf."

"This is so thoughtful. Want a piece?"

He grins. "Clever girl. You want me to risk it first." He plucks out a glob and hands me the bowl. I sit on the steps, tentatively take a nibble, and set the dish down. The brownie has a jerky-like texture.

Jimbo sits on the other side of the somewhat edible offering. The dingy toe of his Converse is flush against the velvet of my ballet shoe. The porch creaks as he moves, settling in next to me. We stare into the woods. The space between the trees is woven with darkness strange for this hour. I hear a faint buzz—like a thousand cockroaches—droning from the forest.

"How are you handling . . . it?" I ask, breaking the silence.

"I don't know Isabel, but Principal Walls was always good to me." He snags another bit of brownie before asking, "Did you get Zadie's text?"

"Yes." I roll a brownie crumb between my fingers, smoothing it into a little ball.

"It's messed up that she wants to run a bonus-tour tonight. I know it's a money thing, so I'm in, but if you don't want to, I'll shut it down. Zadie won't know we talked."

I'll know. Mara's voice snakes between my ears. She's been giddy at the notion of playing herself in the mine again.

I was so relieved not to be alone tonight that I didn't even protest the plan. "I um . . ."

Tread carefully, sweet pea. You wanna be besties with a boy who brings you crap snacks? Fine. But I'm seeing Zadie tonight, and if you screw things up for me . . .

My hand spasms, flinging the brownie ball, which smacks Jimbo between the eyes.

Bullseye.

Jimbo blinks; his expression is dumbstruck.

"I'm so sorry. I-I don't know why I did that."

"Are you sure you're okay?"

"Yeah, I just need a distraction. Let's do the bonus-tour."

Good girl.

In the distance, flashlights flicker and voices call for Isabel. The entire town will search tomorrow, but only first responders are out tonight. The terrain here isn't safe for novices to wander about in the dark.

The star-speckled sky morphs a rusted mine cart into a shimmering statue against the black of the night. I'm no novice, and I walk without a light, letting my eyes adjust. Nothing sparkles in the mine where the dark is pure.

Mara's confidence and a dozen memories of clandestine mine meetups flow through me. I've never done this, but with her inside, my body moves like it's sure of the way. After pulling the metal door open as far as it will go, I duck under the taut chain and squeeze into the dark mouth of the mine. I click on my flashlight, insert my earbuds, select my favorite podcast, *Nothing Bundt Baking*, and put my phone into the bib pocket of the overall dress. Mara was so awful with Jimbo earlier that I'm fighting back with an episode titled "You'd Butter Believe It."

She protests, and I crank the volume. She shrinks to the point where I can't feel her. It'd be nice if we weren't fighting. Listening to the hosts compare Irish and Amish butterfat percentages isn't as comforting as I'd hoped.

It's creepy in these tunnels. I've never done anything like this, tiptoeing in a dark, haunted place. Though I'm upset with Mara and can barely sense her presence, I don't think I'd be brave enough to do this without her.

Grandma never shared her reasons, but she said that the dark entity of the woods was not only present in the mine but more powerful here as well. Even without Grandma's warnings, there are stories. Plenty of people report hearing cries echoing from the bottom of the pit. Everyone knows about the eternal moans from the mutilated miners who never left the Devil's Domain.

It's probably my imagination, but I hear faint groans and sense dread and despair dripping from the rocks. I turn the volume as high as it can go. It's awful here in the dark, shivering on the narrow catwalk, waiting to frighten tourists. I can't believe I let Mara talk me into this.

When we were little, she convinced me to do all sorts of things. Every time I got in trouble, it had something to do with her. Even as I got older, I didn't want to disappoint her. I thought I was over that, but here I am, playing with ghosts.

Taking money for frightening people feels unlucky. In this quiet moment, I decide to give Zadie my share to help with her move. Even though I barely know her, I'll miss Zadie, and I want her to find happiness. I don't want anyone else to feel like a prisoner. She shouldn't stay just because Mara did.

Bat wings flap overhead, and I pull my knees to my chest. I hope the group gets here soon. It's awful waiting here alone.

Nice baker banter, Angsty.

I startle and pause the podcast. I hadn't felt my cousin listening.

What's my consolation prize?

"Huh?"

You're gonna encourage Zadie to leave and give her money as a goodbye present. What about me? I'll be stuck here with you.

"You shouldn't spy on my private thoughts."

She scoffs. *Admit it. This is how you wanted me to find out that you don't care if Zadie abandons me.*

"She has the right to move on. Besides, didn't you break up because of Rhea?"

Fuck you. Mara boils around my heart.

A beam of light shines in the distance.

"Mara . . ."

It's showtime, she snaps.

I turn off my flashlight and get into position.

Behind me, in a not-so-distant cavern, someone—*something*—whistles the tune to "Oh My Darling, Clementine."

Chapter 14

Shirley
44 Years Ago

Robin and Wren tugged at their mother's hands, speaking with rapid-fire excitement about finding a snake under the merry-go-round during recess. Though Shirley was used to how her twins alternated sentences and often spoke in unison, some days, the zealous prattle was exhausting.

"You did the right thing and told your teacher, and nobody got hurt," Shirley cut in. Her head pounded, and she wondered if a vision was coming. Since moving to Vegas six years ago, she hadn't seen any ghosts, but the premonitions never stopped.

"But Mommy, what if it's an omen?" Robin asked.

"My, they are teaching you such interesting words in preschool."

"I learned it from Baba Inga."

Shirley smiled. "Well then, you should ask her what she thinks."

It only took Shirley twenty-four hours of living in Vegas to wonder if she'd made a mistake. She found the locals blunt and the tourists entitled, and she was terribly lonely. She'd gone to the fortune teller's shop to ask for job leads, but when she walked in the door, the plump old woman ran to her, wrapped her in her arms, and whispered, "Oh, my poor little dove."

Inga did find Shirley a job, working in her shop, brewing teas and tidying up. She taught Shirley to read tarot and throw bones, and it wasn't long before Shirley thought of Inga as a freshly forged family.

It was Inga who first sensed that Shirley was pregnant, and Inga laughed until she cried when Shirley sheepishly admitted to a tryst with the lion tamer from a show cycling through. Later, Inga helped watch the girls and taught Shirley how to bake bread and cookies.

"Why is it all dark?" Wren asked now, pointing at *Fortunes by Inga*. The heavy velvet curtains were shut, and the neon crystal ball was unlit.

A stone of unease dropped deep into Shirley's gut. She pushed open the door and called in, "Inga? Are you here?"

"Of course! Get in quick," the old woman snapped, but her face was etched with worry. She sat in a worn armchair by the till and stared at the phone resting beside her.

"What's happened?" Shirley asked.

"Hasn't yet. The phone will ring for you." Inga glanced over at the girls, who, delighted by the dim light, were playing behind the curtains, booing like ghosts. "It's a feeling like I had before my Ivan died. Brace yourself, little dove."

Shirley went cold. This wasn't like Inga. The woman was elderly but not prone to confusion—

The phone rang. Shirley jumped.

"It's for you. I will answer if you wish."

It rang again. Had it always been so loud, so shrill? Her heart sank, it had been over a month since she'd last spoken to Kurt. Did something trigger his PTSD? Shirley reached for the phone, and her fingers froze over the cradle as she spotted Robin and Wren watching.

"I'll take the girls for ice cream." Inga groaned as she stood. The ringing continued as the little girls dashed about fetching Inga's purse and cane.

Shirley held her breath and picked up the phone when the door clattered shut.

"Hello?" The voice on the other line was frantic. "Shirley?"

She exhaled. "Franny? What's wrong?"

"Kurt. He-he was the driver." Franny's voice cracked as a soft thud of a hand covering the receiver muffled a sob.

Her heart seized. "Was there an accident? Is Kurt okay?"

"The bus."

Shirley sank to the floor, the phone cord uncoiling with her.

The bus. Her vision blurred, and her insides twisted. The fence, the toddlers, the portrait. An odd root. A rusty pickaxe. A flashlight rolling down a cavern. The red fuzzy dice dangling in the windshield before a sharp jerk, acceleration, and the bus hurtling into the pit, the bodies flinging inside like clothing in a dryer.

Kurt worked in the mine; he couldn't be the driver. This didn't make sense at all. Franny must be hysterical.

Shirley took a steadying breath. "Were there babies on the bus?"

"No. It was a school field trip. They were coming back from the mine." Franny's voice shook. "Your brother is dead, and he's to blame for fifteen other deaths."

The words were a slap that stunned Shirley into silence. Sixteen people were gone.

This was a tragedy that Shirley knew would come but hadn't been able to stop, and now Kurt . . . She felt feckless and—

"You knew." Franny's voice was flat and accusing.

"Are Dale and Michael okay?" She couldn't ask who else had been on the bus, not yet.

"Shirley! You warned me about the dice. Why didn't you stop him?"

"The dice, I—"

"When Kurt came back from dropping you off in Las Vegas, and I saw them hanging on his rearview, I nearly went into labor. I told Michael what you'd said about if I ever saw red dice hanging in a bus—and Kurt drove a VW bus, and well, Michael said you had a sick sense of humor. Why did this happen?"

Shirley had no answers, and they languished in silence, listening to one another's ragged breaths.

At last, Franny spoke, "Shirley, I think you—" She broke off, leaving hints of a muffled conversation.

"Franny had to see to the boy." Michael Hennessey sounded older than the last time Shirley had spoken to him. "Listen, sweetheart, don't come back. I know he was your brother, but he's a mass murderer." His tone was meaner, too, and if the sloppy edges on his words were any indicator, he was drunk. "There weren't skid marks, understand?"

Shirley felt dizzy and unable to form words.

"Now, I spoke with the Orlich family. They lost their oldest son, Timothy. Terrible, you know." Michael hiccuped. "Anyhow, Orlich Senior says he'll see to cremating Kurt. He doesn't want him buried with the rest of them. You understand, don'tcha?"

"I have to come and—"

"No." Michael's voice went cold. "Now, I'm a nice guy, but you cautioned my wife about the buses years ago. Said something about the big dice—the ones Kurt got in Vegas. He must've been talking about doing something like this for a while. The war scrambled his brain, but you let this happen."

"It wasn't like that."

"Don't come. You aren't wanted."

*

That night, Inga kept the girls and Shirley found an old bottle of whiskey and took a shot before dialing the number of the kind coroner who'd listed her mother's death as accidental.

"Hello?" The man was cautious, exhausted.

"This is Shirley McBennett." The line went still, so still she heard the electricity between them. "I just want the names of the bus victims."

The silence returned.

"Please. I need to know who to pray for."

The man cleared his throat. "The bus had sixteen people aboard. Driver Kurt McBennett, teacher Delilah Walls, students Timothy Orlich, Lillian Hudson, Taylor Miramar, Carmen Redondo . . ."

With a trembling hand, Shirley wrote each of the names down in her composition book. "Thank you," she said after he finished.

The line went dead, and Shirley whispered the names until she recited them from memory like prayers on a rosary. These were people—children—she could have saved if only she'd followed the right thread. The suffering she failed to prevent gnawed at her heart.

Gripping the notebook, she moved into the bedroom. Inside her nightstand cupboard stood a series of composition books. Shirley kept written accounts of all her visions—a habit modeled after her grandmother's midwife records.

Shirley pulled the first down and ran her finger over the lists written in unsteady print. She set aside the journal and moved on to the next one. The more recent books had the toddlers—not her girls but unsettlingly similar—and the bus, as did the current notebook she kept on her nightstand. After a prediction came to pass, the corresponding vision stopped appearing.

She inhaled and flipped through the books. The burst blackberry had the most entries and was the only image appearing throughout all of them. It was her oldest vision, and she was no closer to understanding it than she'd been as a kindergartner. In a ritual of anxiety, she rummaged through the pages of her past and wondered about the visions that had ceased.

She knew the endings of many, like the hiker who got lost in the woods. Shirley had seen the woman's boot with its red laces and the strange metal-looking root repeatedly. Did the woman trip on the root and stumble down a forgotten mineshaft? How could Shirley have stopped that? And why did she continue to see the root but not the boot? There was no one to ask.

In darker moments, she wondered what sort of things her mother had seen. The demon in the woods ran Shirley out of state after one interaction, but that poor woman had daily encounters and managed only by medicating herself into a fog so dense it kept her from noticing when her trucker husband didn't return from that last long haul.

That's when they'd moved in with Grandma Dottie, a no-nonsense midwife who kept her hands busy and didn't make time for the dead. She wasn't without her quirks, though. Time and again, Shirley witnessed Dottie calmly gather her kit before standing by the phone, waiting with her head bowed, hands clasped. Then the telephone would ring. How her grandmother knew when a baby was coming, Shirley never asked. She knew it was something similar to her snippets, something others didn't experience.

Sometimes Dottie would pause at the door and shudder. Those days, babies were born with cords wrapped around their necks, blue or still. Statistically, she lost the same percentage as others in her field. Whatever she knew did little to change fate.

Now, Shirley looked through each of her composition books, searching for what she'd missed, what she *would* miss. The sun set and rose while Shirley performed her futile penance.

87

Chapter 15

Zadie

I conclude the night's tour and try not to gawk at the crowd of thirty-six. They've been weirdly attentive, soaking up my every word. Tonight, this isn't a minimum-wage job; it's a performance. In the saloon, I hum a few bars of the tune the ghost pianist is said to play. One woman even takes notes with a flashlight pen. I'm lit with the energy that comes from giving an exceptional gig. This is the closest I've felt to the exhilaration that came with cheering crowds after Mara and I performed at open mics. It's bittersweet, but reassuring that I can command attention on my own. "Any questions?"

Hands wave in the air. I gulp down my surprise. "Yes." I point to the notetaker.

"Is it true that Mara Quinn was your girlfriend?" Her head is cocked and her illuminated pen poised.

The question makes me gasp. "Who—why do you want to know?"

The notetaker steps toward me. "What are your thoughts on the Walls girl? Do you believe the disappearances are related?"

"I don't want to talk about that."

"Perhaps we can speak later." She moves closer and places a

88

business card in my hand—her cold fingers close mine around the thick rectangle. Blood rushes behind my ears as she finishes. "The disappearance of Isabel Walls must be devastating for you." She presses a hand over her heart.

I nod and look away, taking a moment to compose myself. Thinking of ghosts all night, I haven't been able to take my mind off Mara.

I want this to end. I won't call on Jimbo; I scan the crowd for a less investigative face. "What's your question?" I ask a young guy with a mullet.

"How much does it cost for you to take us to the mine?"

I blink. Jimbo's chin is dangling. Mullet guy isn't a friend of his.

"I'm not supposed to do that," I whisper.

"But you do." A middle-aged woman in a flowery peasant dress locks eyes with me. "I represent a group of clairvoyants. My spirit guide has conveyed that Mara Quinn will communicate with me. She can tell me where the girl is, and we shall save her."

The group closes in around me, waiting for my response. I turn, looking for an out, but I'm surrounded.

"We brought cash." The woman seems to speak for a large section of the group. People reach for their wallets.

I've never been good at math, but I know I can make more tonight than I've stashed away in the past year. "Fifty each," I say, half hoping no one will agree, feeling the weight of the key in my pocket.

Murmurs ripple through the crowd, and the bills pile into my palm. I won't change clothes; I welcome the stiff layers of protection. As we trek to the mine, the crowd buzzes with anticipation, but each step I take thuds with apprehension. This will be my last bonus-tour.

At the gate, the padlock hangs open. It isn't the first time the mine crew has left it unlocked, but it makes me uneasy. When I give my little speech, my movements are heavy with dread. I think of the roll of cash in my skirt pocket and try but fail to shake the thoughts away.

The descent into the earth feels off. Maybe it's the size of the crowd adding extra eerie echoes or my conflicted emotions, but tonight, it actually feels like we're disturbing the ghosts. Over my shoulder, the tourists' faces are eager, salivating for a scare. I hope Audrey's changed her mind about playing Mara. I want these ghoul gawkers to be disappointed.

When I lead the group around the bend in the mine, a click sounds, and a floodlight illuminates the area. The people behind me gasp and stumble.

Flanked by two police officers, Audrey trembles before us, her face soaked with tears. A radio hisses with static.

"We got more trespassers," the smaller of the two cops tells some distant dispatcher. Footsteps echo behind me. The taller officer marches over, shouting, "Nobody move!"

Lights scatter, and footsteps pound into the distance. Without looking back, I know at least half of the group has fled. My stomach drops like a boulder. Wishing desperately for a cosmic rewind button, I look to Audrey. Standing between the two uniforms in her overall dress, she looks like a scene ripped from an alternate universe. *Lost Girl Found.*

The illusion shatters, and my heart catches when the clairvoyant speaks. "Why is that girl dressed like Mara Quinn?"

Chapter 16

Audrey

I can't handle this. Please, Mara, you're better at trouble—you talk your way out of everything. What should I do? Mara?

She isn't answering my silent pleas; my cousin is still stewing over what I said about Zadie deserving to move on. I'm turning into a quivering lump of nerves, and I can't even think. I'm entirely *Angsty Audrey.*

A woman in a petunia-patterned dress stares at me with cold eyes, her glare equal parts repulsion and rage. No one's ever looked at me like that. Like I'm something rotten. I wish I could dissolve.

"She's pretending to be a dead child—disgusting." The woman shakes her head, her anger radiating. "How could anyone do something so terrible?"

My mouth moves as if to speak, but the only phrases threatening my lips are damning.

The radios sizzle and fizz, and even the people seem to buzz. One of the policemen, Officer Donaldson—he plays poker with my dad—has said something. Zadie's looking down, her face red with shame. Officer Donaldson's bushy mustache shifts, and I know he's speaking but I don't register his words.

"What?" I quake.

"Why are you dressed as Mara Quinn?"

"She's my cousin. Was my cousin."

He spits and addresses the leftover group. "Come on, people. Single file, let's go."

Zadie hangs back and reaches for my hand as we walk. When we get outside, she gives me a lace handkerchief—part of her costume—and I realize that tears are rolling down my face. I wipe my eyes and scan the crowd. Jimbo is gone. So many people are glaring at me. I focus on the sky; the stars nestled against the mountains are close enough to singe your fingertips.

"Officers"—the petunia woman has an everybody-better-listen-to-me voice—"those girls are committing fraud. They lured us here under false pretense."

Zadie's fists shoot to her hips. "This was your suggestion. You wanted to use your extraterrestrial powers to gossip with ghosts."

"Extrasensory!" The woman's hands wave with fury. "That girl is dressed as the dead one. Sadie took fifty dollars from each of us to see this fraud."

"Some psychic—can't even get my name right," Zadie mutters.

"She has a key. Everyone's heard of these sightings in the mine. This isn't the first time."

Officer Donaldson clears his throat. "Folks, the mine is off-limits outside of typical tours. I'm going to release you all with a verbal warning."

Zadie exhales with relief. I watch as her shoulders sag, letting an invisible weight roll off. My chest tightens. It won't be that simple. Nothing ever is. Not when anger heats the very air.

"What about our money?" the clairvoyant asks.

"We'll be taking it into evidence. If you submit your information, we'll be sure to get it back to you." There are mumbles as people back away. "Or, we'll donate the funds to the search for Isabel."

The crowd disperses. Zadie tugs at me, and I follow until Officer Donaldson clears his throat again. "Not you two."

*

In my nightmares, I have no control. My legs move like a wind-up soldier, marching me in whatever direction I'm pointed. That's how it felt the first time Mara took over; how it still feels whenever she does so without asking.

Getting arrested is worse. I'm awake and in control, yet my legs jerk forward, my knees hardly bending, and one officer keeps putting her palm on my back, corralling me.

When we stop, she pushes past me, and a familiar scent—a perfume of sap and sandalwood—drifts by, filling me with nostalgia for just weeks ago when I was a victim, not the bad guy. Back then, the officer offered cookies, sodas, and her regrets. Everyone at the police station knows who I am.

When Mara went missing, I received only kind looks and gently worded questions in what they called the soft room. I memorized every paint bubble on those pale blue walls. Even in the parking lot, random people selected for questioning would lose their looks of annoyance, exchanging gritted teeth for slack sorrow when their eyes met mine.

Now heads shake in my direction. There are no tender looks nor considerate eyes. Thoughts and prayers are reserved for victims. I picture Isabel Walls's parents in the soft room, crying while well-meaning people offer them stale Chips Ahoy.

The female officer stops next to a digital camera on a tripod and points to a set of electric-blue footprints painted on the floor. "Stand over there."

The wall is marked with measurements like in the movies.

There's going to be a mug shot of me dressed like Mara.

I take a heavy step and freeze. A man slumps against the wall; his chin-length hair is clumped with gore. He wears a flannel shirt that I'm sure I've seen before. Slowly, he raises his head. I can't look away or move; there's a scream desperate to come out, but I only gape. His face is a smear of skin and blood, and his features swirl together. A bulge with a slit of red—an eye—stares at me. There's something unsettlingly familiar about it. The man's mouth falls open, revealing holes and bloodstained teeth.

"Come on, move it," the woman demands.

At last, I find my voice, "There's a—"

But there isn't.

Only faint lines and chipped numbers are on the wall now.

"I'm not gonna tell you again."

Sniffling, I make my way to the wall as my nostrils fill with the stale scents of burnt rubber, sweat, and rust. I'm standing where the man was moments ago. Fear chokes me as the camera flashes, and I go blind.

Deep inside, reverberating off the chambers of my heart, I hear Mara.

Don't worry, that dude was an echo from way back, like a creepy residue.

"A ghost," I say aloud, but it doesn't sound like anything over my whimpers.

Yeah, but not like me. I got a host—you. I doubt he knows he's dead. That poor bastard is just a memory. Besides, he's gone now.

I squeeze my eyes shut. The camera's flash sears into my retinas; its bright white bolts linger like specters.

Audrey, we'll work it out, okay?

I can't stop crying.

Want me to take over for a while, kid?

"No." With the initial shock of my arrest wearing off, I don't want to give up control.

If there's something, anything, I can do, let me know.

"Just leave me alone for a while, please."

A gentle warmth blooms inside me, a feeling like love swirls in my core before Mara shrinks to the size of a sesame seed and drifts down deep to where I can't feel her.

And I'm alone.

After I'm processed, the officer leads me to the waiting area. Zadie is already sitting on one of the hard gray chairs. Her brown eyes goggle at the popcorn ceiling like she can't believe this is happening.

I sit down next to her and stare at the entrance as if it's a soufflé I'm certain is about to fall. Any moment our parents will come, and I know we're both dreading seeing the looks on their faces. My mother will wait until we get home, then she'll yell until we both cry. That's how our fights go. Dad's only been upset with me a couple of times. He'll give me the silent treatment until he isn't angry anymore.

"Audrey?" Zadie's voice is soft, a whisper, though there isn't anyone near us. "Is Mara in there?"

"Just me right now."

Zadie squeezes my arm and leans in close. "I'm sorry I got you involved in this. I told them it was my idea."

"I could've said no."

Zadie drops her head into her hands. "There's something else I need to apologize for. When Mara told me that she was back, we kissed. I was so overwhelmed I didn't think about asking you if, you know, I could." She peers out at me through splayed fingers.

"It's fine," I say, unable to muster much else.

Zadie lowers her hands. "I think we should—" The Copper City chief of police stomps in, interrupting her mid-thought.

Chief Uckleman—Rhea's dad—glares at us. His body is taut with tension, a vein twitches in his neck, and his dark skin glows as if embers burn beneath the surface. Even his bald head is tinged with orange—like he might burst into flames. Trailing him is the ever-somber and always formidable Richard Orlich, the owner of the mine and CEO of the Orlich Family Corporation.

My heart stutters in my chest as my stomach plummets. Mr. Orlich is Zadie's boss's boss, and worse, the man who signs my father's paychecks, and right now his big hairy hands are fisted at his sides. I force my gaze up, trying to gauge his anger. Against his deep burgundy shirt, his face appears bloodless. His blue-gray eyes scan us; his thin lips go thinner as he shakes his head at our costumes. Wrapping my arms across my chest, I wonder which he finds more distasteful: Zadie as one of his pioneers or me as Copper City's unsolved murder.

Mr. Orlich nods in Chief Uckleman's direction.

The chief sneers, not bothering to hide his disgust. "You girls should thank your lucky stars. Mr. Orlich isn't pressing charges against you for breaking into his mine. He's the reason we're not gonna throw the book at you. Do you have anything you'd like to say to him?"

The wall of water over my eyes bursts. I try to speak, but the words don't come. Leering from above, the men look so impossibly big and powerful.

Zadie clears her throat. "We're sorry." She sounds as pathetic and small as I feel.

Mr. Orlich heaves a great sigh, his big shoulders rolling back before slumping. "When I saw that the chief was calling me at such a late hour, I thought there was news on the little girl."

He doesn't have to say which girl. An unsettling silence falls at the mere hint of Isabel Walls.

"I'm so sorry," I whisper at last, wanting to end the awful quiet.

Mr. Orlich toes at a bubble in the linoleum floor. With his hands shoved deep in his pockets, he looks like a kid troubled by something outside his control. "When I was a boy, a group of us snuck into the mine on a lark. Summer vacation was looming, and we were young and restless. A homeschooled girl named Julie Hartshorne got separated from us somehow. She was soft-spoken and terribly shy. We didn't notice she was gone until it was too late. Her body was never recovered. Not a day goes by where I don't think of Julie."

He pauses and looks at us, *at me*. I nod to show that I'm listening and understand the horrible thing he's confessed. Mr. Orlich shifts, leaning over Zadie, his expression unreadable. "I understand you left Miss Hennessey alone in the mine."

Zadie's face pales. "Yes."

"There is nothing worth that kind of risk. If things went badly—well, you both are acquainted with the pain that comes with losing someone so young."

Shame etching across her face, Zadie hangs her head.

Mr. Orlich turns back to me. "Unfortunately, experiencing one loss doesn't make you exempt from others. Before Julie, my big brother, Timothy, died in that horrible bus incident. I'd never dreamed that morning would be the last time I saw him. The pain doesn't go away. If someone made a mockery of his death . . ." He shakes his head and steps back, addressing both of us. "It's fortunate no one was injured tonight. Teenagers don't realize how fragile life is, if someone fell or . . ." He turns to Rhea's dad. "It's late. I appreciate that you alerted me to this situation. I trust you can take it from here, Chief Uckleman?"

"Of course. Thank you for coming down, sir."

The men shake hands, and Mr. Orlich offers a curt nod in our direction before striding to the exit. We all watch as the night claims the man and the doors swing shut, sealing us in. Hands locked behind his back, Chief Uckleman paces before us like a general.

"In case you have forgotten, this town has an unsolved murder and a missing child. I don't have time for this. What I do have is a couple of orange jumpsuits that'll make it real easy to spot you as you spend your summer vacations picking up trash along the highway." He halts, pivots, and glares. "Report to Officer Donaldson on June first for your garbage bags. Beautify this town, stay out of trouble, and maybe I won't get around to launching a full investigation into your scam. Capisce?"

"Yes, sir," Zadie whispers.

My stomach roils, and I'm terrified I'll throw up on the chief's shiny black shoes.

He snaps his fingers in front of my face. "You hear me?"

I nod.

"Good." Chief Uckleman storms out, muttering something about brats and bullshit.

We're still sitting in silence, unable to look at one another, when my parents come through the double doors.

Momma's face is stained with tears, and her eyes are puffy. Daddy's is blank, and he looks away when our eyes meet, and my heart shatters.

It'll be okay, Audrey. You're still their daughter. I promise they won't stop loving you.

For once, I don't mind Mara replying to my private thoughts.

*

Momma's tirade started the moment we left the police station. Dad spent the ride tight jawed and silent. Now the ride is over, and we're parked under the carport with the engine shut off, but Momma still doesn't stop.

"What are people going to think? My god, when Robin hears what you've done, I can't imagine what this will do to her."

The driver's side door slams shut, and Dad storms into the house.

"Really, Audrey, how do you explain this?"

"I made a mistake."

"If only it were that simple." Momma sighs and exits the car, leaving me behind.

I close my eyes and consider staying in the back seat forever. I wait for Mara to chime in with something sarcastic or offer a shrill impression of Momma, but she's respecting my wishes and giving me space. All of the worst thoughts burn through my mind. I squeeze my eyes tighter. I don't want to think about this anymore, I want things to go back to the way they were.

If I make French macarons tomorrow, I won't be able to focus on anything else. They're the most difficult pastry I know. The notion of measuring and sifting soothes me, and I exhale. Maybe Momma's temper has simmered. I get out of the car; the harsh click of cicadas is more insistent tonight, as if even the insects are furious. I freeze.

A young woman stands in front of our house, watching me.

"Hello?" I don't know when or where, but I've seen her before. She glides under the glow of the porch light. Her eyes are bloody.

Tripping backward, I slam against the car. My hands claw at the handle before I get it open and tumble in. Scrambling, I press down all four lock buttons. She's residue. She can't hurt me. I repeat Mara's earlier words, but outside the woman is closer, her head tilted like she's curious about what I'm doing.

I pull my phone from my dress pocket and drop it, sending it skittering under the driver's seat. I fall to my knees, groping for it, and when my hand grips the cool plastic, I let out a relieved breath. And then gasp, trying to scream, but all I manage is a hoarse nightmare cry.

The woman, a girl really, sits next to me. She holds a finger to her lips, her hand is a grayish white, but her fingernails shine neon with pink press-ons.

The musty mine scent floods the car as my back hits the door, and I blindly search for the handle. I don't dare take my eyes off her.

She offers a sad closed-mouth smile and tilts her head back, revealing tears of curling skin weeping blood down her throat.

"Mara . . ." I croak, trying to summon my cousin to scare off the ghost.

The girl's bloody eyes widen, and she nods.

"Mara!" I try again.

A wide grin splits the ghost's face. Some of her teeth are missing. She points to her neck and then to me.

"Please, I don't know what you want."

She's closer. Her face is near enough to kiss as she opens her mouth and moans.

I pull on the door handle and fall onto the pavement. The girl is out, too, behind me now, standing with her back to the trees.

Blood dribbles from her neck as her mouth drops in a soundless wail, her red eyes burning against the dark. I rip my gaze from her and run.

Chapter 17

Zadie

It's been forty-five minutes since the Hennesseys left with Audrey. I have an idea of what's keeping Mom from picking me up. When she's pissed, she cleans; I picture her slamming around the kitchen, washing dishes, and scrubbing counters. Fifteen more minutes trickle by, and reluctantly I take out my phone. It's been vibrating nonstop, but I haven't had the guts to check it. When I wake the screen, a stream of texts pops, and I want to barf.

The first message is from my boss Jen—small-town news travels faster than mobile alerts can carry them. I steel myself and open it.

DROP OFF YOUR COSTUME AND KEYS TOMORROW. YOUR FINAL PAY WILL BE GIVEN TO YOU AFTER YOU SIGN THE TERMINATION FORM.

Fired, in shout caps, no less. There aren't many jobs to go around, and I doubt my new reputation as a con artist will do me any favors.

I skim through my other texts.

Way to use your dead GF as a flex. UR real sick

WTF is wrong with you?

I heard something about you on the scanner. Are you alright?

That one's from Rhea. I've been avoiding her since learning about Mara. I don't know what to say to her—or even to myself. I doubt anyone's ever had the "listen, I really like you but my girlfriend's back from the dead and I wanna wait and see what happens" convo.

The rest of the notifications are from people I don't hang out with, bored kids salivating for fresh gossip. It's easy to delete them without reading. I've done the town a favor by giving them something to talk about besides poor Isabel. I cringe; I didn't think about the police looking for her in the mine. I'm fine with tricking people like the phony psychic. But the guilt of hurting the search for Isabel digs in deep.

A new message from Jimbo pops up.

Sorry to bail. How much trouble are you in? BTW Big Jim wants to interview you and Audrey for the podcast. He'll pay.

I'm not mad at Jimbo; I'd have done the same. We have a scammer's agreement not to rat one another out. Big Jim wanting to interview us is weird, but the promise of money makes me not care. I reply and then text Audrey.

You okay?

A door slams and I see Mom, her arms swinging in power-walk mode.

The hard line of her mouth and the V of her eyebrows make me wish they'd held me overnight. I rise, but she ignores me and instead asks to speak to Chief Uckleman. The young man at the reception desk looks like he's going to say no, but when Mom leans in, her eyes burning with fury, he doesn't dare. He nods and bolts to inform the chief, who comes out from his office, shakes her hand, and says, "Zadie, tell your mother what you've been up to."

I hesitate, struggling to think of how to explain this mess.

"Go on. We don't have all night," he snaps.

Both their faces are drawn tight, and it's clear neither has the patience or energy to allow for any rationalizations or excuses. I only talk about tonight, but that's enough. The truth stripped bare without justification sounds rotten.

Mom exhales and looks at the chief. "Thank you for your leniency. She doesn't deserve it, but thank you." They pump hands, and Mom pivots and walks to the door. I have to hitch up my skirt to catch up.

"Mom, I—"

She whirls around, pointing her index finger in my face. "Not another word. I never imagined this was possible, but I'm ashamed of you."

Chapter 18

Shirley
40 Years Ago

Shirley folded the eviction notice without reading it; she'd memorized the blasted letter and its legalese. *Fortunes by Inga* and the other shops on the block would be a pile of rubble in a month. Soon, a shiny new hotel and casino would tower over their former lives.

This development was no surprise, but Shirley had only half-heartedly looked for a new location. It didn't feel right to move Inga's place; especially now that she was gone. It'd been over a year since Inga starred a date on the calendar before passing peacefully in her sleep as scheduled.

Losing her was far from unexpected, but Inga had been the stopper on Shirley's barrel of grief. The old woman was the only person she'd spoken to about Kurt and the bus. Inga understood it wasn't sorrow that convinced Shirley her brother hadn't intended on killing those people.

"Little dove, that was not the brother you loved. Poison seeps easily into soft, gentle places," Inga once whispered in her ear before showing Shirley and the girls how to make blini.

Inga had embraced her mysterious gifts, abilities that Dottie ignored and Shirley's mother tried to drink away. Inga built on

Shirley's knowledge of medicinal herbs and added a regimen of divination to their lessons. Now, Shirley held onto a pouch of runes carved into stag knucklebones that Inga had gotten in the old country. When she'd passed them on to Shirley, she'd warned her, "If you're not ready for the truth, don't bother these bones."

The girls would be home from school soon, and Shirley had been gripping the pouch for an hour. Focusing on her question, she closed her eyes and reached her fingers into the cool clicking bones and felt a bit of paper with ragged edges, probably a wrapper. The girls got into everything, and as Shirley hadn't used them since before Inga's death, they probably saw the runes as fair game.

With a sigh, Shirley pulled out the scrap and unfolded it.

Inga's wobbly letters shone in royal-blue ink: *Don't let fear keep you.*

"Oh, Inga." Shirley closed her eyes. She'd come to Vegas to get away from her mother's ghosts and had lost her home. There was plenty Shirley liked about Vegas: It was a transient place where folks came and went without worrying about the watchful hags of gossip and judgment. In a city of anonymity, she didn't have to hide her quirks.

Still, after Inga passed, Shirley felt that old tug of home. Sometimes, she could almost smell the piney mountain air as she walked through the grimy Vegas strip mall where the locals bought groceries. Leaving Copper City was a trade of beauty for twisted neon.

During their Sunday night phone calls, Franny insisted that no one in town held what Kurt did against her. The only person who ever mentioned the dice these days was Franny's now ex-husband, and no one liked Michael, so no one believed him. Even Franny, with some gentle urging from Shirley, had let the premonition go as an unfortunate coincidence. Still, Shirley doubted she could go back without gossip over her fatherless twins and accusing whispers of complicity.

Besides, if she returned, she'd have to contend with the thing that had tried to possess her.

Shirley reached back into the pouch and grabbed a rune. Gasping, she flung the bone across the room as red bloomed along her heartline. She wondered if a scorpion had stung her, but the welt on her palm looked like a burn.

The air chilled as Shirley scanned the room for the rune. It had landed next to a framed photo she couldn't bear to look at or put away. The snapshot was of Kurt, his flannelled back to the camera, one arm dangling at his side with the other propped high against a tree. Pain stabbed behind Shirley's eyes as the photo darkened to a murky green and a foul mist unspooled around the tree branches and bubbled beneath the roots.

The stench of rot filled the air as Kurt turned.

His face was a blurred mess of flesh and blood, and his broken limbs were bent at all angles, rendering him unrecognizable. The frame fell to the floor, the glass shattering. The boulder-battered man gaped as shadows swirled, tethering him to the forest, reeling him in, and then swallowing him whole.

Shirley dropped to her knees and snatched the photo from the shards, slicing her palm. Tears splattered on the image as she looked away from her broken brother.

A fresh-formed fear took over Shirley's mind as she gathered her runes. Were all those awful spirits who tormented her mother just desperate for someone to notice, to help? Was Kurt trapped among them?

Chains of despair clung to Shirley, and she wanted nothing more than to brew hemlock tea and curl up on the couch to sleep forever. But she was a mother. And when she'd chosen to become one, she'd vowed to find the strength that her own poor mother never had. She'd promised to be the parent that she and her brother deserved but didn't get.

The girls would be home any minute. Shirley's hands shook, but she righted the frame and gathered the glass. Among the sharp pieces, she found Inga's note.

Don't let fear keep you.

Shirley made a decision for Kurt, her girls, and for herself.

Fuck fear.

Chapter 19

Audrey

A lazy stream of cool air seeps in through the open window, carting the chirps of cicadas and distant howls of a pack of coyotes. I used to adore the sounds of the nocturnal creatures, but now every noise is jarring. Shame and fear are the main ingredients for insomnia.

Listen, Angsty, so you got arrested, lost your Miss Perfect title, but it's gonna be okay. You gotta relax. The tension here is suffocating.

I pull my knees to my chest. "After we got back, when you were . . . wherever you go . . . I saw another ghost."

Another one? I guess the afterlife has some BOGO special going on.

"What do you think it means? I don't want to be around ghosts."

Present company excluded, right?

"It's freaking me out."

Robin said our great-grandma saw spirits all the time.

"Do you know what happened to her?"

She was a big fan of self-medicating and long baths. She either OD'd or drowned—on "accident."

My fingers flick as if itching to make quotation marks on that last word. I pick up my old stuffed bunny and squeeze. "That's discouraging."

You gotta learn to ignore them. They don't even know you're there.

"This one did. She followed me into the car. She was trying to tell me something."

A prickle of electricity runs through me. I've got Mara's full attention.

Show me.

I try to picture everything: the girl's red eyes, her almost earnest nods, and finally, the desperation of her silent scream.

Mara lets out a low whistle through my lips.

"What do you think she wants?"

Better hair. Or, maybe she wants to be your bestie.

"I don't want to see her or any of them again."

Skip town with Zadie. Copper City is the most haunted place in North America, she says with an invisible shrug. *Did you notice how Auntie Wren seemed more concerned about potential damage to her reputation as a soothsayer than your dead cuz cosplay?* Mara's an expert at changing the subject to whatever she's most interested in talking about.

I bite my lip to stop the quivering. I don't want to cry again; my eyes are swollen already. "Dad wouldn't even look at me. He didn't say a single word."

Oh, Angsty, they'll get over it. You'll always be their golden girl. In a couple of years, this will be their "terrible teen" story to tell. Honestly, they should be grateful for the material.

"At the station, it was like they didn't even recognize me."

Sweetie, the cord-cutting is long overdue. You've never rebelled, and frankly, all that good behavior has stunted you. I mean, that's why you're so afraid to figure out who you are and what you want.

I sit up in bed. I need to make her understand. "I know who I am. I just don't want to see ghosts. I want to be normal."

Then stop channeling Grandma. Staring off into the trees all the time like you're expecting to find something. There's nothing. Just us ghosts. Besides, Grandma was good ol' fashioned crazy.

Despite my efforts, the tears come again. "She wasn't crazy. There's something unnatural, something more than spirits in the forest. She was showing me how to keep the balance."

You believed her "spread the light" BS? There's nothing here for us. For you! Forget the forest. Let's ditch town with Zadie.

My heart aches for her a little. Mara believes she still has a chance with Zadie. I push the thought from my mind quickly and reply, "I can get a job at the market baking bread until Robin's Nest reopens." I stick my chin out, waiting for the blow. Mara doesn't disappoint.

That's what you want to do with your whole life? Bake the same ten loaves on an infinite loop? That's some fresh hell.

"It sounds nice. I love baking."

Done with the conversation, I move from my bed and cross the room to open the top drawer of my dresser. Grandma's old *Viva Las Vegas* fanny pack is there, stocked with herbs. I run my finger along the brass zipper and clutch the pink nylon fabric. Though decades out of style and devoid of monetary value, the fanny pack is the most precious thing I own.

I open it and select a few sprigs of lavender to put under my pillow. The sweet scent wafts in the air, and I can almost feel Grandma's golden presence.

It isn't fair. Audrey, I was murdered *in Copper City, and you want to keep me here as a prisoner.* Mara's panic-infused anger is palpable.

"I'm not keeping you anywhere. This is where I want to be. I know what happened to you was the ultimate injustice, but I can't live your life." I take a deep breath. "And Zadie didn't ask us to go with her."

She didn't ask you. Zadie loves me. She'll want me to go.

My fingers twitch, wanting to form a fist. "Let's talk about this in the morning," I suggest, forcing my hands to relax, to slip the lavender into the pillowcase.

No. You never want to talk about the hard stuff. We're gonna talk now.

"Zadie's ready to move on. She likes Rhea."

The sharp rip of fabric shocks me into silence. I can't release my grip on the fanny pack. My hands pull with a strength I didn't know they possessed, spreading apart the zipper's teeth. The stitches give, and the pack splits in two. Gutted.

The herbs and leaves fall to the floor like dead birds.

"Mara—stop!"

She doesn't.

Our fingers tear the fabric into smaller and smaller shreds. Our feet kick at the fallen morsels and grind them into the hardwood floor. When there's nothing left to destroy, my body goes limp.

Falling to my knees, I examine the wreckage. The bits are too small to fix, but I gather them anyway and clutch the largest piece in my hands. The tears come hot and fast.

I'm sorry, Mara whispers, her form shriveling deep inside.

*

Morning comes, the sun shining on the wreckage of last night. Mara is quiet, but I can sense her like a splinter. Carefully, I collect the remains of the fanny pack, putting every fabric swatch, every sprig into a Ziploc bag.

My phone rings and pings, but I leave it untouched on my nightstand. Zadie will want to discuss last night; she'll want to talk to Mara. It doesn't take a psychic to foretell where her allegiance lies: with her first love come back from the dead, certainly not with the girl she befriended out of pity.

Last night I told Mara I wanted to be normal. I may not know what that actually means, but I don't want to be scared anymore.

That's not asking for much. Neither is wanting to stay in my hometown, the place where I can always picture Grandma. Copper City is a part of me. So is wanting to make others happy in a simple way—by baking. That's all I want.

But that'll have to wait. I need to think, and I need fresh air.

The morning is cool but has nothing to do with my shivers as I stop by the carport where I saw the girl. I step closer to the tree line. The back of my neck prickles. I take another step. "Hello?"

Closer, my entire body tingles.

"You wanted to tell me something?"

Silence. No chirps or wind or anything.

"I'm ready to listen."

Deep from between the trees comes a tiny flash of light.

I move in closer.

Audrey! Stop. There's something wrong in there.

"Go away! I'm tired of you making all the decisions."

You make crap decisions! You couldn't handle Grandma's woo-woo garbage, and you sure as hell can't handle whatever's in the woods.

The image of the scattered remains of Grandma's fanny pack flashes across my mind's eye. In retaliation, I imagine the fanny pack whole and new, then picture Mara shrinking and being stuffed into it.

She gasps.

I wince at the convulsions from her kicks as I push her into the pack and visualize the zipper closing. Finally, I envision shoving the sack deep inside, tucking it under my diaphragm, trapping it and Mara among my organs.

I did it—I got Mara in check. A giddy laugh escapes me, breaking the quiet. My heart seizes. It's too quiet, the air too still.

I see her.

The dead girl stands on the forest trail, waiting.

If I turn away now, I can pretend this never happened. Eventually, she'll find someone else.

This spirit trusts me. My chin lifts; she must sense that I keep the light. Mara says that I'm afraid to deal with the hard stuff, that I don't know how to live. Her barbs still sting, but I roll my shoulders back. Mara's aren't the only words I carry. One of Grandma's mottos was: *Don't let fear keep you.*

I won't let it. Not anymore. I step forward.

My movements are slow, careful, and I feel faint when I'm close enough to see her red eyes and shredded neck. My breathing is too shallow. I think of Zadie and smell an imaginary flower and blow out a candle. Then I close the final space between us.

Smell the flower. Blow out the candle.

The corners of her lips turn up like something close to a smile. Her jeans and baby pink sweater look faded, but so do her skin and hair, as if she's being projected through some artsy filter. She's barely here.

"You can trust me." I don't meet her red eyes. Instead, I fix my gaze on the poufed and sprayed bangs, the cresting wave of hair at the top of her head.

She vanishes.

My fingers feel at the air where she just was. It tingles with electricity. There's a flash, and she's deeper in the forest, paused on the narrow dirt path.

There are countless reasons I shouldn't go, but I need answers, so I follow.

She disappears and reappears multiple times before we exit the dark forest after the staircase to nowhere, traveling down the pebbled street to the old, abandoned houses. Grandma said the cluster of once-homes were long ago condemned and to stay clear of them. I always listened to Grandma, so I'd usually veer the direction of the staircase.

Now, the girl appears next to a small cottage off by itself. I walk toward it, and she nods and vanishes. This time, she doesn't reappear. I bite my lip, unsure of what she wants me to do. I take a ragged breath; it feels like there's glass in my lungs. Maybe she's taking me to the killer, or the ghost girl might be trying to save Isabel.

I wipe my sweaty palms on my dress. I feel for Mara, tucked away; I don't know how long I can hold her. I know she wouldn't want me to go. But I don't trust Mara.

My breathing is steady now. I creep to where the ghost last stood. The house isn't abandoned. Inside, a clock radio flashes 12:00. The window is open and there isn't a screen; it wouldn't be hard to shimmy through.

I'm not going to break into somebody's house. Am I?

No. I formulate a plan: I'll say I'm rounding up volunteers for Isabel's search party, and if things look suspicious, I'll make an anonymous call to the tip line.

The *ding-dong* of the doorbell makes me jump. After waiting a minute, I try again and hold my ear to the door. Nothing.

No one's home. I jiggle the knob. Locked. In my peripheral, I glimpse a twinkle of light beside the open window. Wishing I hadn't worn a dress, I turn over an empty flowerpot to use as a step, pull myself up, and drop into the kitchen. The room is filthy. Flies orbit grimy stacks of dishes that fill the sink. I can't believe

I'm doing this. If I'm caught, will I be considered a repeat offender? What's the sentence for two break-ins in less than twenty-four hours? I bite my lip and hard swallow. It'll be okay. I'll just tell the truth and then I'll get to plead insanity.

Smell the flower, blow out the candle, and focus.

A table is nearly invisible under piles of newspapers and yellow legal pads. I pick up an envelope from a mound of unopened mail for Paul Hartshorne. The name sounds distantly familiar. Water-logged books and old takeout containers reach from counter to cupboards.

I was hoping whatever the ghost girl wanted me to find would be obvious, glistening and ready to pluck like an apple. But this is a hoarder's house, and I don't know what I'm looking for.

I move from the kitchen to the hall crammed with stacks of cardboard boxes. I'll never find anything here.

In the living room, there are more books and more boxes.

Someone coughs.

I step back, causing a floorboard to groan.

A spring creaks, and a snore emanates from the couch.

Heart in throat, I tiptoe closer. An old man is passed out with a remote dangling from a liver-spotted hand. A pair of giant as-seen-on-TV hearing aids rest in a saucer on the coffee table. The panic rises inside me; that man could wake up any moment.

Slipping away, I glance in the junk-filled rooms as I head back to the kitchen, just in case. But Isabel isn't here.

Feet away from the kitchen, the sound of chirping quail drifts in from the window. As I move toward it, something catches my eye. Under a large box, there's an 8'10 picture, yellowed with time. I can only see the forehead of a blonde. I crouch next to it and pull it. The corner rips.

I glance over my shoulder, reassured by the violent snore

coming from the living room. Again, I try to pry the photo out, but it won't budge. I'm going to have to move the junk stacked on top of it. The top box is filled with old homework sheets, notebooks, report cards, and scraps of to-do lists. Pick up eggs, milk, detergent. Post office, perm at 2. Trash. I put it down and pick up the next one.

The bottom of the box gives way, and I watch the torrent of books and papers monsooning down. Hardbacks batter my shins, and detritus falls around me, obscuring the photo.

"What in Sam Hill?"

I kick the books from my feet, losing a shoe, and run, bumping into the kitchen table before slamming my knee against the counter as I fight to get out the window.

Click.

I turn around. The old man is pointing a gun at me.

"Please—don't shoot." I put my hands in the air.

"Who sent you?"

A ghost. "No one. I'm sorry. I-I . . ." I have no words, no explanations.

Wheezing, the man takes a lumbering step forward. He has a prosthetic leg. Even missing a shoe, I can outrun him if he doesn't shoot me.

I swallow. "I didn't take anything. I swear. I'm sorry. Really sorry."

"Why are you here?" he growls, stepping closer.

"I'm looking for Isabel Walls." The half-truth spills from my lips before I can consider how stupid the explanation sounds.

He snorts and lowers the gun. "Did some other kids at the junior high tell you a scary man lives here, and you decided to play hero? You watch too many Scooby-Doo cartoons, young lady." He drops the gun on top of an old phone book.

"I'm in high school."

"I beg your pardon," he gruffs; the sarcasm is unmistakable. "When you get my age, anyone younger than forty looks like a damn kid. What's your name? I'm not gonna call the cops—I should, but I don't like 'em—but I sure am gonna call your parents."

"Audrey Hennessey." My voice is small. I should be relieved he wants to call my parents instead of killing me, but I can't imagine what they're gonna do.

"Hennessey, eh? Your ma's the fortune teller."

I nod, glancing at the yellow phone hanging on his wall. Momma will be livid if he calls her at work when she's with a client.

"She ain't psychic. I like Shirley, though. Good gal, didn't see her at bingo this week."

"She passed away." My voice quakes. I don't add *six months ago*.

"Oh, yeah. Dreadful. God rest her soul." He pulls out a kitchen chair, sits, and groans.

"Move that stuff. You can put it anywhere. Have a seat."

I move the pile of books from the chair to the floor.

"Why'd you think the Walls girl would be here? You oughta tell me if someone put you up to it. Was it the Simmons boy?"

A warm breeze floats through the window carrying a tinge of rot. I force myself to meet the old man's eyes. They sag with wrinkles, intensifying his brilliant green eyes. He no longer looks angry, only curious. I look away, my sight falling on a tower of pastel Tupperware containers.

He hacks a cough. "Forgive the mess. I wasn't expecting any break-ins today."

"I'm sorry."

"Bah. Tell me why you're here, girl."

"I had a sense that led me to your house. I tried ringing the doorbell."

"Your grandmother told me one of you was sensitive. She was the real deal herself, though she never put together how it all worked. Neither of us could quite get a handle on our life's obsessions."

I bristle thinking of Grandma having anything in common with this man. "Did you know her well?"

"Not particularly, but we shared an interest." He gestures to the stacks of books like it's obvious. Most of the titles are about paranormal things like ghosts and aliens. Smaller stacks contain books like *Vanished* and *Lost in National Lands*. Nearest to me is a pile of dog-eared Copper City history books.

The old man rubs his eyes and yawns.

"Something about ghosts?"

"No, well, not exactly. See, it's all connected. Copper City is a petri dish of the uncanny. From the ancients, Bloody Jasper, the missing hikers, the Girl Scout, the bus, Mara Quinn, and now the Walls girl. It's all connected. I'm sure of it. Never quite puzzled it together. I drove my Meredith mad with the research. Course that wasn't hard to do after Julie. Mere took her own life, you know. Out in the woods."

He stops, folds his arms, and looks out the window, his wrinkled face shadowed by a passing cloud. I now understand the box of shopping lists and doodles. It isn't much different than my shredded fanny pack. Sometimes we need to hold on to something.

"I don't blame her. Not one iota." He wags his finger at me. "Hell, I'da joined her, but I can't. Not until I figure out how it's all connected. I have to solve it. For both of 'em." He rubs at his forehead.

My heart flutters with realization. "My grandma used to say that too. That all the strangeness in Copper City is connected." I reach out and let my fingertips fall on the crook of his arm. "She tried to keep everything in balance. She used to tell me to keep the light, do you—" I start, but Paul is shaking his head.

"I-I need to take a little nap. All that yard work earlier beat the tar outta me."

"Okay." I'm confused. Minutes ago, he was going to call my parents. I stand, uncertain.

"Be careful with that boy of yours. I don't like the way he looks atcha. Like a starving mutt." The man shakes his head. "Just be back by supper. Your mother's trying out some new casserole."

"Um. Sure." I give a little wave as I walk from the kitchen.

"Love you, Julie."

"I-I love you too," I call, pushing open the front door—the weeds in the yard stretch past my knees. The poor man has some sort of dementia. I scan the forest for the ghost girl. She isn't there. Maybe she wants me to alert social services to get someone out to help him.

Disappointment knots in my shoulders. The woods feel thicker, darker as I take the path home, speed walking. I try not to think of monsters lurking in the brush.

"It's all connected." I say the words aloud, trying to weigh their validity.

The air ripples and the girl is back, grinning and nodding.

"But how?" I ask before a fist of pain punches me from within. I double over.

The ghost girl and the world around me vanish in a gulp of blackness as Mara takes over.

Chapter 20

Zadie

My cheeks burn as I walk under the missing posters on the doors and windows. Isabel Walls's school picture watches me as I slink through the town to meet Audrey.

Mrs. Valencia—my preschool teacher—glares at me as she staples a flyer to a telephone pole. Swallowing guilt, I tell myself that the precious hour the cops spent dealing with us wasn't a lost opportunity for a break in the case. Still, I know every minute counts, especially in the first forty-eight hours. Tears prick my eyes, and I block my face from view.

I wait for Audrey outside by the flagpole. She shows up looking pale and fragile, but there's a glint in her eye.

"Mara?" I whisper.

She nods and reaches for my hand. My mind flashes to Rhea, and I look around to see who's watching. Despite Copper City's faults, rainbow flags fly year-round, but that doesn't change that people like to gossip, and Audrey isn't a member of the alphabet mafia. I don't want to complicate her life, and I don't want Rhea to find out. Still, it's nice to have a hand to hold.

She rubs her thumbnail against the inside of my palm, something she used to do when she was alive, and any remaining doubts float away.

She catches me staring and gives me a half smile, wink combo: pure Mara. It makes me uneasy.

"Audrey's still in there, right?"

"She's resting deep down, where she can't hear us. She needs a few days off."

Excitement and hot guilt churn in my gut. None of the issues we had when Mara was alive have gone away, and things have only gotten more complicated. Still, my heart beats with the electric notion that I'll be alone with Mara again. It's all so impossible, but when I look at Mara now, I can barely see Audrey.

As if reading my thoughts, Mara squeezes my hand and says, "She's losing it."

"What should we do?"

Another shrug. Mara always had a pull-up-your-big-girl-panties-and-get-over-it attitude, but back when she was alive, she at least *tried* to be helpful.

"The entire town is losing it," I say. "It's all happening again."

"She sees things. Hallucinations. The stress of everything . . ."

We walk the rest of the way up the old stone steps and weave through the hillside path in silence. When we get to our old spot, Mara kisses me, her palms grasping my face, her mouth hungry and desperate. I return the kiss, but I want to talk, to figure out what to do.

When I try to speak, she presses a finger to my lips and shushes me.

I persist. "We need to talk to Audrey before, you know."

"I asked her. She's fine with it, she doesn't want gory details, but she's cool."

At the police station, Audrey said the last kiss was okay, but we didn't talk about anything further.

"Mara—" I start, but she pulls me down to the grass and presses her hand to my chest, laying me down. She straddles me and dots kisses from my forehead to my cheeks, sprinkling little pecks down my neck. The air is hot and smells of pine and earth. The droning of bees buzzing in and out of a nearby hive vibrates around us. Mara tastes like honey tea. No, it isn't Mara. That's how Audrey tastes.

"We should talk," I say. This is reckless, and I need a moment to think. My phone chimes with a text alert. We both stare at the name on my phone—*Rhea*.

"Later." Mara flips over the phone and kisses me again, this time biting my lower lip.

I don't want to fight with Mara, or to think about anything outside of this impossible moment. I roll her over and run my fingers through her spider-silk hair.

Before, our make-out sessions were filled with sweet kisses and gentle caresses. Now, our backs and elbows scrape against rocks. We use our teeth more than our lips. Our hands are desperate, grabbing and clinging. Nothing is truer than pain.

When our hair is full of grass and twigs, we lie with our arms twined together. Watching the clouds drift over the yolk of the sun, we don't speak. What's Mara thinking? I can guess, but I feel so far away from her. School will be over soon, we'll be adults, and I'll be free to pursue my dreams. But Mara? She's tethered to Audrey, and there are no certainties.

I guess a spectral love affair is a fragile thing.

"You look so serious."

"Mara, why didn't you cross over or whatever?"

She scoffs and squints at the sky. "It was all black. I didn't want to fade away from existence. I wasn't ready for that."

She's leaving something out, I can tell by the clench in her jaw, but I don't press. "That's horrible." My mind swivels back to Isabel.

"I dunno. Maybe death is the same as before you were born. It's all nothing. Sometimes, the nothing tugs at me."

I pull the Zippo from my pocket and rub at its scratches. I flip it and watch the flame dance in the breeze. Mara pushes her right thumb through the flame.

I shut the lighter and grab her hand. "Don't do that. You'll get burned."

"I like the pain there." She slides the finger into her mouth.

"Do you think he'll cut off her thumb too?"

"He took mine after I tried to gouge out his eye. So, maybe not."

"You really don't remember who killed you?" I can't help but ask again.

"If I knew, I'd do something about it." She doesn't elaborate on what that something is, but her words are sharp and icy.

We fall into silence until our phones ping in unison.

It's Jimbo; his dad is offering forty bucks to each of us for an interview about Mara's murder. He's got time now.

"You game?"

Mara squints at the sun. "You certainly are."

"I need the money."

She pulls a twig from her hair and breaks it into tiny pieces. "I think you *like* talking about my death." Her tone is bored, but the underlying edge is clear.

"I do not."

She looks at me, cockeyed.

"Sometimes, I *need* to. It's like popping a nasty zit. It's awful, but you're compelled to do it." I make a mental note never to reveal how much time I've spent on Mara's subreddit thread.

"I hate it."

Her tone is hard, and I don't press, even though I'm hungry for information—I crave answers. It's a long shot, but maybe talking about what happened will release a memory in someone else, something important. Something that could save Isabel. "It isn't that much money. If you don't want to talk to him, I won't either."

"I'll do it. I want some say in my press." She kisses my cheek—a fast little peck like she can't help herself. "It's nice being out like this. Don't tell Audrey, but I wish I could take over completely. I'm better at living than she is."

We walk to Jimbo's wrapped in silence. More Mara would be thrilling, but less Audrey makes me queasy. I worry about the whole sharing-a-body situation. Mara has one of those personalities you can picture easily slipping into rude-houseguest mode. She's always needed independence and freedom. Her tether with Audrey, someone who craves stability and safety, is far from ideal. There isn't a good solution. Without Audrey, Mara says she'd be one of Copper City's ghosts—an eternal flicker of energy performing some tiny, endless, compulsory cycle. A fate that's worse than death. But to keep things as is? That's sentencing Audrey to half a life.

I don't know what Mara's thinking, but her words scare me.

On foot, it takes forty minutes to get to the Shady Dell trailer park on the outskirts of town, where Jimbo rents a single-wide trailer.

"Gross," Mara says, eyeing a pyramid of empty Pabst Blue Ribbon cans stacked on the porch as I ring the doorbell.

"Don't forget, you're Audrey and probably excited to go to a boy's house."

"Audrey's hobbies are a freaking mystery." Mara flicks the top can from the pyramid, sending it over the railing.

Jimbo flings open the door and flashes us his crooked-tooth smile. "Come on in."

I go first, with Mara trailing behind.

"Hold up. You got something in your hair." Jimbo's fingers pluck a leaf from the blonde mess, and she swats at his hand. His eyes widen, and he holds his hands up in a "don't shoot" gesture. "Sorry. Um. You guys want a soda or something?"

"Sure," I say, as Mara answers no.

"I'll grab it. He's in the living room. I'll meet you there."

"Come on, *Audrey*," I say, emphasizing the name as a reminder.

"Whatever." She sniffs the air, her nose crinkling. The trailer smells like gym socks and hot dogs.

In the living room, Big Jim Lorenzini fills a flannel recliner. Even slumped over a laptop, he looks enormous. He's wearing a crumpled *Golden Nugget* T-shirt and sweats. It's a far cry from the black-and-vermilion three-piece suit he wears for his shows. That image is still etched in my mind from the dozens of posters that once advertised him around town. In the ads, the tips of his mustache curled just so, and his eyebrows pointed in a way that suggested something sinister. Red foil letters proclaimed him to be both *mesmerizing* and *unforgettable*. And he was.

For as far back as I can remember, *The Great Lorenzini* was Copper City's biggest attraction. He stands, smiling, and I notice his once-brick-wall physique has softened. He still has the pointy eyebrows and mustache, but the edges droop. He smells like sour beer, and it's easy to guess why his Vegas show got dropped so fast.

At my side, Mara stiffens like she's already annoyed with keeping up Audrey's wide-eyed personality.

"Thanks for agreeing to this. The Quinn case has never been more important." Big Jim stands and wipes his hand on his sweats before shaking mine. His grip is too tight, and the sight of his hairy knuckles gives me a chill.

When he reaches for Mara's hand, she flinches and jerks away.

He shrugs and pulls the coffee table closer to the recliner, where cords from a small switchboard, headphones, and microphones snake across the table's surface.

Mara's face has gone as white as her hair, and her mouth hangs open. She's trembling. "Mar—Audrey, are you alright?"

"We have to go. Now," she whispers.

Big Jim looks from his screen. "I'll have the mic set up in a second. I won't keep you long."

"Come on, Zadie." She grips my forearm, her nails digging into my skin.

"We have to leave. I'll set up a different time," I sputter, nearly losing my footing as Mara yanks me from the room.

Big Jim huffs. "I was counting on now. I got a schedule to keep, you know."

"Sorry!" I call over my shoulder.

We push past Jimbo in the kitchen, and I'm about to explain, but Mara won't let go or stop pulling me. She's strong. "Later!" I call to him as the door slams behind us. "What the hell?"

"Keep moving."

"What's going on?"

"It's him."

"Who?"

"Jim Lorenzini. He's the one. He killed me."

Chapter 21

Shirley
33 Years Ago

You're certain you can't contact my Taylor?" Joyce Miramar paused by the exit of Shirley's shop.

Shirley swallowed a sigh and reached for the woman's hands, wrapping her fingers over the dry skin. "I can share what I see in cards and dregs, but I can't call someone from beyond the veil."

"I'll pay double—*triple*—your rate."

"I feel most connected to the spirit realm when I walk in the woods. You're welcome to join me—no fee."

"Do they talk to you out there?"

"No, I'm afraid the conversations are rather one-sided, but I believe they listen." Though there wasn't evidence of Kurt's spirit being trapped on earth, Shirley knew it to be true. She was certain her brother hadn't moved on and felt deep in her marrow that Taylor Miramar had.

Shirley squeezed Joyce's fingers before the woman's eyes clouded and she pulled away. It was unlikely she'd return for another reading, much less a stroll.

Shirley watched Joyce disappear down the winding street and thought about how much money she'd make if she lied once in a while. She closed her eyes and took a deep breath of loamy mountain air.

"Ms. McBennett?" a low voice asked, and Shirley found a young man standing on the sidewalk.

Although she'd been back in Copper City for a few years, she still struggled around the bus victims' families; and two in a span of minutes felt overwhelming.

"Shirley, please." She'd kept tabs on the boy since her return, but she'd never spoken to Jon Walls. "Did you want to come in and have a look around?"

He nodded and brushed past. Perhaps Jon was aware that his mother's killer had once lived upstairs.

Shirley had inherited the apartment from Kurt, and despite offering it to the families of the bus tragedy, no one wanted anything to do with the space.

When she came back and brought her girls, they had a place to go. The antique shop had closed a few years prior, and when Shirley asked Orlich Senior if she could rent the ground floor, she was humbled when he agreed. The apartment was cramped, so the girls slept upstairs while Shirley made a little bedroom out of the shop's storeroom. It was an unconventional setup, but it suited the trio fine.

Sweat slicked her palms as she attempted to read Jon's blank face. He'd been so young when the tragedy happened, and perhaps he felt Shirley shared the blame for his mother's death.

"Do you really see the future?" he asked at last, pausing by the lace-draped table where Shirley read tarot.

She nodded and gestured for him to sit.

He did, his hands gripping the edge of the table.

Shirley perched across from him, pulling her cards from a velvet pouch. "Were you wanting a general reading, or is there something specific you're hoping to learn?"

He shook his head. "Tell me about the bus."

Shirley inhaled sharply. She'd known what the boy wanted but was hoping to be wrong.

"Please, I have money." His voice was hoarse.

"I don't charge for the past." She smiled tightly and pushed the cards away.

"My mother was the teacher on the bus. People won't talk to me about what happened."

Shirley rested her hand on Jon's clenched fist.

He shut his eyes and continued as if he'd been preparing for this moment, "Did your brother ever mention, wanting, I mean . . ."

"No." Shirley shook her head vehemently. "Kurt never expressed a desire for violence."

"They say you knew it was gonna happen. That you said the dice meant that he . . ."

It felt as if a knife had slowly slid up inside her belly to pierce her heart. It was an anguishing ache, but also a pain that paled in comparison to that of the hurt on his face. "I'm so sorry about your mother."

Jon's eyes were hard. "Why didn't you stop it?"

She wished she could say something to soothe his pain, but all she had was the truth. "Years ago, I had a premonition. I saw it happen, but it wasn't precise. Not enough to make a difference."

He stood. "I gotta go."

"Jon—" He was out of the shop before Shirley could finish, and the sound of static spitting from speakers made her turn, expecting to find one of her daughters fiddling with the stereo in the back corner. But the room was empty. Shirley rushed to the radio as it gave a final *click*. A hush weighed heavy on her shoulders as she turned to find a familiar girl standing by the staircase—the girl from the senior portrait vision—a vision she hadn't had in years.

There was no headache. No nausea. This girl was not in Shirley's mind. She was here, one pale hand resting on the banister.

This was the sort of visitor that had tormented Shirley's mother all those years ago, the type that left the woman crouched in corners, pulling out hair by the fistful. This was the spirit of Julie Hartshorne, a girl who'd attended a high school kegger deep in the mine and never came home.

Shirley fought her terror and let out a growl. "Go! You aren't welcome—"

The blood-red eyes stopped her; something horrific had happened. This was not the result of the story Shirley heard when she returned to Copper City. The locals attributed Julie's disappearance to too many beers in a dark place with dozens of pits.

Shirley swallowed and said, "Why are you here?"

Julie lifted her chin and pulled back the fluffy curls from her neck. Someone had slit her throat—no—stabbed it. The wound was a series of deep, angry jabs starring her skin.

"Who did this to you?" Shirley asked as static spit from the speakers.

The girl's mouth stretched in a silent nightmare scream as inky black smoke coiled around her.

Shirley reached into the dark, her fingers curling onto nothing as it and Julie vanished.

Chapter 22

Zadie

There's no one home at Audrey's. Mara flops down on the periwinkle bedspread, her face void of expression.

Questions thunder through my mind so fast, I can't decide what to ask first. Out of breath and stunned, I can't form words. I need to know if she's sure that Jimbo's dad is her killer. I don't understand why she didn't name him before. Mara and I saw Big Jim's show together tons of times, and there are billboards of him that we walked by every day. I'm about to ask when I catch the look of disbelief and horror slathered over her face. Mara is wondering the same thing—why it didn't click before? Trauma scatters memories, so I hedge. "Do you think Jimbo knows?"

Pressing her face against the pillow, Mara shakes her head.

I lie down next to her and wrap my arm across her belly. Securing her as my little spoon, I whisper into her ear, "It will be okay. Tell me everything."

A strange noise warbles out of the girl in my arms, and I gasp with pain as she slams her elbow into my side. I roll away, grasping at my ribs. "Mara?" I yelp.

She's standing, eyes wide and wild. "It's Audrey."

She turns away and stares into the antique vanity mirror over her desk. Her hands rake through her hair before her fingers run over her skin, examining every exposed inch. "What is this?" She whirls around, pointing at the triangle of flesh where her pale neck meets an almost translucent shoulder.

I blink at what looks to be a squished strawberry. A hickey—a betrayal. "I'm sorry."

She paces the room with clenched fists. "You've only known about Mara being back for *one* day. Already you're acting like I don't exist. That scares me."

"Look, it's been a daze. It's unbelievable." I shove my hands into my pockets and run my thumb along the edges of my Zippo.

"We have to cast her out."

"What? Why?"

"She's too strong. She's forcing me from my body." Tears cascade down Audrey's cheeks.

The words dig into me like a dull knife. In life, Mara could be ambitious to the point of ruthlessness, but she'd never force anyone to do something they didn't want to. Still, pushing boundaries, that *is* the sort of thing she'd do. I feel nauseous; Audrey isn't great at advocating for herself.

"I'll talk to her. I know she's stubborn, but I'll get her back in line. I'll make sure she understands that's not okay." I reach for Audrey, but she pulls away. Her eyes have turned icy.

"*You* don't understand. I had to fight to get out. I may not be able to do it again. She's making me *vanish*."

"I-I'm sorry. I'll do something. Please, I can fix this, I swear." My words thump like kicked rocks. There's no truth in my promise—I don't know how to make things better or even where to start. I'm only sure I can't lose either of them. "She said you wanted to be out for a few days. To rest or whatever."

"Mara's a liar." She spits out the words with bitterness.

My heart slams against my rib cage. Mara wouldn't do that, take over, force out her cousin. She wouldn't.

She would, a tiny truth from deep inside of me whispers. It's enough to crack through all the guilt I've shoved way down. It all bubbles up.

"I'm sorry," I say, knowing it's not enough. There's a wall of problems forming around me, and I don't know whether to try to knock it down or scramble over it.

"Help me," Audrey whispers.

"How?"

"I don't know." She fists away welling tears. "I want her gone. It sounds awful, but she's dead. She can't take my life."

It feels like the universe has splintered. I love Mara. Yes, there were issues with our relationship, but it doesn't change how it hurts just thinking about losing her again. I hardly know Audrey, but I trust her. I don't want to, but I believe her.

I beckon Audrey to sit next to me. "I will talk to her. And I won't do that"—I point at the hickey—"again." Relief swells my lungs, but the feeling doesn't last. Audrey won't look at me. "I promise to respect any decision you make—"

"You don't care that Mara is trying to steal my life."

I take a deep breath. It'll never come to that; that isn't who Mara is. "Right now, we need Mara. She says Jim Lorenzini killed her."

Audrey finally regards me, brow furrowed.

"We have to help find Isabel. Big Jim might have her somewhere."

Audrey gives a slight, almost imperceptible nod. "If Mr. Lorenzini killed her, why didn't she say something right away?"

"I don't know. Something sparked her memory when we met with him."

"How do you know she's not manipulating you?"

"She wouldn't—not about this."

"You don't know her like I do."

"Audrey, we need you to keep Mara here, for Isabel's sake."

"No."

"Audrey—"

"Get out, Zadie."

I reach for her, but she jerks away.

"Leave!" Her blue eyes look almost black, and disgust shines from her face.

I nod and shuffle out of the room.

I pause at the front door, hoping she'll call for me, but there's only silence.

My mind shifts through troubling thoughts, unable to hold on to a single idea before a more sinister one takes over. Audrey's anger and desire to get rid of Mara stabs at me before dissolving into Mara's fear-soaked certainty. Big Jim, the killer? He's so charming.

But isn't that what stunned neighbors say after discovering that the nice insurance salesman they've been living next door to for a decade has been moonlighting as a cannibal— "they seemed so nice"? The last time I saw the Great Lorenzini perform, he hypnotized Mr. Rael, the humorless barber, and convinced the man that flames were shooting from his rear. Everyone laughed as Mr. Rael scooted along the stage like a dog wiping its butt on a carpet. But now I wonder what else can he do. Can he wash away memories and lure a girl into the mines?

Another unwelcome thought worms its way through my brain. It's Isabel's second night away. I can't let this happen again—I need Mara. I shoot off a text to Audrey, a plea wrapped in an apology.

No reply.

I could turn left and head to the police station to tell the chief about Big Jim, but he wouldn't buy it. I need evidence or a believable lie to get him to listen—my cheeks heat. The thought of Chief Uckleman spins my brain back to Rhea. Thumbing through my contacts, I select her and type *Hey.* I can't think of anything else to write. I've been ghosting her. I press send anyway. The sensation of stupidity hits simultaneously with the whiz of the message. I let the phone fall deep into my pocket and climb the porch steps, pausing to pet Hobo as he loops through my legs.

The front door is unlocked, which considering recent events, is surprising.

"Mom?" Even though she's still fuming about the mine scam, I want to see her. I'll never admit to anyone how, at this second, all I want is for my mother to hug me tight, stroke my hair, and promise that everything will be all right.

She doesn't answer. I pop my head into the kitchen and check the bedrooms. "Mom?" I call again. Nothing. I go back to the kitchen. Sometimes Mom goes old-school and leaves a note on the fridge. That's when I spot the unlatched dead bolt on the back door.

Not only unlocked but ajar.

I inspect the kitchen. A few drawers are open, and half of the junk drawer contents lie scattered across the counter. "Mom?" It's a small yelp this time. Grasping our old cast-iron skillet with both hands, I lean against the back door and breathe a wordless prayer before kicking the door open and pointing the pan in front of me like a gun.

There's a shriek to my right, and I whirl.

"Jesus, Zadie! You scared me." Mom clutches one hand over her chest; the other is behind her back.

"I thought—what are you doing?"

"Nothing. Fresh air. Why don't you call in some delivery?"

"Are you okay?"

"Just go inside. I'll be there in a minute."

My heartbeat slows to normal, and the adrenaline drifts away. I inhale. A musty, burnt odor hits my nostrils. I look at my mother; one hand is still behind her back. Her cheeks are bright red.

"Oh my god, are you smoking?" It feels like a ridiculous question; Mom is always ranting about how dangerous smoking is, and how she can't believe anyone still does it in this century. She spotted Mara vaping once and wouldn't shut up about carcinogens.

Mom hesitates, gives a what-the-heck shrug, and takes a drag before snubbing out the butt in a rusted Folgers can.

In my pocket, the cold steel of the Zippo burns against my fingertips. I figured my dad was a smoker. Now, I realize that she must have been one too.

"I'm under a lot of stress." She ducks inside without meeting my eyes.

I follow, fighting the urge to call her a hypocrite, a bad example, or perhaps tell her I'm ashamed she's my mother. These insults are all fleeting ideas of revenge for her tirade last night, but I don't voice them. Something must be very wrong for Mom to be smoking—something like her only child canceling college and getting arrested.

"Burritos from Buster's okay with you?" Mom's already scrolling through her phone like she's willing me to forget that I caught her doing something she calls "filthy and stupid."

"Sure. Carne with green and red sauce." I sit on the yellow barstool as she orders. When she hangs up, I clear my throat and force myself to look at her. "I'm sorry about what happened. What I did."

She blinks. "What?"

"Last night . . . The tour, the police . . ."

The red of her cheeks deepens. "Well, that hasn't helped matters. So much is going on."

"Oh, you mean Isabel. I know you tutor her . . ."

"She's a sweet girl. Her poor dad."

"Do you think she'll live?"

Then Mom cries—not little slips of tears but a shoulders-heaving type of crying.

I put my arm around her. "It'll be okay."

She laughs a little. "When did you learn to lie like a grown-up?" She wipes her eyes with the back of her hand. "Zadie, sit down. I need to talk to you."

We haven't *talked* about the incident at the mine, aside from her little ashamed speech. I take a deep breath, wondering if she meant it. We have mismatched visions for my future, but Mom's normally supportive-ish. Disappointing her is actually kinda low on my list. It's somewhere after the Rhea and Mara issue, ghosts existing, and being jobless without a way to leave this damn town. I'm not in the mood for a recap of my arrest. Still, I brace myself.

Mom stares at the table. "They declared Jon a person of interest. So, he's a suspect."

I blink. "Who?"

"Jon Walls. Your principal." She drums her fingers on the table.

"Why?"

"Well, he's Isabel's father, he knew Mara, and he doesn't have an alibi."

Mara said the killer was tall. Mr. Walls is average, whereas they don't call Jim Lorenzini *Big* Jim without reason. Still, Mara spent her last days of life in the dark being tortured; it isn't fair to expect her to know for sure. Years ago, Mr. Walls was our soccer coach. He's normal, to the point of being bland. Did he target her? Could he kill his own child?

"Whoa . . . Do you think he did it?"

Mom lets out a long breath. "No."

"Why doesn't he have an alibi? Wasn't he home with Mrs. Walls?"

"She was in Flagstaff on business. I've known Jon for decades. He's a good man, and he loves his daughter."

I don't think Mr. Walls is the killer; he doesn't seem the type. I wonder, though, does anyone? If it isn't him, the police are wasting valuable time. The killer kept Mara alive for just over a week.

I have to talk to Mara.

"Even when they realize he's innocent, the nasty rumors will linger. That's the worst thing about small towns. A spark of gossip like that, it'll be witch-hunting season."

"It won't be that bad," I offer, "once they prove he didn't do it. Everyone likes Mr. Walls."

She nods, but she's not buying it.

"I don't know what I'd have done if it had been you. Zadie, I—" Her voice breaks and she turns away.

"Mom?"

She opens her mouth as if to speak again but presses her lips tight. She watches out the window. I stand and wrap my arms around her. We hug for a long time. Neither of us moves until my phone's alert chimes.

Hey.

I don't reply to Rhea's text.

After dinner, I text Audrey again and watch the screen until it fades back to black. Sighing, I set the phone down and open my laptop. I need to get the police to investigate Big Jim before it's too late. My fingers hover over the keyboard as I try to conjure the right question to Google. A knocking at my door interrupts my typing of *how to make someone a murder suspect*, and I slam the laptop shut.

Mom pokes her head in. "Isabel's vigil is starting soon. If you want to go, I'll take you."

My chest tightens. Vigils feel like a last resort, and at Isabel's I won't be the victim's girlfriend. I'll be the girl who diverted the investigation.

At Mara's vigil, Mom and I stood at the front with the Quinns and the Hennesseys. Mr. Orlich addressed us one by one. When he reached me, he squeezed my hand, his furry knuckles wrapping around my fingers as he looked me in the eye. Something others had been avoiding. He didn't offer platitudes or condolences. Instead, he leaned close and whispered, "Some losses are exquisite. Grief is deeper than love or hate. Your heart's broken, isn't it?"

It was a strange moment—an honest one. Everyone knew something horrible happened to Mara. We just couldn't speak the words.

"Zadie, I . . ." Mom interrupts my thoughts. "After you graduate, I'm selling the house and leaving Copper City."

"Seriously?" I've been talking about getting out of this place since kindergarten, but Mom's never mentioned wanting to move.

"I need a fresh start. Besides, with you going off to follow your dreams, why would I stay?"

"Is it because of Mara and Isabel, or is there . . ."

Mom sucks in both her lips and regards me as if trying to decide something. At last, she gives me a sad little smile. "Too many bad memories. I haven't told anyone yet, so do me a favor and keep it to yourself, okay?"

"Sure."

"Thanks, Zadie-doll." Mom looks away.

I know with that same sinking certainty I get when a song just isn't right that Mom is hiding something from me.

She rises and gives my shoulder one last squeeze. The door shuts behind her but does little to conceal the muffled sob, the soft sigh of secret tears.

I have to do something—not just for Isabel, but for all of us.

I check my phone. Audrey still hasn't answered my texts. If I go to her house, she'll refuse to see me. Mara is back, but I can't talk to her either.

I can't wait around anymore. It's been over twenty-four hours; Isabel is running out of time. The certainty that Lorenzini did *something* hangs like a weight around my neck. I pull out my phone and text the one person who might be able to convince the cops that they need to investigate Big Jim.

I hit send and hope I haven't run out of chances.

Chapter 23

Audrey

In the bathroom, I press a cold spoon against the base of my neck. When I remove it, the hickey is still just as red. I hate it. The mark has nothing to do with me, yet here it is, aching like a bruise, on *my* body.

Chill, Angsty. It'll be gone in a couple of days. Mara smirks from the mirror. *You should embrace it—people will think you're getting some.*

"I don't want that—don't you dare act like you did me a favor," I warn. "You violated me." In the mirror, my anger morphs into wide-eyed surprise.

No. It wasn't like that, it was just kissing, and it was Zadie. I didn't do anything wrong. I—

"I never said you could kiss anyone—and I don't want you using my body at all." I jab my finger into the glass, and though it throbs, it feels good to tell Mara off.

But how am I supposed to live like that?

"You aren't!"

Angsty—we share a body. We're a team.

"No. You take over my body. You're the villain."

The face in the mirror crumples as Mara retreats so far down

I can't sense her at all. I've won the argument and hurt Mara back. It doesn't feel good like I'd imagined, but I don't regret it.

There's a knock on the door. "Audrey, who are you talking to?" Momma sounds panicked.

I open the door. "It's a video."

"But it sounded—"

I cut her off, "I don't feel good. Is it okay if I stay home? Isabel's vigil, it's just . . ."

Momma watches me like she's afraid I'll shatter. Then she runs her palm over my forehead, and her lips tighten when she doesn't find a fever. She squeezes my shoulder and leads me to the living room. "Why don't you lie down? You look so tired, darling."

If only she knew the half of it. A girl's been stolen, and Zadie believes Mara, a lying demon, over me. A few hours ago, I followed a ghost only to be held at gunpoint by a sad old man. I *am* exhausted. I nod and curl into a little ball as Momma covers me with a crocheted blanket before disappearing to whisper to Dad.

A minute later, he sets a can of ginger ale on the end table. "Keep the doors locked. We won't be long." He looks like he wants to say more but can't find the words.

"Do you want us to stay?" Momma asks.

"I'm fine."

They say goodbye, and I wait for the lock to click before moving from the couch. There isn't much time before they return and, more importantly, before Mara reemerges.

Blanket wrapped over my shoulders like a protective cape, I slip on my shoes, dangle the pouch of runes from my wrist, and head outside. I'm lonely and confused, and the only person I want to talk to is Grandma. I don't know what her runes can tell me, but they're all I have.

I kneel by the trees edging our yard. Holding the pouch

between my palms, I whisper "Where's Isabel?" and select a bone and shine my phone on it. It's blank. Wyrd like before. I set the bone aside, it might be cheating to exclude one, but I need answers.

"What does the ghost girl want?" Pertho. I huff; Pertho is like a Magic 8 Ball declaring: *ask again later.*

I pause, listening, but a thick silence has settled around me. Grandma always said that three was a power number, so I pull one last rune. "How do I get rid of Mara?"

Wyrd.

My heart stutters against my ribs.

I don't know how it got back in the pouch.

The teakettle whistles, and I rush to shut it off, tired of all the noise. As I pour the steaming water into a mug, I catch my distorted reflection in the chrome finish, and my memory flashes to the battered ghoul at the police station. I'd been too scared to truly look at him. Now, I keep coming back to his blurred face; there was something familiar about it. I can't think of it, though; it's like trying to remember a scrap of a dream hours after waking.

I need to stop thinking of ghosts. I'm starting to look crazy. Mara and the rest of the spirits are real—I *know* they are—I also know that sounds insane.

A good night's sleep will help me regain control. It's been weeks since I've slept all night. I let the tea steep. Grandma used to ease my worries and put me to sleep with her tea blended with fresh sprigs of chamomile. There was more to it, though. I swear she could brew moonlight.

I wish Grandma would answer me, but she was a mystery even in life. When we were little, she'd take Mara and me into the forest to play a fairy game where we'd tend to the plants and creatures while keeping clear of a supernatural villain.

Maybe it was never a game.

The notion sends a shiver through me.

I can sense Mara lingering, listening to my thoughts, waiting to pounce. I hurt her—with the truth—but she'll lick her wounds and come back ready to fight. I can't handle another confrontation, not tonight. I can't even handle consciousness. Humming loudly, I go to the medicine cabinet, take a swig of NyQuil, and snap some Benadryl out of the blister pack.

Wait—Audrey, we need to talk about the woods. There's something—

Popping the pretty pink pills, I shut out Mara but not the thought of the woods.

It wasn't the same after Grandma died. I didn't question the changes, the black moss creeping up trees, birds splayed out with their entrails and jellybean organs scattered among Grandma's gardens. I thought the forest was mourning.

Deeper in, things were even stranger. I was always alone, few people in Copper City venture into the woods but suddenly there was evidence of an intruder. Someone who I thought of as the forest artist had fashioned wheels out of branches, created mosaics out of bits of bark, and, most impressively, crafted giant woven gateways that stood along a natural path, like portals to another world.

After Mara went missing, all the whimsical creations were destroyed, ripped apart with their meticulously created remains scattered.

I take big gulps of too-hot tea. I've circled back to the start of this all, the beginning of my loose hold on sanity. Before I even knew Mara was gone, I'd lost something—time.

I'd spied on Zadie and Mara fighting in the clearing and then I was outside the forest. Half an hour had passed. And there was a change in the air, the odor of disturbed earth and a peculiar musk.

The day Mara disappeared, I saw something I wasn't supposed to. It's only a feeling, a scar without an origin. I'd found myself on the edge of the woods, with my hands coated in earth, my fingernails all broken and bloody.

All I remember is that the forest gave me a warning.

Forget.

Chapter 24

Zadie

The house is too quiet. The hall light flickers and crackles as I walk to my room. I feel as inconsequential as a ghost. The bulb strobes before offering a *pop*, followed by darkness.

Plopping down on my bed, I pull out my phone. No answer yet. I put on Zoë Keating and try to lose myself in the haunting chords of the cello.

Body buzzing with the need to do something, anything, I get my laptop and type in Isabel's name. There're already hundreds of results. I click on an Isabel Walls forum that links to a *Copper City Serial Killer* subreddit with new posts popping up every few minutes. There's a lively debate in the comments about whether copper dust in the air has been turning people homicidal since the days of Jasper Dodge. My eyes blur as I scroll and scan. After stumbling on an all-caps rant titled *WAKE UP SHEEPLE! BLOODY JASPER IS STILL KILLING!* I exit the forums.

Isabel has less than a week left if the killer plays to the script. I Google *James Lorenzini*. I move from site to site with increasing speed—there's got to be something.

There's a report of a DUI that features a mug shot of a disheveled Big Jim in a tux and drooping red bowtie. Not wanting to think of my police station portrait, I click over to a gossipy Vegas blog post gleefully announcing his firing after only three performances. Another click leads me to an anonymous showgirl's Instagram post accusing Lorenzini of using hypnotism to put her in a compromising position. On the third page of results, I find his fundraising site. My stomach drops when a giant picture fills the screen. Mara.

I've never seen this one of her. I thought I had every existing image of her memorized. But here she is, leaning against a tree, looking pensive like she doesn't know there's a camera pointed at her. For a moment, I think it's Audrey dressed as Mara. Mara knew she was beautiful and liked having her picture taken, always meeting the lens with a dazzling smile or a knowing smirk.

I enlarge the picture and zoom in until I spot the small mole that dotted the corner of her right eye. After saving the photo to my computer, I do a reverse image lookup and find nothing. This shot isn't copied from somebody's social media; this is an original. Did he take the picture before he decided to kill her or after?

I scan the project's pitch. The bastard is raising money to produce a podcast investigating Mara's death. Only 15 percent of his goal is met. He's trying to shrug off suspicion by looking into the murder. Maybe he's trying to find out what the police know with a bit of investigative sleight of hand.

I need help.

With my phone in my palm and my finger floating over the letters, I struggle to draft the perfect text.

There's a knock at my door, and I drop my phone, sending it bouncing along the hardwood floor. Mom only waits after knocking if there's someone with her. It must be Audrey, ready to talk. "Come in!" I yelp.

But it isn't Audrey.

"Hey." Rhea smiles and holds up a physics textbook. "You didn't forget about our project, did you?" She widens her eyes and darts them to Mom awkwardly hovering in the hall.

"Oh!" I fumble with my backpack.

"Zadie, I know things are . . ." Mom pauses, searching for the right word. "*Crazy,* but you're a senior. You have to keep up."

"Absolutely," I agree, offering my palms.

"It's a good thing you have Rhea for a partner." Mom smiles at her and adds, "Do you girls want a snack? Some brain food?"

My eyebrow rises. "Did you go to the store?"

Mom blushes. "I'm sure I could find something."

Picturing a platter of cereal dust and ancient bread-and-butter pickle slices, I say, "I think we're good."

"Okay. Not too late. The search party starts at seven tomorrow."

"Sure thing, Ms. Slade."

"It's Kate outside school." Mom smiles again, awkward.

"Thanks, goodbye Mom," I say pointedly.

"I'll let you get to it." She does this odd little movement like she's shaking invisible maracas. She doesn't know how to act around people. It's embarrassing, but I think it's a mom thing.

After the door clicks shut and Mom's footsteps retreat, I look at Rhea. We aren't in physics together.

"Can I?" Rhea asks, gesturing to the spot on the bed beside me.

I nod. She sits so close, our thighs almost touch. Her legs are a tawny brown and muscular. Realizing I'm staring, I jerk my head up too fast. She's busy looking at my bulletin board.

I follow her gaze to a sketch of our band logo that Mara did long ago. The *Z* is a lightning bolt. Mara wouldn't want Rhea on my bed. "You didn't have to come all the way here. You could've just answered my text."

Rhea's full lips look pouty when she frowns. She swivels to face me; her long coppery curls sway and cascade with the movement.

She fixes me with those intense eyes. "Oh, I've answered your texts. And you ghosted me. I figured you can't ignore me in the flesh."

"I—"

She holds up a finger. "I'm not mad. Isabel Walls vanishing is a trauma circus for everyone. I get that you're not ready for whatever this is." She pauses and waves her hand between us. "I'm here as a friend. You *really* think you know who took her?"

So my text did get her attention. I fight the warmth budding along my clavicle. I bite the inside of my cheek; I will not blush. "I do."

"Besides the stunt you pulled on the tourists, you're not a liar. Well, not more than anyone else." She scoots back on the bed and picks up Barry-Bear, a one-eyed, balding teddy that's been with me since infancy and that now I wish I'd shoved into the attic years ago.

"So, you don't think I'm crazy?" I say in a joking tone, but I'm genuinely curious. Since Mara's return, I've been wondering.

"No. I think you've got secrets."

My stomach flutters wildly. "Big ones. I need to know you're not going to bolt when you find out."

"I don't scare easy. At the station, I hear a lot of nasty stuff, but I keep my ear to the door. Besides, I'm going to solve Mara's case and save Isabel."

"What about your dad?"

She sets Barry-Bear down and pats him on the head. "Dad's doing everything that's in his power legally. That leaves some potential gaps in the investigation. I can fill those holes."

At this point, no one will listen to me. But Rhea's father is the police chief, and she's got more credibility than I do. She's in the running for valedictorian while I'm graduating by the curls of my cuticles. If I can get the information from Mara, Rhea can pass it on to the people who can do something about it before time runs out. Still, I need to make sure I can trust her. "Why do you want to get involved? I mean, *really*."

She juts her chin out. "You know I'm going to be a journalist, and I want to make a difference. I can crack this case."

"You put a lot of pressure on yourself."

Rhea raises an eyebrow. "Pressure? You're the one trying to be a musician."

I like Rhea. It's not because she's gorgeous, but because she *sees* me. With Mara back, I've tried to tamp down these butterflies, but now they're forcing their way to the surface, and I can't help it.

"What do we do?"

"We investigate. We have an advantage over the cops. You knew Mara better than anyone; together, we can figure out how to bait the killer."

A fist of fear tightens around my heart as I agree. "Let's do it."

Rhea lunges across the bed and hugs me. When she pulls away, her eyes are sparkling. "Let's meet early tomorrow before the search begins. I want to go over our information. Share any theories."

"Okay." I shake her hand. It's cheesy but fitting. This is a long shot, but maybe we can get justice for Mara. Maybe we can save Isabel Walls before it's too late.

Before I can answer, there's a *clunk* at my window, followed by two more. Rhea quirks an eyebrow. I jerk away and brace myself.

Mara.

Chapter 25

Audrey

The last thing I remember is resting my cheek on the pillow.

Now, I see the world through a plastic bubble; everything appears wavy and distant like it's under a film of water. I can't see anything inside my body—only darkness.

Mara broke out and took over as I slept. She's so strong. Did she tell me that she wanted to live more than I did? Or was that a dream?

This isn't, though. Mara's at the helm, steering my body through the world. I woke up fully the other times, knocking her out of the driver's seat. Now, she's unaware that I'm awake. I swallow the urge to scream and fight my way out. If I'm still, I can learn what she's doing.

I already know where we are.

Rocks soar from my hand, hitting Zadie's window with perfect aim. I've never been able to hit a target. Of course Mara is better at manipulating my body than I am. Her confidence trumps mine. She strides over to the window, placing one foot on a spigot and pushing our body up, knowing somehow that the window will open.

I sense the fluttering of my heart as the pane glides open with only a soft scraping sound. Through Mara's gaze, I see Zadie with a golden glow. Even under the plastic protection of the dream-state bubble, I'm aware of my body's reaction at the sight of the dark waves falling around her heart-shaped face. I feel a shortness of breath when Zadie's high cheekbones go rosy over her bronze skin. The love, the desperate longing, oozes into my bubble, and I understand—but don't forgive—Mara's selfishness. She's addicted to Zadie.

A flash of Mara's memories zings through me. It's a montage of them slicing open the window screen followed by glimpses of leaning through the curtains, not waiting to be fully in the room before kissing. Zadie's big brown eyes, with their flecks of amber, lock onto ours, and from deep within, I wish someone would look at me like that. I don't share secrets or adventures with anyone. Maybe this is what Mara meant when she said she was better at living. Her dreams were big and unapologetic, and she was the main character of every moment. In my own life, I'm in the background, even now. Pure happiness floods over my pangs of regret as Mara parts our lips, leaning in as the rest of the messy world melts away.

Zadie pulls away from the invitation to kiss but offers a hand, and we take it, climbing into her room.

Now I feel the tug of need as Mara reaches for Zadie, hungering for her as her scent floods our senses.

Zadie steps back. "*Audrey*, you know Rhea."

My plastic bubble cracks with the sound of a wailing beast. Mara has our eyes fixed on Rhea, and I realize the mournful cry came from within.

Our gaze flicks to Zadie, awkward, embarrassed.

Mara's thoughts pierce my skin, and though I hate her right now, I wish I could hold her as I hear her thoughts. *God, she's pret-*

tier than me. Of course she is. I'm dead. I'm nothing.

Mara is breaking.

Then, ice crackles around me, coating the cracks, freezing the great hurt.

"Hey." Mara is steel now. "Looks like I came at a bad time."

"We were talking about everything that's going on," Rhea offers, crossing her legs and sitting up straighter on Zadie's bed.

Mara leans us against the window. "Are you discussing how useless the pigs in this town are?"

"Audrey!" Zadie warns.

"Oops. I forgot. Your pop's the chief pig, right?" Mara asks, morphing her jealousy into fiery hatred. Calculations and rationalizations float around me like fluff. While I hide from my anger and substitute it with sadness, Mara points her fury like a weapon.

Rhea stands. "Are you upset you got caught swindling people?"

"*Swindling?* Oh my." Mara puts on a shocked face and faux fans herself before allowing our expression to flatline as she moves closer to Rhea. "No. I'm pissed that my cousin was murdered, and the cops are useless, and now another girl is as good as dead."

Zadie moves between them, her palms out like a barricade. One hand is inches away from my body, and my fingers twitch. Mara wants to reach for that hand, hold it, and refuse to let go. She yearns to beg Zadie to pick her, to tell Rhea to get lost. She wants to cry. But Mara was never that type of girl.

"We all want the same thing. Let's not fight," Zadie says.

Rhea doesn't look at her. She glares at us. "I had you pegged wrong. I thought you were this shy, sweet girl. What happened to your cousin was devastating. My father is haunted by the case, and he's doing his best. So please, flip your bitch switch off."

Mara snarls. "Are you going to let her talk to me like that?"

"Both of you need to calm down."

She shakes our head. "I guess I'm not enough for you anymore. Consider yourself free." With that, she tosses our leg over the windowsill and disappears to follow the waxing moon.

"Mara! Wait!" Zadie calls, but we run.

Once out of sight from Zadie's house, our shoulders slump, and Mara sobs. The emotions return, a landslide of hurt, anger, and despair so muddled I know that my cousin doesn't even know what she thinks.

"Mara," I whisper, "it'll be alright. I promise."

With that, the rage returns, and all goes black.

The night is deep indigo when I find myself in the forest. Mara's hiding within, so I can't capture her.

I stand and brush off the needles that stick to my bare legs and shake loose the continents of mud clinging to my dress—the nocturnal creatures stir and chirp. Guided by nightglow, I limp toward the thinning trees, and it isn't long before I exit into the clearing by the bordello. I wonder why Mara brought us here. She hasn't been explaining, only doing. She's reckless. My body aches with the struggle of walking. Dizzy, I sit on the ground. My left hand is fisted, and it takes the full force of my concentration to open it. When my fingers finally splay, a hunk of my hair—roots and all—flutters in the wind.

I've never been so weak and tired before. It's because of sharing the body.

Mara will break us both.

My body. *My* body. Mine. I'll get it back, I have to. When I do, I'll talk to Aunt Robin about reopening the bakery. I'll do more than watch videos on YouTube; I'll apply for a culinary program. I want my own kisses, adventures, and mishaps. The next time my life is on fire, it better be because *I* lit the match.

Mara wants to take over—for good. There're so many holes in my memory; it's frightening wondering what she's done, what she *will* do.

This Mara is so different from the cousin I loved.

Can a soul rot?

The air is cool for late spring. My thin dress isn't enough to keep me warm. Above me, a scatter of stars burns bright. Once, I believed stars were cosmic candles lit to keep us from getting lost. Now, I know they're indifferent.

There's a soft crunching of footsteps in the distance.

I sink back into the arms of the forest, nestling into the base of a large oak. Pressing my face against the rough bark, I don't dare breathe. The thuds of a man's boots echo only yards away.

Shutting my eyes, I try to turn invisible.

The footfalls pause close enough that I hear nostrils flare as if detecting my scent.

Keeping still, I let my eyes open.

A beam of light bumps along the trees as the man whistles a simple, familiar tune.

He is so close.

I wait with only a tree trunk standing between us. Ice fills my veins, and my brain desperately tries to logic the chilly fear away. The man could be a tourist seeking adventure, a local out for a walk, or perhaps even the forest artist.

But my body knows he is not a creator. This man is a destroyer. I hear my heart thrumming. Can he? All four chambers stutter to a halt when a grunt and a throat-clearing hack sound from inches away. Shutting my eyes, I wait for him to speak, to call me out.

A zipper rips through the night, and I dig my fingers into the bark. There's a rustle before the sound of a stream hitting the grass and stones below.

He's peeing.

A dangerous tingle erupts in my chest, and I am terrified I'll laugh. Holding my breath, I mentally measure the ingredients of my favorite cookie: ½ cup caramels, ½ cup chopped pretzels, 1 cup dark chocolate chips, ¼ teaspoon—

"In a cavern, in a canyon, excavating for a mine," the man sings softly, but I hear the words as if he's whispering them into my ear.

Before my panic boils over, the zipper goes back up, and heavy heels crunch pebbles as he enters the trees without a light, marching right by me. The world trembles and creaks as damp, green illumination mists across the forest floor, snaking around my ankles. My mouth opens to scream, but a fist shoots up my throat, blocking my cry.

Mara takes over.

I cling to her like a shadow; before, she'd always shoved me deep into the pit of my soul. Now, she's expelled the bit of consciousness I've been reduced to. Mara follows the light. The man. I scream for her to stop, but she can't, or won't, hear me. No one can. I barely exist.

I let go.

Chapter 26

Shirley
21 Years Ago

Over a decade had passed since Shirley's return to Copper City, and she'd settled into a comfortable routine of roaming the forest in the morning, mixing lotions and drying teas for the locals in the afternoon, and telling fortunes for the tourists until they moved on to bars and shows at night. She'd just pulled the chain on the fluorescent open sign when a knock sounded at the door. Shirley sighed and opened the door to find Richard Orlich standing under her awning.

"Why, hello, Richard. I don't suppose you've come for a reading." She forced a tight smile. It had been ages since he took over as landlord for his father, but still, Shirley felt uneasy around him. His older brother Timothy had been one of the students on Kurt's bus. While Orlich Senior assured Shirley that she was a daughter of Copper City and always welcome, the same warmth did not come from Richard.

"Good evening. Can I have a moment of your time?"

Though he was unwaveringly polite, his presence triggered an uneasiness. "Of course." She stepped aside to let him in and gestured to the sofa, but he held up his hands.

"I'll be brief. The one-hundredth anniversary of the miner

massacre is coming up. I'd like to hire you to perform a séance contacting Bloody Jasper."

"I don't commune with the departed, and if I did, I wouldn't engage a murderer."

"I meant for a *show* at the Silver Dime. The tourists will eat it up. No raising the dead necessary."

"Thank you, but I'm not interested."

Richard didn't move to leave. His mouth opened and closed as if trying to catch the right words.

"Was there something else? Or would you like a cup of tea?" She found Richard's reliance on the town's dark history for promoting tourism tacky. Still, she felt that familiar guilt that came with seeing him; he was middle-aged and had no family left. Shirley knew all too well the loneliness of loss.

"No, I suppose not. You know, you're probably the only person who says no to me in this town. I suspect you enjoy it." His wry smile didn't meet his pale eyes. He gave a little salute and stepped out onto the street.

She secured the door behind him, and when she turned, she found the ghost girl trembling against the wall.

"What?" Shirley snapped, not in the mood for spirits, even Julie.

The girl moaned like a dying beast. She never spoke, her wounds trapping her voice even in death. Shirley had tried Ouija boards and guessing games with Julie, but the spirit was often confused and sometimes appeared as little more than a reflection. There were rare times that Julie was strong and aware, but they always ended with a blackness rolling in, engulfing the girl, washing her out like a stain.

"Please. Tell me what you want." Shirley sighed.

A gray finger slowly reached out and pointed to the door.

"Oh no. I'm not in the mood for a walk. I smell a monsoon, and you'll disappear on me like the other times." Shirley couldn't keep the snap from her tone.

Julie vanished, evaporating like smoke.

Guilt crept across Shirley's chest as she went upstairs. She took out her log and added a new entry before moving on to a crocheting project, but her hands were stiff with dread. Her mind kept circling old visions. It was as if the images were all painted on a vase that was dropped, swept up, and handed to her one sharp fragment at a time.

It's all connected. Those three little words, an oft-repeated phrase from letters Julie's father regularly sent Shirley, stabbed at her. She never answered the correspondence, how could she? It would be horrible to admit to the man that she *did* know something but could only confirm his nightmares, not offer justice or answers.

She fumbled with the crochet needle and tried to lose herself in the rhythm of knots and twists, but her thoughts wouldn't budge from Julie. If she could understand what happened to her, the pieces might fall into place. Julie had wanted her to go outside, so Shirley dropped the strand and walked back down the steep staircase to the shop's front room.

It was a deep navy night, and she couldn't see anything past the picture window. But the prickle of eyes lingered over her skin. She moved efficiently, shutting off the lights and checking the locks, and at last, stood before the glass. The road was quiet, and there wasn't any movement. Yet the feeling persisted, tugging at her like a child who's spotted something shiny and out of the way. Shirley moved to the smaller window facing the end of the street and a parking lot cradled by trees that led to the woods. She put her fingers on the cool pane and pressed her nose to the glass.

Nothing.

But she couldn't look away—something was waiting in those trees. Just as she knew a late summer monsoon would arrive within ten minutes, bursting from the sky with fury, Shirley was confident she was being observed. The sensation differed from Julie's dainty, needle-like presence. This felt heavy and blunt.

After procuring Dottie's old rosary, Shirley left her home, locking the shop door behind her. She slunk along the road, staying out of the scatter of starlight, willing her eyes to adjust to their fullest potential.

By the time she reached the edge of the empty parking lot and a stray drop of rain landed on her forehead, she no longer felt watched. She merely felt silly. Two more raindrops splattered against her skin. She turned to leave, but then came a soft whistling that sounded like the tune the Huckleberry Hound cartoon used to sing. But slower, each beat steady, deliberate, sawing against the night's silence.

"Who's there?" Shirley demanded, sounding much sterner than she felt.

A crack broke the silence as the clouds opened and more warm rain fell.

Julie stood only feet away, eyes beaming red. Phantom blood wept from the wounds on her neck as she mouthed something, desperate to be heard.

Shirley moved closer, knowing she was about to do something incredibly foolish. Taking a deep breath, she let her inner light extinguish. "I'll let you in, just for a moment. You must be quick and tell me everything."

Julie nodded and shut her eyes. Shirley felt the faintest tingling of an outside thought, it was the same sensation as having a word on the tip of your tongue.

A boom shook the earth, and the world went brilliant white as a gritty laugh scratched behind Shirley's eyes. She flung up her mental shields.

The dark returned and a tree in front of her burned, the orange flames furious against the downpour. Embers of pine floated on the wind. Plumes of inky black engulfed Julie, squeezing her until she vanished with the rain.

Chapter 27

Audrey

This may be the end of my existence. Mara pushed me out, I don't think she realizes what she's done. She's always been like that, so intent on getting her way she doesn't even notice who she's knocked over—expelled—to do so. I should be panicking, but without a nervous system to fire off a fight-or-flight response, I just am.

The breeze picks up, wisping me away like dandelion fluff. I drift to a massive tree—an alligator juniper—easy to climb if you're careful not to grab onto a loose scale of bark. This was once my favorite tree. Now, I float up to the nook where two large branches, one above the other, spread out from the trunk, forming a perfect recliner—my old reading spot.

The shoots and needles tremble on the branches. Grinding and crunching rend the night as the world shakes again. Below, the mossy mist dissipates. I lose sight of the man, and judging by the animalistic cry of fury echoing off the trees, so has Mara.

The air smells of rich soil and pine. A small branch shaped like a hook catches my eye, and like a superimposed image, I see my backpack hanging from it. The night flickers and splices with day, and I see pages of a fantasy book.

I reach for it, but I have no fingers. The night returns, and the nocturnal creatures stir and chitter, but they don't hear me. Mara is gone. I'm not sure if she knows she's left me; maybe she does and isn't planning on coming back.

A flash of daylight and the strumming of guitars weave through the forest up to my perch; the book and the backpack shimmer in the sunlight. I've slipped into a mosaic of dream fragments and shards of remembrance. Is this what it's like to be dead, a soul without a host, adrift in recall?

In Grandma's journals, she theorized that a ghost's existence was like a double exposure of their memories laid over the present. The longer they linger, the more fragmented their world becomes. A kind of dementia takes hold as they fade and fray until the spirit is a mere flicker of their most devasting moments.

I've traded places with Mara. I'm the specter now. There's a splash of night, only for a moment. When I blink, I'm reaching for binoculars that my dad bought in the thick of a bird-watching phase. Lenses twisting around my eyes, I peek at the world through a fish-eye glass and find Mara and Zadie.

They act like they're alone in the world as they play their songs, as wind chimes below scatter the melody, providing an eerie undertone.

I move to climb down the tree, to warn them, but the moment I dip a toe downward, it drenches the world in black, and I am nothing but night. An owl shrieks as I wish my way back to the branch. My eyes peer from the binoculars. On a sunshine-yellow blanket, Mara and Zadie curl into one another.

My book is splayed open on a branch, its pages rustling like leaves, beckoning me. I move to place the binoculars back in the bag and catch a flicker of movement from the corner of my eye. One last peek. Though I know what I'll see, the shock still registers. They pull away from each other, Mara gesticulating wildly, anger scrunching her face. Zadie looks desperate, her hands grasping at nothing.

I focus the lenses as Mara stands. Her lips move quickly, offering a short phrase before she picks up her guitar and hurries out of view. I train my sights on Zadie. She's frozen as a bird lands on the blanket, pecking at the yarn, trying to steal a bit for her nest.

Crack. Below, a branch snaps and leaves crumple underfoot.

Startled into almost dropping my binoculars, almost falling, I brace my legs around the branch and look below. Could it have been Mara? She rarely cuts through the woods alone.

The faint whiff of cigar smoke surfs the zephyr.

The pine-speckled earth below me is empty. In the distance, Zadie is running, the yellow blanket waving like a flag behind her. I watch until she disappears down a winding dirt path. There are trails everywhere, first forged in the time of the copper boomers and cowboys. They flow like veins to the quarry pit.

I slip my backpack over my shoulders, shimmy down the tree, and walk to the spot in the clearing where the girls had been. They left a baggie of Aunt Robin's fudge. I reach for it, my fingers gliding along the grass still compressed and warmed from their bodies. I pop a piece of the chocolate into my mouth. As the sugar dissolves on my tongue, I wonder what happened to make them fight like that.

The hairs on the back of my neck prickle, and I whirl around, expecting to see Mara or Zadie return, but I'm alone. Dropping the baggie of fudge into my backpack, I realize I've left my novel in the tree.

Tired, I climb back up only to discover that the book has vanished. *I have vanished.*

Memories. I try to touch my lips, but I have no face, no

hands. Night returns, and the lingering taste of fudge turns to ash.

Splinters of starlight illuminate movements below, my body wandering through a dissipating fog of green. One arm stretched outward, navigating the night, the other gripping the neck of an empty bottle. Wanting to return to myself is only a vague notion, and some part of me knows that the longer I'm outside of my body, the less likely I am to be able to return to it.

Dropping from the tree, I slide in like a finger into sticky dough. Mara shivers as I spread through my limbs, producing weary wiggles with my fingers and toes. The glass slips from my hand and shatters; the scent of whiskey wafts up from the wreckage, or maybe it's my breath. The world sways as I walk, trying to move us out of the forest. It's gone too quiet.

"What did you do, Mara?" My tongue is thick, and the words fall sloppily from my lips.

Bloody Jasper bought us a few drinks.

"You left me out here, alone. You took my body and—"

Tears roll down my face, but for once, they don't belong to me. Mara shakes my insides as her phantom heart beats faster. I feel her reaching for my hand, grasping my fingers from within.

I was never good. Not like you, but I wasn't bad, was I? There's something out here, rotting. Angsty, it wants to take me.

Long ago, Grandma told me bedtime stories about a malevolent spirit lurking in the woods, one that gained power through horrible deeds. My thoughts swim thinking back to the darkness Mara claimed waited for her when she didn't cross over.

Am I evil? she whispers.

A shadow of pity crosses over my soul. "You're drunk. Let's go home." But the moment we take a step, the ground tilts, and we fall, broken bottle bits stab our skin, and the world swirls.

The man is gone, Mara offers, and I nod, and we crawl to the base of the alligator tree. Our skin scrapes the rough bark as we sink against the trunk, and soft whistling sounds from the deep dark, its tune distantly familiar. Our eyes can't stay open as the night swims around us. The whistling shifts into a gravelly song.

Light she was, and like a fairy.

But we are too wasted to worry about a lullaby that is probably a dream. We drift farther away.

You are lost and gone forever. Dreadful sorrow, Clementine.

Chapter 28

Zadie

The sky is cloudless, and the night's cool has given way to warmth. It's strange being up so early, but I'd managed to convince Rhea to keep our morning meeting after the fiasco last night, so I set an alarm and obeyed it.

Nearing my destination, I check to see if Audrey's responded to any of my texts. Nothing. I dial her number and let it ring. Voicemail.

I hit redial, and this time—

"Fuck off."

"Mar—"

Click.

I dial again and get nothing. Maybe she's blocked me.

Sighing, I push through the door to the only joint open at this hour—Cowboy Café—and spot the top of Rhea's curly head in the corner booth. The bell chimes and she looks up. There's already a carafe of coffee on the table and a clean mug waiting for me.

"Mornin'. I ordered," Rhea says. "I had a hunch you like coffee."

I nod and empty two creamers into the cup and pour. Stifling a yawn, I take a long swig of the burning liquid. It needs sugar. I set the cup down and catch Rhea's steady gaze. "So, last night was weird."

She takes a small sip before answering. "Yeah. It was. Especially the part where you called Audrey *Mara*."

My stomach drops. I force a shrug. "Mara's on my mind a lot."

"Audrey pretended to be Mara in the mine." Rhea's tone is mild, but the disapproval is unmistakable.

Shame slithers over my skin. "It's terrible, but Mara would have found it hilarious."

"Hmm," Rhea murmurs. "When did you and Audrey get together?"

"It's not like that." It isn't a lie, but I can tell by the jutting of Rhea's eyebrow that she's not buying it.

"I don't mean to pry, but that looked like a breakup."

I look away.

"Whatever that was, it's her loss."

The waitress plops two plates containing bacon, eggs, and hash browns on our table. "Anything else?" she asks.

Rhea thanks her, and I stare at the meal in surprise.

"What? You haven't already eaten, have you?"

"No, I don't normally eat breakfast."

"Good thing I came into your life." Rhea smiles and shakes a bottle of Cholula hot sauce over her eggs. "You need to eat. It's going to be a long day."

"You got something planned?"

"Besides joining the search party, you mean?" Rhea drops a spiral notebook on the table, flips the cover, and poises her pen. "There's my investigation. You didn't tell me who your suspect is."

I take a bite of the eggs. Bland and already lukewarm. I grab the hot sauce and douse them. "James Lorenzini. He left town right after Mara, and he came back right before Isabel. According to some internet sleuthing, he's got a history of being a creep."

Rhea doesn't move, but the tip of her tongue peeks out over her lips, and I can tell she's waiting for more. "And . . ." I pause; I can't say that Mara's spirit ID'd Big Jim. She'd never believe that. I'm having trouble wrapping my own head around it. "He asked to interview Audrey and me for this podcast thing. He's trying to find out what we know."

Rhea offers a slight nod. "How did he act? Was he nervous? Agitated?"

"I don't know. We were only there for a minute. Ma—Audrey panicked. She recognized him—"

"Of course she did. He's famous in Copper City." Rhea's face screws up in confusion.

"No. Like she had a repressed memory, she thinks she saw him . . ." I chug coffee. "Saw him watching Mara." The lie burns down my throat with the bitter coffee. It's about as close to the truth as I can get.

"Did she tell anyone else?"

I scoff. "Who would believe her? After the whole mine thing, neither of us has any credibility." I shovel hash browns into my mouth.

She chews thoughtfully.

"I want to help save Isabel." I feel like I'm sinking under black water as the realization engulfs me. "But I don't think there's anything I can do." I glance out the window. *Find Isabel* posters hang on every window and door. I want to tell that dimpled face I'm so sorry.

"You know, it's common for serial killers to try to involve themselves in the investigation. I can poke around and see if he's asked to talk to law enforcement."

An idea pops into my mind, and the notion sends a tremor through my body. "I can reschedule the interview. Audrey won't come, but he wanted to talk to me too. Go with me?"

My eyes lock with Rhea's. Asking her is a risk. It's hard enough keeping track of my Mara cover-ups and lies about Audrey without Rhea's sharp observations. Still, Rhea knows her way around an investigation.

Stretching across the table, she grips my forearm and squeezes. "I'm in."

Chapter 29

Shirley
20 Years Ago

Shirley paused from her foraging and listened to the wind. She refused to live in fear, but she wasn't foolish. There was an entity capable of harm, and he didn't care for Shirley.

She could only theorize about who he was and how he gained power, but she was sure her early run-in with the miner had disturbed him as much as it had her. As long as she didn't let him in, she was safe. So she kept her demeanor quartz-hard and took precautions.

She cleansed her home daily, hung blessing bells over the doors, and placed adder stones at each windowsill. Despite her fortifications, Julie sometimes appeared; her presence was not threatening but desperate. Whatever the girl wanted to convey was important and frustratingly outside Shirley's grasp.

Her charms did keep the entity at bay, and she suspected he held the most power while in the wilds. Shirley sensed his hatred as he whistled and crept nearby. She'd scold him whenever he got too close, and he'd vanish. Like most bullies, he was a coward.

Often, she felt him watching.

Like now.

Shirley sighed. The world had gone quiet, and she tasted his rancid energy in the air. She was no longer afraid of him and liked to think that her defiance infuriated the spirit. The heavy presence shifted closer. The entity seemed to have little recourse when she wasn't fearful, and she'd learned to channel her fear into annoyance.

"You have no power over me. Leave," she scolded.

The wind shifted, and the birdsong returned. Her fingers went back to wiggling in the soil, attempting to harvest ginger without losing any of the roots. A soft crunch sounded behind her, but it wasn't the entity.

"Hello, Dale," she said before turning around; he was one of the few people in Copper City who wandered the woods, and she'd always liked Franny's son. Despite having Franny's awful ex-husband Michael as a father, Dale grew to be an introspective and kind man.

He crouched beside her. "Can I help?"

"Certainly." She nodded to the trowel.

They worked without conversation. Something was nagging at Dale, but Shirley didn't press and let the silence have its way. Finally, he wiped the dirt off his hands, staring at them while speaking. "I want to marry Wren."

Shirley's eyebrow arched. "I hope you aren't asking for my permission. She wouldn't find that charming."

He cleared his throat. "Actually, I wanted some advice. Wren says you see things. Know things."

Shirley stopped digging and set her hands on her lap.

"We both want children, well, a child. Maybe two."

"Go on." Shirley met his eyes and gripped his gaze.

"The thing is, mental illness runs in both our families."

Shirley gave a noncommittal murmur. She'd never thought of her mother as afflicted, only haunted. As for Kurt, Vietnam had altered him, but Shirley never accepted that he meant to drive the bus off the cliff.

Dale checked over his shoulder. They were alone, as alone as one could be in the forest. "My dad was a cruel drunk. I don't know how to be a good father."

She squeezed his forearm. "You'll figure it out. You aren't like Michael."

"I want to marry Wren, and I want her to have her dream family. She'll make a wonderful mother. But sometimes I worry"—Dale snapped a stick—"there's something bad waiting. If you could tell me what to avoid . . ."

Shirley laughed, though not unkindly. "I can only divine what cannot be undone, but since you've worked yourself up for a prediction, allow me to give you one on the house."

She wrapped her arms around him and whispered, "Get married. Have a child. Love her. Your life will have great sorrow and great joy. You can't have one without the other."

Chapter 30

Zadie

Rhea insists on paying for breakfast. "I ordered for you."

"Thanks. I'll get you next time," I say as heat rises across my cheeks. Rhea's hair bounces and shimmers in the morning sun. Was this a date? It felt *almost* like a date. I feel guilty, like I'm cheating on Mara—can you cheat on a ghost?

"We should get going. The search party is about to start." She stands, and I follow.

"Oh, and Pop's insisting I be in Officer Donaldson's group," she adds wryly.

"Okay." She didn't invite me to join them. It stings, but it doesn't take a genius to get why she wouldn't ask the local delinquent to tag along.

We walk to school, the rendezvous site, in silence.

Rhea stops short as we near the parking lot. She nods to a patrol car underneath the *Copper City High – Home of the Outlaws* sign. "We shouldn't be seen together. It'll be easier if my dad doesn't know about us. Arrange the interview for later today and text me, okay?" She's already moving away, trying to look like we merely happened to be crossing the street at the same time.

My throat's tight, but I force a nonchalant "cool."

Rhea steps up her pace, stretching the space between us. I want to dissect every word she's spoken. She said she didn't want her dad to "know about us." I know she didn't mean we're *together*, but what if it was a Freudian slip? After all that's happened, I'm not sure she likes me like *that* anymore.

It doesn't matter, though. Audrey won't speak to me and Isabel's missing. I've got to stop thinking about Rhea.

I send a text to Jimbo.

I'm ready to give Big Jim an interview.

His response flashes seconds later.

K. Come by at 6.

My dread gives way to excitement—we may break the case.

Inside the school, the crowd is large and growing steadily. People stream into the open doors of the auditorium to be assigned to a group and location. They move like a concert crowd, bobbing and bottlenecking.

My phone rings, flashing an unknown number. I jam a finger in my ear and answer. "Hello?"

"Hi, Zadie. This is Wren Hennessy. Is Audrey with you? I must've missed her when she left this morning."

"No. I mean, not yet. We're meeting up here soon. I-I think her phone is dead." The fib slips out easily.

"Oh, dear. Have her call me to check in."

"Sure. Of course."

It was instinct to lie because that's what I did for Mara, but not checking in with her mother doesn't seem like Audrey. Concern gathers in my gut.

An old man passes me a Sharpie and a *Hello! My name is* sticker. I hand it to the person next to me and wade against the flow of bodies. Though I want to do everything in my power to find Isabel, right now, I'd be another cog in the search. It's hard to choose, but at this moment, Audrey needs someone—me—just a little bit more.

I'll make it up to Isabel when I face Big Jim later.

I push through the crowd to the back of the school. A couple of people call my name, but I wave like I'm heading to the bathroom. I told Mom I'd see her here, but the throng is so dense that I could say my cell died and I couldn't find her. She won't believe it, but she's been so tired lately I doubt she'll argue. I feel for the Zippo in my pocket and run my thumb along its hinge.

I leave through the broken emergency exit and keep my head down as I pass the searchers. There's an old staircase up the hill I take to avoid the main streets. My sandals smack against the concrete as I climb to the top, cut into the woods, and jog through to the clearing.

I can't go to the clearing—our spot—without thinking of Mara and the final time I saw her whole.

Audrey isn't here. I sit at the heart of the space to think of where she might be, but my mind keeps drifting back to the last time I was here with Mara.

She was furious with me and didn't want to hear my reasoning or even consider that I might not always go along with what she wanted. I brushed off what Audrey said about Mara taking over without asking. My throat burns and the hot sauce and eggs twist my stomach. Just because Mara's back from the dead doesn't mean that she's right.

My phone rings—Mom—that was quick. I let it go to voicemail.

A text pings. *Rhea's here without you & Mrs. Bobo saw you leave. Where are you?*

I hold my finger over the home button as I think better of the dead phone plan. One of us should be at least somewhat honest.

I send her a text.

Waiting to meet up with Audrey.

Almost instantly a response pings back.

Call me now, or we'll be conjoined until you graduate.

Oh crap. I call. "Hey . . ."

"Zadie Lynnette Slade." Mom spits my full name out. She's pissed. She didn't even middle name me when she picked me up at the police station.

"I can explain."

"No. You can listen. You need to be where you tell me you are. Always." Her voice cracks. "I can't lose you. There's a murderer in Copper City, have some sense. Please."

"I'm sorry."

"Get Audrey and come back. Her mother hasn't seen her since last night."

"Okay, okay."

"Check in with the coordinator, and she'll tell me when you get in. So help me, Zadie, if you two aren't back here in ten minutes, I'll divert the entire search party."

"I'm waiting, though, so I'll need more like twenty minutes."

"You'd better tell Audrey to run because I'm giving you ten." She sounds gangster cold and disconnects without a goodbye.

I can't return without Audrey. Once more, I scan the clearing, slowly turning my body, hoping that Audrey will appear, smiling and waving. There's nothing but red boulders, brush, and trees along the perimeter until, at the very edge of the clearing, the near-invisible corner of the old brothel catches my eye.

Mostly concealed by protective branches of ironwood trees, it's been boarded up forever and is easy to overlook. Over the years, I've trained my eyes not to linger on the building. The dappled sunlight plays with the trees' shadows, sometimes forming spectral figures behind the splinter of the visible window. Now, I squint as the breeze stills and the surrounding forest quiets.

I tramp toward the brothel, not pausing to read the long-downed sign warning potential trespassers about the unsound structure. It never stopped Mara and me from going in and exploring. I doubt anyone else has ventured inside; the windows and doors are shuttered with rotting planks, and there's no telltale graffiti or teen paraphernalia. Part of the roof has crumbled, and roots and branches have crept inside.

If Mara wanted to stay low, she might've told Audrey about the secret door hidden in the back wall. We took a blood oath never to tell anyone when we found it. We liked our secrets, and that was one of the best. You can't see the door—it's brick like the rest of the building but has concealed hinges. If you push on the wall just right, it swings open. We found it accidentally when we leaned against the spot together and fell backward inside.

I rush to the back of the building, pressing my hands against the wall looking for the hidden door. Mara and I discussed marking it, but we didn't want to make it easy for someone else to discover.

For a brief time, it was our favorite spot. We poked around and talked about sprucing the place up for a hideout. We never did much, though. The old house is creepier than any of the stops on the ghost tour.

It's a two-story building, the ground floor an open saloon area, empty but for a rotting player piano that rats like to nest in. Old horseshoes hang over the doors in a U position to keep the luck from spilling out. The rickety staircase leads to a second floor with six small rooms. We never spent much time upstairs as entire chunks of the top floor have collapsed.

Once, we left behind old lawn chairs and a box of crackers, and they disappeared. I felt we were being watched. Mara said

I was chicken, but we stopped going inside the brothel without discussion. Later, during my ghost-guide training, I read dozens of stories about Bloody Jasper. That's how I discovered Jasper Dodge was a regular at the brothel.

That's not surprising—it's not like they had dating apps. What stuck in my mind was a copy of an old newspaper story: a sensationalist interview with the brothel madam who claimed Jasper had supernatural powers and could appear out of thin air. His favorite girls found trinkets in their beds; the ones who disappointed him misplaced prized possessions and discovered scorpions in their slippers. But there wasn't any evidence offered in the piece, and it was likely an attempt at wrangling some notoriety. Dark tourism is nothing new.

When I press against the old wood covering a window, a fat splinter slips into my palm. Cursing, I slap the wall, and something feels different.

The hidden door gives way more easily than I remember, as if the hinges have been recently oiled, but that's ridiculous. No one knows about this door.

It's dark inside due to the boarded-up windows. I hesitate, bracing myself for the possibility of finding a body.

"Hello? Audrey?"

No answer.

I poke my head in. Weeds sprout through the rotting floorboards near the door. The old piano has collapsed. Everything else looks the same as I remember.

A loud scraping sound causes my heart to seize. "Mara?" I yell, whirling around. A hawk swoops overhead and out of the open passageway. I gasp and laugh in relief.

My phone chirps. Mom's sent a text. *Is Audrey there yet?*

I push the door back in place and try Audrey's cell again. It goes straight to voicemail. I don't know where else to look. If Mara was leading, this is where they'd be.

There's a creak behind me.

I whirl—nothing—just the breeze through the wood of an old building. I'm scaring myself stupid. The wind picks up, lashing buffelgrass against my calves. Bending to swat it away, I catch a splash of pale blue just yards inside the forest.

The world falls quiet, and my vision tunnels to that familiar hue. I run toward the tree line, sprinting faster than ever before. Certainty causes me to stumble and hit the ground.

The body sprawled before a giant tree trunk belongs to Audrey.

Fumbling on my knees, I reach for her. My hands feel giant and clumsy as I press a palm to her clammy skin and push mud-clumped hair from her face. "Audrey?"

Her eyelids slowly drift apart, revealing bloodshot webs surrounding the blue spheres. She shoves herself upward and grabs the strap of my tank top, pulling me until our faces are inches apart.

"Fuck you, Zadie Slade."

"Mara?"

"What's left of her."

"Everyone's freaking out. You need to call Wren."

"No one cares, least of all you. You're a slut. Worse, you're selfish. A sel-fisssh saa-lut," she slurs, spraying flecks of spit. Her breath reeks.

I pry her fingers from my shirt. "Mara, you got the wrong idea."

"You got the wrong idea," she mimics in a high-pitched tone. "Are you drunk?"

"I scored a bottle of whiskey by the whorehouse." She lies back on the ground, her eyes never leaving my face. "You know, if you weren't so selfish, maybe I'd still be alive."

Her words slice into me. "Mara—"

"You were the first to know I was missing, and you didn't say a word to anyone."

"I-I thought you were avoiding me because of our fight. I didn't know. I couldn't have known something bad happened."

"I'd never abandon you. You're my best friend, my girlfriend, and you didn't even look for me."

There it is. Since she vanished, I've carried the guilt of knowing things might have been different had I only looked past our fight to realize something was horribly wrong. I'd waited to be accused, and when no one blamed me—at least not to my face—I brought it up to anyone who'd listen: Mom, the school psychologist, and the investigators. They assured me repeatedly that I was not the cause of Mara's death, but the wondering never ceased.

I've waited, readying myself for the condemnation, and it's finally come, but the fury I'd always imagined is absent. Instead, it's a deep bruise of sadness.

"I'm so sorry. I was scared you didn't love me anymore," I say, reaching to stroke her cheek.

Slapping my hand away, she hisses "selfish" before lurching forward to vomit. Her shoulders heave and heave until there's nothing left. Her face is pale when she turns back, and her tiny shoulders crumple forward.

"Audrey?" I ask.

Nodding, she continues to cry.

I dial Mom as I wrap my arms around Audrey.

"What's taking so long?"

"Audrey's sick, like with a stomach virus. I'm walking her home now. We're near Durango, heading toward Gulch Road. Can you call Wren and let her know?"

There's a sharp intake of breath on the other side. "Okay. Stay when you get to the Hennesseys', I'll meet you there."

I shove the phone into my pocket and help Audrey stand. Her knees wobble, and her body sways as I wrap her arm around my shoulders.

A cool breeze releases the blooms from a palo verde, creating a flurry of yellow. I sneeze, sending a family of quail darting along the path before us, their topknots bobbing. The Disney movie beauty of this place is a trick. Audrey was once like those cartoon princesses, all sweetness and optimism. But trauma can't be overcome with a freaking song. Surviving isn't inspiring. We're all just scared of the alternative. Audrey is a wreck and getting worse. And Mara? I've truly lost her.

Chapter 31

Audrey

My head pounds as we stumble across the clearing, and no matter how hard I concentrate, my steps go slantwise. I've never been drunk before. I've never even had more than a few sips of alcohol. Mara's stolen both a choice and a first from me. She's turning me into her. Soon I'll be the ghost. The notion floods me with fury, and I wish I could go back in time and be stronger. My knees buckle; I don't know how much she drank from that bottle, but the world is spinning.

Zadie squeezes me tight and yanks me up, securing my arm around her shoulder. Was I slipping away? The earth sways beneath my feet, and it feels like I'm trying to wade through honey.

Zadie grunts before asking, "What happened?"

I remember flashes of the night, of Rhea in Zadie's room, the sensation of Mara breaking. My face smashes against Zadie's shoulder—my head is so heavy—and I have to roll my eyes upward to look at her. "You'd have to ask Mara. But she says she's not talking to you anymore."

"She should tell you at least. You're plastered."

"Do I look ugly?"

"You look like you got super drunk and spent the night in

the woods."

"Oh."

"You okay?"

"Mara's not talking to me anymore either. Or maybe I'm not talking to her. Do you have any water? I'm so thirsty."

"We're only a few minutes away from your house. Come on."

The earth teeter-totters, and I slip from Zadie's side and puddle on the ground. "I need to rest." I could sleep forever.

"The search party could pass through here at any moment." Zadie snaps her fingers in front of my eyes. "Audrey, stay awake."

"You sound like Mara. *Do this, do that. Blah, blah, blah.*"

Zadie tugs at me. "What are you talking about?"

I pull my knees to my chest and rest my face on them. "I told you. She'll do anything to get what she wants. Even death can't stand in her way."

"I'll talk to her, get this all straightened out." Zadie's face screws up with worry.

My mercifully empty stomach roils, so I stretch out on the ground, causing my dress to ride up, but I no longer care about silly things like who might see my underwear.

Tires crunch over gravel as a car stops. Zadie turns, but I know who it is by the screeching of the brakes. My mother parks in the street and runs toward us.

"Audrey!" She falls to her knees beside me.

"She's fine. She's just—"

"Audrey, are you okay?"

"I'm thirsty."

Zadie and Momma hoist me up, holding me between them as they lead me to the Toyota. Zadie opens the back door, and I tumble in. My cheek smacks against the seat belt—it hurts—and I laugh until I'm sobbing.

"Let's get you home." Momma slams the door. "What happened?" she asks Zadie outside. The window is cracked open, but I'd be able to hear Momma's fury even if it was shut.

"I don't know. I found her like that."

"First the mine business and now this? It's obvious she's drunk."

I burrow my face into the seat. I want Momma to stop yelling so I can sleep.

Zadie's response is hard to catch; she isn't yelling like Momma. In this sloppy drunk state, nasty truths bubble to the surface. Mind and body swimming, I can't push them back down, can't ignore the capital T truth. Zadie will pick Mara over me. She already has.

"You're a bad influence. Look at her!" There's a bang on the window. Momma's gesticulating has gotten the best of her. She grips her hand. "Jesus!"

"Can I at least say goodbye?"

The door creaks open, and Zadie pops her head inside. The world pulsates.

"Call me when you feel better. Please." Her voice strains.

I pull my face from the upholstery. "No. I don't want to hang out with you anymore." I shut my eyes and listen to the door slam.

Somewhere along the bumpy road, a gritty male voice knifes into my mind.

I'll help you get rid of them all.

The jolts of the car drift away, and I feel like I am floating. Tendrils of black swirl behind my eyes, coating everything until—

An icy sensation drips over my wrist. My eyes fly open, and I see the ghost girl, her red eyes wide with fear, crouching on the floorboard. Her gray ethereal hand sinks through mine. The girl pulsates with a faint gold aura before vanishing.

Chapter 32

Zadie

I sabel!"

Ten-second pause.

"Isabel!"

The search follows a rhythm. I try to lose myself in the beat: look up, down, and around. Anywhere but Mom's concerned eyes. She thought I should go home, but I want to feel useful, and there isn't anything else I can do for Isa until the interview with Lorenzini. Besides, in this call-and-no-response cycle, there isn't an opportunity for Mom to question me or for me to mull over Audrey's/Mara's last words.

We search every inch of our section, only pausing for mundane items to be bagged for evidence. Near evening, the groups merge with little progress made. Soft murmurs drift through the crowd as hope evaporates. We all know the odds of a happy ending if the missing person isn't found in the first forty-eight hours.

You didn't even look for me. Mara's words echo in my mind. Her parents assumed she was with me, and with the bakery's early hours, they were in bed by eight thirty. Mara's curfew was ten on school nights. I said nothing the next day when she didn't meet me to walk to school. Other people also blundered in those first precious hours: The town collectively assumed that Mara was causing mischief, and Chief Uckleman waited days to call the FBI. Even so, I made the first mistake, and it set off a chain reaction that concluded with Mara's body at the bottom of a pit.

A text from Rhea brings me back to my mission. Isabel is still out there, and I know Big Jim has something to do with it. I can't quit.

The streets overflow with people, but it's quiet.

Mom pats my back as we walk home together. "Do you want to order takeout for dinner?"

My stomach growls at the thought, but I shake my head. "I was hoping to have a study date with Rhea if that's okay."

Mom's eyes narrow. "Are you sure? Don't you want to talk about whatever's going on with you? It might help."

A surge of hot anger cuts through me. There's no way my mother can understand having your girlfriend come back from the dead only to break up with you again. I try not to spit out venom with my words. "There's nothing to talk about."

"Sweetie, I wish you'd let me in. Certain secrets will eat away your soul."

My eyes meet hers, and Mom flinches. Like mother, like daughter.

The old wall clock that hangs over the stove ticks insistently as the silence between us fills the room like smoke. At last, Mom breaks the spell. "Well, I won't worry about your safety if you're at the chief of police's place."

I don't correct her assumption.

Opening the freezer, she prattles on. "You didn't eat lunch, no going anywhere until there's some protein in you." She holds a box toward me, her arms outstretched as if presenting an offering at the altar of some deity. "It was on special. Remember how you used to eat these all the time, even for breakfast?"

"Corn dogs? Seriously? Mom, what if the CrossFitters find out you called corn dogs protein?"

"Fine, then don't eat. I wanted to get you something you liked." She goes to shove the box into the freezer.

"I'll have a corn dog. Hell, I'll take two. I haven't had one since I was a kid."

She pushes the package into my hands. "You're still a kid."

"Mom—"

"Heat me one too." Mom reaches for the wine bottle and fills a jelly glass to the top rim.

I tear open the box and shake out three corn dogs crystallized in freezer burn onto a plate.

Mom sips and says, "I like Rhea. She's a good student."

"You know, most parents don't get to judge their offspring's friends by their GPA."

"Teacher privilege." Mom pauses and clacks her long nails against her glass. "She's also very pretty."

My face heats, and my heart tilt-a-whirls. "Yeah. So?"

She reaches out and tucks a stray strand of hair behind my ear. "So, nothing. Just an observation, one it appears you share."

I groan. "You know it isn't a requirement of motherhood to be so embarrassing."

"It's called sincerity, not as cool as dry wit or sarcasm, but don't worry, there are no witnesses here."

The microwave dings, and we eat our corn dogs. They aren't as good as I remember.

"I'll drive you over when you're ready."

"Hello, *wine*."

She pushes the remains of the glass aside. "I'm fine. I've barely had any, and I won't finish until after I pick you up tonight."

"You're paranoid. It's a five-minute walk."

She fixes me with a stare. "Girls are vanishing into thin air."

"Fine."

She hugs me, and I squeeze back as guilt swells. I hope she never discovers what I'm planning.

Mom's Jeep lingers alongside the Uckleman's house, probably waiting for me to be safely inside before she pulls away. When Rhea answers the door, I rush in, hoping she won't spot my ride, but she does and waves at Mom, who gives the horn two little taps before driving off.

My palms are slick with sweat as Rhea asks if I need anything. Yes, I want to say. I need to know if it's awful of me to want to move on from Mara. I also need to stop feeling this crazy surge of hormones every time I see you.

She's changed outfits since this morning. I've been wearing the same black tank top and cut-offs since the search party. Sure, I've put on deodorant and spritzed my hair, but that's only a slight improvement. Rhea's wearing a short sundress speckled in yellow, red, and orange. She resembles a flame—she literally looks hot. Following her to her room, I try not to stare at her dark legs. I force my gaze up to her hair. It's in a top knot, but with her curls and the elegant curve of her long neck, she looks far from a study buddy.

Rhea opens the door to her room and I'm impressed. Instead of plastic vines hanging down the walls, there's a tiered shelf filled with actual alive and thriving plants. I had a cactus once; despite not needing much, it didn't last long.

She gestures for me to sit on a well-made queen bed. Seeing the smooth snowy-white blanket and fresh crimson pillowcases, I try to think of the last time I made mine. Mara didn't even have sheets on her bed half the time. Rhea's room even smells like fresh linens. Delayed embarrassment hits me. I wonder what she thought about the multiple piles of dirty clothes in my room.

I perch at the edge of the bed and scan the collection of black-and-white photographs artfully arranged on the walls. They were all taken locally. The photos are impressive, expertly lighted, and capture stunning images like a monsoon thunderhead. Only one isn't perfectly in focus. I'm sure it's of Rhea's mom who died when we were in middle school.

The bed shifts as Rhea plops down next to me, commanding my attention. She stretches to grab a tablet on her nightstand, revealing black spandex shorts. It's going to be hard to focus.

She taps on the screen until she's in a notes app. "Okay, I've compiled some research on James "Big Jim" Lorenzini. We know he lost his gig at the Golden Nugget due to a DUI and a serious sexual harassment complaint."

"That's impressive for only being in Vegas a month."

"Yup. He left in disgrace and skipped out on his rent. No red flags about *underage* girls, but he certainly has a reputation for being a predator and all-around creep."

"I only found some of that online."

Rhea beams before looking back at her screen. "Well, the internet's faster at the station. Sometimes I do my homework there, and no one ever logs out of the police database. So . . ." She circles her hand in a "you know" gesture. "What's the game plan?" Her fingers are poised to type.

I shift on the soft blanket, sinking my hands into the deep fluff. "Well, I was planning to wing it."

"Wing it?" Rhea purses her lips in a spot-on impression of Mom after finding out that, yes, I started my term paper the night before it's due.

"Well, we can't just ask him to tell us about that time he murdered Mara or to reconsider doing the same to Isabel."

Rhea nods and taps her chin, maybe being a cop's daughter taught her to take her time answering questions, to be comfortable even while stewing in silence.

Conversely, I was raised by an overanxious oversharer, and the quiet puts me on edge. "I'll figure out how to proceed by what sort of questions he asks me," I blurt out, realizing that (a) this is my actual plan and (b) it isn't very good.

Rhea taps out a note on her tablet. "I think we should consider the different ways Lorenzini might act, so we won't be surprised."

"Okay. The last time I saw him, he was sort of *meh*. Like he almost couldn't be bothered."

"Interesting, I'd wager he's overconfident then. Be sure to make a mental note if anything seems different this time. The investigation could be taking its toll on him."

We go back and forth, Rhea taking notes and providing the most valuable ideas. I want to contribute, but I can't move past the notion that Lorenzini tortured and killed Mara. Meeting with him means putting our lives at risk, and for what—some potential clue?

Reaching out, I grasp Rhea's hand before she can add another bullet. Startled from her task, she blinks and cocks her head. "What if we don't get any proof? Do you think you can convince your dad that Big Jim murdered Mara?"

With her free hand, she pats the back of mine. "Allegedly. I'm not certain either way, and you shouldn't be either. All you have is Audrey getting a major case of creepy-crawlies over him."

"But Audrey knows. She just does—"

Rhea cuts me off with a look. "I'm committed to the truth. If we find evidence that points to the man with the mustache, you have my word, it'll be investigated to the fullest extent."

Another stretch of silence passes before she speaks again. "Let's assume he is the killer. At least your friend, Little Jim, will be there. We don't have time for anything other than winging it, so let's get winging away."

Chapter 33

Audrey

I wake up feeling foggy and lost; I cringe, looking at the dried bits of mud and pine needles that sprinkle my sheets. There's pressure behind my eyes, and when I pinch the bridge of my nose, I recall the man's voice, speaking to me from within like Mara does, promising me he could help me get rid of them all.

The voice left when—I touch my wrist, remembering the chill of the ghost girl. I could see her light, and she got rid of him somehow. At least for now. I don't know who the voice belonged to or why he spoke to me.

It's all connected. Paul Hartshorne's words come back. The ghost girl. Isabel. The other voice. Fear clenches my heart as I consider the meaning of someone else speaking to me as Mara does. I take a breath and scan my body for other presences.

Inside me, Mara is deep in stasis—her version of sleep. I consider boxing her in, but my head throbs, and I know I won't be able to. I don't sense anyone else.

Tiptoeing from my room, I find water, aspirin, and my mother. I force myself to meet Momma's anxiety-ridden face. She opens her mouth to ask questions, but I shake my head, and she sucks in her lips. Tears well in her eyes. I have no answers, and she is afraid to push, terrified I'll shatter. Maybe Momma *can* foretell the future.

Uncertainty and fear threaten to swallow me whole. I need to clear my head, to do something productive. I go to the kitchen and, ignoring my body's fresh bruises and aches, I preheat the oven and measure out the ingredients. Smells invoke memories, and so do recipes. I want to inhale vanilla and nostalgia. I need to go back to a time before everything went so wrong. Even if only for a few minutes.

Sprinkling flour over the worn wood of the table, I pretend I'm helping Aunt Robin stock the bakery with Valentine treats. We woke before dawn and made hundreds of heart-shaped cookies. Mara popped in and out, obnoxiously tugging on apron strings, demanding balls of dough dipped in confectioners' sugar. She never actually helped, but nonetheless, Mara was part of the process. By the afternoon, Aunt Robin was teaching me the wet-on-wet method of icing the cookies and it wasn't long before I could pipe intricate lace patterns onto blushing pink hearts.

My cousin wanted to leave a lasting mark on the world. But I'm most satisfied when I add tiny flourishes of ephemeral beauty. Savoring the quiet, I shut down all thoughts of the many things I can't control, and focus on piping, alternating between Victorian curlicues and floral patterns. Lost in the calm of creation, I startle when the kitchen timer buzzes.

My eyes refocus on the finished cookies lining the countertops, and the frosting bag slips from my hand, splatting on the floor and oozing red. The last row of cookies is decorated crudely. One reads *Bloody Jasper was here.*

A laugh rumbles from within me. *You should have seen your face!* Mara can barely contain herself. I grit my teeth and with a single sweep of my arm, I slide all the cookies into the trash.

Oh! Angsty—you didn't have to do that. I was just teasing.

"You did it again. Took over without asking."

It was a joke.

"It isn't funny. You're making me crazy."

I was trying to lighten things up.

"I won't let you do this anymore."

Come on, Audrey.

"Leave, Mara."

I feel her pluck from me, getting as far away as she dares.

I stare at the ruined cookies in the trash, the jagged *Bloody Jasper* dripping at the top of the heap.

"It's all connected." I whisper the words, trying to gauge if there's any truth to them. The ghost girl led me to the old man, and while he wasn't all there, he seemed the most coherent when he spoke of the uncanny. Paul Hartshorne said there was a connection between Bloody Jasper, the bus, the missing hikers, Mara, and Isabel. I can't think of any links between the serial killer miner and Isabel. Over a century spans between them.

In the six months since Grandma passed, I've missed her daily, and now I need her fiercely. She'd know what to do, or at least where to start. In my room, I gather Grandma's runes and am about to cast them when my eyes fall on the box of her journals stored in my closet. I settle cross-legged and look through one. There isn't much logic to follow, and they span almost an entire life. Though Grandma had a knack for interpreting dreams, they're not dream journals. Despite snippets of texts having dream-like qualities, nothing is mentioned outside of real life.

Stifling a sigh, I go through each book. There are hundreds of listings for a "burst blackberry" and dozens of mentions of an "odd metal root" but no elaboration for either. One page has only the letters *J.H.* scrawled at the top followed by a long list of dates.

My legs are cramping as I select a newer composition book. Only a handful of pages have been written in. The index shows six mentions of the bus. The first five are nearly identical lists: the bus, the fence, twin toddlers, and a metal root. But the last . . . I grip the paper so tightly it tears from the spine.

Bus crashed into open copper pit. 16 dead.

I run my finger over the list of names, many of their surnames familiar, and freeze at the last one. *Kurt McBennett.*

A wave of nausea crashes over me; my body is still hungover from Mara's bender. I squeeze my eyes shut. Kurt was Grandma's older brother; she didn't talk about him much, and I always thought he'd died in the Vietnam War—an assumption no one bothered to correct. The bus tragedy rates high among Copper City's campfire stories, sparking the rumor that handprints will appear on your windows if you park near the cliff.

There's a memorial plaque at the pit, but Kurt's name isn't listed with the others. Bile rises in my throat. My great-uncle was the driver; there's a killer in my blood.

I shut the notebook. A clock ticks from the hall, and the bathroom faucet drips as my heart thuds. I can't connect Kurt killing himself and fifteen people to Mara or Isabel, but it's too big of an event to ignore. In middle school, a girl once told me to go drive a bus off a cliff. At the time, I thought it was the meanest thing she could think of. Now I wonder why no one ever told me the truth about my family.

My mother is in the living room waving a selenite wand in a cleansing ritual.

"Where's Dad?"

Her arms fall to her side as she takes me in. "Work. Sweetheart, you should lie down."

"How come you never told me about what Kurt did?"

The wand slips from her hand and shatters on the floor. She looks from the crystal shards and back again as if trying to divine an answer and then kneels, collecting the fragments.

"Momma?" I step forward, standing over her.

She gazes up at me. The lines around her eyes have deepened in the last few days, and her mouth has thinned. "It hurt your grandmother too much. Kurt wasn't evil, though some people say that." She stands and guides me to the couch by my elbow. "He was mentally ill, more than anyone realized. Why are you asking about him?"

I grab Momma's hand and grip it tight; I don't want her to avoid answering. "What do you mean by mentally ill?"

"Oh Lord, sweetheart, did someone compare you to him? Because you're not like that. I promise."

"Tell me."

She shifts, trying to pull her hand back, but I grip tighter. "Well, he quit his job at the mine because he hallucinated in the tunnels. He heard voices, and that's all I know."

I release her hand. My entire body pulsates with a potent mixture of pain and fear.

Momma leads me to my room, where I lie down and flutter my eyes shut, holding my breath until the door closes and her footsteps disappear.

The memory of Paul Hartshorne's shotgun keeps me from sneaking out to visit him, but he had an old wall phone in his kitchen, so I pull up Copper City's directory and search for his name.

I hard swallow and enter his number. The phone rings and rings until—

"What?" Paul wheezes.

"It's Audrey, Shirley's granddaughter."

"I don't know any Shirley."

"Please, I was there the other day, and I was hoping you could tell me more about how it's all connected." He doesn't respond. "Mr. Hartshorne?"

"Amy—you're Julie's friend. She isn't home yet."

Julie was the name he called me last time. My heart sinks to my feet. He isn't lucid. "Oh." My voice breaks. I'm losing hope.

"You in some kind of trouble?"

"Yes." I pause, wondering if this is a mistake. "That's why I called. You said it's all connected. I need to know how."

"You're the kid who broke in."

"I-I called this time." I don't mean to sound flip; his drifting from past to present is unnerving. "Please, tell me how the bus is connected to Mara and Isabel."

"Has someone been talking to you?" His voice is muffled, like his lips are right against the receiver. "If they start talking to you, it's over."

"Who?"

"Whatever you do, stay outta the mine. It stems from there."

"What does?"

"Evil." The line crackles.

"Mr. Hartshorne?"

He doesn't answer.

"Please."

"I'll have Julie call you back when she gets in."

"Sure," I say, disappointment blooming in my chest as the line dies.

I don't set down my phone; I type *Julie Hartshorne* into the search bar. My heart stutters to a stop at the image of a pretty girl with poufy bangs.

It's the ghost girl.

More than thirty years ago, she went missing in the mine. It's all connected.

Feeling faint, I wander to the bathroom and splash cold water on my face. My eyes sting as the droplets roll over my skin, and Mara looks back at me.

Audrey, who's Julie?

I drop my voice low. "Another dead girl. It's connected, her death and yours. And to Isabel. Maybe more."

That picture on your phone is from decades ago. Terrible shit happens in this town. Big Jim would've been a kid.

"Grandma saw Julie—J.H.—she listed the dates in her journal." Right and wrong are blurred now, and I can't think straight. My body hasn't truly slept in days. All I know for certain is that I'm in a fog surrounded by dead girls.

Are you gonna try and link the Girl Scout that got eaten by a cougar to me too? We should get to Zadie to find out what she's doing about Lorenzini. He killed me, and I know he took Isabel.

"But—"

We're running out of time.

Chapter 34

Zadie

After doing a final run-through of our flimsy plan, we head outside, and Rhea opens the passenger side door of her car for me. The Honda is tidy, but it's older than we are. Still, a car is the one thing I've struggled not to spend my get-out-of-Dodge money on. I envy Rhea's speed at getting places and the privacy and freedom. *Isabel may never get to drive.* The icy thought douses my longing as Rhea turns into the Shady Dell trailer park.

We are going to have a chat with a killer.

We park on the lawn next to a pickup on cinderblocks. "You ready?" Rhea asks.

No, but Isabel needs me. "Yes," I say. "You?"

She nods, and we leave the Honda.

Jimbo sits on the stoop drinking a soda. His eyes widen at the sight of Rhea, who smiles, and I wonder if she wore the tight, fiery dress as a distraction tactic.

"Hey," I say, sinking next to Jimbo.

"I heard about Audrey." He looks out into the distance; his jaw is tight, and his eyes are watery. I forgot he's sorta friends with her. My chest tightens.

"She'll sleep it off," I say.

Jimbo crushes the can. "Getting drunk isn't like her."

I don't ask how he heard the details; the entire town will know by now. Instead, I stare at the birds that gather along the power lines, glaring back at us.

"Everything's rotten in this town," Jimbo says, jabbing his phone. "I gotta go."

My heart shoots up to my throat. "Go where?"

"I got called in to pick up a shift."

"Oh. Okay." I can't ask Jimbo to stay without arousing suspicion. We're gonna be alone with Mara's killer. I sneak a look at Rhea; her face is neutral but her knuckles blanch from gripping her phone. I've put us both in danger.

Jimbo opens the door for us, and we go inside. "Hey, Jim? Zadie's here."

My lungs are tight and my breathing shallow, like I just ran the mile. I focus on breathing in and out as I try to relax my face. I can't look like I know what Big Jim's done, what he's going to do.

Big Jim appears in the hall, his form nearly eclipsing the narrow space. The trailer's low ceilings make him look even taller. He holds a computer cord, the wire wrapped around one hand and gripped in the other like a garrote. When he smiles, his eyes are cold.

He strides over, a citrus scent rolling off the sharp points of his mustache as he gets closer. "Nice to see you again, Zadie," he says, his voice oozing with a politician's charm. When he spots Rhea, the tip of his tongue juts out slightly before he shoves the cord into his back pocket and offers her his hand. "James Lorenzini, call me Jim."

She takes his hand and daintily shakes it while ducking her head as if Big Jim's presence is overwhelming. "I'm Rhea. It's a pleasure to meet you. I've seen your show a million times, and you never picked me."

I goggle at her. Her concise, crisp voice has gone girly—high and extra breathy.

"Really? I must be insane. When I get my show going again, I'll need an assistant. You look like you'd fill out the costumes nicely."

She giggles, and Jim turns to lead us into the living room. Catching the WTF look on my face, she gives a curt nod to Jim's broad back. So, this is her strategy, dumb and cutesy, to gain his trust. She didn't offer her last name, keeping the family badge hidden.

I'll play it simple: nonthreatening sad girl misses her girlfriend. It isn't a stretch, but I'm not much of an actor, and there's no way I can—or want to—pull off the sexiness Rhea effortlessly drips.

This time the coffee table is free of the coiled nest of electronics, only marked by a yellow legal pad covered in tiny block letters and a remote. Jim's cleaned up. He's fresh-shaven and wearing dark denim jeans that look too tight but expensive, and a baby-blue button-down.

He's playing a part, too, the role of too clean-cut to be a kiddie killer. The realization chills my blood. Something made him change his strategy. The makeover might mean he knows that I suspect him.

"Sorry your friend couldn't make it." Big Jim smiles at me.

My shoulders tense as Jimbo waves at us and thuds outside, the screen door clattering behind him.

"You ladies want a beer? Or we got whiskey and coke." He stands in the doorway to the kitchen as if ready to take my order.

"I'm the DD," Rhea chirps. "Maybe next time."

Big Jim points finger guns at me. "You?"

"I'm not twenty-one."

"I won't tell if you don't." He winks at me, and my stomach turns.

I'm playing the grieving best friend who doesn't *know*, so I smile and say, "In that case, I'll take a beer."

He grins and pops into the kitchen, and I hear an echo of one of Mom's favorite lectures. *"Never accept a drink you didn't see made or opened."*

Usually, I don't worry about getting roofied, but with this guy . . . I dash into the kitchen behind him. He's at the fridge; he turns around, holding two unopened beers.

"Just wanted to see if you needed a hand." I sound so lame. He'll catch on if I'm not careful.

Jim pops off the caps using an opener bolted to the wall and passes me one. "I'd offer you food, but the boy doesn't keep any in the house."

"It's cool," I say, sounding anything but. I sip from the beer; it's thick and nearly black—strong, disgusting stuff—the kind of beer that'll knock me on my ass if I finish it. Peeling the label with my nail, I take only a few sips. Big Jim raises an eyebrow and steps closer as I clutch the cold bottle.

My heart punches against my ribs. This man kidnapped, tortured, and killed Mara, and I've brought another friend to him. A murderer is standing over me, and if he decides to, he has the power to take everything.

"It's okay to be nervous. It's a difficult subject." He pats my back, and I cringe as he moves past me into the living room.

My shoulders scrunch, and I fight to relax them. It's like his touch has marked me, and I want to scrub at my skin until it's raw.

"Shall we?" he asks.

I take my beer and sink into the furthest chair. Rhea is looking at her phone, which she stealthily slips into a pocket hidden in the folds of her dress. Big Jim sets his drink on the coffee table and disappears into the kitchen.

The heavy bass of rushing blood crashes behind my ears.

He returns with two wooden chairs and takes them into a large storage closet at the end of the living room.

"The audio I was recording was trash, so I've built a sound-proof room. It's a tight squeeze, and I only got one mic, so we'll have to huddle close," he says over his shoulder as he clamps and adjusts a microphone onto a TV tray stuck between the two chairs. My lungs tighten. He wants me to shut myself in a freaking closet alone with him.

"You okay?" Rhea mouths.

I'm not. I'll never be okay if Big Jim is walking free. I definite-ly won't be okay stuck in a tight space with that animal.

I take a swig of beer. My hands tremble as I set the bottle down on the coffee table.

"Rhea, I apologize my studio isn't large enough to accommo-date you. Perhaps I can interview you another time?"

Disgust flashes behind her eyes, but she recovers quickly, of-fering a giggle and a dimpled smile.

"Ready, Zadie?"

There's no chance of ever being ready, but I nod. He places a big hand on my shoulder and gestures for me to go in first. Feeling the strength of his hand, the size of his fist against my skin, I freeze. It'd be easy for this man to do serious damage. Shrugging him off as I enter, I select the chair the laptop doesn't face. A bare light bulb offers dim illumination, casting the old pillows nailed to the walls in yellow light. Mini roadways of cords covered in silver duct tape crisscross the floor and exit under the door, because this is a closet, and there are no outlets.

When Big Jim enters, his form blots out the light, and a massive black shadow falls over me. He pulls the door shut—it's covered by a woolly army blanket that's stapled along the edges—and I eye the knob. The only way out of this room is through Lorenzini.

The tray table jostles as his body passes it before settling into his seat. Jim sits with his legs spread wide, forcing me to cross mine so his jeans don't rub up against my body.

The air is hot and stale, and I feel trapped. When the light bulb flickers and dims, I want to knock over the table and run out the door.

I calm myself with the idea of Rhea just outside, ready to call the cops if needed. I release a breath—I can't panic, not now. I focus on the questions we brainstormed to wheedle information about Isabel.

I still feel his hand on my shoulder, as if that brief contact has left a lasting imprint.

Big Jim shuffles through a stack of index cards and lays them out in a tarot spread on the tray. He touches the rectangles thoughtfully and slides them around. Notes are written in red in the center of each card, I squint and try to read them upside down, but his handwriting is a series of indiscernible knife-slash lines.

At last, he seems satisfied with the arrangement and looks up. "I'll do an intro later, so we can jump right in. Ready?"

"Sure." My voice sounds small, and all I want is for this to be over. But I'm doing this for Isabel. For Mara.

"Hello, Zadie. Thanks for agreeing to talk."

"Hey."

A flicker of annoyance flashes across his face before it returns to its neutral performance mode. He reaches out and grasps my hand. "Relax," he commands before releasing his grip and leaning back.

"Tell us about Mara."

"Mara was my best friend. My girlfriend."

I wait for his next question, his fingertips tapping like rain-drops on the cards. He's waiting for me to give him more. Sighing, I add, "I met Mara when we were little. Her family lived down the road from my mom and me. She looks—" I pause to correct the tense. "Mara looked sweet, but there was this edge to her. She had a take-no-prisoners-or-bullshit attitude. She was fiercely loyal." This time, I didn't have to think about the *was*.

Towering his fingers, Jim leans in closer and mouths "relax." He selects an index card and runs his finger along its borders, clearly a fan of ASMR. He licks his lips and lets his voice roll out like an old-timey news anchor. His first questions are easy; he selects his cards without reading them and removes them from the table as I answer. Big Jim's face remains neutral, as if he knows what I'll say. It's unnerving how much he knows about me, Mara, and Audrey. I tell him as much. He smiles and drums his fingers lightly.

"I researched. *Relax*." He keeps his voice low and smooth, honey dripping over a glass, and I sink into the depths of the wood chair. Melting. Big Jim's finger slides to the next question on the TV tray and taps the card. He looks up, and his pale blue eyes are icy. "Tell me, what happened to Mara?"

I can't even consider what I'll say before the words spill out. "We were being watched. Someone chose her. Took her. Killed her." I blink hard. A faraway clock punches out the seconds, pounding alongside my heart. It all makes sense as snippets of memories float in my mind like drifting pollen.

"Why do you think that?"

Leaves rustle, and there's a woodsy scent in the air. My skin prickles in recollection—the clearing. It's impossible, but I don't fight it, not even with a woodpecker thrumming somewhere in the distance.

Sunshine warms my skin. "We both had this feeling there were eyes in the forest. We'd joke about ghosts. We brushed it off. Once, we'd brought snacks to this clearing, and the food disappeared while we practiced guitar. Someone must have been right there, and we saw nothing. Strange little things like that happened all the time."

Sliding his finger along another card, he speaks softly, "Did you tell anyone about those 'strange little things'?"

My cell phone rings, and I jolt like I've been startled awake. The fiery illusion I was in control is put out with the ice-water realization that my thoughts were being plucked from my head with suggestions, and I'd willingly strung them together into a story.

Big Jim grunts and tilts his head as if stretching his neck.

Ignoring the ringing, I point my finger at him. "Did you"—I choke down a cocktail of shock and fear—"did you hypnotize me?"

"Even a great hypnotist can't put someone under who doesn't want to be."

It isn't a no, and Big Jim was never just a *great* hypnotist; he was exceptional—he could have been the best in the world if it weren't for his vices.

No, he hadn't performed some trick. The Great Lorenzini broke into me and stole all my control.

I can't stop shaking. "You did something."

"I suggested that you relax, nothing more."

I pick up my cell. It vibrates in my palm—Rhea's calling. I don't answer; I can only stare at Big Jim. This hasn't gone the way it was supposed to. I came here for information on Mara and

Isabel, not to get put under by this monster.

"Let's get back to the interview. You want that forty bucks, don't you?"

"Did you hypnotize Mara?"

His eyes narrow and turn stormy as he stands. "This isn't going to work." It isn't a denial.

"Why are you really doing this?"

"Podcasts with less of a platform have gone viral and solved other cases. This town knows me, trusts me. People will talk to me when they won't go to the cops. I'm doing my part to catch the killer."

"By hanging out in a closet?" I fix him with my gaze. "While that bastard is busy torturing poor Isa or waiting to get back to her." I glare a moment longer, hoping he'll flinch or react so I can be certain.

He merely shrugs. "I'm not paying you."

Shoving my way out of the closet, I bump into the tray table, and the note cards tumble down, their questions unanswered. Rhea is perched wide-eyed at the edge of the couch, her finger poised over the screen of her phone. When I get close enough, I see she's dialed a nine and a one and is ready to press one again. I shake my head, and she exhales, wiping her face of fear and anxiety with one breath, and then smiles warmly over my shoulder in Big Jim's direction.

I grab my bag.

"Interview's over?" she asks with bubblegum sweetness.

"Yes, Zadie was illuminating." The hot air of Jim's breath rankles the tiny hairs on my neck.

He's smiling tightly, but his eyes shoot a warning.

"Yup. I told him everything I know."

"Almost forgot—your fee." He plucks two bills from his wallet.

"You said you weren't gonna pay."

"I was teasing. You shouldn't let yourself get so carried away." He holds the folded twenties out and smiles.

Not knowing what kind of game he's playing, I reach for it. He doesn't let go; he waits for our eyes to lock. He whispers, "If you let me, I can help you remember."

I shudder as he releases the bills. My steps are as wobbly as a new colt's. "Come on, Rhea," I say hoarsely, but Big Jim gets between us.

Handing Rhea a shiny gold business card, he says, "Give me a call this summer. I'll be working on my act. If you want in, we'll have some training to do."

The desire to smash a bottle against the coffee table and shove it into Jim's throat is almost too powerful.

"I'll call you as soon as school's out," Rhea chirps. I know her excitement is false, but her flirtatious complicity is a knife twist in my belly.

Outside, every dog in the trailer park is barking in a clash of yips, bellows, and howls. I want to yell at them all to shut up—to get out of my head.

Rhea rubs my shoulder. "You were in there so long, I got nervous. You okay?"

It hadn't felt that long, but the back of my shirt is damp with sweat, and my neck aches like I've held it at an odd angle for hours. Even my head pounds hangover-style. "I'm fine."

"You look like you want to stab someone."

"He did it."

Rhea's eyebrow arches.

"No proof. Just a feeling. He plays mind games, and he's a total sleaze." I want to tell her how he messed with my head, how I lost control. But one glance at Rhea's calm, logical face, and I keep quiet. Sure, she'd be sympathetic, but she wouldn't believe it.

Not entirely, at least.

"Did he say anything strange? Or comment on Isabel?"

"No. Nothing. It was a waste of time."

Rhea stops walking and grips my arms. "It was a long shot—one we had to try."

I wish I could share what I *did* learn—why Mara didn't remember. He hypnotized Mara, lured her away, and killed her. James Lorenzini is a man who can recover lost memories—and I'm sure he can force you to forget.

Chapter 35

Shirley
18 Years Ago

Shirley felt like a giddy fool, smiling as she examined the freshly completed pink crocheted blanket. In a month, she was going to be a grandmother—twice. Both of her girls were pregnant and due within a week of one another. The town was titillated by the novelty of pregnant identical twins walking around. *The Copper City Crier* even did a feature on them, falsely stating that they shared the same due date, but Shirley supposed it made the coincidence more fun. Wren knew her baby was a girl, but Robin wanted to be surprised and opted not to know the sex.

Shirley opened her bag of butter-yellow yarn and smirked. Robin was also having a girl. The old wives' tales about carrying high, battling heartburn, and craving sugary sweets indicating a girl, in this case, were true. Shirley *knew*. Still, she bought yellow yarn because the blankets were for the baby shower, and she didn't want to spoil the surprise.

Three rows into the pattern, Shirley's fingers clamped around the shaft of the needle as she felt a stone of dread drop into her stomach, sinking deep.

Steeling herself, she moved to the bookcase and flipped through a composition book until she found the entry about the toddlers. There it was. Near-identical blue-eyed babies sitting on a yellow blanket. Worry wrapped around her.

Perhaps it was a mundane foretelling of her granddaughters intermeshed with that other nastiness. That's what she hoped, but her gut sensation told her otherwise, and the yellow yarn pooling on the bed shone like a harbinger. She wondered what threaded the bus to Julie Hartshorne, her granddaughters, the odd root, a pickaxe, and a flashlight rolling in a cavern. Shirley shoved the yarn into the bag and put on her good walking shoes. It was time she paid a visit to Copper City's favorite conspiracy theorist.

Shirley hesitated with her fist raised to knock when the cottage door swung open.

Paul Hartshorne's bushy eyebrows scrunched as he leaned against the open door. "What happened?"

"I—" Shirley couldn't remember the last time she'd been at a loss for words.

"Well, come on in then." Without waiting for a response, Paul led the way to the living room and sank onto the couch with a grimace and a grunt.

"Are you alright?" Shirley asked.

"Fine." He shook his head. "It's this damn socket, I put on a few pounds so now it rubs, that's all." He gave his prosthetic leg the finger.

"I make an aloe and jojoba oil balm that—"

"Is this a sales call, Shirl?" Paul's eyes burned through hers. "Or did something happen to make you take my letters seriously?"

"I'm going to be a grandmother." She clasped her hands. Paul's first letter had come when she'd first arrived back in Copper City. He felt their misfortunes were connected and believed an evil lurked in the bowels of the town. Maybe it was unkind to throw out the letters, but it grew easy to ignore his pulpy prose that arrived unstamped, twice a year, on the anniversaries of Kurt's and Julie's deaths.

Of course, she'd stood in Paul's yard many times, having followed Julie's spirit. But she couldn't face a grieving man only to share that his daughter had been brutally murdered and now wandered the woods like a wretch.

She swallowed. "You'll be disappointed to know I don't *see*, not in the way you seem to think I do, but I am sorry I never responded."

He stared at a framed portrait of his daughter hanging loosely on the wall. "It's all connected. What happened to my Julie, your brother. It started in the mine, there's something evil that lives there." He nodded to a stack of mold-speckled town history books leaning against a sagging bookshelf.

Shirley considered the titles before commenting, "You mean Jasper Dodge."

"It was there before Bloody Jasper. That bastard was just willing to embrace the dark." Paul fished a toothpick from his shirt pocket and stuck it between his teeth.

"I don't understand, what was here before?" Shirley asked, her thoughts drifting to what her grandmother had called the entity, the wrongness that resided deep in the woods and underneath in the mine.

"My letters explained it," Paul gruffed as he crossed his arms.

Shirley nodded slowly. His letters were ramblings full of contradictions. She changed the subject. "You wrote that you worked with Kurt."

Paul nodded. "Briefly at the mine."

"Do you know why Kurt quit?"

"The mine isn't a place to be by yourself." He shifted his leg.

"Was Kurt alone on his last day?"

"Yeah."

"Did he say what he saw?"

"No. A few of the fellas heard screams in the Devil's Domain. Seen people who weren't there outta the corners of their eyes. That sorta thing." He cleared his throat, and Shirley waited. "Sometimes, I'd hear Kurt talking to himself. Like he wasn't alone. After the bus, they figured he had schizophrenia or something."

"But you didn't?" Shirley asked, her voice quiet and prodding.

"His last day, I heard him talking to someone. Arguing."

"About what?"

"Dunno. Couldn't make it out. I went to get him and a man—" Paul stopped and his eyes bore into Shirley's. "A miner I believe to be Bloody Jasper—passed right through me. That's who he'd been fighting with."

Shirley pressed her lips together, not trusting her voice. Some days she believed it was Bloody Jasper that sent her running to Las Vegas. On others, she thought it was the entity taking on a familiar legend as its form.

"Jasper Dodge is no ordinary ghost. He's an evil stain on Copper City." Paul's gaze settled on his moldering books. "After he was killed, the obvious murders slowed down, but the disappearances never did."

"Why did you write me?"

"We're the same. We both lost someone and know the official story's nothing but bunk. The rest of this damn town ignores it, keeps clear of the woods, and they turn their heads to overlook the rot. Maybe we're all infected."

"Julie was murdered." The words left Shirley's mouth raw.

"I know." Paul's eyes glisten. "But it's more than that. Meredith saw Julie after. Said something was chasing our girl even in death. That's why my Mere . . ." Paul pulled out a handkerchief and blew his nose.

Silence stretched between them until, at last, Paul cleared his throat. "Kurt was murdered too. There's something here, something with a fetish for collecting souls."

When Shirley left Paul's cottage, she had more questions than answers. All she was certain of was that the entity roaming Copper City took her brother.

Everything was connected.

Chapter 36

Zadie

The sun is setting, and cotton-candy clouds fill the sky. It's ridiculous how pretty such a terrible place can be. I was naïve to think I could do anything to help Isabel Walls or to discover the truth about Mara.

Rhea and I climb into the Honda. I'm about to tell her that Big Jim hypnotized me when the phone buzzes and flashes the word *Mom*.

"You should get that." Rhea nods to my phone. "She likes me. We don't want that to change."

Rolling my eyes, I answer, "Hey."

"Zadie-doll." Mom releases a great breath. "Do you need me to pick you up? You're not walking."

"Rhea will bring me."

"Have her drop you off by eight thirty."

"Eight thirty? I'm not twelve, and it's the weekend."

"There's a murderer out there. Nine thirty, final offer."

"Fine." I hang up and look at Rhea. Her body looks relaxed behind the wheel, but her face is serious with thought. "Thanks for coming with me."

"Anytime. I tried listening at the door while you were playing seven minutes in hell with Lorenzini, but it was too muffled. Got any adult-free suggestions on where we can go to debrief?" Rhea asks, letting her hand fall on my forearm.

I'm still for a moment, analyzing the touch, but she moves it back into position on the wheel and it's like it never happened. I want to obsess over everything Rhea does, but I need to focus on saving Isabel and getting justice for Mara. Hormones will have to wait. I roll down my window hoping the night air will smack some sense into me.

"I know somewhere. There's this clearing, it's the last place I saw Mara alive." My heart skips a beat as I say it. I showed the police the clearing, but they didn't find anything there. Still, telling Rhea about our secret place feels like I'm betraying Mara to the max.

Rhea's eyes light up at the suggestion. "That's a great idea, we might spot something the boys didn't."

It's only three minutes down the road before I tell her where to turn in. It's the parking lot nearest to the clearing. She looks up at the darkening sky, pops her trunk, and removes a hurricane lamp. I raise an eyebrow when I see the contents of her trunk. A foldable shovel, a tool kit, a bag of kitty litter, and a clear Rubbermaid tub stuffed with what looks like camping supplies.

"One of my dad's conditions for me driving is that I'm prepared for the zombie apocalypse."

"Do you throw kitty litter at zombies?"

"Naturally. It also helps with traction if you're stuck in the snow, not that Pop would let me drive in any sort of flurry." Rhea grins. "Shall we?"

We skirt along the road and then break for the dirt path, hidden by tall grass and weeds, through the woods. She follows me as I weave through the wide, stretching cottonwoods that conceal the clearing.

"What's that building?" she asks, frowning as her eyes appraise the foundation.

"The old brothel."

"Why hasn't Mr. Orlich turned it into some tourist destination?"

"It's falling apart. It'd be more money to fix it than that place could ever bring in."

"It's weird. I thought I'd been to all the historic spots in Copper City."

"Mara and I found it on accident years ago."

"Hmmm." Rhea cocks her head, gazing at it from a different angle. "No plaque, so the historical society must think it's useless. It's strange that Orlich didn't have the building demolished. He's had kids' forts torn down for being eyesores."

"Maybe he doesn't know about it. You didn't."

"It's beautiful here," she says cautiously, an unasked question hovering between us.

I nod; it is pretty, but it looks different now. It feels off-kilter. "This is the spot. I stood right here, and Mara ran that way, through the trees." I say the words like a newscaster, like they don't have anything to do with me, but there's a lump in my throat.

Rhea sets down the lamp in the center of the clearing. The sky is turning navy, and the buzzing of insects fills the air.

My neck tingles, and I jerk my gaze to the trees. *We were being watched.*

That's what I told Big Jim. He put me under to discover what I know and if I'm a threat. But I'm not certain he was the one watching us. After years of being a skeptic, Mara's return has made me question if the woods really are inhabited by something supernatural.

"You okay?" Rhea sits on the patchy grass and motions for me to join her.

I glance back at the forest: There's no glowing eyes or monster action. It's just boring trees. That's all. "Yeah."

Rhea watches me, a curious expression on her face.

Desperate to end the awkward moment, I blurt out the first nonsense that pops into my head. "Did you know that this was one of Bloody Jasper's favorite hangouts?"

It's slightly pathetic that my main well of conversation topics comes from things I learned at a minimum-wage job I got fired from. I guess it could be worse; at least I'm not trying to impress Rhea with an expertise in deep fryer oil.

"Really?"

"Well, back then, it was every miner's preferred extracurricular, but the ladies working here claimed that ole Jasper could appear out of thin air. The thing is, though, some of the girls went missing, and Bloody Jasper likely had something to do with that."

"Huh. I never heard that part before. That would be a great research topic for a paper."

"Uckleman, you love school, don't you?"

"I like knowing the answers."

I try to think of a witty retort, but she shifts and her fingertips brush against mine. I can't keep getting distracted with wondering about Rhea.

I'm not sure what's going on between us or if I have any sort of chance with her. There were a lot of uncomfortable questions I left unasked with Mara.

The last time I was with Mara—the alive Mara—was the first time I didn't go along with one of her schemes. I've been blaming myself for not agreeing to run away with her. It would've been an adventure, and she'd still be alive.

I know that sort of magical thinking is dangerous. I also know that if I'd been more honest about my feelings throughout our relationship, maybe Mara would have reacted differently to being told no.

Now, the sappy part of me fantasizes about Rhea's soulmate potential, while my realist side knows she's my best resource in finding Isa, but already, I haven't been open with her.

I straighten and look into her eyes. "I'm going to make things awkward. I'm enjoying our friendship, and no matter what, I want us to keep working together to find Isabel. It's distracting, though, because I keep wondering . . ." I falter, there's too much to say, and I don't know where to start. I want to ask her if I can kiss her, but the words won't form.

"Um. Before, it felt like there was something between us. It might be wishful thinking, but I'm wondering if you're gay. I am—gay, not just wondering." It's like watching myself fumble in a movie, the words tumbling out, each lumpier than the last. I wish I'd shut up, but I keep going. "Not that anything will change anything either way. I don't want to do something, um, unwelcome." I have the urge to shove a fist in my mouth just to keep it from saying anything stupid.

In the flickering lamplight, Rhea stills in thought before tucking a sprig of curl behind her ear and saying, "Well, I'm a three or a four on the Kinsey scale. If you want to define me, I'd say bisexual. I don't engage much either way because if I brought a guy home, Pop would show him the contents of the gun safe. When I told him I liked girls, too, he said it was a phase I'd grow out of, which is insanely irritating. So, I'm doing the monk thing until I move out."

"That sucks about your dad. My mom's pretty understanding, but nosy."

"Did she know about your secret relationship with Audrey? Was that going on before Mara . . ."

I bite my lip. Whatever I tell Rhea about Audrey will sound like a lie after she saw her come through my window. "I know what it looks like, but we aren't and weren't together. It's just complicated."

"Hmm. You know, I've been trying to figure you out." There's a cracking in the distance, and we both go quiet for a moment, waiting for more. All is still and silent. She continues, "I listen to your music. You pour a lot of your soul into the lyrics, laying it all bare like you aren't afraid to be vulnerable, but when I'm with you, it feels like you're holding something back."

The joy drains from me. "What do you mean?"

"You're so certain that Lorenzini killed Mara. I have a hunch you have a good reason to think that, but you're not telling me."

It isn't a question, and Rhea's eyes are pinned to my face. I sigh. "I *do* have a reason, but the source of information . . ."

She jerks from sitting to kneeling and grips my elbows with her long fingers, her nails piercing my skin with red crescents. "Tell me."

"Rhea, do you believe in ghosts?"

Her hands go slack, and her face droops with disappointment. "Zadie—"

There's a *thwack* sound, and the hurricane lamp explodes. I shriek as a hail of hot glass assaults us, and the darkness takes over.

"What the hell?" Rhea stumbles to her feet.

"Did it explode? Maybe it got too hot?" I switch on my flashlight app and try to scan the tree line, but it only illuminates a few feet into the night.

"Nuh-uh. Not possible." Rhea's face is hard.

"Then, how?"

"Sssshhhh."

Nothing—

—then a *crack* sounds from the brothel side of the woods.

"It came from over there." I point to our right.

"Who's there?" Rhea calls in an authoritative tone. She sounds brave, but when I reach for her hand, I grasp trembling fingers. There's no response, but in the distance, a pack of coyotes howl, celebrating a kill.

"Let's go."

We move quickly, abandoning the remains of the lamp and dashing through the darkness back to the parking spot.

Twice, strange noises sound behind us, following our trail. We move faster. The breeze smells of rotting meat, and I wonder if a mountain lion is stalking us. I turn around, expecting to see a pair of glowing yellow eyes, but all I see is the black landscape.

We make it to the car, and there's another *crack* as Rhea fumbles for her keys and drops them in shock. I scoop them off the asphalt, unlock the driver's side door, and dive in, stumbling into the passenger seat as Rhea jumps in beside me. I grab her things and chuck them into the back seat as she starts the car. She skids out as a loud *thwack* sounds from behind us.

"Something hit the bumper," I gasp.

"Don't care. We need to get outta here."

Blood pounds in my ears, and though it's a warm night, I'm chilled to the bone. Someone watched Mara and me in the woods. Someone chose Mara from that same spot. Someone was watching us now.

Neither of us speaks until Main Street. "What was that?"

"I don't know. Maybe . . ." Rhea pauses. "We scared ourselves after the lamp exploded?"

"You said it couldn't just explode."

"I have to look into it. Tomorrow, let's go back and collect the pieces. Maybe there's a clue like fried wires or footprints."

"Sure thing, Detective, and if there's no evidence, maybe we should contact the Copper City Paranormal Society and see if there are any reports of Bloody Jasper being on the prowl."

"I can't tell if you're joking." Rhea side-eyes me.

I can't tell either. Nothing seems plausible. My heart is beating so fast that I'm even considering the possibility of the boogeyman chasing us. Before I open my mouth, red lights are flashing in the rearview. Rhea curses and pulls over for the black-and-white.

"Pop's gonna be pissed," she grumbles. "Just don't say anything . . . You know, unless they ask." Rhea rolls down her window.

We sit stiffly as a figure appears and a light beam falls across Rhea's face before hitting mine.

"Hi, Frank, what seems to be the problem?"

"Well, hi there, Rhea. You know there's a kidnapper on the loose." He says this half joking, half admonishing.

"I'm dropping my friend off."

The light shines back on me, and I shield my eyes with my hand. "Is that Zadie Slade, Copper City's favorite con artist?"

I want to give him the finger, but even I'm not stupid enough to antagonize a cop.

"Does Chief know who you're hanging around with these days?"

"May I ask why you pulled me over?" Though there's a tinge of annoyance to her tone, Rhea sounds calm. "I wasn't speeding."

"Your taillight's busted."

"Huh. Which one burnt out?"

"Not burnt out. Busted. Did you back into something?" He leans in closer. "Or did you flirt with a softball player's boyfriend? Looks like someone took a bat to it." He winks.

I try not to make a face.

"Not that I'm aware of. Though it sounded like a rock hit the bumper earlier, I'm guessing that's what did it."

"See that you get it fixed. Go straight home after you drop her off." He lowers his voice, but I hear him clearly. "I don't want to have to tell Chief about the company you're keeping."

Rhea's shoulders tense, and her knuckles whiten against the steering wheel. "Anything else?"

He raps his fist on the hood of the car. "I'm just saying take care, Rhea, that one's gonna end up like her mother."

"What? Like a math teacher?" I blurt out, clenching my fists. I don't understand what he's insinuating, but from that smirk on his face, it isn't good.

He huffs, shakes his head, and says, "You ladies have a safe evening now."

We watch from the rearview as he swaggers back to the patrol car.

"Dick," Rhea seethes.

"What was he trying to say about my mom? She's squeaky clean."

Rhea looks down at her hands and licks her lips. She starts the car; it's almost curfew.

"Wait, what about my mom?" I ask.

She lets out a long breath as she turns onto my street. "Well, you know they interviewed her about Mr. Walls."

"They work together." Mom hasn't brought up being called into the station, but I'm not about to admit that.

Rhea nods. "You know, the whole Mara in the mine trick bothered a lot of the force. They'll be jerks to you until they get a new dog to kick."

The adrenaline of this strange night is wearing off. "Should we have told Officer Douche about what happened in the clearing?"

She parks in front of my house five minutes before curfew. "He wouldn't be the right one to trust. Let's go back in the morning and look at the lamp. It may have all been a series of odd occurrences."

"You don't believe that, do you?"

"No. But he's not a nice guy, and anything involving you, well, let's say it won't be taken seriously."

"Are you going to get in trouble for hanging out with me?"

"Pop will be annoyed, but nothing I can't handle."

"At the search party, you didn't want to be seen with me."

Rhea unbuckles her seat belt, leans closer, and grasps my hand. "I'm sorry. That was lame of me."

I stare at our clasped hands, and I think of Mara.

I love her. I always will, but death changed her. Still, looking at Rhea makes me feel like I'm cheating; but I can't build a future with a dead girl. I squeeze Rhea's hand.

She opens her mouth to say something, but I move in, almost placing my lips on hers in a silent question.

Her mouth meets mine in answer; Rhea's lips are full and soft and taste like pear lip balm. Her hands cup my face, and my fingers swim in her curls. Our bodies are so close I can feel the beat of her heart against mine.

The endless succession of passing headlights makes the world feel like our own personal disco. My lips feel raw, and my foot falls asleep and goes tingly. I don't care. Kissing Rhea is my favorite thing in the world, and I never want to stop because we'll have to speak when we do, and I have no clue what I should say.

Rhea pulls away first and flops back into her seat, her expression unreadable. She drums her fingers on the steering wheel. "I'm not gonna be your side piece. We can be friends if you're still seeing Audrey, but this . . ." She pauses to swing her hand like a pendulum between us. "This can't happen again."

"We aren't together."

"You don't sound all that certain." Rhea looks cross. "Let me know in the morning."

"Okay," I say, wondering if I'll ever stop feeling guilty about Mara.

"Will you be up for investigating tomorrow?"

I nod. "Text me when you're ready." And before I can second-guess myself, I add, "I want to be with you. Just you."

We fall back into each other's arms and don't stop kissing until Mom's ringtone blares from my phone.

I don't answer the call because Mom's standing on the front porch, watching. I give Rhea one last peck, open the door, and say, "She's not gonna buy the study-buddy story anymore."

I feel airy as I bounce up the porch steps. Mom's annoyance shows in her arms-crossed stance, but she doesn't say anything as she disappears into the house. The sensation of Rhea's kisses dances on my skin until I spot the *Bring Isabel Home* flyer on the door. I go cold, and Mara's accusation of my selfishness comes flooding back. I'm supposed to be trying to find Isabel. How much closer did she get to death while I was fooling around with Rhea?

I vow to make a difference, even if that means confronting Lorenzini.

Chapter 37

Audrey

Audrey. Audrey. Wake up. ANGSTY!

Rabbit holes, Isabel in a hellish upside-down wonderland, a pinwheeling-eyed Lorenzini, something that stinks like rotten meat, and a . . . But the peculiar dream dissipates from my mind until even the smallest fragments dissolve into a low-grade panic that niggles at the back of my neck: There was something I needed to remember.

AUDREY VANESSA HENNESSEY!

"Stop, just stop. Please, I'm so tired." Mara won't leave me alone. She won't stop screaming in my head, demanding that I talk to her. She's been yelling off and on all night. Dead girls don't need sleep.

AUDREY! The noise rings through my bones. When I don't respond, my hand jerks up from underneath the pillow, grips onto my hair, and pulls.

"Stop!"

The grip remains, but the yanking halts. She's waiting.

"I'll give you five minutes if you promise to let me sleep," I plead into the darkness.

My hand falls to the mattress, and Mara quiets. I feel her

heavy nod inside me. I climb out of bed and tiptoe to the bathroom. Closing my eyes, I flip on the light before letting them flutter open and adjust slowly. I climb onto the counter, my feet resting in the sink, my back to the toilet, and my body pointed toward the medicine cabinet.

It's easier to talk to her this way, watching my lips say her words and her expressions take over my face. Yes, it's unsettling watching someone inhabit your body, but it's better than having a conversation in the dark, wondering if you're going crazy. Hugging my knees to my chest, I gaze into my reflection and wait. It hurts to stare this closely at myself; my skin has gone blotchy, and purple crescents sag under my tired eyes. I focus on my constricting pupils.

"Well? I'm listening."

With a jolt, my eyes roll skyward, and after a flash of light, Mara's cool expression takes over. "Just waiting for you to get settled. Jeez, don't be so pissed. It isn't a good look for us."

"Please, tell me what you want."

Mara twirls my hair and licks my lips. "Did you forget Isabel Walls?"

"No. But if the police and the FBI can't save her, I don't know what I can do."

"Look, I've been awful, and I'm sorry or whatever, but with Isabel's disappearance, I realized a few things and needed to complete a few *tasks*. There's just one thing left to do, and I'm trying to be more respectful by asking first."

"You want to take over my body again?"

"It's *our* body. I didn't choose you. I died and found myself in your boring little life. Neither of us chose this." Mara leans forward like she'll crawl out of the mirror.

"Stop." I press my palm against the medicine cabinet as if

keeping her away is that simple.

The eyes in the mirror fill with tears. "Don't you get it? You're my jailer. At first, I thought this was my chance to be with Zadie again. But it's so much bigger than me. I was brought back to stop him. To save Isabel. I need a few hours to resolve things. Then maybe I can move on. You can understand that, can't you?"

I touch her mirrored face. "I understand."

Mara looks off into the distance. "I'm sorry this happened to you. If I could stop existing or leave without getting stuck forever in Copper City, I would."

"Really?"

"Kid, you know we'd both be happier if I was gone. The truth isn't pretty or polite, but as they say, it can set you free."

"What are you planning?"

She sighs and clacks our nails against the sink before locking eyes with me.

"We're going to kill James Lorenzini."

Chapter 38

Zadie

re you sure this is where we were?" Rhea asks when we get to the clearing. All evidence of the hurricane lamp has vanished.

"Look, the grass is smooshed here. This is the spot. Someone cleaned it up." I run my fingers through the grass until I find a small shard of hard plastic. I hand it to Rhea.

She squats beside me. "The sun's only been up for an hour. Either they got here really early, or whoever did this came back last night."

"But why?"

"Because they shot out our lamp." Rhea looks grimly triumphant.

"What? There wasn't a gunshot. We would have heard it."

She grasps my hand and helps pull me up. "I told my dad about the taillight, and he had a look at it. He found a pellet. Someone shot the lamp with a pellet gun. If it were pumped already, we would have only heard the shot. If the gun was fired at close range, we might have conflated the sound of the shot with the explosion of the lamp."

I glance around nervously, wondering if someone is watching us. The hairs on the back of my neck prickle. With her arms akimbo, Rhea pivots slowly, scanning the tree line and stopping when she faces the brothel. "We sat side by side with the lamp right in front of us. So, they shot at it at an angle."

"They must have been hiding behind the brothel." It's surprising how normal my voice sounds. My mind races with the idea that someone was watching us, waiting with a gun—even if it was just a peashooter.

"Think we should investigate?" I ask. Rhea's brow is drawn, and I can tell she's worried.

"Okay. Get your cell out. Be ready to call 9-1-1."

I pull my phone out, and I'm grateful to see a stubborn little bar on the screen. Cell reception is spotty in the clearing, and it's almost nonexistent on cloudy days.

We head for the brothel. The scattered patches of tall grass look as if they've been trodden on recently, but it's possible I did it when I was here before. The windows and doors remain boarded up, and nothing looks disturbed. It's silly, but I don't mention the hidden entrance to Rhea. That's one of the last secrets I shared with Mara when she was alive. Besides, it's clear by how decrepit the inside is that no one's been in there. Well, no one living at least.

Goose bumps rise across my back as I think of Mara and me in that abandoned building, the vanished items, and the sensation of being watched. Spirits. The realization startles me. Maybe there's more to this than Lorenzini having a thing for murder. My heart thuds hard against my rib cage; maybe the rumor that Bloody Jasper killed Mara isn't so far off.

But ghosts can't do anything.

They *can't*.

I watch as Rhea crouches, getting shots of the crushed grass.

Moving methodically and steadily, she captures every angle of our picnic spot. I join her, and together we edge around the building, scanning the grounds for footprints or signs of disturbance. There's nothing.

"Do you believe in ghosts?" I blurt out and instantly feel foolish for repeating the question from yesterday, to which she'd responded with such disappointment—right before the lamp exploded.

Rhea cocks her head to the side as if rolling each word in her mouth before letting it tumble past her lips. "Pop's seen one at the station, and he's not one to tell tales."

"What about you?"

"I've never seen a ghost."

"Do you believe in them?"

Rhea smirks. "It's not that simple, because so many people I trust have had experiences. But I don't."

"Fair enough." I deflate a little; I can't tell her about Mara.

"We better hurry. The morning briefing starts soon," Rhea gasps, looking at her cell.

"I know a shortcut through the woods."

"Is that a good idea?" Her brows knit. Most people in Copper City keep clear of the woods.

"It'll give us more time to snoop around your dad's office."

"Fine. Keep your phone out just in case."

I reach for Rhea's hand and squeeze it. "The path is by that big tree." She squeezes back.

I'm estimating how many minutes of kissing I've bought us when I stop short at the alligator juniper. It feels like someone has reached into my chest and ripped out my heart. I can't speak.

"Zadie? What's wrong?"

I point. Punctured on a scaly bit of bark is a page ripped from

The Zaras notebook that went missing with Mara. The sheet has snippets of a song and notes written back and forth—specks of dark brown dot the paper. And someone has circled a single word in thick red ink. Mara's writing. My name.

Zadie.

"What is that?" Rhea leans in as close as she can without touching the page.

It feels like I've been doused with ice water. "It's from a notebook Mara and I kept. She had it when she was taken." I reach for the page to pluck it from the branches, but Rhea grabs my arm.

"Fingerprints! I'm calling it in." She lifts her cell to her ear, and I see her dial again.

"Dead zone," I mutter.

Rhea snaps a picture of the paper hanging from the branch. "Let's get out of here. It feels—"

"Like we're being watched?" I add, glancing around.

Rhea paces, holding her phone in the air, searching for a signal. "Come on." She grabs my hand. I'm about to head for the forest path, but she shakes her head. "No shortcut. We don't want to be isolated. As soon as I get a cell signal, I'm calling my dad to come down."

We dash toward the nearest road, each taking turns glancing behind our shoulders. I'm panting by the time Rhea stops to call her dad. It only takes minutes for him to pull up beside us in a patrol car. He opens the back door for us to get in, and my stomach flips. This is my second time in a cop car in only a matter of days.

Chief Uckleman drives us as close as possible to the clearing. After I point out the path, we're left inside the car while he investigates. The chief returns grim-faced. He climbs into the driver's seat and addresses us in the rearview. "There's nothing there."

Rhea checks the time on her cell. "It's been ten minutes. How could it vanish?"

He starts the engine. "You're certain that it was from Mara Quinn's notebook?"

"It was our notebook, and yes, I recognized her handwriting and the song lyrics."

"Do you know where the notebook is now or who might have it?"

"Of course not." My eyes meet his in the mirror.

He nods. "I think it's time you come down to the station and chat."

My gut drops.

"Why?" Rhea's gaze shifts to her seat belt.

"Later." His voice is gruff.

"I-I need to talk to my mom first."

"We'll talk to her together. She's already scheduled for an interview."

"What? Why?" I'm baffled.

"Let's see if your mother's available now." Without leaving room for argument, he turns toward our hillside neighborhood.

There isn't time for this. I glance at Rhea. Her face is screwed up as if she's also stuck without a solution.

I text Mom, and she doesn't answer. It's Sunday morning, and she *should* answer; usually, she does with near-telepathic swiftness. My mouth goes dry.

The police radio crackles as we turn onto my street. Chief Uckleman answers, his voice low and clipped.

Rhea locks pinkies with me and whispers, "Keep calm."

"Okay."

Chief Uckleman opens the car door and pierces me with his dark eyes. "Grab Katherine. We'll wait."

I nod. I can't lose any more time; my best bet will be to convince Mom to tell the chief to shove off. It's an effort to walk up the path to our house when my body is desperate to run. The door is locked. Aware of the cop car loitering behind me, I grope in my pocket for my keys and open the door. My heart knocks loudly against my chest.

"Mom?"

No answer. There's a note on the table. *Running an errand.* What errand could she be doing this early? Hardly anything is open on Sundays in Copper City.

She's lying. The very notion gives me the creepy-crawly sensation of a spider legging across my skin. Isabel's disappearance has kept me from questioning the smoking and other secrets Mom's hiding. It's like I'm standing on the edge of a cliff, squeezing my eyes shut, pretending if I don't open them, I won't have to face the drop.

Taking a deep breath, I run back outside. I've made a choice, and I don't have time to second-guess it. Chief Uckleman gets out of the patrol car when he sees me, his large form looming over even the light bar on top.

"My mom's in the shower. We'll drive down as soon as she's ready."

Uckleman shrugs. "I'll wait."

"No—Mom said—"

"I insist." With a rap of his knuckles against the top of the car, he ends the conversation.

"Okay." Shit, shit, shit. I glance toward the patrol car, hoping to send Rhea a psychic signal, but I can't see her through the tint.

Inside, I call Mom, but it goes straight to voicemail. "Call me. Don't come home—call first." I'll catch hell for this later—I lied to the police chief. But I bought myself ten, fifteen minutes maybe.

Less if Mom shows up.

I choke back the panic. I need to think.

There's a connection between Mom and Isabel. Something bigger than tutoring. There must be. Why else would the police want to interrogate her? Raking my hands through my hair, I make a choice. I'll give myself five minutes to ransack Katherine Slade's life and hope to hell I find whatever I'm missing.

Hobo springs into a Halloween cat pose as I barrel into Mom's bedroom. We both know I might not like what I find.

The last time I snooped through Mom's stuff, I was eleven. She was out and I was bored. I wasn't really expecting to find anything, but there was an orange Nike box under her bed. Nothing else was there, so I knew it had to be something. Inside was a small notebook, a photo strip, and a Zippo engraved with leafy swirls. The four little photos were of Mom and a Mexican man with earlobes nearly identical to mine. The pictures were blurry and faded by time, but were possibly the only pictures of my parents together in existence.

Only two pages of the notebook were used for a list of Mexican surnames starting with the letter *S*. It bothered me she couldn't remember his name. That she'd lost her phone with his number before she'd even left Rocky Point. My father never knew I existed. Before putting the box back, I pocketed the Zippo. I wanted something that belonged to him, something I could pretend he gave to me.

Sure, I got my brown skin and dark eyes from him—I don't even look related to Mom—but I always wanted something more. I always wondered if he saw me, would he know I was his?

I force the past from my mind and take a deep breath. I have to move.

I squat and look under her bed first. The Nike box is where I left it all those years ago, and judging by the layer of filth coating the orange cardboard, it hasn't been moved since. Besides a collection of dust rodents, there isn't anything else.

Scanning the corners of the room, I wonder where Mom would hide evidence of whatever secrets she's keeping. I check the closet first: A line of shoes standing sentry, clothing, purses, and belts, but nothing else.

Holding my breath and praying *not* to find any sex toys, I slide open her bedside drawer. There's a flashlight and some other innocuous items, and a crumpled piece of paper. My hands tremble as I remove it.

Lines are scratched through and whole paragraphs are scribbled out, but I can make out enough. *Too much wine. Lonely. This can't happen again. We couldn't have known.*

Nausea shoots through my stomach.

I slam the drawer. The strange moments of past days fall into place: the two wine glasses, Mom's smoking, the little lies. The night Isabel went missing, Mr. Walls was here, with Mom.

That cop's comment about me being like my mother comes back with a sting.

Mr. Walls is married, and he's the only suspect in his daughter's disappearance. Jesus, Mom's his alibi. She'd lie for him—if she believes his innocence.

I wonder if it's possible Jon Walls killed Mara.

No. My money is on Lorenzini—Mara says it's him—but Mr. Walls knew Mara. Mom wouldn't fall in love with a killer. There'd be signs or giant red flags. Peeking out the curtain at the waiting police cruiser, I think of the history of warnings my mother has missed or ignored. She likes to see the best in people. She'd rather swallow lies whole than question her preferred reality.

There's a chance Mr. Walls has something to do with his

daughter's disappearance. The crime might have nothing to do with Mara. Maybe he was trying to use coincidence as an advantage. Cheating doesn't make you a murderer, but it sure doesn't make you look innocent. The sound of his wail at the assembly echoes in my mind. I don't think Jon Walls did it, but he and my mother are in serious trouble if the real kidnapper isn't caught.

After expelling a heavy breath, I move through the house quickly, sliding a pocketknife into my jeans opposite my Zippo.

They estimate that Mara was kept alive for six days. Isabel's been gone four.

There's no time for caution.

A pounding knock reverberates from the front door just as I slip out the back and run as fast as I can.

Chapter 39

Shirley
10 Years Ago

In the woods, the entity was watching. Shirley cursed herself for being in the proximity of the old brothel; that wretched spirit had more strength here. She rose from her crouch, dropping a sprig of rosemary into her fanny pack, trying to move as if she were unaware of the rotting scent that hung heavy in the air.

She moved down the route, hoping to clear the orbit of whatever had its sights on her. The mechanical whir of a palo verde beetle shattered the silence. It flew into her forehead, causing her to stumble. She never cared for those roaches with wings. It flew at her again. Hastening her step, she swatted as it came a third time.

Something snared her foot, and she went sideways. A sickening crack rang in her ears, the earth around her caved in, and she fell hard into a black pit.

The sky-blue splinters seemed impossibly high above her. Her skull throbbed, and her stomach churned. A concussion then—wonderful. No, it was more than that. It was like someone had shoved a finger into her head and waggled it about. Inky black flooded her vision, and the pain intensified—a burrowing, gnawing sensation as if something were eating through her brain.

Shirley cried out.

Gotcha.

The entity—he was killing her.

"No!" she yelled, but the agony kept her down. The edges of her vision bled, and she couldn't see outward.

After Kurt had died and Shirley fell into deep despair, Inga told her never to let grief blot out her light.

Now, Shirley channeled her agony into a golden flame and pictured it expelling the void. The world strobed as she focused, sliding the shards of black from the soft gray crevices until there was only a sliver the size and shape of a fine cactus needle left. Try as she might, she couldn't get that last piece to budge, so she wrapped the splinter in a flaxen twine of light.

*

Shirley woke on the damp, mulch-blanketed earth. She didn't remember what had happened. Her head felt vised.

"Wonderful. A concussion," she murmured, sensing déjà vu as she groaned and looked about. She guessed she'd fallen ten feet. The pain was electric.

She remembered to breathe. She wouldn't be one of those poor fools who made things worse by panicking. Inga had always said that panic could wait.

Shirley vowed to soak in the tub after getting out of this pickle. Her head throbbed, and a vision of a medical donut flashed in her mind's eye. She guffawed with relief. So, she'd have less dignity, but she would live. She wiggled both sets of toes. When she shifted her left ankle, she grimaced. Sprained. The rest of her leg felt tender but in one piece. Her tailbone hurt something fierce, but she suspected that her ample bottom and decades of gathered mulch had kept her back from shattering.

Wren had told her to buy a mobile phone, and Shirley had laughed. Cell phones were for doctors and drug dealers. She'd allow Wren an "I told you so" after this and then get a Nokia. It would be nice to have some handsome fireman rescue her rather than yell herself hoarse until someone came.

Carefully she moved herself to a seated position and called out, "Hello? Anyone there?"

A dark shadow drifted above, blotting out the sun. Shirley's head pounded, a pickaxe vibrating in her vision. She blinked it away. Overhead, the shadow didn't move.

"Hello?" she tried again. Nothing. The darkness of the sky increased. She wondered how long she'd been unconscious. She'd thought it'd only been minutes. Dread crept over her, and unease twisted inside.

"Silly woman," she scolded herself. "You're going to be alright. You saw the darn donut. You'll have a bruised ego and behind. That's all." To soothe herself further, she closed her eyes to call up the image of the cushion, but nothing came. All she could summon was a hazy memory of it. That had never happened before. She tried again, but the only vision she could conjure was the pickaxe. It came sharper than ever before, and she could taste the tang of the rust, feel the splinters of the handle, and hear the zing of the blade slicing through the air.

"Help!" she screamed, though she knew with cold certainty that no one was around to hear her. The forest had fallen silent.

Shirley forced her body up; the tiniest weight on the sprained ankle caused her to gasp in pain. She leaned against the wall, supported by her good leg. The shadows above covered the exit as if night had fallen.

"Oh, no." Shirley squeezed her eyes shut. Electricity floated in the damp air, and chills of certainty ran through her.

This was a trap.

When she was small, their cottage had mice. Her father had set glue traps all around. Most of the rodents were discovered alive and discarded. But two stuck in Shirley's mind, even after all these years.

The first was the mouse she discovered next to the fridge, eyes wide in static panic, its tiny gray hairs standing on end. The poor creature had died of a heart attack. The second mouse left behind a pair of bloody paws. It had chewed through its own legs to escape. Her father predicted they'd find the rodent dead, bled out somewhere nearby. But they never did.

As the putrid scent of rot filled her nostrils, Shirley wondered what sort of mouse she was.

A heavy dragging sound approached from the distance— along with a faint whistling. The entity was coming for her.

Shirley's knees gave way, and she crumpled to the earth. She'd be the mouse who died of fear then.

Little dove, whoever dug this hole needed a way out.

"Inga?" Shirley whispered. But no reply came except for the slow, serrated whistling.

She pulled herself back up, the pain shocking in its intensity. Someone had built this place and gotten out somehow. A rope would have rotted away, and ladders could be removed, but Shirley had to try.

With little light to guide her, Shirley smacked her hands along the wall, feeling the cold rock and earth. She had daughters who needed her and grandchildren whom she intended to spoil.

At last, her palm slapped against something metal. The rung was rusted through and covered with muck; she gripped it and slid her good foot along the wall until it hit the lowest bar. Gingerly she placed her injured foot on it and winced as she shifted her weight and stepped fully on the ladder.

Something growled from outside the hole.

She froze. She couldn't think of an animal in her forest that made such a guttural sound.

"Damn you," Shirley spat back, and reached for the next rung.

The pain of moving her injured ankle made her bite her lip to keep from screaming. The tang of blood flooded her mouth. She clung to the rung; she'd only gone up four. How many more to go? Ten, fifteen, twenty? Steeling herself, she took another step.

The air was frigid and black. The whistling slipped in through her ear, each note felt like a shard of glass jammed into her brain.

Shirley pulled herself up and up, each step sending a crashing wave of pain over her. It was worse than delivering the twins. She'd never thought anything would compare. But this . . . She focused on each step as if it were a contraction. She breathed out on the pain. Up and up, she went.

"*Out,*" she huffed as she emerged from the pit, pulling herself out and sobbing warm tears of relief.

The clouds shifted, and the light returned. Her ankle throbbed, but it was nothing compared to the splinter of pain lodged in her head. A concussion, she reassured herself again.

A dog barked in the distance.

"Help me!" Shirley called.

The barking, accompanied by footfalls, came nearer as Shirley summoned the vision of the medical cushion at last.

Chapter 40

Audrey

I don't trust Mara, but she's all I have. If Isabel Walls can be saved and killing James Lorenzini is the only way to do it . . .

But I feel that tingle, that intuition Grandma was always urging me to follow, so I tell Mara about Julie, the bus, the entity in the woods, and all the cracks forming between worlds. For once, she listens and waits until I'm finished talking to speak.

How did you keep this from me? Her tone is near reverent. *I ought to give you more credit, Angsty.*

"You should." I can't stop the yawn from escaping me. My legs unfurl from the sink, and I walk back to my bed, unsure who is controlling them. We overlap now, like a double exposure.

We collapse on the bed. We are vulnerable, I can't keep my barricades up, and I see truths in Mara I suspected but never confirmed.

I see wisps of unfulfilled wishes, the longing to time travel, to change a million tiny details so that she could be alive. She shudders inside, and I feel how she aches for her parents, her body. She stiffens, hardening, and I see her love for Zadie has turned to bitter obsession. And deep at the center of it all, I find her dark truth. If she could, she would take over my body completely. She's relieved that she can't—she'd never be able to forgive herself—but she knows, if given the opportunity, she wouldn't be able to resist breathing again.

Inside, she puffs herself up, ready for a fight, but I am so tired. "Oh, Mara."

She deflates. *I won't do it. I'm not anywhere close to being able to. If I kill Lorenzini, I know I'll be able to leave. It won't be an issue.*

If that doesn't work, I'll cast her out somehow.

She bristles at my thought but doesn't argue. *Our body needs rest. We have a big night ahead.*

I want to say it's my body. Mine. But I don't have the strength. Though it's only afternoon, our body is too tired. We do need rest.

Together, we slip away.

*

A clatter at the window disrupts our dreamless sleep. I should be alarmed, but I keep my eyes shut, nuzzle my face farther into the pillow, and slip back into the sweet nothing.

Fingers squeeze my forearm, and a voice whispers my name.

Inside, Mara tugs at my bones. *Sleep. I'll handle this.*

My soul sinks back, but not all the way. I watch, but it's as blurry and far away as when my wisdom teeth were pulled and I spent the day drugged on the couch.

Mara rolls to face our visitor, and Zadie's eyes go wide as they travel over the bruises on my arms. We look away.

"So, I'm on the run," Zadie offers. "But I'm not in costume this time, so the mug shot will be way less embarrassing."

Mara allows for the tiniest smile and, as if taking that slight upturning of lips as an invitation, Zadie sits on the edge of the bed.

"Sorry to wake you. Are you okay? You don't seem like the sleep-all-day type." She's smiling, but her eyes are wide with worry.

"Okay? I feel like week-old shit."

"Mara?" Zadie grins, and adrift in the ether, I feel betrayed.

My head nods.

"Is Audrey there too?"

"She's resting." Mara pulls herself up on her elbows, stacks the pillows, and leans back into a seated position.

I fight to keep still, out of notice. Mara thinks I'm unconscious. I dread what she'll say and do when she thinks she's unsupervised, but I need to know.

Zadie's gaze glides over the crisscrossing cuts and eggplant-colored bruises along my arms. "We have to talk."

Outside, the whir of propellers cuts through the morning, and they both turn toward the noise. "Sounds like old Orlich's donated more choppers. Not that that'll help, since I'm sure little Isa's in a hole somewhere."

"*Mara.*"

"You know Orlich's a rich dick."

"He put up a lot of money trying to find you."

"Dirty old family money. And this missing girl shtick is giving the town's profile a boost. He has to pretend to care." Mara stretches and yawns before asking, "Do people think Bloody Jasper's ghost took Isabel?"

She's being sarcastic, but I can't help but think about what Paul Hartshorne said about everything being connected. Bloody Jasper murdered sixteen people and dumped them in the Devil's Domain, where Mara's body was later found. The mine is the same place Kurt heard voices; the field trip was coming from there when he steered the bus into the pit. Julie Hartshorne was lost forever in the tunnels. They've searched the mine for Isabel, but miles of the passages aren't mapped. It's still possible she's there somewhere.

Zadie wraps her arms around herself. "Not that I've heard. But it wouldn't surprise me. Listen, we gotta talk about Lorenzini. We're running out of time."

"We? I'm officially out." The sneer in her tone is unmistakable.

The *chop-chop-chop* thrum of the blades lifts away as the aerial search moves on.

"Please, Mara. I need you—both of you—to save Isabel. How's Audrey holding up?"

Mara wriggles us up to sit a little straighter. "I hear some of her thoughts. Usually, her inner monologue is boring as all hell—*I should make rhubarb* cherry *pie instead of rhubarb strawberry— wouldn't that be wild! Oh, how I wish I had a truffle hog*—but it's juicier now that she's gone coo-coo-ca-choo crazy. Can't blame her, though. She's worried about everything: Isabel, her family, you. Makes sense she's having psychotic delusions."

The smirk that slithers over my face makes my stomach turn, and I hate Mara.

Zadie's face is ashen. "Is she . . . functional?"

"Meh." She wobbles our hand in a "so-so" motion.

"And you? How are you doing?"

"The body's beat up and sleep-deprived, but I've been worse. I died once, so you know, I'm peachy."

I can't stand it anymore. I rear up, ready to take back my body, when I feel a fist slam into my middle, knocking me to nothing. Invisible walls close around me. Mara's using my lockdown method against me.

Through my now-bleary vision, I watch as Zadie leans in closer. "Listen, I'm going to find Isabel. Come with me to see Big Jim."

I slam into Mara's barricades, trying to fight my way out.

Mara grips the thin bedsheet as I kick. "I remembered something. Before he took me, Lorenzini was doing weird stuff out in the woods." I scratch and pull. She coughs and points to a bottle of water on my nightstand. "Hand me that, will ya?"

Zadie passes it to us, and Mara chugs from the bottle. Water cascades from the sides of my mouth and down my chin, and the sensation tells me I'm close.

"Like what?"

"Just strange things like twisting branches together. Maybe he was building a trap. I asked him about it and . . ."

I stop fighting. I haven't heard any of this. Mara squeezes our eyes shut. "I ran. It's hard running off the path in the forest. There are so many roots and rocks waiting to trip you. He got me, and he hypnotized me. You know the rest."

"How did he hypnotize you when you were trying to get away?"

Mara's anger tints my vision red. "Are you suggesting I wanted to be tortured and murdered?"

"No! I'm sorry." Zadie gulps. "I wasn't thinking."

Mara leans in close as a nasty anger sizzles inside, the Zadie love all but evaporated now. "So, how's *Rhea*?" She makes the name sound like a curse.

Zadie shifts, her face reddening. "Get dressed. We'll confront him and find out where Isabel is."

"That's a stupid plan. I want revenge." Mara is distracted by her fury; she doesn't sense my prison crumbling until it's too late, and I lunge from within, taking control.

Zadie grasps my arm. "Don't shut me out—think about Isabel. Mara!"

I exhale, releasing my cousin's pent-up rage, and fall back on the pillow. "Hi, Zadie."

"Hey," she says. Her face is uncertain.

"I can't control Mara anymore." I fight to keep my chin from quivering.

"Audrey . . ."

"We're going to snap my soul like a wishbone."

Zadie reaches out and squeezes my hand. She always seemed more mature, more capable of being in the world than me. But watching her stumble around not understanding what Mara has become makes me realize she's naïve. She is no closer to stopping this than I am. The tears come hard and fast.

"Sssshhhh. Audrey, don't cry. Mara's difficult right now. The whole Isabel thing is messing with her."

"That and Rhea. I'm surprised she talked to you at all."

"I need to find out what else she knows about Lorenzini. I'm going to see him again."

I grip her hand. "There's more to it than Lorenzini. It won't end with him. Besides, we can't trust what Mara says. She's using us."

"What do you mean?"

"I'll come with you to see Big Jim. But then I need you to help me with something. Promise?"

"Okay . . ."

"We need to get rid of Mara."

Zadie flinches, and I see my nails have dug into her skin. I move my hand away.

"Audrey . . ."

"She's destroying me."

Footsteps echo from the hallway. For a moment, Zadie looks like she'll faint, but she takes a long breath. "I won't let her hurt you. I'll do whatever it takes to . . ." She pauses. "I'll get rid of Mara."

The footsteps come closer.

I glance toward the door. "I'll meet you by the path in ten minutes. Don't let my mother see you."

"Audrey, I—"

The footsteps stop outside the door. "Honey? Can I come in?"

"Just a minute," I call before mouthing "go."

Zadie shoots me one last look before disappearing out the window.

After taking aspirin and drinking a full glass of water like a good girl, I nestle back into bed and let Momma kiss my forehead. The moment she shuts the door, I fling off the covers and dart into my bathroom.

I climb into the sink; I need a face-to-face with Mara. These past days with her have given me a lifetime's worth of hurt and betrayal. I hate confrontation, but she's like a ballooning blood vessel in a brain. You can only ignore the headaches so long before it explodes.

I smack the mirror and watch my reflection go wide-eyed. "So, you think I'm crazy?"

"I was venting."

"Well, I feel crazy, and that's because of you. If you keep taking over, I'll tell Momma everything."

"Angsty, they'd lock you up."

"No. They'd lock *us* up. Understand?"

A silence follows, stretching until Mara snaps, "Yeah. I get it."

"Good. We need to catch up with Zadie."

Mara softens. "Today, together, we'll end it. With Lorenzini dead, you'll get rid of me. We'll both be free."

"How can you be sure?"

"He killed me. I'm certain." She shows me an image of his face, his lips whispering "forget," and a trill of déjà vu trickles down my limbs.

Leaning my forehead against the bathroom mirror, I whisper, "I don't think I can kill someone, not even him."

The reflection's palm reaches out as if to stroke my hair. "You won't. I'll do it, it's my destiny. And once he's dead, I'll be able to leave."

"But everyone will think I'm a murderer."

"You'll be a hero. If we get rid of him, Isabel will have a chance."

Isabel. This is more than my cousin's revenge fantasy. Even if we don't spare Isa, we could keep other girls from the same fate.

Pulling away from the medicine cabinet, I ask, "How would we even do it?"

A wicked glint sparkles in Mara's—my—eye. "Great-Great Grammy Josie's Derringer."

Shutting my eyes, I picture the pocket pistol in the curio cabinet. At every family gathering, Dad removes the tiny gun from its display and tells the story of Josie Hennessey foiling a liquor store holdup with the ivory-handled weapon. The ivory has yellowed, and some intricate engravings along the barrels have been rubbed out by time, but as Dad says, "the thing still shoots." My parents aren't gun people, but they collect knickknacks, tchotchkes, and vintage signs that decorate the sitting room. Next to the Derringer, they keep an antique red-and-green Remington carton that once contained twenty bullets but now only holds three.

Reading my thoughts, Mara says, "That'll be enough."

I nod and climb down from the sink. The hem of my nightgown is damp, and coldness brushes along my knees. "It'll be hard to sneak it out of the living room."

About that . . . I already stashed it under your bed.

I'm too tired to scold her for stealing more of my life.

After this, I won't take another second. Cross my heart.

Together we slip on a pair of boots. Mara retrieves the pistol, pushes on the lever, and opens the double-barrel to load the chamber as Dad demonstrated on many Christmases. She shuts it with a satisfying click and slips it neatly into the boot shaft. Our lips spread into a smile. I'm having trouble telling who's who.

I grip my hands on the windowsill, ready to climb out like Zadie did, but my knees knock, and I nearly fall.

One of us needs to have complete control, Mara says pointedly.

"Me."

Just until we find him, okay? Then let me take over to—you know.

"Fine." Strength returns to my limbs, and I land outside without making a noise. Pain shoots up my calves, but I'm in control.

Chapter 41

Zadie

At the edge of the Hennesseys' property, I find a set of fierce brown eyes glaring at me.

"Rhea, what are you doing here?"

She doesn't answer; instead, she turns on her heels and power walks away so fast I jog to catch up. "Slow down. I'll explain everything, but I need you to come with me to Lorenzini's—"

"No. When you pulled that runner, I figured you had an actual lead. Why else would you royally piss off my father? But then I watched you crawl through her window."

"There's no time. I needed information on Big Jim," I pant, quickening my pace to keep up with her long, angry strides.

She halts, and I stumble. We've reached her Honda.

"Rhea, stop! We need to talk."

She yanks open the car door, and I jump back to avoid getting a chest full of metal. "What the hell?"

Her beautiful face shows none of its gentleness. Her full lips pull into a tight frown, and her eyebrows arrow downward into a scowl. "Tell me what exactly is going on." She points her finger as she spits the words.

"I don't know what you're talking about."

"Let me save you some time. The window was open; I heard *both* your conversations."

Oh, god. I study Rhea's face; she doesn't look confused or scared. Just livid. My body feels like it's sinking. "I know it doesn't make sense—"

Rhea cuts me off. "Oh, it makes sense, and it's disgusting that you're taking advantage of Audrey."

My jaw falls open in disbelief. "It's a crazy situation, but I'm not doing anything wrong."

She folds her arms across her chest. "Pretending she's your dead girlfriend is despicable."

I wish this conversation wasn't happening. I can't stand the way Rhea is looking at me, and I know when I explain, I'll lose her. Struggling to meet her gaze, I know I don't even have a good lie. I'm stuck with the truth. "She's not pretending."

"You're saying she *is* Mara?"

"When Mara died, she came back, sort of. She's been inside Audrey since the funeral. I know it sounds impossible, but it's her." Tears spill from my eyes.

Rhea's face softens. "I get why you'd want to believe that. I pretended my mom's cancer was a cover, that she wasn't dead but just on a secret mission for the CIA, and one day she'd come back. But I gave up on that crap when I was twelve. You gotta stop. You're hurting Audrey by enabling her delusion."

"It's real."

Rhea scoffs.

"She knows things that only Mara could. Things about our relationship, our secrets. She knows because she *is* Mara."

Rhea doesn't speak. She settles into the car sideways, resting her head in her hands. I sit on the curb and try to steady my breathing.

"If Mara were back, her murder would be solved, and Audrey would be able to convince more people than just you." She shakes her head, swings her legs into the car, and puts the key in the ignition.

"Mara told me it was James Lorenzini."

"But she waited until another girl was taken?" Rhea shakes her head. "Listen to yourself."

I want to beg her to believe me. But from the look on her face, I know there's nothing I can say to make her understand. "Please . . . Come with me." I cringe. I sound pathetic.

"No." Her eyes narrow at something behind me. "Jesus. Does that look like a sane person to you?"

I whirl around to find Audrey, wild-eyed, wearing a slip night-gown and combat boots.

"I'll help her. We just have to do this first. For Isabel."

"You gotta fix yourself before you try to help anyone else."

It would feel better if she'd kicked me in the ribs.

"The cops are looking for you."

Stepping back, I don't answer, and Rhea slams the door and drives away.

As the car disappears along the winding road, Audrey's fingers lace through mine, reminding me that there are horrors to deal with.

"Are you sure you're up for this?" I ask.

She nods, her expression stiff and determined. "Whatever happens, I want you to know that it was my choice." The voice has Audrey's signature softness with the razor-sharp edge of Mara's confidence. It's an uncanny blend, but I don't have time to question it.

"We'll have to cut through the forest. Chief Uckleman's looking for me."

Audrey squeezes my hand in response, and together we enter the woods to follow the main trail that leads through the center and lets out near Jimbo's trailer park. We don't speak. The only sounds come from the pine needles that crunch underfoot and the near-constant vibration of my cell. It seems Mom's found out that I gave Uckleman the slip.

"Zadie?" Audrey speaks my name like it's an apology.

"Yeah?"

"When this is over, Mara's agreed to leave."

"Oh." I don't know what else to say. The idea wrenches my heart. I only had her back for a moment.

Deeper in, the ground goes soft, and mud squelches underneath our feet. I'm trudging forward when Audrey tugs on my wrist.

"The forest artist came back. Look." With her free hand, she points out hanging spheres of looped branches. There are at least twenty that dangle from trees like holiday baubles.

I stare at them in wonder. They are intricate and look like something a wood nymph would make. I reach for one of the loops and run my fingers over the braided wood strips. I wonder why someone made this, taking the time to create something that hardly anyone will see.

Mara said Big Jim was building something like a trap. Hands that could produce such tight weaves and configurations could easily make something sinister. Grimly I imagine a cage falling on a kid in the woods, something that could perform its duty and then be easily broken down to nothing but a pile of sticks.

My phone vibrates furiously. When I check it, I see dozens of texts and missed calls from my mother.

"You should message her that you're safe," Audrey says, placing one of the loops over my head like a glowstick necklace.

She's right. "Okay, just give me a sec." I stare at the screen, scrolling through the increasingly frantic messages. The phone trembles and buzzes in my palm as I struggle to compose the right words.

Finally, I text:

I'm okay. I'll explain later.

"Let's get going," I say, reaching into my front pocket. I pull out the knife to make sure it's still there. The Zippo tumbles out and lands on a patch of damp earth, and for a moment, I consider leaving it. It's foolish to pretend it's anything more than an old lighter.

Again, the cell vibrates in my hand, and I shove it into my front pocket, impulsively grab the lighter, and slide it down into my back pocket.

"Ready, Audrey?" I look up, and she isn't there. "Audrey?"

Whirling around, I call for her and spot her boots standing in the mud. I rush to them but can't figure out where she went from there. I call her phone, and it goes straight to voicemail. Rhea's right, Audrey isn't stable, and now she's wandering the woods.

"AUDREY!" I scream, sending birds shooting out from the trees. No reply comes. Maybe she went home or ahead. Her voice is so soft I might not have heard her tell me. I need to keep going for Isabel. I'll find Audrey on the way.

I choke down the panic and move forward. The woods have grown thicker and darker.

A few more minutes of walking, and there's a flicker of movement and human sounds ahead. Audrey. Relief swells in my heart, and I wade through the brush to get to her. A branch causes me to stumble, but I right myself before the fall, straightening in time to see Big Jim step into view.

He hacks and spits on the ground before nodding his greeting. Beside him are a black duffle bag, a pile of sticks, and a half-used twine ball.

Chills of electricity rush through my limbs, and my body readies to bolt. But I can't run away, not when I've stumbled on the very person I was looking for.

"Hey, did Audrey come through here?" I ask, forcing a casual tone when all I want to do is scream.

"Nah. Nobody comes through here." Lorenzini steps closer to me. His eyes are bloodshot, and his face is blotchy. A sloppy grin slithers across his face as he reaches out. I yelp as his giant hand moves to my throat. He grips the branch loop and laughs mirthlessly.

"Never thought of these as a fashion statement."

I swat at his hand, and he releases the necklace and runs his fingers through his hair, causing it to stick out at greasy angles. He leans against an ironwood and stares at me. "Well, whaddya want?" The smooth-talking mesmerizer from the interview is gone, and all that's left is an angry drunk.

"I need to talk to you."

"Is that so?" he scoffs, and snaps a branch off the tree. "Well, spit it out."

My mouth is dry, my tongue feels fat. "You were here, in the forest that day."

Big Jim's bleary eyes focus on me. "I'm in the forest a lot of days, sweetheart. I work on multimedia art like that piece you've helped yourself to. You're gonna have to be more specific."

Grounding myself, I take a deep breath. "Is the day Mara Quinn disappeared specific enough?"

He grumbles, bending down to remove something from the duffle bag at his feet.

I jump back and yell, "People know where I am!" The lie is

shrill and watery.

Big Jim raises an eyebrow as he waggles a cheap bottle of bourbon at me. "That's nice, little girl. Good to take precautions, but I'm just gonna have myself a drink. Why don't you sit down?" He gestures to a boulder.

I don't sit. Instead, I palm my pocketknife, holding it tight enough for its tiny screws to impress stars on my palm.

"Want some?" he asks. I shake my head. He unscrews the cap and takes a long pull from the bottle. Smacking his lips, he releases an "aaaahhh."

"Where are you keeping Isabel?"

"My boy tells me you're bright. To be honest, I don't see it."

"I know you took Mara. You killed her." I release the blade at my side, nicking the skin on my middle finger.

If he notices the knife, it doesn't worry him. Even with a weapon, he has over a hundred pounds on me. If he attacks, I'll go for his neck. The thought burns through my mind like acid. My entire body vibrates with adrenaline. Big Jim lifts the bottle to his lips but doesn't drink. He sighs and sets it down in a thick V of space nestled between trunk and branch. He rubs his palms against his temples.

"I never touched that poor girl."

"You were with her in the forest."

He nods slowly. "As I said, I'm here a lot, doing my art. It's a strange place, even for this town. Haunted, you know."

Rage boils over in me. "You saw her, and you took her!" My arm darts forward, pointing the knife.

A genuine smile lights up his face. "I like your moxie, but if you're gonna threaten someone with a blade, you should be close enough to stab 'em."

I don't have time for his nonsense. Faking confidence, I set my face into hard lines. "I'm not leaving until you tell me everything."

"You're understandably upset. Take a deep, deep breath. We can talk when you're calm."

His voice is now smooth and deep, like the tone he used before. I bite my lip until I feel pain and taste the rusty blood. "Is that how you got Mara and Isabel to go with you? You put them under?"

Big Jim stares down the trail for a spell before answering. "I got nothing to do with the Walls girl."

"And Mara?"

He releases a slow, sorrowful breath. "I *saw* her that day; I was working on these chimes. I always wanted to be an artist, but nobody gave two shits about my creations, so I did it for myself. I saw Mara in the woods a lot back then."

"You were the one spying on us."

"You weren't there, and I'm not some Peeping Tom." He fumbles for his phone and checks the time.

I'm losing him. "You say you saw Mara a lot?"

"It was strange how she wandered the forest alone, most kids don't come this far. Not Mara, though. Brave girl. I'd hide when I saw her. I didn't want to scare her." He pauses, lifting the bottle again, studying it, trying to decide whether to drink or not to drink.

"You didn't want to scare her but you—"

"I never touched her. Shut up, and I'll tell you everything. I came back to solve the murder." He takes another swig. "But then a different girl goes missing. And I realized I'm not as smart as I thought. Nothing makes sense."

"You didn't come back to make money off her murder?" I don't bother hiding the salt in my tone.

"I gotta piss." He turns and staggers a few feet away, disappearing behind a tree.

It's a struggle to make sense of what he's saying. Worse, it's hard to stay calm, and I wrap my arms around myself to stop shaking. Lorenzini is deceitful and drunk. I don't know how to piece together what's true and what's meant to make me doubt Mara. He made it sound like she was always deep in the woods, but that isn't right. We were practically conjoined, and Mara and I didn't gamble on breadcrumb trails.

Lorenzini couldn't have seen Mara—not if I wasn't with her. But Mara's doppelgänger, Audrey? She's always alone.

Jim stumbles back and regards me blearily, "You still here?"

"The girl you saw in the woods was more than once?"

"Nearly every day."

"It couldn't have been Mara. She was always with me. If you're telling the truth, that was Audrey."

"You mean that skittish lil blonde? Nah. The girl in the woods was confident. You could see it in how she moved. It was Mara."

"But I was *always* with her. You saw Audrey!" The realization stabs at me. Sweet little Audrey, quiet and eternally obedient. She would have been the ideal victim; *she* was the one the killer was after.

"I know what I saw." Jim chugs the remaining brown liquid before spiking the bottle.

I jump, waiting for the sound of shattering glass, but the bottle only bounces. Plastic.

Big Jim towers over me. "I saw *Mara* that day, and she was running. That kid was terrified. She smacked right into me. Said she'd seen something in the woods. Someone vanishing into thin air. Didn't make a lick of sense."

I step back and grab my phone. Heat radiates from Lorenzini, and he's so close that when a drop of sweat drips from his nose, it lands on my shoulder. My finger moves to dial for help, but he chuckles and makes his way back to the duffle bag.

He removes a cigarette from a crushed pack, lights it, and takes a long drag before speaking. "I grew up in Copper City, so I'm not what you'd call skeptical. Hell, I swear I saw Bloody Jasper in the theater once. Anyway, Mara was in such a state. I knew she'd run afoul of something or someone bad. So I hypnotized her. Told her she saw nothing, that it never happened. I told her to forget."

A clump of ash falls from the cigarette. "I went home and got wasted. Next day, I sobered up, and it's all over town that the girl was missing."

"Did you report it?"

"I couldn't go to the cops. I was on all sorts of junk and had no alibi."

"But you didn't tell them you saw her, and she was afraid—"

"They knew about the time she'd gone missing. I didn't have any useful information."

"Still, you should've—"

"I had to be in Vegas. I thought she ran away and that the whole thing would blow over. When they found her body . . ." Big Jim stubs out the cigarette before wiping at his eyes. "I didn't touch that girl, but I'll never forgive myself. I came back here to make it right."

"You can't make it right. She's dead." My voice is cold, but I don't care. I've wasted enough time.

Though I don't want to believe him, I do. Big Jim doesn't know where Isabel is.

Chapter 42

Shirley
8 Years Ago

Insomnia kept Shirley twisting in bed. The night hadn't gone as she'd hoped, and dread buzzed around her like mosquitoes. Wren was doing fireside readings for a women's retreat, and Shirley had offered to have Audrey spend the night. When Shirley invited her other granddaughter, she'd had the phone on speaker when Mara responded, "Nah, sounds boring. No offense, Gramma."

Audrey's face had crumpled, and the nine-year-old acted more pensive and withdrawn than usual. Despite the disappointment, Audrey fell quickly into the untroubled sleep of a child who'd spent the day drinking in fresh mountain air.

Sometime deep into the witching hour, Shirley woke under a sheen of sweat. The mattress creaked as she shifted, getting on her elbow to check on Audrey. Haloed by moonlight, the child murmured to a ragged bunny cradled in her arms.

"Audrey," Shirley whispered, wondering if she was actually awake. As children, both twins had talked in their sleep, and Robin even sleepwalked a few times.

But Audrey turned, her eyes wide and alert. She gestured for her grandma to come over. Shirley's body ached as she moved it from sleep and limped over to crouch beside Audrey.

"Did you have a bad dream, dear?"

Audrey shook her head.

"Do you need to use the toilet?"

Again, she tossed her pale hair; her small jaw was set tight.

"It's late. Lie down and go back to sleep."

Audrey craned her neck to look out to the staircase's landing. Shirley shot her a look, and the girl lay on her side. "Did you know about the lady, Grandma?" she asked, fingering the bald spot of her rabbit's left ear.

"I don't know who you mean."

"She was sitting over there, watching me." Audrey pointed to the landing.

A knot noosed over Shirley's heart. She peered out to the stairs, making a show for the child. "There's no one there. It was just a dream."

"No." Audrey's little voice was firmer than Shirley had ever heard it. "I was awake. She left when you got up."

The noose tightened. "I didn't hear the door."

"She didn't use it. She just . . ." Audrey squeezed the bunny and rubbed its ear with renewed vigor. "She stopped being there."

"Oh. I see." Shirley thought of her mother screaming in empty rooms, ripping out her hair, drinking and dosing away the demons.

"You don't believe me."

"Darling, I do." Shirley patted the girl's arm. "Do you think you can fall back to sleep? Are you scared?"

"She wasn't scary. Just sad. Her eyes, they were red." Audrey's body curled tight with her words.

Shirley's soul seized. What did Julie want with the girl? "Did she do anything?"

"Nope." Audrey yawned, her eyes fluttering.

"Have you seen others like her?"

"With red eyes? No."

"I mean, other people no one else sees."

Audrey sighed, her eyes pulling closed. "Not people. But other things, 'cause nobody else pays attention."

Shirley was about to ask another question when the girl let out a soft snore. Audrey didn't seem bothered by the vision; that was something. Shirley took little solace in the girl being untroubled; Audrey didn't understand what it meant. One day she would, when others treated her differently or when she saw something that transformed her life.

*

The following day, Audrey's keen eyes spotted a cluster of mushrooms nestled between the roots of a tree. "Look! Can we use these for something?"

Shirley crouched beside her. "Well, that depends on whether or not they're poisonous. They might be puffballs, which I prefer sautéed. Or they could be death caps. Those will kill you within twenty-four hours, no matter how you season them."

Audrey recoiled.

"Death caps are only deadly if you ingest them, so why don't you pick one, and we'll decide what's for supper."

The girl selected a mushroom as Shirley pulled a small knife from her belt. "What colors do you see?"

"It's all white."

"No green or yellow tint?"

Audrey shook her head.

"Well, that's encouraging. The only way to be certain is to open the mushroom from top to bottom." She took the mushroom and bisected it. "Lovely, see how it's like a marshmallow? These are puffballs. Let's get a handful for tonight. Now, if it had ridges or gills, it would be a death cap, and we'd leave it be."

As the girl gathered the puffballs, Shirley felt a headache coming on. Not a migraine signaling a vision, but the kind that had plagued her since her fall down the old shaft. The headaches all splintered from the same spot. She pictured a shard in her brain getting pressed deeper in whenever the entity was near.

The wind shifted, and Shirley's nostrils flared with the scent of rot. She grabbed Audrey's arm. "Do you feel that?"

"What?" The girl's eyes were wide.

"The change in the air."

"Like a bug zapper feeling?" Audrey asked, her voice filled with uncertainty.

"If that's what you sense, make it a statement. Give your words power."

"I taste sparks and feel sizzles."

"Well done. I want you to tune in whenever you feel that electricity. When the forest goes quiet and the air changes, it means something."

Audrey raised her hand in the air and wiggled her fingers lightly, as if testing the current.

Shirley looked up to the top of the trees. "Do you hear any birds?"

"No."

"See creatures of any kind?"

Audrey paused. "No. What does it mean?"

"A predator. Something unnatural."

Audrey rested a palm against a tree trunk. "What's it hunting?"

"Power, fear. I'm not entirely sure, but the fact that you're sensitive to it makes you potential prey. It enjoys frightening folks."

Audrey's face paled, but she showed no other signs of distress. Sometimes, Shirley questioned if the girl believed the more fantastic things she shared. Mara was a born skeptic. Audrey was quiet, overly polite, and impossible to read. Shirley wished the girl would push back occasionally.

"What can it do?" Audrey asked.

Shirley inhaled. This was the right moment. "My mother saw spirits from the time she was a girl. They never harmed her physically, but mentally, they took a toll on her." Shirley fiddled with a mushroom. "There's an entity in these woods. You must guard your mind."

"How? I'm scared of everything. A ghost or Bigfoot . . ."

Shirley smiled. Audrey had seen at least one ghost, but she said nothing about last night's forgotten encounter. "I don't think you have to worry about Bigfoot. As for the ghosts, most spirits are lost, trapped in a world they no longer belong to." Shirley looked up at the canopy of leaves, fighting tears. Sometimes she sensed her brother just out of reach. "If you are stern, you can tell them to go away or move beyond. If you sound frightened, I'm afraid they won't listen."

"I don't think I can sound stern."

"Practice with alive people. Have boundaries, and when someone doesn't respect them, let them know. Don't apologize or hedge. Just tell them. If you can get over your fear of disappointing the breathing, it's easy to face the dead. Ghosts are simpler."

A slight pink tinged Audrey's cheeks, and at that moment, the girl reminded Shirley of her mother, gentle and sweet. Undeserving of misfortune. Yet that made her more susceptible.

"You're sensitive to the other side. That's why we spread light and keep the balance, but if you aren't careful, you'll call spirits to you. They might try to stay. If you see or sense the uncanny, it's best if you demand they move on. Most of the time that'll work. This entity is different. When you feel that bite of electricity, surround yourself with golden light, follow your intuition, and keep out of his way. Never let him in. Never let any spirit in."

The shard in Shirley's mind throbbed. *She'd* let the thing in. Now it felt like an antenna to the entity was lodged in her brain. He fed on fear and tracked her, waiting to trick her into another one of his pits. She often tried to expel the splinter, but time and her own light held it in place.

Audrey's blue eyes were hyper-focused.

"I want you to practice boxing different emotions, not discarding them but moving them around to be reopened later. You must learn to control all that's inside you. If you are afraid and can't put away the fear, I want you to mentally wrap yourself in whatever feels safe."

"Okay." The girl shifted from foot to foot, wafting nervous energy.

The rotting scent grew thicker. In the distance, Shirley spotted Julie watching them. The ghost lifted her arm in a wave. Blocking the view of the spirit, Shirley reached for her granddaughter's hand. "Let's go home."

Audrey nodded, and the pair followed the twisting path out of the forest.

Chapter 43

Audrey

Deep in the trees, there's a green mist, and for a moment, Julie—the ghost girl—winks into view. We've been following her for a few minutes when I realize I can't see Zadie. I didn't have time to explain, and I only had seconds to slip out of the too-big boots, grab the Derringer from the shaft, and tiptoe into the woods.

I call for Zadie and wait, but all is quiet.

It's better if she isn't here for this, Mara murmurs.

When Julie doesn't reappear, we follow the current of electricity until we are at the core of the woods, where it's darkest. The memories come back as vivid and strange as a fever dream. This is where I saw the man grab Mara and pull a root that triggered the earth to swallow them.

How had I forgotten? There was a secret elevator in the middle of nowhere. If I'd remembered, I could have told the police or the FBI that there is a platform in the forest that's disguised so it looks like just another patch in the quilt of forest.

I forgot. But somehow, I held on to a slippery thread of the truth. If I follow the string to its source—the concealed memory of Mara's disappearance—it knots together with a presence, with Isa.

The old mining tunnels are everywhere, Mara says.

I know about the tunnels—everyone in Copper City does. Along with fire and active shooter drills, we had mine safety seminars in school. Teachers and parents begged us to look out for old planks of wood, a telltale sign of forgotten shafts abandoned after the copper boom. Back then, no one bothered to keep track of the hundreds of tunnels.

With the right equipment and know-how, Big Jim could use the tunnels to sneak around undetected.

"Remember the stories about Bloody Jasper being able to appear and disappear from the earth?"

Yeah. That's probably where Lorenzini got the idea.

A gentle wind rustles my nightgown, and I smell lavender laced with rot. "Grandma used to come here; she was searching for something. She used to say there was something wrong with the forest."

A wry smile tugs up our lips. *Grandma was psychic,* Mara says in a near-reverent tone. *I just never believed. I made fun of her once when I heard her whispering to a lost soul. I think she was looking for Uncle Kurt.*

"Is she a ghost too?"

No. I would've seen her. I think satisfied people move on. That's why I need to kill Lorenzini.

We walk through the forest, our eyes scanning for something dark and familiar. There's no twisted oak that sparks recollection or an X that marks the spot. There *is* a sensation, though.

"It's too quiet. No birds," I say.

It smells like decay.

The memory of Mara sinking into the earth, and the dreams of Isabel falling, match up with this place. I gaze at the ground as if daring it to shudder.

Yes, that's where he is, Mara urges, interrupting my thoughts. *We wait for him to come up for air, then kill him.*

Remembering the big, quiet man, I close my eyes. What had he whispered? Oh yes, he warned me not to return. He told me to forget, and all went black.

My body goes rigid. We're here; we *must* be.

Let me take over our body, Mara says. *We'll share one mind.*

I agree, and my limbs tingle with sleep. Gun in hand, Mara moves us closer and closer to the point of no return. I let her watch my memories of Big Jim Lorenzini, hypnotist and artist of the forest, telling me to forget. He said those velvety words, drying my tears with his calm demands, commanding my memories away. What could I do but obey? He held my hand and told me nothing had happened. His eyes were red with burst vessels, his words slurred but still powerful.

We reach the spot, and together we stamp along the forest floor; we pound our fists and listen for hollow thuds.

This is how the man finds us, on hands and knees, ten feet away from the platform.

"Audrey Hennessey?" The big man smiles with flames erupting behind his eyes. "What are you doing here?"

For a moment, we are still.

We remember *everything* now.

All goes quiet as our vision periscopes, zeroing in on his inhuman heart beating underneath a dull gray shirt. A slow, lazy breeze rustles dry leaves, and we can taste salty sweat twisted with the tang of blood in the air.

This man is not James Lorenzini—but he is the killer all the same.

We stand, aim, and fire.

The man startles, but he doesn't go down—the bullet lodged

itself in a tree. "Hey!"

We step forward, squeezing the trigger again.

He jerks sideways, but he doesn't look afraid, only angry.

I try to run, but Mara holds our body in place, binding our two souls with pure fury. She releases a banshee battle cry, and the remaining bullet spirals wildly, leaving the man unharmed.

He laughs, a cold hacking sound that shakes our hands, the useless gun falling into a bed of pine needles. "John Wilkes Booth killed Lincoln with a pistol like that." The man steps nearer. "However, Mr. Booth was aware of the model's flaw. It has an inaccurate shot, so best to use it at a very close range." His eyes narrow, and he licks his lips. His arms stretch outward, reaching.

An unholy trinity of girl, ghost, and feral madness, we lunge at him, baring our teeth and nails.

He laughs as we make contact, but a gasp of pain betrays him.

Raging, we fight, hiss, kick, bite, and spit. We want to force him to feel our pain and try to shred him into bits of bloody matter. A fist connects with our cheek, and we see every star in the galaxy as we enter a black hole and he takes us down.

Down.

Down.

Down. And we vanish like the others.

Chapter 44

Zadie

I'm trying to decide which trail to take when a realization hits, piercing my heart like a bit of jumping cactus. Mara was an accident; the killer wanted Audrey. She's in danger, and he could be hunting her right now. Blood thrumming, my fingers fumble with my cell, trying to call Audrey again. Voicemail.

In desperation, I call and then text Rhea: *Call me if you see Audrey. Please.*

She doesn't respond, and the sinking sensation in my gut tells me Audrey didn't go back to town.

The trees stretch above, pointing to a sky I can hardly see. I'm not sure what I'm looking for. I venture deeper, and the bars on my screen disappear one by one as civilization falls farther away.

My fingers twitch, and I hear music. Even as the world falls apart, my brain thinks in melodies. The notes drift, and if I follow them, I'll get lost.

I consider the legends of Copper City. Not just the ghost stories, but the more recent tales about missing hikers and the Girl Scout who disappeared on a campout sometime between s'mores and sunup. She had a name once, something pretty and vintage, like Heather or Veronica, but she's gone down in local lore as the Girl Scout.

And there's something about the clearing, the brothel. That's where I get a prickling sensation at my nape, the feeling of eyes on me. I change direction and head toward the clearing.

A branch cracks in the distance. I whirl around but see nothing. I go in deeper. Another sharp sound echoes. I move faster, following a near-forgotten path. I imagine long-silent tunes on the breeze and know that this is the way.

Following the trail, I stop every ten feet to look up, down, and around like searchers are instructed to do. If you simply walk through, you might miss something: a scrap of torn fabric, a message in the dirt, the sole of a shoe connected to a body. I find nothing.

I hike along, forcing the bad thoughts from my mind—there's still hope, there must be. Stop. Look up. Down. Around. Repeat. Stop.

I blink, sink to my haunches, and press my fingers to the dirt.

The trail has been unremarkable until this point. Sure, there have been a few spots where it's clear that search and rescue has combed through, but the windy days have brought a fine dusting of sand and pine over those places. Here, the ground is freshly trampled, mussed with divots and slicked down steps. Plants are squashed and branches and brambles bent, all evidence of a struggle. And then, I spot a funny-looking root, it looks man-made. I'm crouching to examine it when light glints off a nearby tree and I spot a bullet lodged in the trunk. I swallow. There's a faint sulfuric tang in the air. I circle the area looking for where the disturbance leads.

It goes nowhere.

It starts and stops in one place, like the width of a sumo ring. I scan every inch of the earth, trying to make sense of it. I call the names aloud, "Mara! Isabel! Audrey!"

No answer, though I knew there wouldn't be.

How can the signs of disturbance just suddenly stop? I pull out my phone, but the signal is gone. So I move forward, pausing every few feet to scan. After losing Mara only to have her come back to me, I believe in ghosts. But this is different. What spirit is powerful enough to steal people, hiding them as quickly as acorns shoved into pockets?

There isn't anything more for me to discover here. I move on.

It's quiet until my phone pings, and with one flickering bar, the text messages load. Jimbo, Rhea, Mom. All questions and no answers. I try to answer, but the bar vanishes quickly, and the signal drops.

A crow squawks warnings from a spindly branch as I enter the clearing. The brothel waits, crouching among thick trees. Someone—*something*—lives there.

I jog to the building and peer into a gap between the rotting boards that seal the window. It looks the same as last time, except—I suck in air like I'm drowning—there's a pile of notebook paper in the center of the grand room. I can't read what's written on the pages, but I can see a disemboweled notebook, a swirling wire spine and a worn red cover. *The Zaras.*

A monsoon of blood rushes behind my ears. I pull out my phone and call Rhea, she answers but all I hear is a garble of static and syllables before the signal vanishes altogether. I could run closer to town, call from there, and get a detective to come back with me. I think of the last time we ran for help, only to have the sheet vanish before we returned. They might not believe me, and what if I manage to drag a cop back and the notebook remains are gone? I need proof, a clue for them to hold, to take me seriously.

I check over my shoulder before moving around the back.

I peer through the slats; the brothel stands gutted and empty.

Still, my hands shake as they press against the back wall, my fingertips turning red, then white as I dig them against the entrance.

It moves as if taking a slight breath, and I grit my teeth to put my whole weight into it.

The stupid door is fickle.

I chew on my lower lip as I slide my fingers over the seam of the secret entrance. If it's somehow blocked, wouldn't that mean whoever was sealing the way is inside?

Once more, to be sure, I move about, peering into every crack, every gap, and every hole. There's no one.

After a deep breath, I slam my shoulder into the door. It takes three tries, but the door shudders and pops on the last smash.

Chapter 45

Audrey

Everything hurts. My temples pulsate, and blood dribbles from my split lip. I try to shift into a more comfortable position, but even the slightest movement strains my shoulder. It's like all my tendons are on fire.

It isn't fair. I was supposed to be a baker with simple ailments—sore arms from hauling bags of flour and wrists that need braces after decades of stirring and kneading—nothing more. I didn't ask for fame, fortune, or even a happily ever after. I just wanted to decorate cakes, but I'm trapped in the cold dark, waiting to die.

Mara is so small now. I feel her huddling deep inside me, quaking.

"You were wrong," I tell her. "We set out to kill an innocent man."

Lorenzini isn't a saint. Her words are raspy. She's been screaming.

"Neither are we. Why did you say it was him?"

I can see your dreams.

I shake my head. There's only black here, but she can feel my movements as I feel hers.

Big Jim was in all your nightmares. I saw him in the woods the day it happened. Mara heaves a great sigh. *Maybe it was the day before. Time blurs together. So many things pointed to that man, and when I saw him—our nightmare come to life—I was so effing certain.*

"You were wrong," I say again. I can't help it; I don't speak up enough, and though it's too late, I owe it to myself. "So wrong."

She scoffs. *Yeah—dead wrong. I never thought I'd end up here again.*

"This is the place?"

Yes. Her voice drops to a whisper. *It's a dungeon. There are spirits here. Before, I was so afraid when I'd hear them. But it was nothing compared to when he was here.*

Fear grips me in an icy fist. "What's he going to do?"

I'm so sorry. Mara is barely a whisper.

"What should we do?"

I can't go through this again. I can't. She's shaking violently inside me now.

In the dark, there's nothing to count, and I can't think of a single recipe. Anxiety hacks don't work in true danger. My teeth chatter, and cold sweat drips down my spine. A groan emits from somewhere deep in the black.

Mara's trembling hand grips my heart. *Listen, Audrey. You don't need to be brave. I want you to know that you'll only feel so much pain before your mind shuts it out. It'll be awful, but I promise that the worst parts will be over quickly. The hurt will stop, and you might see everything happening from above. That's good. It means it's ending.*

The noise grows louder.

Terror fills me as I mouth her name, "Mara . . ."

I can't stay. I'm sorry. I love you, Audrey.

She shrinks to a speck smaller than the tip of a cat whisker and sinks so deep within me that I can't feel her. "Mara!" I scream.

"Come back!"

The only response comes from the black as something coils around my ankles, snaking its way up my body. I kick out, and it constricts. It wraps around my knees, and my hands grope to find whatever cords bind me, but there's nothing.

I remember my grandmother's long-ago words and imagine a bright white light filling me, pouring out, breaking through this thing's hold on me.

Then there's a sensation of a thousand beetles scurrying across my skin, my soul.

I hold on to the light, refusing to let it go even after the presence has lifted.

I cling to my inner fire as the screams begin.

With a sizzle, like a match being doused, what little light I manifested evaporates. "Wh-who's there?" I ask, pressing my back against the jagged rock wall. It could be the evil spirit trying to trick me or, "Isabel?"

The screams give way to croaks and sobs.

I pull myself up on the rocks and try to swallow the pain of moving my body. "Isabel Walls? I'm Audrey Hennessey."

Sniffles are the only reply. Judging by the distant dripping and the echoes, this basement, cavern, or whatever, is enormous. The black cold of this place threatens to swallow me whole. I shut my eyes and picture Grandma. She'd tell me not to panic, that panic could wait until I was home safe.

It must be Isabel; something akin to hope fills my chest with warmth, and I realize I'd been thinking of the girl as one of Copper City's ghosts.

I stand on quaking legs and reach out. "Isabel?" I call, inching forward.

Piles of debris meet my shins and feet. A few steps produce

soft thuds. I try not to think of dead rats.

"Are you hurt?" I know the answer.

He's hurt her in ways I never want to think about, in ways that make you loathe this world and the monsters who dwell in it.

A tiny groan sends a fresh prickle of knowing—of fear—down my body. I'm certain Isabel is the source of the noise, just as I'm sure she's broken. I don't know if she can speak or if she'll ever want to again.

"Isabel?" I try again, but she's gone silent. I stumble around in the black, but it's like trying to find your way in a dream.

Once, Grandma left me in the heart of the forest. I'd seen a spark of light in the mulch and knelt to pick up what I figured was pyrite. It was a tooth, roots and all, with a gold filling. Realizing what it was, I startled and dropped it, and I was alone.

Grandma had mentioned abandoning me in the pines before, insisting I could easily find my way out if I only let myself listen, feel the vibrations, and follow the tug of home. I did none of those things but found my way out three hours later to where Grandma sat at the edge of the woods, crocheting and waiting. She'd bristled at my anger, telling me I'd have been out in fifteen minutes if I'd only followed my instincts.

In this place, a cavern of unknowable size, I have no choice but to try what Grandma suggested. I close my eyes, take a deep breath, and listen. I push past the familiar sounds of my blood and heart, and tune into something farther away, ragged.

Something on the left.

I move slowly, shifting by degrees whenever a shiver, a scent on the air, or a pluck on my heartstrings dictates. As I inch along, my right palm finds a cold and jagged rock wall. I slide my fingers across it, trying to divine where Isabel lies.

I trip over a stack of what feels like papers, and my knee explodes with pain as I land on the hard ground. Biting back tears, I stand and move. My foot kicks something soft.

Isabel whimpers. *She* is the soft something.

"Isa!" I drop and feel for her, and my hands find a shaking creature whose body is cold, near freezing. With great care, I pull her to me and feel her rabbit heart beating against my chest.

"Sssshhhh," I murmur, though she's quiet. It's what Momma did when I had bad dreams. "Hush, love."

Her hair smells like sour milk. I wish I could tell her that we're sharing a nightmare, that we will wake soon. But I know better. Wishes don't come true.

Isabel nuzzles into my arms, and her tears are as cold as snowflakes. She is dying.

I found the lost girl and joined her.

Chapter 46

Zadie

My first steps into the brothel are rigid as I inch forward, keeping my back to the wall and my knife ready.

My eyes move across the grimy walls and floors, searching for signs of other intruders. No one is hiding in a corner ready to pounce. Still, I creep along like a cop casing a scene in some movie, except there's no backup coming. Every creaking floorboard shoots ice through my heart, and it isn't until after I pop my head into the great room and find no one that I exhale.

Beads of sweat rise along my spine, and though it does little to soothe my frantic body, I tell myself a lie: I'm safe, and soon Audrey and Isabel will be too. Clicking the knife shut, I drop it into my front pocket next to my cell.

I take a deep, steadying breath; the room tastes as damp and coppery as the mine. I squat in front of the scatters of Zaras papers and fight the tears that prick my eyes when I see the bubbly loops and swirl-dotted i's of Mara's handwriting.

It's hard to move past the hurt that the destruction of the notebook stirs in me, but I came in here for a reason.

The outside wind filters through the brothel's many openings, whistling with ghostly enthusiasm. The noise is distracting, and the cool licks of air that tickle the back of my neck make it hard not to jump every few seconds.

To calm myself, I whisper my mantra: Mara. Isabel. Audrey. Justice for Mara. Safety for Isabel. And Audrey . . .

After I take this evidence to the cops, I'll find her. When we are safe, I'll help Audrey see Mara off to the unknown. I'll say goodbye.

The thought of losing her for a second time is like being told I can never listen to my favorite song again, but Mara doesn't belong here anymore. She can never find happiness living as a pale shadow of her former self. It's time for her to move on. Audrey still has a chance at life.

The Zaras papers will bring Mara justice, and maybe then she'll be able to rest. I nudge the sheets together, careful not to let my fingers press against the surfaces. It takes minutes to slide the sheets into a manageable pile. I pinch at the stack and stand slowly.

I'll take this straight to the police station and hand it to the head FBI person. They'll stake out the brothel. Whoever left this will come back.

Flushed with adrenaline and hope, I feel warm optimism flowing through my veins. I'll give the investigators the case on a silver platter. I won't fail Isabel like I failed Mara.

A creak splinters the silence.

Chest tightening, I turn, my eyes focusing on the shining metal of a shotgun.

Click. The trigger pulls back.

"Drop the papers. Put your hands on your head and kneel."

Richard Orlich towers over me, holding the gun steady and aiming at my heart.

The notebook pages flutter, encircling my stunned body as

I do what he says. Where did he come from? The door is still boarded shut, and the secret entrance isn't open wide enough for him to shimmy through without making a racket.

He's like Bloody Jasper, appearing out of nothing.

He emits a low growl, and I grip the top of my head and sink down, kneeling among the lost pages of my past.

When I was five, I was skipping ahead of my mother on the way to the farmers' market when I heard a loud, almost mechanical whirring. My mother yelled *"Jump back!"*

But I didn't. I gaped at the rattlesnake coiling at my toes, the pearly rows of the rattle quivering furiously. The snake's mouth spread wide, its black tongue hissing between fangs. My mother's arms wrapped around my chest and yanked me out of striking distance.

There isn't anyone to pull me away, but I can almost feel Mom's wiry arms around me as I stare into the double barrels of the gun.

Weapon trained at my head, Orlich slinks forward, his boots only producing the lightest sounds. His worn, wrinkled face cracks open with a cruel smile.

He chuckles softly. "Used to be, I had to take girls. Now, they come to me." There's a grit to his voice that I've never heard before.

My mind echoes with the memory of when I saw Mr. Orlich at Mara's candlelight vigil. *"You're heartbroken now, aren't you?"* He wasn't honest or empathetic; he'd been licking up my sorrow, savoring my pain. Now he doesn't have to hide his evil.

I've got to do something. I can't wait for the snake to rise and strike. But I can't see how this will end without me dying. "I don't know anything. I didn't get a good look at you. You can still let me go."

"You're a terrible liar, Zadie Slade." His words ooze around me. "Now, be a good girl, keep one hand on your head, and turn out your pockets with the other."

Hope is foolish when a child killer points a gun at your head. You do what they say, wishing, praying, pleading with both God and the Devil to make the bad man let you go. Holding on to that tiny shred of faith, I reach down to pinch at the insides of my pockets and watch as my cell and knife clatter to the floor.

Orlich kicks them aside, keeping the double barrels glaring at me as he squats to pick them up. He scoffs at the blade, shaking his head as if trying to hold back a laugh. The implication is clear: *You thought this little knife would protect you from me?*

His calloused finger scrolls through my unlocked phone, and he chuckles as he reads aloud a new text. "Where are you? I'm worried. Call me."

He spikes the phone to the floor. The screen shatters, but that's nothing compared to what his boot does to it, stomping until my phone is nothing but chunks of circuits. "It's a pity you didn't tell anyone where you went."

My hands are numb against my skull; my arms are so heavy, yet I can't drop them. I can't catch my breath; it's like someone is kicking my chest every time I empty my lungs.

He's going to kill me.

I don't want to die. The panic-laced thought is all I have. *I don't want to die.*

Everyone dies, but I'm only seventeen. Except so was Mara, and Isabel is thirteen. Nothing about my life or lack of years matters to this man, this monster. Still, when I can gasp out a word, it's only to beg. "Please."

He licks his lips with the tip of a pale tongue, and my stomach churns. "Keep your hands on your head and stand up."

I could run, but he'd blast me in the back before I got to the door.

I want my mom. I want to tell her I'm sorry, and I want her to make it all better. Instead, when Orlich barks at me to stand again, I obey. Gesturing with the gun, he makes me move toward the room with the decaying player piano.

This can't be how it ends. I try to fight through the dread to form a plan.

He'll have to take me out of this place. If he doesn't, Rhea knows about the brothel, she'll tell her father, and they'll save me. I grasp on to that morsel of hope.

If he makes me leave, I'll scream as soon as we're near people. I'll run when he puts the shotgun down. He can't keep it pointed at me forever.

And if he takes me to the woods to shoot me, I'll bolt and hope he misses.

Air slips into my lungs easier now. I can do this; I'll survive. I'll see my mom again. I'll—

"Look down. See that little hole in the wood? Hook your finger in it and pull up."

The floor is a cobbling of old rotting boards, and the wood's natural patterns are concealed with decades of grime. Countless splits, pocks, and tiny wormholes mar every plank. I don't understand what he's asking or why he wants me to stick my finger in one of those nasty holes. I think of Mara's severed thumb and wonder if this is some sick trick.

"What? Why do you—"

He kicks my calf hard, and I smash into the ground. "No questions. Just actions."

My leg throbs as my hands fumble over the gritty floor, my fingertips dipping into crevices but finding nothing.

Orlich toe-taps a board and snarls, "This one."

The hole doesn't stand out from the others, but when I slip my finger in, it goes knuckle-deep, the inside smooth and cool.

Still confused, I grip with my finger and yank. The panel of wood opens soundlessly. Underneath is a steel door with a keypad.

"I made improvements to the original trapdoor." He thinks I'm impressed; it's evident in his tone. "The code is 1-8-9-7. Punch it in, and when it opens, climb down, or I'll drop you."

My fingers tremble so wildly that I grasp my hands together, steepling my pointer fingers. There are no electronic beeps when I hit the buttons, only four dull thuds. There's a click of release, and I open the steel door, revealing a wrought-iron ladder descending deep into the earth. A single caged bulb offers little illumination.

"Now," he growls, prodding me in the back with the gun.

All wisps of hope vanish as I climb into the pit.

The trap door shuts, eclipsing the outside world before I reach the bottom.

The bulb flickers off, and all that's left is cold, dank dark.

Encased in blackness, I scream as fiery panic fills my body.

I scramble back up the ladder, my fear-slicked hands slapping against metal. I only stop climbing when my head collides with the hard steel of the trapdoor. I grip the rust-coated rung as my head gets that bleeding-but-not-really sensation, and my body shudders.

My only choices now are to curl up and wait, or do something. Wrapping one arm around the topmost rung, I push with all my strength against the cold steel, trying to budge it open. It's locked and too heavy. Besides, Orlich is on the other side.

My feet meet each step with defeat until I hit the hard dirt and let my body crumple onto the cool earth and weep.

A skittering echoes through the pit; it's the sounds of a rat's nails and the least of my worries. My thoughts are a blur of "if onlys" and "should haves."

Mostly, I wish it was yesterday or any other day.

When I run out of tears, I wipe my face with the hem of my shirt and hear a soft noise.

"Who's there?" I ask, scrambling to my feet.

"Zadie?"

"Audrey!" I swipe in the darkness, searching. "Where are you?"

"I-I don't know."

In this place, words bounce and echo; it's nearly impossible to tell where they're coming from. "Hold still. I'm coming to you."

"Okay."

I move to where I think she is. When I nearly trip over a pile of debris, my heart climbs into my throat—it's awful not knowing what I've stepped into.

I shuffle and wave my arms in the dark. When my hand finds a forearm, I cry out. Arms wrap around me, and soft lips whisper into my ear.

"Shh . . . It's me. You found me."

I gulp down cries and wrap my arms around Audrey. I'm relieved it *is* her and horrified that she's here. We hold each other, our panicked heartbeats slowing and syncing together.

"Isabel's here too." Audrey's lips press against my ear. "She's barely alive."

I croak into the darkness, "How long have you been here?"

"It feels like forever."

"Oh, Audrey, how did he take you?"

She gives a bitter little laugh that threatens to turn into a cry before answering. "Mara planned to kill the Great Lorenzini. It looked like we had a chance in the woods, and I wanted this to be over. I guess it was lucky we found the real killer instead. I didn't want to be a murderer."

"Wait, you were going to kill Big Jim?"

"Only when I thought he murdered Mara. It probably wouldn't have worked anyway—it didn't on Mr. Orlich—we only had three bullets."

Stunned, I blink as if I could wake up from this bizarre nightmare. This morning I thought I knew who killed my girlfriend, only to discover hours later how wrong I was.

Big Jim. Orlich. The only thing they have in common is their height.

It felt important earlier when I put together that Audrey was the intended victim. Now, it doesn't make a difference. Still, I grip Audrey's elbows, wanting to know she is looking at me even though neither of us can see. "The day Mara went missing, you were in the woods, and you saw Orlich take her."

"I couldn't remember." The pain in her voice is unmistakable.

"Jim Lorenzini was drunk in the woods that day. He said he saw Mara freaking out about something, and he hypnotized her to forget it."

"That doesn't make sense."

"You're right. It doesn't." I squeeze her elbows. "Because it was you. Audrey, *you* saw Mara getting kidnapped, and you freaked out. You two look so much alike that he thought . . ." I don't know what else to say.

Audrey falls silent, and I wish I could see her face; instead, I run my hand along her cheek, and she lets out a gasp of pain.

"What happened?"

"Orlich," she intones without emotion.

"Jesus. When we get out of here, I'll take his gun and kill him."

She doesn't answer, and I can hear a far-off dripping. "Is Mara around?" I ask, hopeful that she is and has a damn good plan.

Her voice turns thin, like she's speaking from beyond. "She's hunkered deep down. She'll come back when she senses you're here. She'll want to say goodbye."

I grit my teeth and think of Mara. That bastard killed her, and I'll make this hard. All I have left is fear and anger. At least rage will be useful. I'll *force* him to remember me by leaving marks he won't be able to hide.

I'll make him regret everything.

Chapter 47

Audrey

Time passes, and Zadie sings softly. Lyrics slip into being, filling the cold air with a sweet sadness. For a few precious moments, I lose myself in the music, but when the final chorus ends, I realize it might be the last song I ever hear.

Terror rises inside me like a blaze. My eyes search the blackness; we might as well be lost in outer space. I struggle to steady my breathing, and Zadie shifts beside me.

"Smell the flower, blow out the candle." She holds my hands in the dark as my huffs and gasps stabilize into smooth inhales and exhales.

Finally, I'm able to speak. "I never got to make croquembouche. I've never kissed anyone as me. What if we never see sunlight again?" Each *never* and *last* stings like a papercut until there are a million slices across my soul.

"When does he usually come back?" Zadie asks.

I don't blame her for changing the subject; we don't have the words to talk about our looming deaths.

Isabel doesn't speak, so I answer, "I'm not sure. Where did you climb down from anyhow?" The light bursting from above was both blinding and terrifying.

"There's a trapdoor in the brothel. How did you get here?"

"The same way he took Mara. A tunnel in the woods."

Zadie sighs. "I don't understand what this place is."

"It's always dark." Isabel's voice is small and hoarse. She has a coughing fit, and I pull her in closer. Comforting Isabel Walls might be all I accomplish in this life, but at least that's something.

It's nothing.

"Who—" The air stills. The weight of Isabel is gone. I'm not cold anymore, I'm—

You're nothing.

The voice bursts inside me, pulling me under into an ocean of unknowns. I can't feel Isabel, can't hear Zadie. I'm somewhere else, and I'm not Audrey anymore. I have no body. I can't think of a single recipe or even why I would want to. I'm vapor, I—

The void churns.

I've been waitin' for you, darlin'.

"Get out!" I scream.

A cruel laugh erupts all around. *Oh, lil darlin', you're in me now, and it's time we had a proper introduction.*

The nothing dissipates and I'm in a body, but not mine. My hands are a man's, with broken knuckles and black fingernails. They're gripping a pickaxe, and I stare in awe as green smoke spills from a crevice, gliding through the air.

See that? the gritty voice purrs. *I was chosen. This is the moment when I became a god.*

The putrid scent slithers inside, carrying an ancient power. A surge of supremacy rushes through me with the realization that now, I am more than just a down-on-his-luck miner with an empty belly. I am so much more than a mere man, I am a twister of power, an unstoppable force.

That's right, I became a god set to devour the whole damn world.

"No!" I cry. I don't want these nasty emotions twisting with mine, this hatred bubbling like tar. This is not who I am. I'm Audrey Hennessey, I—

Am Bloody Jasper Dodge.

A wave of absinthe crashes, and I see those same hands wrap around the pale neck of a woman with rosebud lips and a snub nose.

She thought she was too good for us. Didn't know her place. So, we taught her.

The woman tries to pry his fingers from her throat.

"Who's we?" I ask, desperate to distract him, praying he'll stop.

That's a loaded question, lil bit. Now pay attention.

She fights until she's like a kitten batting at string. Even after her eyes bulge and her arms fall, he throttles her until she slumps, lifeless. His laugh cuts like a serrated knife.

"Why?"

Even a god's gotta eat.

A twinkle of light rises from the slain woman's chest, drifting skyward until—

—a fist of black-green smoke wraps around the light, extinguishing it.

See, darlin', when you take a life, you can feed off it for an eternity, but you'll always hunger. There's no pleasure like feeding.

There are other women—some girls. I lose count. Then come the miners. The sickening crack of the pickaxe as it splits a skull. The squelch of brains when he pulls his weapon from a man's eye socket.

A chuckle rattles my consciousness. *I was insatiable.*

The setting shifts to the Rusty Spur Saloon. I watch the faces of a dozen people as bullets find them. The saloon door swings open—another blast—and I recognize the sheriff's star and the blood dripping from its points. The rest of the posse aim their weapons.

All goes black. A gripping sensation. And despite thirteen bullet wounds gushing blood, a flat refusal to leave.

I was still a young god then.

The visions take on a hazy, colorblind quality. I watch hikers get disoriented and fall into abandoned mine shafts. I feel their minds as he slithers through them. The clothes change, as does the manner of death as time progresses. The victims are no longer suffering mishaps. They are being hunted. Bloody Jasper started by possessing cougars. But he pushed until he could take a human. He could influence some, forcing them to do terrible things. Soon, he could stretch the time between possessions; when he was well-fed, he was powerful enough not to need a body to do his bidding.

See how I evolved, lil bit? I can satisfy myself on fear, build muscle on others' trauma, but I sought the tastiest morsels.

A flash of green, and I'm inside Kurt's bus as it flips. Back-packs and bodies swirl like the innards of a kaleidoscope. Each revolution brings screams and snaps of bones. Red droplets splat like raindrops. The cries cease, and there are only thuds.

My favorites are the ones with bright souls, he drawls with a sigh.

Another strobe of brilliant light, and I am the ooze that lines the walls of the mine. I watch as a group of giggling teenagers break off from a party in the main cavern to explore, carrying cheap wine and smoking Marlboro Reds. They break off into pairs, making out in different tunnels. The ooze slips silently along the rocks, following one couple. I recognize the girl with a start. Julie Hartshorne. The young man with her, tall and broad, is Richard Orlich. I know him by the ice-blue eyes, cold even in youth.

I want to look away, but I am the slime, the thoughts that

whisper suggestively in Richard's head as he trails his fingertip through the ooze. When Julie refuses Richard, Bloody Jasper stokes the coals of his hatred, and assures Richard that he is righteous in his anger.

My hands are Richard's. I want the vision to stop, but I'm living it. Strangling Julie as she begs hoarsely. Then she fights, acrylic fingernails breaking off against hairy forearms. Fortified by rage and the spirit, Richard throws her against the rocks before pulling a corkscrew from his back pocket and thrusting it into her throat, again and again. She fights until she doesn't.

A surge of power rushes through Richard. He has taken something that can never be returned.

I taught him what it's like to be a god. When he panicked, I lapped up his fear. I'd been bored—it was fun taking on a protégé. Richard was eternally grateful when I showed him where to hide the body. The silly boy didn't even think to pretend to look for her, to yell the girl's name, till I told him to. Everything Richard Orlich knows comes from my lessons. 'Fraid, there ain't much else to do with him.

I wanna try a new flavor. You come from an exquisite line, darlin'. The light drove your great-grandmother crazy, and that ole bitch Shirley never took a shine to me. But you, you're special. I reckon after years of being a doormat, you'll revel in playin' God.

I feel what he feels, the thrill of owning a heartbeat, stopping it. Viscous glee slides through my nonexistent veins.

No! I hate this.

There are others. So many others. I can't see or feel anything other than what this entity—Jasper Dodge— shows me.

I got a little something for you, darlin'. Something you've always craved.

I watch him hurt her.

I watch Mara die.

Chapter 48

Zadie

Isabel's words wind around in my head. *It's always dark.* We're deep underground where night and day don't matter. I wish I had my phone.

It hits me. Orlich didn't have me empty my back pockets. He assumed that I was wearing useless girl jeans whose back pockets can't hold a credit card. I check mine now, find my Zippo—bless you, boy pants—and ignite it.

Aglow by the flame, Audrey blinks. "Huh. Couldn't have thought of that earlier?" The lower tone and sarcasm are unmistakable.

"Hey, Mara." I wonder if she's still mad about Rhea. Funny, I choose a living girl over Mara, and I might be dead anyway. "It's good to see you."

"I came back to see if Audrey was still alive." Mara sounds younger now. "I wasn't going to take over, but she isn't here."

"What?"

"I dunno, she's like catatonic. I can't find her inside."

I swallow. "Let's focus on getting out. We'll deal with that later." I can understand why she'd shut down, but it complicates things. Still, one problem at a time. I need to check on Isabel and

296

find an escape. I take a deep breath and turn toward her, crouching beside her body. Isabel's pupils are dilated into black holes, and she squeezes her eyes shut as I run the flame over her.

It hurts to look at her; her clothes are dirty and torn, her lips are cracked with dehydration, and her eyes are ringed with heavy circles. She's been tortured in unspeakable ways. I lightly stroke her forehead and stand to explore the pit.

"It won't do you any good." Mara's tone is flat. "The first stage is denial. I should know. I've been there—here. You should jump ahead and accept that you're already as good as dead."

Isabel whimpers, curling into a tight ball.

"Don't say another word unless you plan on helping."

"Sorry, Z." And she does sound remorseful. I know the harsh bravado is a coping mechanism; I also know that she's probably right.

I look around. There is a mildewed pail of water that I suppose Isabel has been drinking from. I don't see a flashing exit sign or any conveniently placed weapons. So, I keep going.

Under the pale halo of the Zippo, I find a jar of BBs, confirmation that Orlich shot out Rhea's taillight. Then there are stacks of newspaper clippings. The freshest are about Isabel; beneath them are Mara's articles. Deeper in, there are ones about Victoria Azar, the Girl Scout who was supposedly eaten by a mountain lion years ago. The stack tumbles over. The paper at the bottom is from the 1980s. My mouth goes dry as I read the article's title. *Local Girl Julie Hartshorne Presumed Dead Three Months After Disappearance.* I recognize the name from what Orlich said at the police station.

There are more stacks and piles; there are more girls.

I move away from one hill of detritus to another. There are entire mountain ranges of clutter here: old bottles, rusted antiques, and even a blanket we left at the brothel. Was Orlich always lurking just out of sight?

Is that where he picked out Audrey? And later confused Mara for her? I shake the filth from the blanket and take it over to Isabel, who cries out when I touch her before shuddering back to sleep as I tuck the felted material around her body. Her head rests in Mara's/Audrey's lap.

We don't have long to get Isabel out; she needs medical attention. She's shivering nonstop and hasn't strung more than a few words together at a time. Audrey or Mara stares into the blackness; her pupils don't register my light. They've given up.

I force myself to continue. I find more junk, including shards of glass, old books, and gardening supplies—nothing that will make a good weapon.

Kneeling, I examine a hefty burlap sack containing fertilizer. The label image is a cartoon miner swinging a pickaxe under a speech bubble proclaiming *Bodies make the best fertilizer, but Simmons makes the second best!* Did Orlich save the bag because it had a lame serial killer reference? At Graveside Tours, he was known for his Bloody Jasper fetish.

I need to find the tunnel, but the dark stretches on and on.

Giving up on the junk, I keep exploring. The pit narrows and extends into a bottleneck about fifty feet away from the girls. I hold the flame far in front of me, my thumb growing raw from constantly having to reignite the Zippo.

The fourth time, I shake the lighter before the flame bursts forth. In the glow, I spot the exit, and my heart threatens to erupt. Tears spring to my eyes.

A large wooden door stands between us and freedom. I twist the brass knob—locked. The door must lock from the outside, there's nothing to pick. I slide the Zippo into my back pocket and slam my body against the solid oak.

Nothing. I haven't budged a splinter. Fear gives way to fury and my fist goes flying. The punch does nothing to the door and blood drips from my throbbing fist.

A hand brushes against my hair, and I scream, slapping into the dark. "It's only me. Save your strength and take it all out on Orlich."

In this space, I can't tell if the flat voice belongs to Mara or Audrey.

"If we could get through there . . ."

"We'd have to find our way through the maze. I think these were Bloody Jasper's tunnels. It would make sense how he could kill so many people and disappear."

"It's so twisted. Orlich's even made improvements," I mutter, holding my busted left hand to my mouth before reaching for the lighter; I want to see my friend.

Her skin shines like a lunar surface in the flame; her eyes are slits in the center of purple bruises. I look away. I don't want to know what he's done to her; I don't want to imagine what he will do to me.

"Look, Zadie."

I turn back to her, and the firelight glimmers on the surface of a shard of glass she holds up. "A weapon, good thinking."

"No. It's more of a preventative measure; this is how we keep Orlich from killing us. We do it ourselves."

I don't know what to say; suicide can't be our best option. "Mara?" I ask, fighting the quiver in my voice.

"I'm not really either anymore. I know whoever I am, I don't want to be anywhere near Orlich. Before you came here, he told me he'd find you and said he would kill you slowly and make me watch . . ." she says.

"Let's stick him with the glass. We could surprise him."

She shrugs and examines a decaying buckskin jacket she pulls off an old saddle. An orange tin clatters to the ground.

I pick it up and drop the container immediately after reading the words *Hodgdon's Rifle Powder*. "Hold this." I thrust the Zippo at her and grope for the tin.

Careful not to get it too close to the open flame, I examine the small metal container. It's rusted and dented, but it's nearly full.

Years ago, a local kid found Civil War–era gunpowder, and the accidental explosion he caused was news for months. Blowing out a slow, steady breath, my body stills, and my mind clears as if I've suddenly gone from cowering in a hurricane to standing in the eye of the storm.

We have gunpowder, paper, and a bag of fertilizer. I wonder how much fuel the lighter has. "Shut off the light."

"Why?"

"I don't want it to run out. I have a plan. We blow up the door."

"You're insane. That'll kill us all." The voice is 100 percent Mara now, and it's clear she doesn't care for the big bang option.

"Maybe so, but it's better than Orlich killing us."

"A little bloodletting will solve the same issue and hurt a helluva lot less."

"If the explosion works and breaks apart the door, we can run out through the tunnel. We'll get burned, but we'd have a chance at living."

"Maybe we should brainstorm less agonizing ways to die? Like slowly getting devoured by ants?"

From the corner, Isabel hacks and coughs before moaning.

I drop my voice. "I agree. But Isabel doesn't have much time. Even if this doesn't work, we might destroy his tunnels, or at least make it harder for him to do this to anyone else."

"Zadie . . ."

"He's going to come back when he's done establishing an alibi or whatever. Then he'll kill us."

Our hands clasp together, and we fall into silence.

At last, Mara speaks. "I'm leaving. I can't die again, and I want to give Audrey her life back. It's awful timing, but giving her a few minutes of peace is the least I can do. When she comes to, tell her I'm sorry. It wasn't fair to make her live half a life. And you, I love you, Zadie, and I want you to be happy. If you make it—and if anyone is bullheaded enough, it's you—I want you to love a living girl. Even if it is that skank Rhea."

"Mara—" I begin, but her fingers press against my lips, and she kisses me. A soft, lingering goodbye before her body slumps against mine.

"Mara?"

There's no reply. I light the Zippo once more to find only Audrey's blank face.

Chapter 49

Shirley
6 Months Ago

In the heart of the woods, Shirley paused to look at the sun's reflection sparkling between her feet. It was the anniversary of the bus tragedy. Each year the families of the victims met in the church, and though no one showed Shirley any animosity, she was never invited.

So, she came to the wilds to mourn Kurt. She'd never stopped looking for her brother, and a handful of times, she'd felt he was near. She walked the trails and spoke softly to him, assuring Kurt that she knew the truth.

A groan caught her attention. Julie stood yards away, her bloody mouth agape.

"What is it?" Shirley asked. But a force like a swinging pendulum slammed her to her knees. The shard in her mind plunged deeper, splintering her skull.

She grimaced and tried to pull herself up, but the invisible force walloped her again. Her fingers fought to grasp the pull-tab zipper of her fanny pack. She needed to call for help.

A dark chuckling wormed into her head, digging holes in the lobes of her brain.

"You have no power here." Her words were a series of gasps

and winces.

Power? Says an old hag who plays cards and sells spices.

She tried to summon the light, but the world grayed. "Get. Out."

No use. I killed you long ago. It just took a bit.

With a hacking laugh, the voice tore from her.

She did not fight as the shard, imbued with so much of her light, pulled free. A blood vessel deep in the prefrontal cortex of her brain burst.

Shirley's body no longer followed her commands. At last, she understood the blackberry vision. This was how she was to die. Black tendrils encircled Julie, who waited in the trees with her hands clasped over her heart. Shirley wouldn't be joining her.

Pain and fear evaporated with a gentle breeze. With every breath ticking away like seconds on a clock, Shirley saw the faces of all those she loved. A smile crossed her face, and she whispered, "Keep the light."

The world went black and then winked into brilliant gold.

Chapter 50

Audrey

Bloody Jasper's tour ends with my grandmother. We watch her from above. He licks his invisible lips as she meanders down the path. His trigger finger quivers as she passes underneath. He dives, pulling me with him. Like a bullet, we pass through gray tufts of hair and then skull. We bite into a swell of blood inside Grandma's brain, bursting the artery like an overripe berry in the brambles.

Grandma crashes to her knees. Her hands fly to her head, pressing, reaching as if she could pluck out the pain and eradicate Jasper Dodge. The adrenaline of victory surges through the cloud of energy, pulsating like a heartbeat.

You shoulda let me in.

Near corporeal now, Jasper crouches in front of Grandma and holds her face in his hands. This is for me. He wants to make me watch as her lips twist in agony and a trickle of blood spit dribbles from the corner of her mouth.

He forces me to meet her pained eyes, and Grandma's expression changes to defiance. Her teeth grit even as anguish keeps her on the ground. For a second, I think she can see me, but I'm not really there.

That's when she mouths her final words and winks.

A sharp, hot pain pierces my palm, and I know what I must do. I breathe. I take in all the air, fear, and energy that's powering Jasper. In the vision, Grandma collapses, her eyes close as her head falls into a nod. Her lips twitch in a near-smile as I breathe in her last breath before bursting back into my body.

It's dark and cold.

"Oh . . . no. We're still here. I thought maybe . . ." Maybe this had all been some terrible dream, but I'm in the black without hope for starlight to guide me.

"Mara says goodbye. And that she's sorry." Zadie sounds haggard.

"Oh" is all I can manage. That two-letter word contains a universe of grief.

Zadie lights a roll of newspaper as a torch. In the flame light, she looks like a sugar skull. "We have to work quickly. We're gonna blow the door before he comes back. Get Isabel ready?"

I nod, cradling my grandma's faith in good overcoming evil. Next to me, illuminated in light, is Isabel. She looks like a broken doll. "Isabel?" I ask, nudging her shoulder. Her eyes flutter. She is awake, but barely. "We're leaving. We need to get as far back as we can." I wrap a buckskin jacket around her shoulders, hoping it'll shield her.

"I want my mom."

I kiss her forehead and whisper, "Me too."

Zadie and I line the door with gunpowder and fertilizer, and we shove crumples of newspaper under the inch-wide gap. This plan is the only one we have, and I'm grateful for it. Still, the blast could kill us. Or, if it doesn't, and the door remains standing, fire will fill the pit. As it consumes decades of old garbage, we'll choke on smoke and get eaten by flames. Horrible, but better than a fate dealt by monsters. When we're done, my heart pounds as Zadie and I crouch beside Isabel and help her stand.

Her legs wobble so much that we carry her away from the door. "Isa," I start carefully. "If you can, run with us to get out. Use all your strength. Once we're through the flames, we'll have more time, and we'll be able to carry you. But we have to go through the fire first. Do you think you can do that?"

She nods uncertainly. The ember glow of the torch reveals how battered her body is.

"If you can't, we'll carry you. We'll go home together." These are promises I can only hope to keep.

"Are you ready?" Zadie calls from the starting line of her gun-powder trail.

The stacks of newspapers and junk remind me of Paul Hartshorne's house and Grandma's notebooks. "Wait. We should gather some evidence."

"Won't we be evidence enough?" Zadie asks.

"In case . . ." If we die, someone might find our bodies and discover a clue that puts away Orlich and hinders Bloody Jasper. It's a grim thought, so I mimic Grandma's defiant face.

I fold a clipping about Julie and a printout from the *Bring Isabel Home* website and tuck them in Isabel's pocket. There could be fingerprints. Maybe Paul Hartshorne will figure out how it's all connected.

Zadie shakes as she speaks. "I'll light it here and come to you. Then we'll throw on the blanket and run through the blasted door. Ready?"

Holding the blanket, I crouch beside Isabel, steading my arm to pull her back up. "Ready."

Zadie giggles nervously. "This is ridiculously dangerous. I mean, so is dying."

"At least we're not alone."

A bang echoes through the underground room. My breath and heart catch in my throat. I pull Isabel into me and whisper, "You're not alone."

Zadie stomps out the torch just before the heavy door opens. Paper kindling scrapes and crunches along the earthen floor as a pair of boots stomps in. Isabel whimpers into my ribs.

A pale yellow ray spears across the space, slowly sweeping, bumping over piles of junk as a looming figure appears. He wears rust-splattered overalls. A pickaxe stained with a century's worth of blood dangles from the carpenter's loop. Zadie said he had a gun, and I wish he hadn't replaced it with the cruel arched blade. Bullets are at least quick. The beam from the old-fashioned lantern hovers on me as the scent of burning oil mixes with the dank musk of the underground.

"Come here." Mr. Orlich's voice is hard and cold.

Trembling, I ease Isabel down. My legs shake.

"You were the one I wanted. Mara had moxie and was brave. She died all the same, but I craved you, my shy little flower. Come to me. It'll be worse if you don't."

A hoarse sob sounds from the ground, and in the dim light, Isabel cowers.

Caught in the lantern's path, I take a breath and find my voice. "You don't have to do this."

"I said, come here," he growls.

I raise my palms, trying to feel the light inside me, but there's nothing. "My uncle was the driver of the bus that killed your brother, Timothy."

"Here. Now," he growls, one hand gripping the hilt of the pickaxe.

Three soft clicks sound behind me. The Zippo isn't lighting.

I step forward, closer to this demon. "Kurt was under the

influence of an entity—Bloody Jasper. My uncle didn't want to kill those people, just like, deep down, you don't want to kill us, Mr. Orlich."

A smile stretches across Orlich's face. "Your uncle wasn't worthy. He was a callow man terrified of shadows and bumps in the night. Jasper Dodge ended him and chose me as his successor, and I run this town like a king. I've done more for Copper City than anyone. I am the protector of this land, and everyone is grateful to me, except for your grandmother and some others who don't know their place. I was gonna fix you."

He reaches for me and I dodge. Orlich snarls.

"Bloody Jasper's been feeding off you, and he's bored. He told me so." My words are desperate. Crouched behind me, Zadie's Zippo produces only dull ticks barely audible above Isabel's sobs.

"Jasper's mine. I use him." Orlich grabs at me again, and I dart the other way as he slides the pickaxe from its loop and twirls it.

"He belongs to an ancient evil. I saw. If you let us go, we can—"

"We're done playing."

Zadie is in my peripheral. Her eyes are on Orlich's feet—they're planted in gunpowder. A flicker sparks behind Zadie's back. I hold my breath.

"Hey, Orlich!" Zadie calls, her voice quavering.

"Quiet. It's not your turn yet."

"Burn in hell!" she screams, and the lighter soars, cutting through the black like a comet. I picture a golden light guiding our little fireball of hope to the gunpowder. The metal clatters against the stone, and for a fraction of a heartbeat, I fear we've failed.

Then there's a *pop,* and the Zippo morphs into a bolide.

Orlich's eyes turn to glowing orbs in the darkness as his feet ignite and fire dances up his legs. He hurls the lantern while gripping his pickaxe, the handle aflame. The bright licks of fire reveal that the door is ajar.

Clutching his pickaxe, Orlich falls onto the cave floor, kneeling into the fire, trying to put out the flames. He doesn't scream in agony or writhe in pain. Instead, he growls as he slaps his bare hands against the fire.

I pull Isabel up, but she weighs heavily on me, and I have to drag her. We slam into Zadie. She takes Isabel's other side, and with her help and my heart pumping pure adrenaline, we hurtle forward, skirting the edges of the growing flames. Isabel's long fingernails dig into my neck as Orlich howls the inhuman shriek of a monster.

He lunges as we run past him and throws his pickaxe, nearly hitting me as we dash around him. Something jerks us back, tugging at us like a fishhook. Isa cries, tumbling from me, but I reel her in as my body crashes against the rocks, cushioning the blow for her.

But Zadie—

—fingers claw at her legs, trying to drag her into the fire.

"Zadie!"

"Run!" she screams.

Orlich's hands are on her, one over the other, pulling her body closer to the flames. Her fingers rake the ground. I roll Isabel off me and try to grab onto Zadie, but my hands are slick with sweat, and I can't get a grip on her.

Zadie kicks, her heel connecting with Orlich's nose. I grab her arms and pull. He doesn't let go. Zadie slams both feet into his face. He howls as I yank her from the pit, and together we hoist Isabel.

The flames leap higher, and I scramble to grab the axe. It's hot and heavy, but I can't leave it, I don't trust it out of my sight.

"Audrey—come on!" Zadie calls, and we run through the open door into the dark veins of a tunnel.

The light fades behind us as we move forward into nothing. When we reach the first fork, my lungs collapse, and I fight to breathe.

Gasping for air, we set Isabel down and fall to our knees. Each breath feels like a kick in the lungs, but we're alive. I feel a pang for Mara. There's no scent of bittersweet chocolate and no twitches from within.

I linger on my senses; underneath the acrid smell of the fire, there's a familiar musk. "We're in the mine."

"Shit," Zadie wheezes.

"We-we can find our way out." My eyes burn with smoke and tears. I think of Grandma and feel for that "tug of home" but find nothing.

A gravelly laugh travels through the tunnel.

"No!" Zadie's fingers dig into my arm, her other hand pointing at Mr. Orlich. His body jerks violently with each step, with one foot dragging behind. Spikes of flame burn along his limbs and across his neck, illuminating the bloody long-toothed grin that doesn't leave his face.

There's a soft thud at my side as Isabel faints.

"Back off, Orlich!" Zadie screams. She doesn't know. Doesn't realize that this isn't Mr. Orlich, not really. Not anymore.

I grip the pickaxe, wondering if I have the strength to swing it.

The figure lurches closer, whistling now. It's a tune I recognize, one I've heard in this mine before. The repetitive notes puncture my mind, and I feel like I'm fading away, but I recall Grandma and force the golden light through my body.

What once was Richard Orlich stands feet from me, his gory mouth glowing with embers.

"Audrey—" Zadie screams before going slack.

The cracking of bones echoes in the cave as her body contorts, and her head jerks around, cocking toward me. A rictus grin cuts across her face.

"Zadie?" It isn't her. Not right now. I know it—but I don't want to believe it.

The whites of her eyes have gone toxic green.

"Please, Zadie." Terror tells me to run, but despair holds me in place.

"Well, hello there, lil bit." The voice is deep and gritty.

Zadie lunges, knocking me to the rocky earth. Her hands shoot out and grip my neck. I pull at her arms, scratch at her hands, but my vision tinges with red, and I feel my soul slipping from my body.

My arms fall, and I focus everything I have left on my fingertips finding the wooden handle of the pickaxe.

"Please," I croak.

Her nails pierce my throat as I smash the wooden handle against Zadie's head. She doesn't scream. Doesn't make a sound as her hands release, as she topples over.

Orlich's smoldering corpse casts a glow over Zadie's face. I scramble back, ready for her to wake up fighting or for Jasper to reanimate the smoking body before me. Every inch of me aches and my head throbs with a skull-cracking headache I should—

My arms jerk forward and my hand slides over Zadie's throat. Soft and warm.

Electricity twitches my fingers. They grip.

Zadie groans. I can't move my hand from her neck.

"Atta girl. Squeeze. Concentrate. Pinpoint the exact moment

she ceases to be."

"NO!" My cry echoes off the rocks.

"She'll be lost and gone forever. Dreadful sorrow, Zadie-doll." Bloody Jasper Dodge cackles, sending sparks from the corpse's mouth. He intends for me to host a kill for him.

"I won't!" In the smoke-filled cavern, there is no light to call. My arm jerks violently, and now both hands are on Zadie. I cry for my fingers to release and press my legs against the wall trying to push myself away, but soon it feels as if they've been crushed. My fingers dig-dig-dig into her.

Audrey! Let go—you have more power than him! Mara's voice feels far away.

The corpse staggers forward.

If I let go, it'll end me.

Let me help, Mara whispers. Picturing the pickaxe just out of reach, I wait for her to understand; I feel her nod.

"She's dead." At last, I can let go. I push my friend away. Her stillness is unsettling.

Orlich's corpse offers a slow clap. Embers sprinkle from between charred fingers. "Girl, I was afraid you'd be like your grandmother—" Jasper slaps at a flame on his elbow as if it were a mosquito. "Powerful mind but no fun at all."

"What do you want from me?" I ask hoarsely, my mouth full of ash.

The corpse gestures to its roasting self. "Occasionally, I require the use of a body, an occasional loan between feedings. All you gotta do is let me in." Cinders fall as he moves closer.

Inside, Mara is coiled, ready to spring; I show her the pickaxe again. A cruel smile spreads across our face.

"Never," I spit as Mara weaves through me, snatching the handle in a blinding fury of speed and force. Together, we swing the axe. It plunges into Orlich's skull, and we jerk it, pulling the body along, slamming it into the rocks.

I shiver as Mara peels away. Still, I swing over and over again until there's nothing left but pulp.

You can stop. He isn't going to get up.

I drop the axe and stumble toward Zadie. I fall to my knees and touch her neck. I hold my breath, my hands shaking too hard to find what I'm looking for. Mara washes over me, stilling my fingers, and together we find that faint, stubborn, little pulse.

My tears fall hot and fast. I move to check on Isabel. She's even colder now, her breath ragged. "How will I get them both out before he-he—" But a sob cuts me off.

It's okay. We'll—

The temperature drops, and the air crackles.

Bloody Jasper Dodge stands before me; his form is composed not of flesh but of green mist. Hoping that he still thinks Zadie is dead, I yank Isabel up and drag her along as I take off. There is only dark, and when I can't run anymore, I tuck us into a nook in the rocks.

The air sizzles with an electric current. Weak and full of grief, I scramble for a plan. Nothing comes. So I push Isabel out of reach.

You filthy, lyin' bitch. You're gonna die slow.

I stand and plant my bloody bare feet. I think of Grandma. Even in death, she believed I could defeat this entity.

Invisible talons snatch at my head, their sharp points sinking into my skull, and lightning pain radiates throughout my body.

Beg me.

There's a hint of bitter chocolate in the air. Mara wraps herself around me like a blanket. The talons dig deeper.

"Help!" I call out, and Jasper chuckles.

Julie Hartshorne materializes beside me; her presence joins

Mara in shielding me, and I feel the smallest relief until a new wave of hurt crashes over my body.

This is my rodeo. Tell your ghoul to git.

"Never." But he is getting stronger. I need more help. There are spirits Bloody Jasper damned to an eternity in Copper City and there are others who stayed, hungry for justice. Hoping I'm right about the familiar flannel, I imagine the blurry-faced specter from the police station and cry out "Uncle Kurt?"

A twinkle of gold illuminates the battered spirit, and when he nods, I see a flicker of a face I recognize from pictures. Uncle Kurt has Grandma's eyes.

An animalist growl echoes through the cave as a burst of raw energy hits my chest, leaving me gasping for breath as the air grows colder.

I picture every face I saw tumbling inside the bus and, one by one, the victims come, shimmering as they surround me, yearning for justice. The dark still weighs on my body, but the pressures are shifting.

Jasper flickers before me, his body dimming as his grimy hands solidify, wrapping around my neck. I don't flinch. I look him in the eye, and I call to the miners. They crawl out of the shadows with their rock hammers and chisels, their eyes trained on Jasper. He is so full of rage he doesn't see that we are surrounded. His hands squeeze, and I'm floating.

I no longer feel the fingers gripping my neck. I feel nothing but will myself not to let go, to stay in this horrible place, just for a little bit longer.

Hold on if you like, girl, he roars. *I don't mind delayed satisfaction.*

I need more help but can't move my lips. Still, I quiet my mind and summon the lost women of Copper City. The brothel workers appear with hands on their hips, ready for whatever may come.

The spirits surrounding me send specks of light, and the pain returns, but that is a good thing. I'm still alive. Luminescent flecks gather in my hands. My palms glow, but Jasper is blinded by hate. He lifts me higher in the air, and my toes dangle far from the ground.

A glimmering gateway splits the black behind Jasper. Grandma steps through. Pride shines from her eyes as she mouths "now."

I lift my arms, press my hands into his chest and let light explode from them.

Bloody Jasper Dodge's mouth gapes open as golden beams shoot between the gaps in his teeth, the rays burning through his chest. I raise my hand higher, stretching my fingers, feeling the intersection of my life and love lines splitting as the brilliant shard from Grandma soars from my palm and bullets through Jasper's skull.

I fall to the ground as he explodes into a cloud of copper dust. The spirits dive in, devouring the flecks, dividing his essence among themselves. They gobble him up and vanish.

Julie smiles at me. Her eyes are green and bright. Uncle Kurt is no longer broken. He whispers something to Grandma before they both wrap me in an embrace. My grandmother's lips feel like a rose petal brushing my forehead just before she and her brother slip through the veil.

Mara peels from me like a sunburn and is the last to go. She doesn't vanish like the others. Instead, she waves at me, granting me a sheepish smile as her shimmering form walks toward where we left Zadie.

I collapse on the ground, cradle Isabel, and let the dark engulf us.

Chapter 51

Zadie

I'm all by myself. Maybe they got out. I hope they did so it'll be worth dying alone. An eruption sounds from down the tunnel, and the ground shakes, and bits of rocks rain down. That was a shit-ton of fertilizer.

The mine rumbles. The smoke might not kill me—the caverns could collapse instead. My head pounds, and everything aches. When I asked Mara what it's like to be a ghost, she said, *"Nothing hurts. Well, nothing physical, anyway."*

The hellish heat and agony I feel must mean I'm still alive. My body wants to give up, but I have to know what's happened to the others. "Audrey? Mara?" I call.

There's no answer.

I crawl forward, wincing at each movement. Patting the ground, I don't find any rails or anything familiar. The earth rumbles below, and I fall.

Hot smoke crashes over me in a wave of cinders, and I choke on a mixture of ash and blood.

Another, more violent, explosion shakes the earth.

A rock smacks my shoulder, and while I register the impact, I don't feel it.

The pain is gone, and it feels like I'm floating.

I close my eyes and pretend that I'm being rocked to sleep, that I'm not alone, that I'm not imagining the sensation that Mara is nearby. I'm drifting into oblivion when I hear a clatter, softer than the falling rocks. But I can't see anything. All is dark as the world crumbles around me.

My eyes fall shut again. The clatter—a rolling noise—continues, and I stretch out my unbroken hand. Something plastic and cylindrical bumps against my fingers.

Feeling the plastic, I find a button and press it. A ray of light cuts through the blackness.

I have a flashlight.

I point it toward where I heard the noise, but there's nothing there.

"Audrey?" I call.

"Zadie?" Her voice is weak but not too far. Gripping the flashlight, I crawl, pain shooting through me as feeling returns to my limbs. The rumbles and crashes are farther away now; still, the tunnel is thick with smoke.

We continue to call for one another until my light finds them. I collapse next to Audrey and touch Isabel. Her skin is cold. I let the light fall on the girl's face. Holding my fingertips over her mouth, I sense a tiny puff of breath.

We lie on the ground as hot smoke billows over us.

My body wants to stay down forever, but I'm not ready to give up. Not yet. "If we find the tracks, we can follow them out." I shine the light along the ground. Nothing. I look for tunnels, but we're at a dead end. The way we came from is filled with smoke.

Audrey squeezes my hand.

I wish I could say goodbye to Mom, to Rhea, hell, even to Copper City, a place I thought I'd never miss. My head feels heavy, and my thoughts are fuzzy except for one: I can at least say goodbye to Audrey. A person who was there for me when I needed someone the most. Rhea's accusation still niggles at me because she's right.

"Audrey, I'm lucky to have you as a friend, even for a short time." I swallow, searching for the right words, but there aren't any. "When I was alone with Mara, I only thought of my own happiness. I'm sorry."

There's a deep intake of breath beside me before Audrey speaks. "Thank you for believing me. I'm glad you're my friend."

The earth shakes, and rocks fall until the tunnel is blocked.

"No." It's all I can think to say. The flashlight flickers in my hand, the battery dying.

Audrey jerks up. "I smell chocolate—Mara's nearby. Shine the light again. Look everywhere."

I do it, not because I think it will help, but because she asked. The light catches a glistening metal knob just yards away. "Audrey! Look, there's a door."

Crouching, I get to the knob; it is cold and solid in my hand. I turn it and push.

The egg-shaped entry creeps open, and under the flashlight's shine, I gasp in recognition. We're in the Devil's Domain, where Bloody Jasper dumped the miners' bodies so many years ago. The outside of the door is all rock. I've walked by it dozens of times and never suspected anything; I knock on it to make sure it's real.

I know the way out.

Although the smoke thins out in the Devil's Domain, the journey to the mouth of the mine is a long one.

Audrey and I wrap Isabel's arms around our shoulders and carry her along the tracks.

She hasn't regained consciousness, and every few minutes,

when one of us stumbles or collapses, we check for a pulse.

Exhausted, we force ourselves up. We don't have the energy to speak; we simply move forward.

At last, we come to the entrance, the end, and the sight of orange sunlight lasering in from the gaps around the double doors is the most beautiful thing I've ever seen.

Together, we stumble to the doors and push. The metal shudders but doesn't give. We try again, and I hear the telltale clink of metal against metal.

The doors are chained shut, and I can picture the padlock and feel its key in my hands on so many bonus-tours; I never imagined myself trapped on this side.

"Don't worry. I can squeeze through, remember?" Audrey says woozily, letting go of Isabel, and I feel the girl's full weight.

Blinking, I watch her press against the door, trying to shimmy through. But she can't get an arm or even her fingers out.

"They shortened the chain," she gasps.

My legs crumple underneath me.

We were so close. The tears come as hard and as fast as a monsoon. My good hand goes to Isa's throat, searching for her fading pulse. I feel her chest and then hold my fingers over her mouth. "She's . . . not breathing."

"HELP!" Audrey starts kicking the door, trying to snap the chain.

"She's . . ." I don't want her to be, so I don't say the words. Instead, I say, "I'm going to keep trying."

"Me too." She keeps kicking.

I lay Isabel on the path, clear ash from her mouth and nostrils, and begin chest compressions with my good hand. Audrey kicks and pleads and pounds against the door until—

"Hey! They're in the mine!" a male voice yells.

"I got bolt cutters in my trunk," a girl replies.

Audrey freezes, her fist still raised. "Did you hear that?"

"Yes!"

She kneels beside me as I place my ear on Isabel's chest. As faint and soft as a distant drip, I hear her heart.

It is the sweetest sound I've ever heard, and I promise myself that one day I'll record her heartbeat and set it as the baseline for a song.

Audrey squeezes my hand, and together we pull Isabel up. We huddle by the doorway, listening to the sounds of the padlock snapping in two, the chains dropping on cement, and at last, the doors scraping open.

The world is pure white but for two silhouettes.

I shut my eyes against the bright light of the new morning. The tide of adrenaline ebbs from my body, and I stumble.

Rhea grabs my arm and sets me on the ground while balancing Isabel and placing her beside me. Jimbo holds Audrey upright until she sways dangerously in his arms. He lays her down. "They're all hurt."

Rhea presses a phone into his hand. "Call 9-1-1."

My eyes flutter when I feel her hand sweep along my brow. Her coffee-and-shea-body-butter scent is a welcome change from the stench of fire.

"Hey, Rhea," I rasp. "I'll give you an exclusive interview. Just promise to think about forgiving me?"

Full lips brush against my forehead. "Hush now. Help is on the way."

My fingers travel to Isabel's neck, and I rest the tips against her barely-there pulse. In my other hand, I grip the flashlight, afraid to let go.

I squint at it, recognizing the black plastic and the Graveside

Tours' tombstone logo. Laughing to myself, I mouth the words printed on the flashlight:

A light from beyond.

Chapter 52

Audrey

Mara used to tell me I lived life all wrong. She mocked me for being too polite, too earnest, too *Angsty Audrey*. Days ago, when we were so deep underground, when breathing became cumbersome and death seemed inevitable, I realized my cousin had been right about some things.

Dying has a way of forcing you to reckon with all the wasted moments of the past: the countless times I didn't speak up, didn't go after what I wanted, didn't follow my heart. Worse still were the moments I spent choking while I glimpsed images of a lost future.

As the smoke crashed over me and ash burned my eyes, I saw an herb garden of tiny glazed pots sitting on an unfamiliar windowsill with a view of the mountains that I've loved forever. Another blink and there was a magnificent gingerbread castle, complete with winding turrets I knew my hands were intended to sculpt. Finally, as rocks crashed around me, I was haunted by a set of twin boys. They followed me down a sun-drenched forest trail, their storm-gray eyes replicas of Grandma's.

That was the moment I grasped the extent of Mara's fury. I understood the searing pain of all the could-have-beens. To be a ghost is to comprehend, but not accept all you've lost.

She's gone now.

At least, she isn't in me. I haven't heard or felt Mara since the mine. Though sometimes I catch a whiff of bitter chocolate, and I tell her that it's okay—she can move on from this world.

If it is her, she doesn't answer.

Mara does things in her own time. That's always been her way.

The quiet is an awful relief. I'm free to make decisions without guilt. But I feel lonely sometimes. Mara's left a void. One that's hard not to fill with grief and regrets.

Grandma used to say, *"You can't change the past. But you can learn for the future."*

There's a lot—good and bad—to learn from Mara.

"You alright, Audrey?" Jimbo fidgets with the nurse call button, his finger ready to press should I give him the command.

This is now. This is my hospital room. Taking a deep breath, I inhale the sweet scent of flowers, which makes me want to bake lilac shortbread. I'd gotten lost inside myself; I'm trying not to do that so much.

I'll be fine. The thought rings true, and I smile. "I'm good."

Jimbo drumrolls his fingers along the bedrail before gripping it and looking up at me, his face serious. "Can I tell you something weird?"

"Sure."

"I mean, it's bizarre—like you probably won't believe me." His eyebrows scrunch as if gauging my reaction.

"Try me," I say, reaching out and patting his calloused hand.

"When I was eleven, I stole a little dragon statue from your grandma's shop. She caught me and scared the hell out of me cause of all the witch stories about her."

I shift, rustling the stiff sheets. "Did she put a curse on you?" I smile. I'd forgotten how she used to hex kids she caught stealing candles and pocket stones. She never called parents, or police, just muttered gibberish and waved her hands a bit. None of the would-be shoplifters ever tried again.

"Not exactly. She told me to keep the dragon, but in exchange, I had to vow to watch out for her youngest granddaughter. She said one day, you'd need me. Everyone I told the story thought it was one of Shirley's pranks, but when I saw you reading in the library years later, it all felt true."

I nod. "Sometimes, she just knew things. What are your plans now that you've paid off your debt?"

Jimbo strokes the scruff forming on his chin. "I dunno, it's a super nice dragon. It has a crystal eye and all, so I'm at your service until Shirley says otherwise."

A smile warms my face. Grandma was always urging me to make friends. She'd be proud.

Chapter 53

Zadie

The best part of being on oxygen support is that no one expects you to answer questions. That's the only good part, but it's important to look for silver linings.

So far, the words I scribbled on Rhea's notepad in the ambulance—Orlich did it, he's dead—have satisfied the investigation, but I've been dreading the official interview.

I haven't needed extra air in two days. My nurse brought me pancakes this morning and whispered that she heard I was getting released. I raised my marshmallow-wrapped arm and said, "Thumbs up."

My heart's not in it, though. I kinda wish that they'd put me in a medically induced coma because I'm not ready to process anything.

"Hey, Zadie-doll," Mom chirps, entering my room holding a bouquet of balloons and a bubblegum-pink bear that's the size of a kindergartner. "More gifts from your admirers."

"Oh, joy," I wheeze. Flowers, cards, candy, stuffed animals, and other get-well-soon crap fills every flat surface.

"Did you want to keep them or regift them to the children's ward?"

"Regift." Between Audrey and me, we've given every kid here at least one stuffed animal. I glance over at my tray table, checking that the souvenir flashlight is still there. Rhea claims I wouldn't let it go, and when Officer Donaldson tried to collect it for evidence, I hit him with it.

I don't remember that, but I hope it's true.

We'd have never made it out of the mine without the flashlight. It's likely one that a visitor dropped on a bonus-tour, but my heart tells me it's more than that.

Turning back to Mom, I ask, "So are the rumors true?"

She drops the bear to the floor, and the balloons bump against the ceiling. "Yes." Her face has gone ashen. "Jon Walls and I had a-an indiscretion. It's over."

"Awkward. I already knew that, and we don't need to discuss it. I was asking about me getting to go home today."

Mom's face is pinker than the bear's. "Oh. Well, Dr. Freeman needs to examine you and give her okay first, but it's a possibility. Wren said they're releasing Audrey today."

"Will I have to talk to the feds today?"

Mom sits on my bed and strokes the Band-Aid leftover from the IV port on the back of my hand. "No, baby. Eventually, you will, but the lawyer says your statement can wait a few more days."

"Good."

"There are two other things we need to discuss. They can wait until you feel up to it, but I don't want you to think I'm keeping anything from you."

My throat hurts, and I gesture to the water jug and cup next to my flashlight. Mom fills it and passes it to me.

I chug and wipe my lips with the back of my good hand. "Just tell me."

"Well, I got a job offer in California that I haven't accepted yet. I wanted to see what your plans are. I'm assuming you're taking the reward money and hitting the road?"

I gesture to the water jug again and drink slower this time. The mayor of Copper City stopped by with a giant cardboard check the other day. I was too hopped up on painkillers to remember most of it, but the town voted to split the *Bring Isabel Home* reward fund and then some between Audrey and me.

After years of fantasizing that a lump of money would fall into my lap, the actual check is paralyzing. "Where in California?"

"San Marino. Suburb of LA." She smiles at me. "You could come with me, check out the music scene. You'd have to go to community college if you want to live rent-free, though."

"I've been thinking about going to school to be a music teacher in case the singer-songwriter thing doesn't work out."

"That's very wise." She pats my leg. "I want you to know that even without this whole action-hero thing, I'm proud that you're my daughter."

I fight the tears that prick at the corner of my eyes. I've been crying way too much lately. "Thanks, Mom. You said there were two things?"

She pales slightly but nods and removes an envelope from her purse. Pinching both ends, she walks over. "I received this from FedEx yesterday." She sets the open envelope on my lap.

"The story's gone viral . . . along with a picture of you. Apparently, you are the spitting image of your grandmother. Your father is very excited to meet you." Tears fill Mom's eyes, but she's smiling.

I lose my breath and my stomach gets that rollercoaster loop feeling. I accepted long ago that I'd never meet my father. It's overwhelming to have your whole life change, even if it's for the better. I read the name on the return and laugh until I cough and Mom pats my back. "My dad's last name is *Estrada*? All these years we were looking for an Oscar with an *S* last name!"

Mom's face is Tapatío red. "Well, I'm prone to mistakes." Her words hang in the air as I press the button that raises the head of the hospital bed.

"About the Mr. Walls thing, I get it, being lonely, I mean. People don't make the best choices when they're hurting."

Mom sniffs. "Thanks. Speaking of Mr. Walls, he and Clara would like to have us over for dinner sometime to thank you for saving Isabel."

"That sounds incredibly awkward."

"I plan just to drop you off unless you want me to stay."

"Gee, thanks."

Mom straightens the little table. "Dr. Freeman will be in soon. Why don't you rest up so we can bust you out of here?" Mom grabs her purse. "Do you want me to get you a Snickers or something?"

"Nah. Could you stay, though? I don't want to be alone."

"Of course."

*

After being cleared to go home, I dress in sweats and a T-shirt and leave Mom to disperse the flowers and pack up the cards as I head down the corridor to talk to Audrey. The door to her room is ajar, and my good hand freezes midair when I hear a girlish giggle.

"Please don't do elf accents!" Audrey squeals.

I peek inside. Jimbo is perched on Audrey's bed, holding a fantasy novel.

I knock.

"Come in!" Audrey calls.

"Hey, you excited that we're getting out?"

"Yes! I'm tired of having my vitals checked." Audrey beams. "Did you hear? Aunt Robin's back. I told her about my idea to add a tea shop to the bakery, and she loved it, and we're gonna be business partners."

Mara's mother is returning. It feels like the explosion in the mine actually put bits of Copper City back together.

"That's great," I say, shuffling from foot to foot.

Audrey seems different—confident and happy. I smile a little too broadly, stalling, trying to think of how to ask about Mara without alarming Jimbo. "Speaking of your Aunt Robin, has anyone else popped up?"

Audrey offers a sad little twist of her lips. "No."

Nodding, I say, "Just checking."

"Did they tell you the plan?" Jimbo asks, setting the book down.

"What plan?"

"They're going to sneak you ladies out through the parking garage, so you don't get swamped by reporters. They're gonna send nurses in wheelchairs out the front way as decoys. You're freaking famous."

"Not what I want to be famous for, but you know." I hold up my bandaged hand, a reminder that I'll be taking a forced break from guitar.

"You gonna let people sign your cast?" Jimbo asks.

"Nah, it'd look lame if only you two sign it."

"Oh, Zadie, don't be silly. I bet you could get the cops to sign it." Audrey smiles.

My heart flinches at the mention of cops; I need space. "Well, I'll see you later for Operation Discharge."

"Gross," Jimbo says, and Audrey rolls her eyes.

I shut the door and close my eyes. I've lost Mara all over again, and with sinking certainty, I know Audrey has a better friend now.

I feel alone.

"Hey, stranger."

My head swivels down the hall, where I find Rhea leaning against the wall. "Hey. I didn't see you there."

Hope catches in my throat. I haven't seen Rhea since the ambulance ride. Our only contact has been one awkward phone conversation where I didn't have the nerve to ask if I had any chance with her. I guess that doesn't matter since I'll be moving, still I don't want to leave with the Mara fight hanging over us like a storm cloud.

"I hear they're letting you out." Her eyebrow juts up, and my knees go weak.

She holds out her arm, and I loop mine through hers, grateful for the support.

"Walk and talk?" I ask, choking down nerves.

"Sure."

We're at the end of the corridor before I find the words. "I'll never be able to explain what happened between Audrey and me. Mara was—" I swallow. "It isn't something I'd believe if I hadn't experienced it. But it's over."

She offers a small nod.

I continue, "Rhea, I'm grateful for every moment we spent together, and I'm sorry for how I handled . . . everything."

Rhea stops walking, and we both lean against the wall and watch as an orderly pushes an empty stretcher by. "Your mom told me about the move."

"I wish I had more time to prove to you that—" I stop, noticing the wide, wicked grin breaking across Rhea's face.

"You forgot, didn't you? Girl, you get a pass because you foiled a serial killer. Remember where I'm going to college?"

I blink at her, and she rolls her finger in a "come on" motion.

"You're going to UCLA! I'll be living—"

"Just thirty minutes away, I mapped it."

"Does this mean . . ."

"We've got some issues to work through, but yes, I'd like to be with you, Zadie Slade."

I rest my cast on her hip and ask, "Can I kiss you, Rhea Uckleman?"

Chapter 54

Audrey

The woods feel different now. The rotting scent has dissipated, and the birds never stop singing. I walk to the heart of the forest without fear and go to the abandoned stone staircase and climb to the top, sit on the landing to nowhere and let my feet dangle. I give thanks to all the spirits who showed up to help me vanquish Bloody Jasper.

It feels like it was all a dream. For a few days after the mine, I thought my confrontation with Bloody Jasper was a hallucination. I told no one.

When I brought a plate of honey-drenched sopapillas to Isabel's house the day after she was released from the hospital, she told me she thought for sure we'd died. She saw a cyclone of spirits with me at the center.

We laughed about it, and I didn't burden her with the truth.

Now, I think of the departed who gathered to help me defeat Bloody Jasper and hope they felt justice and moved on.

The first night in the hospital, I awoke and found Paul Hartshorne standing by my bed. He saluted me before disappearing from this world. Paul's obituary says he passed away peacefully in his sleep the same morning we were rescued.

I adjust the Graveside Tours fanny pack on my hip. It's a goodbye gift from Zadie. Today I've filled it with rosemary, anise hyssop, and lavender. I've been working on a tea menu for Robin's Nest. There's much to do in the coming weeks before the grand reopening, and I feel slightly anxious about not feeling anxious, which is silly and carries its own sweet sense of well-being.

I lie back and watch the lazy clouds drifting above and know that I'll always find my way home.

Epilogue

Mara

No longer tethered to anyone or anything, Mara Quinn drifts through Copper City, observing. She starts her day at Robin's Nest bakery, where the ovens once again fill the streets with the scent of sweet bread.

In the kitchen, Audrey holds her chin at a high angle, and a halo of newfound confidence surrounds her. Mara can almost taste the bittersweet cocoa powder puffing into the air when her cousin taps a metal sifter over babka. The care in Audrey's movements and the preciseness of her measurements leave Mara certain that her cousin is well suited for a life of creating edible happiness.

Best of all, she likes watching her mother's flour-coated fingers working the dough into various shapes. She remembers those hands resting atop hers while directing the rolling pin. Impulsively, Mara reaches out and tugs at her mother's apron strings. Robin Quinn's eyes go wide, and she smiles before shaking her head and whispering, "Silly woman, imagining old times."

In the afternoons, Mara finds herself in the clearing. The brothel has been leveled, and the rotted beams and debris carted away. She watches as laborers busy themselves creating something new. When she first saw the foreman unfurl the plans for an outdoor stage, her spirit filled with bliss and lifted high above the top of the tallest tree. It took almost a full day for Mara to drift back to earth.

Now, she enjoys reading the placard that glistens in the sunlight: *Future Site of the Mara Quinn Amphitheater*. From the conversations she's eavesdropped on, she knows this project was Zadie's idea; she can think of no better use for the clearing.

Mara ignores the shimmering portal that has taken to appearing everywhere she goes. It calls to her, but she isn't ready—not yet.

She goes to the community gardens when Zadie meets with Isabel Walls. The younger girl reverently holds Mara's old guitar despite the inherent comedy of trying to mimic a person strumming with their wrist in a splint. The girls sing old Zaras songs, and the portal looms larger behind Mara.

Not yet.

Most nights, she sits on the rooftop with Zadie. Sometimes Zadie speaks to her, but Mara can only listen. Tonight, when Mara arrives, she finds Zadie resting her head on Rhea's shoulder. Their pinkies entwined, they whisper sweet things that Mara isn't supposed to hear.

There's a U-Haul truck parked in the Slades' driveway. Mara sits on the hood and watches as the night grows darker, not moving until the sun breaks through. She's on the lawn as Audrey and Jimbo arrive carrying trays of warm prickly-pear empanadas and butterscotch scones. Respecting her cousin's space, she hovers beside Audrey and whispers: *You know how to live. You're gonna have an epic life.* Mara doesn't believe she can hear her, but a small smile tugs at the girl's lips and Mara is grateful.

Rhea brings coffee and a handful of police officers who carry out boxes and load furniture into the truck. At noon, the Walls bring pizza, and Isabel cries when Zadie gets into the passenger side of Rhea's Honda.

Mara waves as the truck, the Honda, and the helpers drive away, disappearing over the horizon.

The portal swirls, glittering and pixelating, growing larger by the moment. The sweet scent of lavender tea, which reminds her of Gramma, emanates from the glistening space. Mara takes one last look around Copper City and makes a final wish as she soars into the air and dives through the portal, on her way to whatever comes next.

THE END

Acknowledgments

I was a lonely kid who hid inside books. They taught me almost everything I know, especially this: If you're going on a journey, you'll need help. Find your friends.

Writing this book was a hell of a trip, and I owe many thanks.

To Lora Durance (who writes as River K. Scott), for being my first writing friend and infinitely more. She taught me what a comma splice was, edited thousands of my pages, showed me how to mix a Sweet Sonoran Heat, and is forever imprinted on my soul.

To my brilliant agent, Ellen Goff, for her insight and persistence and to the amazing team at HG Literary.

To Amanda Manns, Krysta Winsheimer, and Creature Publishing, I couldn't ask for a better home for Audrey and Zadie. Special thanks to Luísa Dias for creating such a creepily beautiful cover design.

To my phenomenal Pitch Wars mentors, Andrea Contos and Kay L. McCray, thank you for pulling my words from the slush.

To Breanna, aka B. Nacole, for reading the earliest draft and for your valuable feedback—especially when it came via GIFs and memes.

To Christy Donahue for being my creative cheerleader and fellow dream chaser.

To the little writing communities that have welcomed me. Groups like the Quokkas, The Bi+ Book Gang, and the 2025 Small Press Debuts kept me sane.

To my parents, for taking me to the library and for buying me countless Babysitters Club and Goosebumps books. You started this.

To my family, thank you for leaving me alone in the closet so I could chase words. Home is my favorite place because I get to be with you.

And finally, to Spoony, my first reader, harshest editor, and most giving friend. You know all my secrets. IBLLY.

L. L. Madrid lives in Tucson where she writes moody stories about misfits. L.L. is a recipient of the HWA's Mary Wollstonecraft Shelley Scholarship. She is a member of the Bi+ Book Gang, a Pitch Wars alum, and a graduate of the Odyssey Writing Workshop. Her short stories are scattered across the internet.

Creature Publishing was founded on a passion for feminist discourse and horror's potential for social commentary and catharsis. Our definition of feminist horror, broad and inclusive, expands the scope of what horror can be and who can make it.